Also by Antoine Vanner:

The Dawlish Chronicles

Britannia's Wolf
September 1877 - February 1878

Britannia's Reach
November 1879 - April 1880

Britannia's Shark
April – September 1881

Britannia's Spartan
June 1859 and April - August 1882

Britannia's Amazon
April – August 1882
(Includes bonus short story *Britannia's Eye*)

Britannia's Mission
August 1883 – February 1884

Britannia's Gamble
March 1884 – February 1885

Being accounts of episodes in the lives of

Nicholas Dawlish R.N.
Born: Shrewsbury 16.12.1845
Died: Zeebrugge 23.04.1918

and

Florence Dawlish, née Morton
Born: Northampton 17.06.1855
Died: Portsmouth 12.05.1946

Britannia's Innocent

The Dawlish Chronicles

February – May 1864

By

Antoine Vanner

Library of Congress Cataloguing-in-Publication Data:

Antoine Vanner 1945 -

Britannia's Mission / Antoine Vanner.

ISBN-978-1-943404-16-2

(The Dawlish Chronicles Volume 8)

Cover design by Sara Lee Paterson

Published by Old Salt Press

Old Salt Press, LLC is based in Jersey City, New Jersey with an affiliate in New Zealand

For more information about our titles go to www.oldsaltpress.com

To learn more about the Dawlish Chronicles go to:
www.dawlishchronicles.com

Britannia's Innocent

Introduction

In November 1863 the new king of Denmark, Christian IX, was prevailed upon by a government that had wide popular support to sign a new constitution. Doing so violated the terms of the "London Protocol" of 1852 which recognised a "Danish Federation" which linked the duchies of Schleswig, Holstein and Lauenburg by personal union under the king with the Kingdom of Denmark. (See map). Austria and Prussia, the two great German powers, both with legitimate interests as regards these duchies, demanded withdrawal of the new constitution. Under pressure from Prussia, the rising power in Germany under its "Iron Chancellor" Otto von Bismarck, the Danish government abandoned Holstein and withdrew its army back into Schleswig.

Danish intransigence on the issues at stake, fuelled by widespread enthusiasm for the "November Constitution", and built on overestimation of its own military capacity, led to an ultimatum from Prussia and the Austrian Empire. When this was rejected, their forces crossed into Schleswig on February 1st 1864. War had commenced.

Denmark, facing overwhelming enemy strength, found itself without allies since the London Protocol, which it had breached, was recognised by Austria, Prussia, Russia, France, and Great Britain. The Danish army placed its confidence in occupying the Danevirke, a thousand-year old system of defensive earthworks that stretched for some twenty miles across Schleswig. Within two weeks this position proved untenable in the face of modern weaponry and the Danish army – poorly equipped and inadequately supplied, but defiant, withdrew in appalling winter conditions and headed north and north-east.

A protracted agony had just commenced…

Denmark
November 1863

Vendsyssel(D)

North Sea

Kingdom of Denmark
shown in white

Jutland (D)

Zealand (D)

Baltic Sea

Funen (D)

North Schleswig

South Schleswig

Danevirke

Holstein

Prologue

North Schleswig

Sunday, February 14th 1864

This was not a retreat. Defeated armies retreated. His force was headed for a new position from which to maintain the fight.

Saabye had drifted into sleep with the thought. It was with him again when his orderly pulled his boots on for him, the only items he had taken off for a week. His four hour's rest had done little to relieve his exhaustion and he was numb with cold, his breath cloudy in the faint light of the man's lantern. Around him, other bodies lay half-hidden in the straw piled on the barn's floor, greatcoats clasped around them, heads swathed in whatever they had begged – or taken – from villages and farmsteads passed on the previous day. He had asked to be woken at five o'clock These worn-out men, most of whom had stood-to for the first part of the night, until relieved by others who were now shivering at their posts, could be allowed another half hour.

Major Valdemar Essmann, Saabye's deputy, was waiting in the chill darkness outside.

"Any change?"

"They haven't moved, Friherre." Essmann always addressed Saabye by his title of nobility, not by his military rank of colonel. He pointed towards the line of yellow pinpricks winking in the east.

They must be the camp-fires of the Austrian cavalry that had been keeping pace at three or four miles' separation. They had made a brief attack on the head of the straggling column just before dusk, and their accompanying light horse-artillery had even managed to get two four-pounders into position. When they fell back, they left behind seven of their number dead and one of the four-pounders and its limber captured. A small victory, but bought with four Danish deaths and a half-dozen wounded.

"They won't attack again," Saabye said. "Not today at least. They're as tired as we are. But they'll keep us under observation, keep up with us, report back our movements."

And that was what he wanted, though he had not shared it with his officers yet. He wanted that cavalry to follow him, and to draw behind it the Austrian force that was thrusting northwards along the central spine of Jutland. He knew of it because the single squadron of Danish

8

dragoons that had attached itself to his column had reconnoitred efficiently despite the melting snow. There was Austrian infantry to the east, several battalions at best, an entire division at worst, several artillery batteries too and supply wagons following.

There would be another hour before the sky would brighten in the south-east but now sergeants were rousing the men packed in the village's cottages, barns and stables, urging quick preparation of food. They had been the lucky ones. Further back, men had no option but to bivouac in the open, grateful for the lee of a bush or the ground beneath a wagon.

"Still northwards then, Friherre?"

Saabye nodded. The question had been a courtesy only. Essmann knew that there was no hope now of establishing contact with the main Danish army. Not with that Austrian division so close, and beyond them the feared Prussians, dogged, superbly trained, driving forward remorselessly, intent on forcing battle before the Danes could regroup or dig defences.

"Northwards," Saabye said. "Further northwards."

He still kept the ultimate destination to himself. Ninety miles yet to cover, paralleling the West Jutland coast along what were little more than cart tracks. Another eight or ten days at the pace that the exhausted column was now making. And that took no account of the possibility of further swoops by enemy cavalry or for the arrival of more snow.

But at last there would be a place to make a stand, a place he had known since childhood, a place where superior numbers would count for little against an entrenched force, however small.

A thorn in the enemy's side.

Not one enemy side either, but two. Prussian or Austrian, it did not matter. The more that would pursue him the better. He would draw strength away from the enemy's main thrust and in time . . .

He shook himself from what might yet prove a dream. Even before a wintery sun rose in the south-eastern sky his force must be on the move.

*

Saabye steeled himself before entering the village church. He had been a soldier for a quarter century, had fought the Prussian enemy fifteen years before. He had not flinched under fire – he had surprised himself – and he carried with pride the scar on his left cheek that dragged the eye above

9

it permanently half-open. But battle had not been the worst of it. He had never come to terms with the aftermath of wounds and suffering, of the lingering despair of others who knew that life was being dragged painfully from them.

He reached for the iron ring on the door, turned it, entered. The smell was like a solid wall of foulness. The church had been converted into a makeshift hospital and the few lamps cast weak light and deep shadows. Pews, their backs smashed off, had been pushed together to make beds. Extra blankets and counterpanes taken from the villagers had been used to swathe the sick against the cold. Persistent coughing from a dozen throats provided a background to louder moans, to babbles of delirium, to intermittent piercing screams from a far corner.

A burly figure lurched towards Saabye, eyes red-rimmed, blood spattered on his face and spectacles, as shocking as that staining the apron drawn over his mud-caked uniform. Surgeon-Major Gustav Hartling was clearly fatigued to the verge of collapse.

"Three gone, colonel." The voice weary. "There never was much hope."

"Gunners?" The Austrian cavalry that had driven at the horse-drawn nine-pounders yesterday had hacked furiously before they were driven off. Their sabre cuts had been deep, slicing flesh and shattering bone.

"Yes. Yes, gunners," Hartling said. "I'd no option but to amputate." He held up his hands in hopeless acceptance.

The news would travel fast, Saabye knew, spreading despondency though ranks mainly filled with conscripts so recently pulled from farm or workshop and so hurriedly trained. They had shown stolid endurance so far. He feared to speculate how much longer that could persist.

"And these others?" He gestured to the swathed figures lying on the floor in the straw-strewn spaces between the undamaged pews.

"Pneumonia. Fever," Hartling said. "Bad feet too. A few will lose toes, maybe feet. There'll be more like them."

Useless mouths. Encumbrances. Many most likely doomed.

"They'll have to stay," Saabye said.

"And myself, colonel? Should I stay too?" Hartling must know the answer already.

"I'll need you." Saabye tried to make it sound more like a request than an order, though both knew that it was.

"The pastor told me that there's a doctor in a village six or eight miles from here. On the coast," Hartling said. "He offered to take a message to him, to bring him here. And to see that these sick are taken in by families when we're gone."

"Tell the pastor to keep a record. When all this is over there'll be compensation for anyone who helps."

If Denmark won't be bankrupt, Saabye thought. But I'll pay from my own pocket if necessary. My estates are big enough to stand it.

He turned to go, ashamed that he was glad to leave the stench of misery behind. He knew he would be abandoning more men like these in the small towns and smaller villages still ahead.

In the south-east a blood-red sun had just risen and was streaking long shadows across the barren winter landscape.

*

It was of no benefit that the temperature had risen slightly in the last two days. Advance over roadways' frozen ruts had been hard enough but now the feeble warmth had brought mud rather than relief. Deepened by the fall of every boot or hoof, the sludge made every step an exhausting misery. It was bad for those at the head of the column, incalculably worse at the tail. There, wheels inched forward only because men strained on the spokes while struggling horses sunk to their bellies. Occasional pistol shots announced the despatch of some wretched beast, a leg broken, or exhausted beyond its strength.

Saabye ranged back and forth along the column, riding when the ground permitted but for the most part plodding on foot, an orderly leading his mount behind.

It was the ninth day since the Danish forces had fallen back from the massive Danevirke defensive line. It had been a stupidity ever to have considered manning it, Saabye thought, one to crown that yet greater stupidity that had precipitated this conflict, the wilful provocation that had lost Denmark sympathy across Europe and left her to face her enemies without allies. It would have taken five or six times the men available, and ten times the artillery, to have defended the Danevirke's nineteen miles of antiquated earthworks effectively. Only the arrival of massive Prussian and Austrian forces – mobilised faster than ever anticipated – had forced recognition of reality, that withdrawal was the only alternative to immediate and absolute defeat. Snow and darkness had hidden the stealthy desertion of the Danevirke's trenches and redoubts. Only massive pieces of garrison artillery, too heavy to move easily, had been left behind, securely spiked.

It was noon now and Saabye stood by the roadside, sheltered by a hedge from the rising east wind. He wanted the men to see him, to know that he too was cold and tired, that he asked nothing of them that he did not demand of himself. Two infantry battalions and three batteries of supporting field guns had already toiled past, the units with which he had manned the redoubts on the extreme right of the Danevirke. The order to withdraw from there had arrived late but it had been executed without raising an alarm among the Austrian outposts freezing in the darkness to the south. Only daylight alerted the enemy that the defences had been deserted and by noon their forces were driving through and past the earthworks, unopposed, as the entire Danish Army withdrew north-eastwards.

But not quite entire…

For Saabye had realised almost immediately that a massive enemy force had thrust itself between his command and the tail of the main Danish withdrawal. Meeting a bloodied squadron of the 7th Dragoon Regiment had confirmed it. Half its number had been lost when it blundered into an Austrian column in a snow storm. Contact had been lost with the rest of the regiment and its major had been killed. His nerve-shattered deputy was glad to place the squadron's remnant under Saabye's command. And in the days since, those dragoons had been a godsend, paralleling the column's march, probing eastwards. And always finding, always falling back to report continuing Austrian advance.

Saabye himself had joined one of the reconnaissances, had seen in the distance the huge dark blocks of advancing Austrian infantry, had survived a half-hearted pursuit by enemy cavalry, had confirmed that any attempt to break eastwards through such forces could only be suicidal. There was nothing for it but to keep heading north close to the coast. There would be no directives from the army's supreme command. He was on his own.

And it was then that the idea had come to him.

A thorn in the side.

The wind was rising, a howl now, the cold more intense by the moment, but still Saabye stood by the roadside. The units that had been under his own direct command, both infantry and artillery, had passed him, but now others were acknowledging his salute as they trudged past. His had not been the only units to have been cut off and many others had suffered in bloody skirmishes before accepting reality and turning north. The remnants of two grenadier companies slogged past – regulars, pride still palpable in the weary determination of their tread – and after

12

them half an infantry battalion, mostly conscripts whose brutal peasant lives had inured them to fatigue, had left them little expectation of comfort. Behind them came the most valuable acquisition of all, five batteries of nine-pounder field guns and two of twelve-pounder howitzers. A Major Stavald, who clearly loved his guns, had brought them without loss of a single barrel through mud and slush and a brutal encounter with enemy cavalry.

And then the lumbering wagons and the hopeless misery in the uncomprehending eyes of the straining horses. Men who had fallen exhausted by the wayside crouched between the crates and barrels and boxes of already depleted supplies. It was the food that would give out first, Saabye knew. In another two days only the farms and villages ahead must provide it, whether willingly or not, and horses must be taken too, despite all pleading.

At last the rear-guard, three companies of light infantry, unblooded yet, but struggling with determination through the mire churned by those who went before.

Saabye had kept count. Upwards of four-thousand men, of four-hundred horses, of some forty field-pieces and twenty howitzers. And their ammunition, their precious, invaluable ammunition.

It was the best part of a brigade, in peace-time terms, and by some gift of providence every officer was less senior than himself and willing to submit to his command. And there might yet be help from another source...

The stupidity that had brought on this unnecessary war still angered him, but his country had been invaded, and he was damned if he was to stand for it. He sensed something of the same among the men, even the illiterates of peasant stock. Some would fall out, sick or frost-bitten, and there would be a few desertions, and perhaps a need for summary justice, but he would carry the great majority with him to the barren spit of land still eighty gruelling miles ahead.

A thorn in the enemy's side, an irritant without strategic significance, but one that for honour's sake alone would draw enemy strength away from the battles, far to the east, that would determine the war's outcome.

Saabye – Colonel Friherre Axel Saabye – heaved himself into his saddle, turned towards the column's head.

Tonight he would share his intentions with his officers.

And there would be a special role for Major Essmann.

Chapter 1

The envelope that lay on his plate when Dawlish came down for breakfast carried a crest. Mrs. Gore, his old nurse, now the housekeeper, was standing back from his chair, her curiosity poorly suppressed. The others – his father, his brother James, his sister Susan – were seated already and watching with no less inquisitiveness.

"It's just come, Nick," Susan said.

He hoped for a moment that it was from the Admiralty – confirmation of his promotion to sub-lieutenant, for he had passed the examination with ease – but as he picked it up, he saw that the crest was heraldic. Bears rampant on either side of a quartered shield, a plumed helmet above. And a Latin motto that defeated him.

"Pejus letho flagitium." James must have examined it already. "Disgrace is worse than death."

The postmark said Taunton, the envelope addressed to Midshipman Nicholas Dawlish. Mention of the rank displeased him – he did not want to be reminded, felt already that he had advanced beyond it. But the only person whom he knew who was from Somerset still held that same rank also.

"Noble friends you must have now, Nick." A hint of resentment in his father's voice. Market town solicitors moved in humbler spheres.

"From some beautiful heiress who loves you madly, I hope," Susan was laughing. "Go on. Open it, Nick. You can see that we're all agog."

He could never refuse his sister. He slit the thick cream vellum envelope open with a table knife, unfolded the two sheets within. The handwriting was untidy and instantly recognisable. He had heard it criticised often and harshly. Midshipman Albemarle FitzBaldwin seldom earned his superiors' praise.

"It's from a friend," Dawlish said. "He was on *Nile* with me. We came back from Bermuda together."

He scanned the letter quickly – references to a ball, to good shooting and good hunting also – but it was the suggestion in the last paragraph that surprised him. They had been friendly, but never close.

"An invitation," Dawlish said. "To stay a week. Two if I'd like." No need to bring a gun and there were mounts enough in the stables, FitzBaldwin had added.

"Tell me that he's a rich and handsome young lord who's looking for a wife. I'll be expecting you to introduce me," Susan said. "And tell me he's got a beautiful sister who's longing to fall in love with a dashing young naval officer."

"He's not a lord," Dawlish said. But he knew that FitzBaldwin's uncle was. "And if he has a sister, he's never mentioned her." Though he had not met him, he knew that FitzBaldwin's father was also in the service, a senior captain, widely admired.

"You'll go, Nicholas?" Something like envy in his father's voice.

"After I've seen Uncle Ralph's farms."

"We could do that tomorrow," James said.

And so it was decided. Dawlish telegraphed that he would arrive at Melhill Priory in two days' time – February 17th. A wire came in return that afternoon. FitzBaldwin would send a dog-cart to meet him at Taunton station.

*

He had been back in Shrewsbury for a fortnight but he was not sorry to leave for a few days. The homecoming had not been as he had imagined it during the previous two years. The assignment to HMS *Nile*, flagship of the America Station, had meant only dull routine, one midshipman among many, but the illness of a junior lieutenant on a small gunvessel had rescued him from it. Appointed temporarily to HMS *Foyle*, he could stand as watchkeeping officer, take responsibilities and opportunities he could never have had on the larger ship. He had imagined that his stories of *Foyle's* action against a makeshift rebel navy off Colombia and of chasing a Brazilian slaver would have impressed his family, that his delight in night watches on calm seas, with a phosphorescent wake glowing astern, would have fascinated.

There had indeed been polite appreciation when he had arrived in early February. His father had nodded grimly and knowingly as he listened, as if he too had once faced similar risks, even though he had never travelled further than London. Susan had been pleasurably horrified by the account of the slave ship, would willingly have hanged its captain, had she been a man herself. Mrs. Gore, his old nurse and now the housekeeper, had wept and held him to her, had thanked God for his safe return. Only his elder brother James, now working with his father, listed in solemn silence with something like longing in his eyes.

It lasted a week and then there were no further questions, not even from James. It was not that he had bored them, Dawlish realised, not that pride or love were lacking, only that they could not imagine – could not sense – the feel and dangers and joys of that great world outside. And that world, not Shrewsbury, was his now. There was a barrier between him and his family, unwelcome but inevitable, one that could only strengthen in the future. He loved them, always would, and they him, but he could never be close to them again.

He had hunted once since he returned, mounted on his father's sturdy hack, a mare who had never taken a fence and who demanded laborious detours to find gates. James, on his own powerful gelding, had been with the leaders, disappearing from view almost from the start, clearing with abandon obstacles which wiser riders might have avoided.

Dawlish found that he was glad that he himself had not been in at the kill.

"You missed it, Nick," James had said. "A great big dog-fox."

It was the only time since his return that he had sensed something of the fire that had been his older brother's when growing up.

"The chase was enough," Dawlish said. "It's been two years since I've ridden. I'll ache for a week."

But there was more to it than that. His true blooding had been on that dreadful day at the Taku Forts five years before, not the smearing of his cheeks with a fox's shreds by a Master of Foxhounds when he was nine years old. It seemed a squalid mockery now, worsened by the memory of the other riders' applause and congratulations that had flattered him at the time. His profession might demand killing, but he hoped now that he would never have joy in blood, whether of a man or beast.

The nearest of the farms he had inherited from his uncle lay fifteen miles to the south-west and he was pleased by James' suggestion that they ride there rather than take their father's trap. It took four unhurried hours, the morning still and cold, the trees and hedgerows bare. The difference of seven years between them seemed nothing now and there was a satisfying feeling of warm companionship of equals.

"They're making hardly a penny," James said as they rode. "It's poor land to begin with and prices for anything they produce are low."

Rented out to tenants, the six farms were managed by an agent. James scrutinised the books at intervals. If he had resented the farms being passed to his younger brother, he never showed it, and Dawlish admired him for it. It would be another three years before he himself would come of age and he knew that even then he would be glad for James to continue the oversight. Glad too for what they represented, a last link to his uncle. He had loved and admired Ralph Page when he had spent months with him in France in the last year of his life. The clean air of the spa-town of Pau had not saved him. Only now did Dawlish appreciate the full tragedy of the naval career cut short by consumption, the heartbreak of talent unfulfilled, of achievement denied. It had been the same disease that had taken Ralph's sister, his own mother. He could recall her only as a vague presence – she had died when he was four – and not as the living person whom James and Susan remembered. But he still missed her.

"You'll have to raise the rents," the agent said as they rode away from the last of the farms.

"But they're still profitable," Dawlish said. A hundred and four pounds, seven shillings and ninepence three farthings had been credited to his account this year. He did not doubt the figure – James had checked the books. It was a fortune compared with the just over thirteen pounds that the navy paid a midshipman each year.

"A profit, you say? It's touch and go," the agent said. "One bad harvest will wipe it out, leave you in debt. And repairs can't be put off forever. The roof at the barn at the Shotford place won't last more than another year, and you've seen the cow-byre at Darkhampton. And the tied cottages at Alfield are –"

"I'll discuss it with my brother." James' tone indicated that the matter was closed. For now.

As they rode back together James said "It's got to be done Nick." He had seen that he had been moved by the squalor in the cottages. "If we sugar the pill, do some of the repairs, we can justify rent increases. Not much, five percent say. You wouldn't be the only one doing it."

Dawlish didn't answer immediately. He had seen want in those cottages, the smell of poverty, grudged courtesy from the fathers, misery in the faces of worn-out women, resentment in the glances of the unkempt children. Several of the older sons had left for Australia, one for America.

"I don't need the money this year," Dawlish wondered if he would ever want to take it from those people, need it as he might. "Spend it on the Alfield cottages. And a new well too. With a pump." There had been typhoid there, a mother and two children dead, the well, sunk centuries before, contaminated by a cess pit.

"You're sure, Nick?"

"I'm sure. Just let me have two tenners. That'll be enough. The Navy covers board and lodging. I'm waiting for another ship. I'll be looked after."

"And raise the rents?" James said. "Maybe not five percent, but two or three perhaps?"

"No. Maybe next year."

"You've got a good heart, Nick. Like Mother."

But it wasn't that, Dawlish thought, not that sort of goodness. It was for himself, it was to combat the oppression of spirit that had so often come upon him since that terrible day at the Taku Forts, the awareness of suffering, of the world's unheeding cruelty. He could not avoid it — nobody could, however much they ignored it. Better to face it with courage and compassion and integrity like he had sensed in that Major Gordon whom he had encountered at Pekin.

They dined at an inn just south of Shrewsbury, nobody else in the small parlour. Neither raised the matter of the farm rents again. The conversation was inconsequential — domestic matters, James' hunting, Mrs. Gore's recovery from recent illness — and yet Dawlish felt quiet joy in his brother's company.

But a surprise when at last they rose to leave.

"I envy you, Nick" James's voice was sad, almost bitter.

"Why?"

"You've got the world, Nick. I've got —" Words failing, hands raised in a gesture of bewilderment, even of despair. "You can't know your future except that there'll be opportunities, not years of that wretched office, the petty lawsuits, the wills, the rights of way, the covenants — I can see it all already" The words were pouring in a torrent now. "I'll be father's partner. I'll be respected, a churchwarden, an alderman perhaps, probably mayor someday. And I'll yearn through long months for the hunting and shooting seasons to start and in between I'll pore over Bible commentaries and I'll marry some friend's sister — a decent girl, no doubt, but no different to a hundred like her in our circle — and I'll tell myself I'm happy and I'll know that I don't believe it. There'll be forty, fifty, maybe sixty years of it."

"There's still time," Dawlish said.

He knew that James had dreamed of going to Oxford, had once spoken of taking Holy Orders, for he had always been devout, still was. But he must have known then already that there could be no hope of it, that, though there might be money enough, his father would not hear of it. Three generations of Dawlishs had been attorneys. There must be a fourth.

"There's still time," Dawlish said again. "You could –"

"It's getting late, Nick." The tone said it all. No further discussion. Resignation. "It's time to go."

They rode back in silence.

*

Albemarle FitzBaldwin met him in Taunton and drove the dog-cart himself.

"I'll be glad to have you here, Dawlish," he said. "The place is dull. It's been full of father's friends. Strange fellows, some of them – comings and goings and talking with each other with low voices and long faces and only remarking on the weather to me when I come by. Only one of 'em is interested in the shooting – and it's excellent – and none of them ever rides to hounds, and that's damn good also around here."

"Your father's here? The captain?"

"He's always here these days. He's on half-pay."

Another captain waiting for a ship in a navy that had more captains than ships. Even one with a reputation like Montague FitzBaldwin's, earned in the Kerch Straits and at the Bogue Forts.

"Is your uncle at home too?"

"His Lordship?" The tone not quite contemptuous, dismissive rather. "He's always here, always has been. You won't see him, Dawlish. He never leaves his bed, he can't, poor fellow, he never has for all his life and he's –" A finger raised to the temple, the gesture eloquent yet unpleasant.

The house was less grand than Dawlish had expected, a Tudor mansion with soaring chimneys that had been ruined by jarring additions in differing styles in the centuries since. The ruins of the original Melhill Priory stood close by. Some astute earlier FitzBaldwin had done well out of the dissolution of monasteries. It was even less impressive within, shabby even.

They arrived there late, with just enough time to change for dinner. Dawlish was grateful that he had declined a servant's offer to unpack for him, for he found that Susan had sneaked in the slippers she had embroidered to welcome him home. Florid and gaudy, they were objects that he would never want anybody to see, on or off ship, and yet she had spent long, loving hours on them. But the sight moved him, and brought

19

back memories of her care for him when he was little, and for the joy and laughter she had brought into a motherless family. It could not be long before her kindness and vivacity would attract some suitor. Whoever he might be, he would be a lucky man.

For all his formidable reputation, Captain FitzBaldwin, tall, heavy and florid, seemed genuinely welcoming, more relaxed, less aloof, than any captain could ever afford to be at sea.

"We've a mutual friend, Mr. Dawlish. Sam Caulfield. Spoke highly of you. More than anybody ever says about you, do they, young Al?" He clapped his son on the shoulder and both laughed.

Dawlish was surprised. Samuel Caulfield, *Foyle's* captain, had always been sparing in his praise, had been remote even in the close confines of a gunvessel. The nearest he had come to familiarity had been recommending and lending books – Carlyle, Macaulay, Prescott. But he was professional, decisive, principled, the sort of officer Dawlish hoped to be himself.

There were no women at dinner – no sister, as Susan had hoped, and Captain FitzBaldwin's wife was dead. Albemarle was an only child. In time, as his father would most probably be before him, he would be Lord Yarlington in his own right. The health of the invalid upstairs guaranteed that.

Three others at the table besides Dawlish and the FitzBaldwins, father and son. Formal introductions. A Mr. Elmore Whitby, anything between thirty and fifty, his grooming impeccable, his dress immaculate, what looked like diamond links in his shirt cuffs, an air of what Dawlish judged to be insincere cordiality. An American, introduced as Mr. Bulloch, with no further clarification. And a Colonel Blackwood, grey, slight but wiry, the captain's age. Dawlish recognised him.

"You won't remember me, sir, but I saw you at the Summer Palace in Pekin." A Royal Engineer, Gordon's superior. He had two arms then. Now an empty sleeve was pinned to his right breast,

"A bad business that. No pleasure in burning it. No option, though." It had been a reprisal for a hideous atrocity. Blackwood winked, as if sharing some disreputable secret. "I hope you got something out of it before those French blackguards did."

"No, sir."

But it had been tempting, as the French and British forces had vied with each other in the looting before the fires were lit. Men had fought over jade and ivory carvings, silken robes, exquisite porcelain, smashing much in their haste and greed and treading it underfoot. It had been the sight of officers as shameless in their plundering as private soldiers that had disgusted and restrained Dawlish.

Talk of China persisted through dinner – reminiscences from Captain FitzBaldwin and Colonel Blackwood, and Dawlish prompted to tell about the Taku assaults. Blackwood made no mention of his missing arm. Conversation drifted to the Crimea – Blackwood had been at Sevastopol and Whitby mentioned having been there too as a lieutenant in the 17th Lancers. Other than a reference to having served in the American Navy, Bulloch contributed little other than questions. Yet for all the easy conviviality, and FitzBaldwin's efforts to draw his son and Dawlish in on something like equal footing, there was a sense of artificiality about it, a conscious effort to steer the talk in an innocuous direction. It was confirmed when the port was passed.

"I know what you young fellows are like," FitzBaldwin said. "Dreading old chaps boring each other and eager for billiards. So I don't mind if you'd like to leave us to it. Enjoy your game."

His son was less than happy when they reached the billiards room.

"They'd like us to think it's business," he said, "but they they'll be swapping smoking-room stories the gov'nor thinks we're too young to hear. I'll wager that that Bulloch fellow has some choice ones."

"Who is he exactly?" Dawlish was imitating his friend's more expert chalking of his cue and trying to appear accustomed to doing so himself. The game was new to him.

"Bulloch? Damned it I know. Only got here yesterday with Whitby. and going off with him again in the morning. All hail fellow, well met, and good for a cigar but he doesn't give much away about himself. The guv'nor seems to like him though – all three of them were shut up together most of the day. Like all the others."

"Others?"

"Several came traipsing through in recent days. Blackwood's the only one to say longer than a night. Whitby's like a shuttlecock. He's been here three times."

"Who is he?"

"Something to do with the court, don't ask me what. But listen here, Dawlish, are we going to play or not?"

Dawlish was the guest. So he played.

*

21

Colonel Blackwood joined them for rough shooting in the estate's woods next morning. Lack of a right arm was no obstacle – he had brought an adapted gun with him. Complicated strapping held the butt to his shoulder and he was as adept in breaking it and reloading for himself as he was in aiming and firing. Two spaniels flushed out wood pigeons – easily brought down – but the rabbits which bounded suddenly from cover were harder targets that only Blackwood hit. As the morning wore on however Dawlish recognised strain in his face, saw that each shot must now be causing pain in his shoulder. He was fumbling slightly as he reloaded but Dawlish looked quickly away lest he be seen noticing it.

"I won't be embarrassed if you'll lend a hand, Mr. Dawlish. I'm short of one myself." No hint of a call for sympathy, something in the tone conveying mild frustration rather than resentment.

Dawlish helped, did so for the remainder of the morning. It had been enough for him to have brought down two wood pigeons, his conscience salved by assurance that they would go too an estate employee's family.

"You've been itching to ask me how it happened," Blackwood said as they headed back for lunch. "My arm. People always are, but they're too embarrassed to ask."

"In China, sir?"

"That's what others mostly assume. Nothing so glorious, though. A bloody stupid accident after I got home. A shoot like today and an idiot to my right. Little more than a scratch, but it went septic. Gangrene then. Nothing for it but to come off."

"Are you still serving, sir?"

"On paper, but I live in hope. There've been one-armed officers before, generals even. Raglan would have been no worse – and no better either – if he'd had two instead of one."

It rained heavily that afternoon. Courtesy as a guest demanded that Dawlish feign enjoyment in two hours' billiards with Albemarle but he was glad afterwards to escape to the library. Several days' Times and Morning Posts and the week's Illustrated London News lay on a table but the bookshelves held nothing published in the last half-century. The FitzBaldwins were clearly not given to literary pursuits. It did not matter. Dawlish had wanted to read Gibbon and now he had his chance. The elegantly bound edition had never been read – it needed a paperknife that he found on the writing desk to cut the pages – but he was entranced by the language as much as the content as he settled into an armchair before the fire. He read until dinnertime – Blackwood was the only other guest now – but he could not avoid more billiards before he went to bed with The Decline and Fall's first volume.

He was glad that it rained the next day and that he could retire to the library after breakfast. He found Blackwood there already.

"Take this with you. I've finished it." The colonel reached out the Morning Post a little later. It had been fascinating to see how he flicked the newspaper open, folded it, held it, read it, flicked to the next page, all with his one arm. "Not good news for the Danes, I fear."

Nor was it. Their hastily mobilised army was in retreat in atrocious conditions – in mud and sleet, when not in snow and ice – from vast earthworks like that great semi-circular rampart shown in an artist's sketch in the Illustrated. Outnumbered by Prussian and Austrian forces, capitulation must be all but imminent. Dawlish felt little interest. It was a land war. The Danish navy was respected and had nothing to fear from Prussia's negligible maritime forces. And the Austrian navy, based in the distant Adriatic, must be a still lesser threat. But even if the Danes had a ten-times larger fleet, it could not decide the contest ashore. Sea power had its limits.

Continued rain and sleet afforded two further comfortable days' reading, punctuated by more billiards – Albemarle was all but proud that he never read a book – and a visit to the stables to talk horseflesh. Nobody proposed church on the Sunday. The next day was clear and they hunted. Dawlish had never been better mounted and, heavy as the going was, he enjoyed the chases. Shooting the next day, Blackwood again an agreeable companion before he left in the afternoon. Captain FitzBaldwin neither shot nor hunted but remained closeted in his study.

"I'm damned if I know what the guv'nor's up to," his son said. "Half-a-dozen telegrams arrived for him yesterday and one of the footmen's been twice to the post office in Taunton with replies."

But the captain was good company after dinner that night. Thirty-seven years' service had generated a fund of stories, even if his son had apparently heard them all before, and he made no hint about younger men wanting billiards.

"You've enjoyed yourself, Mr. Dawlish?" the captain said the morning he was due to leave.

"Splendidly, sir."

"Why not stay on a little longer then? You'll be welcome."

Dawlish did. even though he felt a little guilty at being glad not having to return so soon to Shrewsbury.

The next day the house filled with guests. Blackwood was back, and Bulloch too. Whitby was the last to arrive.

And with him he brought a Mr. Essmann.

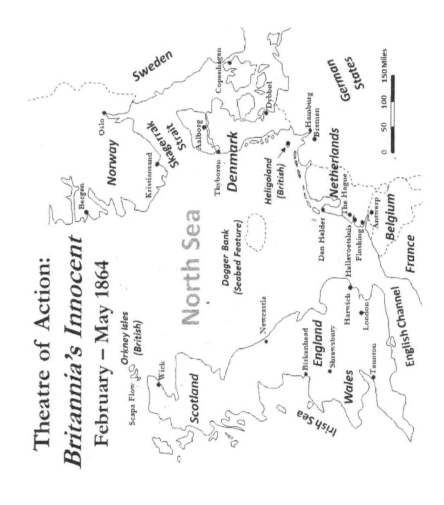

Theatre of Action:
Britannia's Innocent
February – May 1864

Orkney Isles *(British)*

Scapa Flow
Wick

Scotland

Bergen

Norway

Kristiansand

Oslo

Sweden

Skagerrak Strait

Aalborg

Copenhagen

Denmark

Dybbol

Thyboron

Heligoland *(British)*

Hamburg
Bremen

German States

Netherlands

The Hague

Den Helder

Hellevoetsluis
Flushing

Antwerp

Belgium

Newcastle

North Sea

Dagger Bank *(Seabed Feature)*

Harwich

London

France

English Channel

Birkenhead
Shrewsbury

England

Taunton

Wales

Irish Sea

0   50   100   150 Miles

25

Chapter 2

"The guv'nor doesn't want us here tonight," Albemarle FitzBaldwin said. "He tipped me a sovereign and suggested that we take the dog-cart over to Taunton and have a good dinner. There's a theatre there too. We could see whatever's playing, he said."

And better than a theatre was a second-hand bookshop. The second and third volumes of an incomplete set of Gibbon cost a half-crown. The bookseller threw in a battered Motley's Dutch Republic for another shilling. Whatever his next ship, Dawlish would not be short of reading.

It was raining when they retrieved the horse from the livery stables. The evening had been enjoyable. The dinner had been passable, the small theatre shabby and half-empty but the travelling company's performance – a one-act farce and a three-act melodrama – made up with desperate energy what it lacked in subtlety and talent. Albemarle had already drunk too much before a last brandy each sustained them for the cold drive back.

They arrived at the Priory well past midnight. One window was still lit up – Captain FitzBaldwin's study. The curtains were open, two oil lamps burning, and a glimpse showed him in what seemed earnest discussion with Whitby, Essmann and Bulloch. Chilled by now, Dawlish went straight to bed.

He was later than usual to the breakfast room next morning and found only the captain there.

"A good night, Dawlish? You don't seem too worse for wear. I hope my son's the same. No sign of him yet. The kedgeree's good by the way."

Dawlish loaded his plate at the sideboard and the captain waved towards the chair across the table from him. A footman brought toast and coffee.

"Bad weather this." FitzBaldwin gestured towards the heavy rain outside.

"Very bad, sir," Dawlish said.

"Better than snow at this time of year, though. Good for the winter wheat."

The conversation was forced – memorable snowfalls in earlier years, damages by high winds, flooding – and Dawlish felt uncomfortable, as if under scrutiny. He ate quickly.

"If you'll excuse me, sir." He had finished, was standing up. The library beckoned.

"I'd like a word with you, Dawlish. It'd be better in my study."

Dawlish's heart thumped. He was a guest here, generously treated, but he was still a midshipman, and FitzBaldwin was a captain, something godlike. Requests like this – politely phrased orders – seldom boded well.

FitzBaldwin had sensed his concern. "No, I'm not asking for tales out of school about young Albemarle. Even if I did, I doubt you're the sort who'd tattle."

A coal fire was glowing in the study's grate. FitzBaldwin motioned that Dawlish take an armchair to one side of it and sat at the writing desk himself.

"Al tells me that your father is an attorney?"

"A solicitor, sir. In Shrewsbury."

"And your uncle was Ralph Page?"

"You knew him, sir?"

"Not well. I just met him once or twice. A good man and a fine officer, I understand."

"He's dead. Six years ago." The loss still painful.

A pause that seemed to last for aeons, coals settling in the fire, a ticking clock, rain gurgling in the gutters outside.

"This isn't an easy thing to say," FitzBaldwin broke the silence. "Not easy for you to hear either, but I'd be doing you an injustice if I didn't say it. Don't be offended."

Dawlish felt his heart pound, his mouth dry, his brain racing to identify some forgotten dereliction.

"You're a nobody, Mr. Dawlish. You're a gentleman, but you're a nobody."

No hint of malice in the voice, but the words were devastating, humiliating, nonetheless, and all the worse for coming from a man he had come to like and admire. But not to be accepted, even from a captain.

"My father's a gentleman and –"

"A nobody also. A small-town attorney, a decent man no doubt, just as your uncle was a respected officer. But nobodies, both of 'em."

Dawlish stood up. "I thank you for your hospitality, sir. I'll be leaving this house directly." He moved towards the door.

"Sit down. Sit down, Nicholas." FitzBaldwin had not used his name before. "Hear me out. I told you this wouldn't be easy."

Dawlish sat down. His hands were shaking.

"I've seen you, and I like what I've seen and what I've heard. Sam Caulfield's no fool and he was damn impressed by you. More, I fear, than

27

anybody's ever been by Albemarle. But there's another difference between you and my son. You've got no great expectations and he has, not in the navy maybe, but here. By no merit of his or mine. Did he mention that my brother is upstairs? Lord Yarlington. Whom everybody is too civil to mention?"

Dawlish nodded.

"He won't live. Not long, and that'll be a mercy for him. And I'll take his seat in Westminster in coronet and ermine robes and all that flummery and Al will take it after me. Inheriting it won't make me leave the navy, because I love it, but Albemarle will, because his heart isn't in it. He'll be more than happy with what's here."

Almost three-thousand acres, Dawlish had heard. And this house, its walled garden, the stables, in all likelihood a fortune in Consols also…

"And you'll only have the navy, Nicholas."

The farms too, Dawlish thought. A hundred pounds or so in a good year. And in a bad… He'd already witnessed the genteel poverty of so many officers, even of captains, keeping up appearances while haunted by fear of half-pay.

"There will always be opportunities, sir." He wanted to believe it.

"It's not Nelson's navy anymore. No big war in prospect, no prize money, little opportunity for a nobody, however talented, to stand out and reach senior rank unless he has influential friends."

The next words, honest but chilling, were inevitable.

"You've got no such friends, Nicholas."

"I'll make my own way. I'll do it on my own."

He wanted to rush from the room, but he was damned if he was going to retreat. He'd stand his ground.

"I'm trying to help you, Nicholas," FitzBaldwin said. "Advice I'd give Al if he needed it. I'm telling you that you need somebody who'll remember your name. Somebody who matters."

"It sounds sycophantic, sir." His uncle would never have made such a bargain.

"Nothing to compromise your honour, Nicholas. You might never meet the person and I've no doubt that your service would be just as meritorious if your name were never known to them. But such a person needs to know it and remember it, and recognise it when it crops up."

Put that way, it didn't seem dishonourable. Not completely.

"There's an opportunity now," FitzBaldwin said. "An opportunity to get your name remembered. It won't come back."

"What is it?" Dawlish found his mouth dry, his voice hoarse. He was wondering if he should even have asked. But he had.

"I can't tell you yet. Only that you may never get another chance like it. If you say 'Yes' you'll find out today. If it's 'No' then you'll leave immediately, in amity, and forget I've ever spoken to you like this."

He thought of Shrewsbury. His father, his sister, his brother, his old nurse. Loving him, proud of him. But he was already separated in spirit from them, always would be, and they had no conception of the world he had chosen, nor could they help or guide him in it. But the man now speaking to him with apparent goodwill did. And he was a respected officer, courage proven, generous and decent as he had proved himself in his own home, honesty unquestioned. There could be nothing dishonourable…

"It's about these visitors, is it, sir?" Words to buy time as his mind raced.

"You're not blind, Nicholas."

"Is it about Denmark?"

"Yes or No, Nicholas?"

"The person you mentioned, sir. Is —"

"Yes or No?"

And still the coals settling in the fire, the ticking clock, the rain gurgling in the gutters outside.

"Yes," he said.

*

The train must be nearing Harwich now and Dawlish took one last look at his sketch before he began to tear it up, first in two. The closed compartment had afforded privacy to draw it but he would not want to have it found on him if…

"Hold on, Nick," Albemarle FitzBaldwin said. "Let me have a last look."

He took the two pieces, held them together, scanned the drawing, its plan and profile, the annotations.

"You've got a bloody good memory, Nick," he said. "I didn't take in half of this."

But it wasn't just a good memory, Dawlish knew. It was concentration, an ability to focus on a subject and note the smallest details. Remembering came easily afterwards. He'd once thought that ability a universal one but contact with his contemporaries had shown it to be otherwise.

"We'll see her soon enough." Dawlish took back the torn sheet and began to rip it into yet smaller pieces. He did not need it anymore. Making the drawing had made the ship real to him. And he felt something more, something like a hunger for her, humble though his role on board would be

He'd sketched the *Galveston* from memory of the drawing that Bulloch had shown him while Captain FitzBaldwin had injected his own comments at intervals. Whitby watched as an adult might when amused by children's enthusiasm for a simple game.

"We got her out of Lairds just in time," Bullock said. "The Yankees were pressing for her to be detained. They didn't want another *Alabama*. We couldn't trust the government here not to yield to them."

Bulloch's pride was obvious as he mentioned the raider. The Confederate States' Ship, CSS *Alabama*, had slipped out of Laird's Birkenhead yard eighteen months before and had been devastating maritime trade of the Northern States ever since. Prizes had been taken – dozens, most of them burned, a few retained to send captured crews to safe ports. She had ranged over the Atlantic and Indian Oceans, had struck even within the Magellan Strait. She was still at large, with Union cruisers in a so-far futile pursuit.

"Nobody ever believed the story about your new ship being ordered for Ecuador." Something like mocking satisfaction in Whitby's voice. "Calling her the *Manabí* didn't fool anybody, Bulloch, not your Union friends, not Her Majesty's Government. You weren't going to work the same trick twice."

Bulloch ignored the gibe. Dawlish felt himself liking the bearded American with the deep sunk eyes. It was easy to imagine him on a ship's bridge, easy too to recognise resolution under the slow soft drawl, the over-courtly manners.

"She's the *Galveston* now, sir," Bulloch said.

"Not until she's fulfilled her obligations," Whitby said. "Three month's service from the date we accept her, Bulloch. You know the terms."

"I think our young friends are more interested in the ship herself," FitzBaldwin's tone was conciliatory. "Let's take a look at 'em."

Dawlish's gaze had been fixed on the drawings already spread on the table. Not just the hull, but the wickedly curved ram bow. And most of all the wonder that he had seen in sketches in illustrated papers that showed armoured vessels battering each other on American inshore waters. A turret.

FitzBaldwin's finger swept over the drawings and Dawlish saw that he too was entranced by the concept's daring. A steamer, her brig sailing-rig all but nominal, nineteen hundred tons, just over two hundred feet from ram-point to counter. Two thousand horsepower and twin shafts, ten knots achieved when she had sped out from the Mersey, had turned south at Anglesey, had forged southwards through the Irish Sea. And armoured with six-inch thick plates along the sides of the hull above the waterline.

"But only two guns," Albemarle said. He too must have accepted an offer like that made to Dawlish – his father might have allowed him no option. FitzBaldwins were not expected to shirk challenges. "It looks like too much ship for too few cannon."

"Two three-hundred pounder Armstrongs," FitzBaldwin said. "Landing even one shot will sink any ship afloat."

And that was the intention, Bulloch told Dawlish later that day when he had encountered him in the library, poring over an atlas.

"She'll break any blockade," he said. "The Yankees have nothing to match her. Charleston, Wilmington, Mobile, any port in our hands, she'll clear the Yankees from their approaches and she'll hold them open afterwards."

Dawlish had seen blockade runners clustered at Bermuda, fast, lean vessels crammed with weapons and medical supplies and waiting for dark nights to run westwards past the Union patrols. Not just with necessities for waging war either. Fortunes were made by shipments of luxuries unavailable within the beleaguered Confederacy. Clearing the access to any of the major Southern ports would bring trifles no less than essential supplies and weaponry flooding in.

"Will breaking the blockade win the war, sir?" Dawlish had asked

"We won't win it, not outright, not in battle," Bullock said. "We don't need to. We've just got to hold 'em long enough to get recognition. By Britain, by France. Get the Confederacy recognised as a sovereign state. And then the Yankees will back out of it. They're sick of it already, they've lost so much. They're not defending their own homes, their lands, their own sacred institutions. But we are."

Dawlish had learned from FitzBaldwin what James Dunwoody Bulloch was. Not just an officer with fifteen years' service in the United States Navy who had resigned to make a fortune in merchant shipping. He was now an agent of the Confederate States, sent to purchase supplies in Europe, to broker sales of the cotton brought out by the blockade runners, to order warships from British and French yards and get them armed and manned.

For which the money had now run out.

"There'll be an election in the north in November," Bulloch said. "Lincoln won't win it, not with all the blood he's squandering like water. There'll be some other candidate who'll see sense, who'll accept the inevitable, recognise us, sign a peace. We've just got to make them bleed for every foot of ground they try to take between now and November."

And the *Galveston* would support that bleeding. But only if certain other conditions were fulfilled first. Because for now she lay in Antwerp, her presence tolerated by corrupt Belgian officials and her single turret empty of the two Armstrongs cannons that were even now being shipped from Newcastle. And before the Confederate colours could be raised there was an obligation to be satisfied, one that would pay for her arming and her manning.

A three-months obligation.

Cold air flooded into the compartment as Dawlish lowered the sliding window. It was late on this winter afternoon, light fading, landscape bare, the first lights of evening winking in distant cottages as the train rushed on. He tore the drawing's pieces into yet smaller fragments and then released them into the blast outside.

Twenty-four hours from now he would be on board the *Galveston*.

But that would not be her name.

Not yet.

*

At the Priory, earlier that morning, Blackwood had asked him to join him on a last rough shoot. Dawlish had liked him, felt that the feeling was mutual. Stray references had indicated that the colonel's only son had died of fever during his first season in India.

"Bulloch's funds have run out," Blackwood told him. "There was barely enough to have Laird's release that ironclad. Whitby got wind of it, pulled a few strings in Brussels and settled with Armstrongs for the guns, paid for their shipment. And he's negotiated loans on impeccable security and he's covering all the other costs also. Your pay, mine, all the rest of 'em"

"Who exactly is Mr. Whitby, sir?" Dawlish tried to sound casual as he reloaded Blackwood's shotgun. He had been showing signs of pain after a dozen shots.

Blackwood laughed. "You know that the group I'm recruiting isn't to be called the Alexandra Legion or Alexandra's Own, not under any circumstances? But you know the name and nationality of a certain august personage's wife?"

The name said it all. The Prince of Wales' Danish wife, Alexandra, had given birth to an heir the previous month, just as her father's kingdom was being plunged into war and invasion. The rejoicings in England for the birth had been lavish and it was impossible to imagine her husband denying her anything. Not even a small army to help uphold her nation's honour.

"Whitby's her secretary," Blackwood said. "British father, Danish mother – he speaks the language perfectly. He did well enough in the army but he's done better as a courtier and he knows bankers too. He's been the go-between. He's managing the finances."

"And Mr. Essmann?"

"Major Essmann. The lady's cousin sent him from Denmark with news of where his force was headed. Essmann's a damn resourceful fellow. Came across in a fishing boat, landed near Berwick. Never rested until he got to Marlborough House."

Residence of the Prince and Princess of Wales.

And the Princess's cousin, the man whom Blackwood was gathering a force of unemployed ex-soldiers to support, was a Colonel Friherre Axel Saabye.

"There was talk of a legion as soon as hostilities became inevitable," Blackwood said. "The prince was all for it. He even talked about leading it himself, though no one thought he was serious, and he wasn't. Just a small addition to the main Danish force, a token, a gallant gesture. And just enough to irritate his mother – he likes doing that – and to spite his sister."

His mother, the Queen, still in extravagant mourning for her sainted German husband. His elder sister, married to the son of the Prussian king, already mother of an heir.

It was public knowledge that there had been little love between princess and prince, sister and brother. She had been their father's favourite and he his disappointment. Rumours were widespread that the Queen held her son responsible for his father's death, the worthy man's will to combat the typhoid that had killed him weakened by revelation of the prince's squalid affair with an actress. Britain was officially neutral in the conflict between Denmark and the German states but there was no doubt where the sympathies of the Queen and her elder daughter lay. That was enough to turn the prince into an ardent supporter of his wife's homeland.

"There's no value in the legion – sorry, the volunteer force – joining the Danes' main army now," Blackwood said. "Since it retreated it's being penned in against the eastern coast by the Prussians, and the Austrians are driving north up central Jutland. Saabye's force – a ragtag collection, but with fight in them – is moving up the west coast. He's headed for a position that could be bloody nearly untakeable if he gets entrenched in time. It's a place called Thyborøn. And that's where Alexandra's Own – no, the volunteers – will support him."

"Is the *Galveston* to support him too, sir?"

"Floating artillery, Dawlish. Floating heavy artillery."

Sworn to secrecy, assured that the period of his absence would be covered by a delay at the Admiralty in assigning him to his next ship, Dawlish was privy now to the outlines of the plan.

Support by land, support by sea.

Blackwood's deputies had assembled the best part of two companies of discharged soldiers at Hull, as many of them as possible sappers or gunners, and due to by shipped in secret across the North Sea by chartered steamer.

And at Antwerp the *Galveston* was swinging at anchor in a little-used side-channel of the Scheldt river. She was still just partly manned. Like the *Alabama*, her crew were British seamen lured by high pay, commanded by an ex-officer of the United States Navy.

Blockade-run cotton had paid enough for her iron frames and plating, for her engines and boilers and masts. But not enough for the Armstrong three-hundred pounders she would need for breaking the Union blockade, nor for their munitions, nor for coal to feed her furnaces, nor for food and wages or bounties for her mercenary crew. Those costs had been advanced by Whitby and *Galveston* must earn them before she could at last head across the Atlantic.

Earn them off the Danish coast.

And under the Danish ensign.

*

34

The lights of Harwich slid past in the dark, on both sides at first, then on the right only. The moon's reflection on still water confirmed that the train had run on to the quayside. The brakes squealed. Masts and rigging outlined in stark black against the brighter sky, a glow above a funnel, lanterns suspended above semi-circular paddle boxes and passengers from another train filing up the gangplank to the nightly mail-packet.

There must be a pillar-box on the station platform, Dawlish thought as he lifted his valise down from the rack above the seat. He had a letter to post to tell his family that he had been called away. On naval business.

It wasn't quite a lie.

CSS Galveston – alias Odin

Builder: Lairds Dockyard, Birkenhead
Launched: November 1863
Completed: March 1864 (at Antwerp)
Displacement: 1900 tons
Length: 207 feet overall
Beam: 40 feet
Armour: 6" Side Belt, 9" Turret

Machinery: 2000 Horsepower, Twin Screws
Speed: 10 Knots (Max.)
  7 Knots (Cruising)
Armament: 2 X 9". Rifled Muzzle-loaders
  Armstrongs, 300 lb. Shells
Complement: 125 (Ideal)

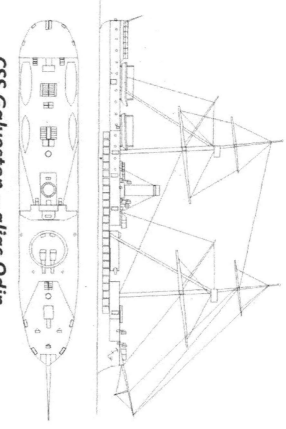

Chapter 3

The packet docked at the Dutch port of Flushing just before dawn. Dawlish hoped that he and Albemarle FitzBaldwin looked like young gentlemen down from Oxford who were embarking on a European tour. He beckoned to a porter to carry their valises ashore, then followed. Lanterns threw yellow light and long shadows in the customs hall but they were waved through without inspection of their luggage. They pushed their way out into the damp cold through the bustle of other travellers. A small throng was waiting outside, hotel servants offering accommodation, bleary-eyed clerks sent to meet arriving businessmen, an old couple rushing forward to embrace a woman and her two children.

"This way, gentlemen."

They had not noticed him glide up behind him and the words were heavily accented. He was shabbily clad, nondescript. They followed him in silence for a hundred yards along the quayside. He paused in a wall's shadow, fished in his pocket and handed each a small envelope with the feel of a few coins inside.

"You've enough there to get you to Antwerp." He nodded towards a small river steamer. "You'll be met there." He turned and walked away.

Many of the passengers from Harwich boarded also, serious-looking men with briefcases – Antwerp was a major trading and commercial centre. Though Belgian, much of the exports from the German States, beyond to the east, passed through it.

Dawlish and Albemarle stayed on deck after the vessel pulled away and headed upstream. A blood-red sun hovered low in the south-east and cast cold light on the broad grey River Scheldt – some three miles wide at this point. Level land extended on either shore, protected by dykes high enough in places to cut off the view and to indicate that the ground behind was below river level. At intervals there were windmills that looked forlorn as they stood unmoving in the still cold. Glimpses of fields, flatter than any billiard table, some bounded by ditches rather than hedges, thatched farm houses and barns, red-tiled roofs clustered around dark church towers. The river widened to perhaps five miles, large islands of dark silt exposed by the falling tide, the navigation channel at the centre marked by buoys. For this was an international waterway, free navigation guaranteed by treaty, even though the land to south and north was Dutch territory, and would be almost until the outskirts of Antwerp.

Dawlish found the view depressing and the chill was eating into him. There would be hours more of this — some forty winding miles — and he was glad to adjourn with his companion to the warmth of the men's saloon ahead of the spindly funnel. It was thick — choking — with tobacco smoke but at least there was hot coffee to be had, and a breakfast of ham and eggs. Afterwards he drifted into uncomfortable slumber on an upholstered bench, lulled by the beat of the craft's paddles.

The view had little changed when Dawlish came on deck again two hours later. The bows were headed north-eastwards now, the river's breadth undiminished, but the extent of the exposed mudbanks confirmed that it was low water and progress was faster. Far astern he could see the roofs and spires of a substantial town. He consulted the small guide he had brought. It must be Terneuzen, a small port on the southern shore with canal links, the book said, to Ghent to the south.

He could not put off any longer the action he had shrunk from since leaving the Priory. The French-stamped envelope, postmarked Pau, had arrived on the last morning. It had been redirected from his father's house by Susan — her handwriting was unmistakable — and he suspected, feared, that its news was bad. He ripped it open and a found a single sheet.

Since he had joined the navy, he had written twice a year, in French, to Madame Sapin, the lady — he shied away from the word mistress — who had comforted his uncle's last years. She had been like a mother to himself, her daughter Clothilde like a sister, when he had been there during his uncle's final months. Her replies, warm and affectionate, had always reached him. But none had come in the last twelve months. Desperation had prompted him to write to the Reverend Augustus Lyall, minster at the Anglican church at the spa town, to ask for information. He remembered him without fondness.

The clergyman had not wasted words in his reply. He had enquired about the person — he made the word seem indecent — to whom Mr. Dawlish had referred. She had died in February of the previous year. He understood that a Roman curé had denied her burial in a church graveyard, in view of the life she had led, but another had relented. There were conflicting stories as to what had become of her daughter but there was some evidence that she had left Pau with an army officer. A married man and not her husband, he underlined. And he hoped that Dawlish read his bible daily — he had chosen a profession that exposed young men to many temptations.

Dawlish felt the same desolation as when his uncle had died. It wasn't just Madam Sapin's death – the lack of letters had led him to fear, even expect, that. Far worse was what might have become of Clothilde. It would have broken his uncle's heart, as it now broke his own. He crunched the letter into a ball and was about to throw it overboard when he hesitated, opened it again, read it once more. It seemed even worse a second time. At last, he cast it away.

Cold as it was, he had no desire to re-enter the saloon's fug and he remained on deck as the steamer followed the channel's windings. The land to either side was no more inspirational than before but the river had a fascination of its own, its traffic constant upstream and down. Steamers ploughed onwards under their own power, many large sailing ships and even more smaller ones were ghosting in the light airs, others, and strings of barges too, were under tow by thrashing paddle-tugs. Outside the borders of the main channel, flat-bottomed craft with brown sails and huge lee-boards navigated the passages between the silt-islands with the confidence of long experience. The *Galveston* had come this way under cover of darkness, Bulloch had told Dawlish, secrecy assured by liberal payment to an expert pilot and to a dozen officials onshore.

The river narrowed, a half-mile wide and then a quarter, and grew ever more sinuous. Soon after midday Antwerp was growing on the horizon. One last loop, low swampland to starboard, but on the other bank moored shipping, wharves, warehouses, narrow channels leading off the main stream, gated docks, carpets of flat barges. Then on to the city itself. A turreted medieval fortress lay directly on the river, a quay extending on either side with a frontage of high brick-built houses, splendidly ornate. Soaring behind them was the majestic tower of the cathedral and the hint of yet more splendour beyond. Dawlish's guidebook had told him that the city was magnificent, but this excelled all expectation. Regret stabbed. He would have no opportunity to explore.

They landed, shuffled through the small customs shed. Outside it, cabs taking passengers away, families reuniting. Unspoken but mutual alarm that there was apparently nobody to meet them – they had been given no address. Two well-dressed young men trying with little success to look casual and inconspicuous must be easy to identify. The contact, when he finally came, was in threadbare civilian grab and spoke with an accent recognisable as Liverpudlian. No name, no introduction.

"Better carry your own baggage. Pay him off." He gestured to the morose porter they had engaged. "Just follow me."

A small steam launch was moored at steps some three hundred yards beyond, two men making some adjustment to its exposed engine, seamen by the look their clothing. Dawlish and Albemarle took seats in the cockpit and the craft cast off, swung into the stream and headed back downriver.

"Is it far?" Albemarle asked.

"Far enough," the man at the tiny helm said. Words spoken in what must be a Flemish accent, the tone indicating no desire for conversation.

Dawlish found himself losing track after the launch left the main channel and began to thread its way between moored shipping and barges, turning up smaller waterways, past slipways with coastal craft drawn up for repair, smoke and steam billowing from straining cranes, open-fronted workshops, the glow of small furnaces, the slap of overhead belting, the clanging of hammers. On through the labyrinth – narrower channels, river tugs and barges here – and patches of open swampy ground. The overall direction, as best Dawlish could judge, was north-westwards. At last the bustle fell away astern and there were only open muddy banks. Then a last turn, and into an all but empty side-channel of the main river that Bulloch had mentioned.

And there, moored fore and aft, lay the craft whose features and dimensions Dawlish had already memorised, whose outlines he had sketched on the train. As yet, he could see her only stern-on, her half-painted hull black and steaked with rust, hinged bulwarks lying down along her flanks to expose her deck, two ochre-painted tripod masts – no shrouds – and a single black funnel amidships, smokeless for now. The turret was hidden by the superstructure but the absence of any other ship alongside – and one should have arrived from Newcastle by now – indicated that no guns nestled yet within the iron drum.

"Bloody ugly looking, isn't she?" Albemarle said.

"No," Dawlish said. "She's beautiful."

He was entranced. He had served on minor gunvessels and on a twin-deck ship of the line with ninety guns that would have seemed out of place at Trafalgar only because she carried a tiny steam engine as an auxiliary to her sailing rig. Large or small, all had been wooden-built and even the most traditionally-minded officers admitted the uncomfortable truth that such hulls would be doomed if exposed to explosive shells.

But what lay before him now was something wholly different, an iron ship with iron armour, designed from the outset to withstand pummelling by solid shot, to shrug off explosive rounds. Driven by a powerful steam engine, roles reversed so that now it was the sails that were auxiliary, she could manoeuvre independently of wind to carry two of the heaviest guns afloat to bear on any enemy's weakest spot.

He knew that he was looking at the future.

The future he wanted.

*

The man with long hair, close cropped beard and grimy face looked no different to those with whom he had been straining to drag a winch into position. He wiped his hand on his grease-stained dungarees and held it out.

"Welcome on board, gentlemen." The accent was similar to Bulloch's. "Woodham Lorance. Captain, Confederate States Navy."

They introduced themselves – mention of the rank of midshipman embarrassing.

Lorance must have noticed that, for he laughed. "Watch-keeping lieutenants as soon as we're battleworthy, gentlemen." He glanced towards their clothing, tweed travelling suits and coats, Albemarle's with a cape. "You've brought a change, I hope. Working rig?"

They hadn't. Suitable clothing would be provided, Captain FitzBaldwin had said. Practical, without insignia. Lorance had heard nothing about it however but he called a man over to get them kitted and get them back to him. There was work to be done.

All that was available were coarse dungaree jackets and trousers like Lorance himself wore. Stiff and dirt-engrained, they looked – and smelled – as it they had never been washed. Dawlish felt revulsion as he pulled them on in the small cabin he would share with Albemarle. The furnishing was incomplete, indeed hardly started – bare iron-plate that should have been wood-panelled, rust on the deck, unvarnished bunks without matrasses, no cupboard or closet, no writing desk. The *Galveston's* departure from the Birkenhead yard had been hurried indeed.

"I'm damned if I'm wearing these rags. And those boots! A tramp would turn up his nose at them!" Albemarle hadn't changed his clothes, was looking at Dawlish with disgust. "We're officers, Dawlish!"

"You saw what Lorance is wearing himself?"

"He's an American! Those fellows think nothing of getting their hands dirty, un-officerly as it might be. You saw him slaving with those common seamen."

"I thought the better of him for it," Dawlish said. "You can see the state of this vessel? There's still so much to be done."

"Not by me, Dawlish. Not that type of work. Doesn't the fellow know that he's on board by sufferance? That it's my father who'll command her when he gets here?"

"You're going to tell Captain Lorance that?"

"I'll be courteous," Albemarle said. "Courteous but firm. That's it. If the fellow's a gentleman he'll understand."

They went on deck. A flat-top barge had drawn alongside and coal was were being hoisted onboard. Lorance himself was one of the men lugging sacks to the circular coaling hatches and emptying them into the bunkers below. A dark cloud billowed up from the opening as each load fell.

"Here, young fellows!" Lorance called. "Lend a hand!"

His eyes were set in light circles on an otherwise blackened face. A flash of anger in them as he took in Albemarle's unchanged clothing. But Albemarle was standing his ground and glancing towards Dawlish for support.

"Captain Lorance, sir! A word with you!" A quaver in his voice.

Lorance approached and flapped the sack he had just emptied. Dust and particles fell on Albemarle's well-polished shoes.

"You'll have a word with me when I ask for it. Not before." Lorance had brought his face close to Albemarle's. "You understand, sir?" The words so low as to be almost inaudible.

"My father —"

"Will brook no more insubordination than I will. You understand, sir? Good! Here's a sack! Take it! You can see what's needed."

Albemarle was looking down on his elegantly-cut suit. His father's own tailor had made it for him, he had told Dawlish. Twenty-two guineas.

"What are you waiting for, Mr. FitzBaldwin? The work won't do itself. And you, Mr. Dawlish, why are you standing around? You'd better get busy too."

Lorance turned on his heel and strode to the growing heap of sacks at the deck edge. He swung one on to his shoulder and joined the line of men carrying them towards the coaling hatches. Dawlish followed. He found the weight almost too much for him, and he staggered beneath it, but, when he had emptied, it came back for another. And another, and another.

Albemarle joined the line too and his clothing was soon little better than Dawlish's, and worse for the work in hand. The sacks were still

42

swinging up from the barge and long hours stretched ahead to fill the bunkers.

And Dawlish knew now the sort of man who had brought this ironclad here.

One he might not like – though he was unsure about that – but one he could respect.

*

The galley was as unfinished as so much else of the ship but there was a stew of indeterminable sort to bring warmth after two chilling hours of coal-heaving. Darkness had fallen but work continued after the hurried meal, not coaling now but fitting of equipment that had been brought in crates from the builder's yard. Both engines had been ready for sea, the result of two days and nights' frantic effort to finish installation. Completion of all else had been left undone while the threat of impoundment by the British government had hung over the vessel.

Dawlish learned as much as he laboured in the engine room. Lorance had sent him there to assist eight tradesmen in connecting piping, hammering flanges tight, replacing packings, lubricating bearings, running copper tubing and mounting gauges. These men from Laird's yard, and a dozen others like them, had accompanied the *Galveston* on her flight. They worked throughout the passage against the promise of twice their normal wages and a further bounty before they left for home. A handful of seamen, several of them ex-Royal Navy, had brought the vessel here on similar terms. More would be needed if this was to be a fighting ship and these Captain FitzBaldwin would bring from Britain in the coming days.

Exhausting as it was, hands numb from cold, Dawlish felt satisfaction in the work. On HMS *Foyle*, when not on watch, he had spent hours in the engine room, fascinated by the machinery and learning its purposes. He had admired the skills of the men who tended it, even if their chief was barred from the wardroom by carrying a warrant, not a commission. Steam would be essential in that future he wanted and he shared none of the scorn for it as a begrudged necessity that so many sail-obsessed officers professed. But the engine he was now crawling under was more powerful than any he had seen before, a thousand horsepower, and another like it lay alongside to drive together the twin shafts and screws.

They worked until nearly midnight, would start again at daybreak. White frost had settled when Dawlish came on deck and the cold made him shiver. The glow of a portable forge forward, and the noise of hammering, confirmed that riveting was still in progress. On much of the decks and upperworks one rivet in three had been omitted to speed completion. Now that lack was being corrected. Further aft there was activity around boat davits that had been lifted on board earlier. Dawlish had last seen Albemarle working there.

"Happy now that you signed on, son?"

He recognised the accent even as he turned.

"Tired, I'll guess? But worth every drop of sweat once we've got to sea." Lorance was even filthier than Dawlish had last seen him. He fished in a pocket, drew out two cigars. "You smoke, sir? Good. Not Havanas, Sumatras only, but just about the best that's to be found in these parts."

Dawlish took one – he had picked up the habit in the West Indies and still felt a little guilty about it. Lorance struck a match on his thigh, held it for Dawlish to draw in the flame, then lit his own.

"You know that you, me and your friend are the only officers on board yet," Lorance said. "You seem game enough even if he isn't. I'm putting you to work in the turret in the morning."

"What work, sir? I haven't seen inside it yet."

"I'll show you."

The twenty-two foot circular drum was positioned a third of the vessel's length back from the bow. The surrounding deck was bare of planking – there had been no time for that – and the cambered metal underfoot was slippery in the frost. The turret lay in a gap between the deckhouses extending ahead and abaft of it. With their sides angled off the central axis, they narrowed almost to sharp points close to the drum so as provide the guns it would contain with the widest possible bearing. A hundred and thirty degrees arc on either broadside, for both guns, Dawlish recalled, and ten more for a single weapon. Fire directly ahead was impossible but the manoeuvrability provided by two screws would all but guarantee that any target could be at the mighty Armstrongs' mercy. The hinged bulwarks were down now but when raised would provide substantial shelter to crew on deck during passage.

"Look in there," Lorance held up a lamp to illuminate one of the two oval gun-ports in the turret face. The sidewalls were revealed as two layers. "You see the armour – nine inches of iron here. Six at the rear. And the teak backing it? Twelve inches of it and a half- inch of iron behind that again to hold splinters. There's not a gun afloat that can penetrate it."

They entered through a manhole at the rear. The lantern threw deep shadows but enough light to show the two slides on which the guns would be mounted, the racks along the sides, now empty, for storing charges and shot and shell, the beams overhead for the chain hoists that would lift them to the muzzles. There was no roof to the drum other than a canvas tarpaulin stretched across. It felt cramped already and it would be worse with cannons and munitions in place and fourteen men to load and fire them.

"How's it turned it, sir?"

"That crank behind you, and that gearing, Dawlish. Like a winch. Same on the other side. Two men to a crank. Damn hard effort, but it should be possible to manage a complete rotation in under two minutes. You can't see the roller-bearings underneath. That's where the problems are. We'll need to go below to take a look."

Dawlish could sense the older man's elation, a hint of delight in challenge. And for all the easy familiarity, he saw that it was not to be taken at face value. This man could seem everybody's friend, be nobody's.

Access to the space beneath was through a manhole. A circular track there supported the turret, stout verticals beneath carrying the weight towards the keel, a pillar as the central pivot. Glimpses of gear-toothing on the track's inner edges and of the conical rollers on which the whole assembly would rotate.

"It's jamming, won't shift, that's the trouble," Lorance said. "The whole damn thing will have to be jacked up and the rollers realigned before the guns arrive. That's your job."

"I'll do my best, sir, but —" Dawlish began.

"No experience of the like? Me neither. But the Laird's people know what they're doing even if they're not doing it fast enough. You'll need to oversee them, keep their noses to the grindstone, not accept excuses. Know when the foreman is talking sense, get the feeling of when he isn't and put the fear of Christ in him if it's needed."

"When will the guns be here, sir?"

"Two days, maybe less, so you're going to have this thing rotating smoothly be then."

"It'll be done, sir." The responsibility was at once flattering and frightening.

I'll rise to it, come what may.

"Time to get some sleep, Mr. Dawlish. It'll be a long day tomorrow."

In the cold, bare cabin Albemarle was already asleep on the lower bunk, a blanket clutched around him. Dawlish swung his valise on to the upper – he would have no other pillow. He climbed up and wrapped his own thin blanket around him. He was cold, miserably cold, but he slept anyway.

Chapter 4

The work next day – February 28th – was brutal and slow. The four jacks available proved insufficient to lift the turret above its track. Time was lost when Dawlish went in the steam launch with the foreman to seek more. They found four of sufficient capacity at the third small repair yard they visited. Negotiation of rental terms was difficult – a mixture of Flemish and broken English on the yard owner's side, English only on the other. It was mid-afternoon before the extra jacks were in place and lifting could commence. It took two hours to raise the turret six inches so as to expose the rollers. They were pitted with rust, the track also. The missing rivets had allowed sufficient water to enter the hull during transit to splash high enough with the vessel's motion to damage surfaces that should be mirror smooth. They never would be again, Dawlish recognised, and the best that could be done was to scour away the rust with wire brushes and to lubricate heavily with grease.

Lorance looked in twice to check progress.

"We can drop the turret by midday tomorrow," Dawlish told him. "We'll have to work through the night."

"No later than midday, Mr. Dawlish."

It would mean cajoling, confrontation if necessary. It was Dawlish's first experience of working with civilians and he didn't like it. Three were dragging their feet but most of the others seemed to have some pride in their work and were putting their backs into it. Even the best of them seemed to complain incessantly and volubly. The foreman was surly and clearly resentful of Dawlish and a few did not hesitate to answer back. It was only the promise of another bonus – "Whitby can afford it", Lorance had said – and the threat of losing it, that kept the work progressing.

Activity on deck was no less intense, not just continuing riveting and davit-mounting, but hoisting of the yards and gaff and setting of the running rigging. Powerful as the engines were, the *Galveston's* brig configuration was an essential auxiliary for lessening dependence on coal supplies. Lorance seemed everywhere at once, moving from one work-group to another, tireless and resourceful, impatient of delay, quick with solutions to make up for lack of supplies or equipment, always ready to throw his weight on a straining rope or take a turn with the riveting hammer.

Dawlish was bolting down a plate of stew that evening when Lorance approached again.

"You might be interested in this, Mr. Dawlish." He extended a newspaper folded on an inner page, an article framed by rough red pencil strokes. "Looks like our friends are holding their own for now."

The Times, yesterday's.

"It's much the same story in this one too."

The Morning Post, also yesterday's.

Dawlish scanned the articles. Both newspapers had correspondents in Denmark and both reported that the Danish army had ended its retreat on the east coast, was making a stand there. At a location called Dybbøl – he wondered how it was pronounced. A strong position on the east coast, according to the journalist, one separated by a two-hundred yard strait from the island of Als.

"The only smart thing they've done so far," Lorance said. "Digging in. Hoping the enemy will beat themselves to death against entrenchments."

The Danes had gone to earth along a two-mile arc across a peninsula, with the strait to their rear. The labour needed, in atrocious weather, had been all but superhuman and large redoubts were under construction at several points.

"Do you think the Prussians will do that, sir, beat themselves to death?"

"They're not fools. They won't storm earthworks, not yet, even if they're incomplete. They'll wait, build up their forces, artillery as well as infantry, wear down the Danes by a protracted siege"

. Dawlish read on. There seemed to be no correspondents elsewhere in the country but rumours indicated that the Austrians were pushing northwards through Jutland. Nor was there mention of the Danish force on the west coast about which Essmann had brought news to Britain.

Cleaning and polishing the rollers and track went more slowly than hoped. The midday completion target was not met and the work that dragged through the afternoon hours was only finished just before the next sunrise. Dawlish had expected reproof from Lorance but got none. His body was screaming for sleep as the jacks were reversed and the turret settled again on its circular track.

Time now to test rotation. He stayed below to watch the rollers – he had all but come to know each one individually, had smeared them with grease himself, had laid them gently within the cage that held them apart from each other. Lorance was now in the drum above, heaving with three others on the cranks.

Nothing at first, gasps of effort, calls for two others to join in, still no movement of the gears. Fear unspoken that the mechanism remained stuck, fear that was gone suddenly with the first judder. Movement then, the aligned marks that Dawlish had made on the turret base and on the track jerking apart, stopping, jumping forward again – a sixteenth of an inch, an eighth, a quarter – and then settling into a steady creep. Lorance yelled for the men with him to keep grinding the cranks. The turret rotated on, the rollers rumbling as they crept around the track. A quarter turn was completed now – Dawlish had counted forty-three seconds – and the motion was smooth as the heavy drum's momentum eased the burden on the men straining overhead. The full rotation took twenty-seven seconds longer than the two minutes Lorance had hoped for – and this was without the extra weight of the guns which were yet to be installed. But it was a start.

Two more full rotations confirmed that the problem had been solved. The turret was ready to receive its guns, the *Galveston* her bite.

Dawlish's elation was greater than his exhaustion when he finally collapsed on his bunk.

*

His sleep was short, for the ship from Newcastle had arrived, piloted in darkness up the Scheldt, guided to this anchorage by a Belgian customs launch. Local officials were not just turning a blind eye, rather were they complicit – for price – in the *Galveston's* presence.

Captain FitzBaldwin had come with the nondescript steamer, some sixty seamen with him, most British, many ex-naval. A half-pay Royal Navy lieutenant introduced himself as George Killigrew.

"You look like scarecrows." FitzBaldwin was regarding his son, and Dawlish, with amusement. "Earning your keep, I'll warrant. But we've brought decent clothing."

They were woollen uniforms, naval pattern, thick greatcoats also, coarse linen shirts, warm undergarments and decent sea boots. And no insignia of rank.

The tramp steamer moored along the ironclad's port side. Tarpaulins were stripped back to reveal the two great gun-barrels resting on wooden cradles abaft the foremast. Neither ship had the capacity to lift them – that must wait – but transfer of stores began immediately.

Organising the newly-arrived crew into watches must wait also and every hand was set to hoisting sacks and kegs and crates from the steamer's hold, swinging them across to the *Galveston* and manhandling them to storage. The effort ran in parallel with progress on the fitting out.

Lorance had already struck a deal with a ship-repair yard for the hire of a barge with a stiff-leg derrick – the manager was confident that it was good for a twenty-five ton lift. Dawlish went in the steam launch with the message that it was now needed. Get positioned tonight, hoist in the morning.

"It's not available, young sir." The manager, Mijnheer Reynders, regarded Dawlish through a cloud of cigar smoke and did not rise from behind his desk. "It's needed urgently by another customer. You can tell your friends that they'll have to wait, young sir." The man's English was perfect but his tone was mocking.

"It looks idle to me." Dawlish could see it through the window. It lay against the wharf, several flat-top barges tethered on her other side, all equally deserted.

"Urgently needed, young sir. Tomorrow and the day after also."

"You made a bargain, Mijnheer," Dawlish said. Lorance had told him the terms. Exorbitant, a seller's market. Immediate availability guaranteed, priority over all other customers.

"There's an English expression I've heard," Reynders said. "Don't send a boy to do a man's job. If your baas is interested then he can come himself to talk about it. Tell him that something might be arranged."

"Thank you, mijnheer." Dawlish hoped his anger and humiliation did not show. "I wish you good day."

He was trembling as he walked back to the launch and told its seaman to head back to the *Galveston*. He was already decided on what to do and it did not involve relaying Reynders' demands.

Back on the ironclad he sought out FitzBaldwin.

"The derrick's on its way, Mr. Dawlish?"

"It'll be here by sundown, sir."

FitzBaldwin had seemed impressed when he witnessed rotation of the turret. Lorance had given full credit for it to Dawlish. Something that might be presumed upon.

"A small favour, if I may, sir," Dawlish said.

"A favour?"

"Six men, sir. Just for an hour or two. Veterans. Ex-Navy."

"You're not going to tell me why, are you Mr. Dawlish?"

"I'd prefer not to, sir."

50

"Find Bob Hopper. Tell him I sent you. He was my coxswain once."

Hopper was grizzled, sinewy, had a mouth set in what might be permanent disapproval. Dawlish told him what he needed. Five other men, well able to look after themselves, best if Hopper knew them personally.

"Carrying anything, sir?"

"Belaying pins should be sufficient."

The steam launch threaded its way back towards the repair yard through the maze of channels. Dawlish felt the men's eyes on him, turning away when he glanced towards them. None was younger than his mid-thirties, all had an air of hardness about them, a sense too that transition to civilian life had not been easy. He knew that they were evaluating him, had seen countless young gentlemen before him, would be merciless in their judgement.

I'm not just doing this for the derrick alone. It's for trust, for authority. My authority. I need it from the start.

It was two years since he had first led men older than himself ashore. It had been life and death on the coast of Columbia and it was not here, but the same fear of failure nagged him as it had then.

Now the repair yard. A dozen men replacing plating on the hull of a coaster on the slipway, more on smaller craft moored along the wharf, others visible in the open-fronted workshop beyond. It was impossible to know what loyalty they might feel to Mijnheer Reynders.

Dawlish marched up to the office, a long wooden hut. Two seamen took their place at the door – nobody else to be let enter. The remainder followed him inside. He brushed aside the protests of a clerk in the outer room and made for Reynders' office. The manager himself, alarmed by the commotion, met him at the door.

"We've come for the derrick," Dawlish said. "I expect it's ready."

Reynders retreated to put the desk between them.

"Daar uit! Daar uit!" He had lapsed into Flemish, voice quavering, eyes locked on the belaying pin that Hopper, behind Dawlish, was beating gently on the palm of his left hand.

"Call your foreman," Dawlish said, "and the skipper of that tug I can see out there that's needed to tow the derrick. You've got instructions for them both and I've no time to waste."

"Nee! Godverdomme nee!" Reynders was turkeycock red. Veins bulged in his neck above his collar.

"I haven't got all day."

"I'll have the police here! You can't –"

"Do you think they're not being paid too, mijnheer?"

Dawlish knew it – Lorance had told him. Not just the police either. The burgemeester, several city councillors. "They'd throw their grandmothers into the bargain too if it was worth their while," Lorance had said.

"Nee, Godverdomme! Ik doe het Godverdomme niet en –"

Hopper's belaying pin crashed down on the desk. It shattered a coffee cup and showered its contents over Reynders' waistcoat.

"You heard what the gentleman said, mijnheer. That he hasn't got all day."

Reynders saw the sense of it. He called the clerk and spoke in Flemish. The man was back five minutes later with the foreman and the tug's skipper. From their expressions Dawlish gathered that they were amused, had little sympathy with their master. The skipper assured Dawlish in broken English that the derrick was indeed available and the tug's steam up. It had been shuttling barges all morning. Instructions then from Reynders – words as reluctantly drawn from him as teeth – and the skipper and the foreman left to execute them.

"I'm sure you've got work to keep you here until the derrick's on its way, Mijnheer Reynders," Dawlish said. "Two of my men will keep you company. And they'll like some coffee while they wait. A cigar wouldn't go amiss either."

It took an hour to shift the barges moored alongside the derrick. By mid-afternoon the great rectangular box that supported it was following the underpowered paddle-tug through the labyrinth of waterways towards the *Galveston*.

"Any problems, Mr. Dawlish?" Captain FitzBaldwin asked when he came on board.

"No problems, sir."

"And Hopper? Satisfactory?"

"Very satisfactory, sir."

As darkness fell the derrick had been drawn in along the outer flank of the steamer and secured there. Ready for the first lift tomorrow.

*

It took two days – and nights – to arm the *Galveston*.

The transfer had to be in two steps, first to lift the guns from the steamer to the derrick's barge, then move the barge on the ironclad's other side, lift them again and drop them into the empty turret. The derrick had been positioned so that its boom lay directly above the barrels – eighteen tons apiece – on the steamer's deck. Strain as it might, its steam-driven winch proved incapable of lifting the first. The pistons flailed, slowed, stalled as the cable slack was taken up, as it grew bar-taut, as the barge heeled slightly with the pull, as the blocks at the tripod's apex trembled under the strain.

The cable snapped with a report like a pistol shot. Men dived behind the nearest cover as it whipped down across the deck, writhed, weakened, lashed down a seaman with its last convulsion. The injured man, his clothing shredded by the parted cable to reveal his chest lacerated, his rib-cage shattered, died choking in his own blood an hour later despite the efforts of the Belgian doctor for whom the steam launch was sent. *Galveston* had suffered her first loss even before leaving neutral waters.

The derrick structure itself had proved sound – Reynders had not lied when he had guaranteed it for twenty-five tons. The problem was the cabling – the load on it had to be reduced. There was nothing for it but to double the blocks to increase the mechanical advantage. It took time – hours – to reconfigure the blocks and to thread the cabling around them.

Darkness had fallen before the first barrel eased up from its cradle and was swung across to the derrick barge and set down there on a bed of old railway sleepers. It was after midnight when the second barrel lay alongside it. And all the while the other work continued on the *Galveston*, riveting, rigging, painting.

The barge was repositioned during the night, to the *Galveston's* starboard flank, ready for the morning lift. In the cold early light, the derrick's boom hoisted the first barrel and swung it over to above the turret – the tarpaulin had been stripped away from its open top. Dawlish waited inside with four Laird's workmen, ready to guide the barrel down by ropes attached to either end. Lorance was perched on the rim above to direct activity from there. The barrel inched down, swinging slightly, until it was a foot above the mounting slide and was held there. Dawlish's crew hauled on the ropes to kill the swing, and he called up to Lorance that he was ready. The barrel dropped and the trunnions settled into the bearings that awaited them.

The second lift was delayed by a steam pipe failing on the derrick's winch. It took until late evening to fabricate a replacement, install it, fire up the boiler again and raise steam. It took to midnight to install the second barrel. Dawlish and his crew stood-down.

He found FitzBaldwin waiting for him on deck when he emerged from the iron drum.

"Satisfied now with the turret, Dawlish?"

"Yes, sir." More than happy. Proud.

"That's just as well then. Consider it your charge. Choose your crew tomorrow. I suggest Hopper – he's familiar with heavy guns. Nothing like these though, but he'll manage. He'll help you select the crews."

"Thank you, sir."

He hid the trepidation rising within him, remembered what he had been told by Samuel Caulfield, the aloof captain of HMS *Foyle*.

You'll never be asked to do something you can't do. It may be difficult, but you can do it.

And he would. From this moment he was gunnery officer of the *Galveston*.

Another step away from being a nobody.

*

FitzBaldwin himself accompanied the dead man's body to the cemetery with his weeping bother and five of his friends. Albemarle had gone the night before to arrange with the vicar of the church that ministered to the English community. He brought back a coffin. All the mourners had enlisted together at Newcastle, Dawlish learned, dockers or warehousemen who had had found life outside the navy less congenial than they had anticipated. The gloom that had pervaded the ship since the accident seemed to lift slightly after the launch left. It might not have been a formal naval funeral but FitzBaldwin's decision to be at the graveside when the minister spoke the last words had earned respect from the crew.

And a crew they were now becoming, no longer an all but random collection of discharged seamen. Some had answered a bland newspaper advertisement or had heard of it from a friend already committed. FitzBaldwin himself had contacted others, men who had served with him and who, often nearly destitute, had written to him earlier to ask for references. A few, mostly from Liverpool or Birkenhead, had relatives serving on the *Alabama* and had heard of the virtual fortunes they were earning. Similarly lured, several of the Laird's mechanics had volunteered to remain on board to tend the boilers and machinery.

The newly arrived Lieutenant Killigrew saw to assignments to watches, preparation of duty rosters, recording of supplies, readying for sea. For *Galveston* was all but a fighting ship now, armed, manned, coaled, provisioned, yet she still lacked the training, the repeated drills, that would weld ship and crew together into a single weapon.

Work resumed after the funeral party had left. Dawlish and Hopper supervised transfer of the munitions carried from Newcastle. Silken powder bags in tin cylinders were stacked vertically in the racks around the turret's interior, solid shot and explosive shells with them. Long crates containing Enfield rifles were lugged across.

"She's got a bone in her teeth." Hopper nodded towards a steam launch – not the *Galveston's*, for it had a striped awning aft – that was coming fast down the channel.

Dawlish recognised the figure standing in the bows, the elegance of his clothing at variance with the bleak brown river and its muddy banks. Mr. Elmore Whitby. Secretary to the Princess of Wales. And the man with him was James Dunwoody Bulloch, Confederate agent.

The launch drew alongside. Lorance, also alerted, welcomed them on board. Heads together, a few words exchanged, obvious concern, and then they disappeared aft.

Albemarle joined Dawlish.

"Had you heard anything about them coming here?"

Dawlish shook his head. "Your father said nothing?"

"No. Lorance neither."

They went back to their tasks, heard nothing more until an hour after FitzBaldwin's return from the burial. He too had gone directly aft and must be closeted with the unexpected visitors.

"Captain's compliments, Mr. Dawlish, sir." A seaman knuckling his forehead. "He wants to see you in his quarters."

The semi-circular saloon at the stern would have been comfortable, even luxurious, had it been completed with wooden panelling. Now all was bare metal plating, rust-streaked, glinting with drops of condensation, an inadequate coal stove failing to heat the space. A camp bed lay to one side. Three deal tables, kitchen chairs, a battered desk and several cupboards, last-minutes purchases from a second or third-hand dealer before the hasty escape from the Laird yard.

"Sit down, Dawlish." FitzBaldwin said.

He was seated at the largest table, Lorance, Whitby and Bulloch with him. Faces as grim as those Dawlish had seen on HMS *Plover's* bridge as she had nudged up the Pei-Ho river towards the Taku Forts. Towards slaughter. What appeared to be a chart of the Scheldt estuary lay before them. Killigrew entered as Dawlish sat, Albemarle just after.

"These gentlemen have brought news." FitzBaldwin said.

"There's some of it good," Whitby said. "From Denmark. It came across with another fishing boat. Colonel Saabye's force is getting entrenched."

"May I ask where, sir?" Killigrew asked.

"Somewhere called Thyborøn, on the west coast. Scarcely even a village, but it's on a peninsula. It could be a damn nearly impregnable position."

"And the Austrians?"

"They're digging in too. They haven't forces enough yet for an assault. But they will have – more are moving north."

"There's worse news." FitzBaldwin said. "Tell 'em, Whitby."

"Mr. Bulloch and I have come from The Hague this morning," Whitby said. "A friend at our embassy there had warned us that something was in the offing. We went across from London yesterday for confirmation."

"The Union Navy," Bulloch's voice bitter. "A frigate. The *Conewago*. She arrived in Cherbourg three days ago. She coaled, needed a few repairs because she'd hit heavy weather on the way across, but we've got a report that she was readying in a hurry for departure. She might already be at sea. There's no doubt she knows our whereabouts. She'll be heading up the Channel to wait outside the Scheldt for us."

"There's more," Whitby said. "My friend at the embassy arranged a meeting for us with a senior Dutch official. The sort who provides information for a price. It seems the American ambassador has brought pressure to bear to stop this vessel passing down to the open sea."

"It's Dutch territory on both banks.," Bulloch said. "The Scheldt's an international waterway and it should be no business of the Dutch authorities. But the Yankee ambassador's been quoting all sorts of legal pretexts. That this is an armed ship, not commissioned by a sovereign nation. Virtually a pirate."

"And a duty incumbent on every civilised nation to detain it," Whitby said. "Suppression of brigandage at sea, upholding of peaceful trade, strict interpretation of neutrality, all virtuous stuff. The Yankees have made threats too about trade relations, not so veiled either, and trade's the Dutch lifeblood."

"The upshot is that two Dutch warships are being sent to Flushing," Bulloch said. "A gunboat from Hellevoetsluis – that's nearer – should get there today. A frigate from den Helder, their main base, sometime tomorrow. It'll all be very polite. A request to heave to if we drop downriver, discussions, arguments, quotes from treaty small-print. But long enough to give time for the *Conewago* to reach the mouth of the Scheldt."

Dawlish guessed what was coming when FitzBaldwin leant over and swept his hand across the river's winding fifty-mile course.

"Ready or not, that's why we're leaving tonight," he said.

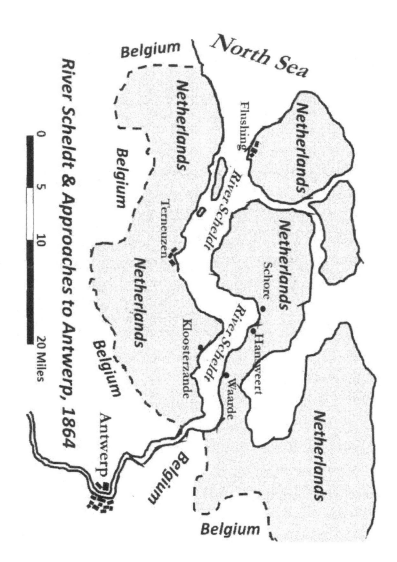

River Scheldt & Approaches to Antwerp, 1864

Belgium

North Sea

Netherlands

Belgium

Flushing

Netherlands

Netherlands

River Scheldt

River Scheldt

Terneuzen

Schore

Netherlands

Kloosterzande

River Scheldt

Hanweert

Waarde

Belgium

Netherlands

Antwerp

Belgium

Belgium

0

5

10

20 Miles

Chapter 5

The sky was only partly clouded and the waning moon gave little light as the *Galveston* edged from the side-channel and into the Scheldt's mainstream just before midnight on March 5th.

Dawlish was on an improvised seat on the turret's inner wall, looking forward across its edge towards the dark river and darker flanking banks ahead. The tarpaulin cover set aside, the turret's interior was open to the sky.

The guns were manned below him. He had spent the hours prior to departure drilling their crews – if the confused sequence of mistakes could indeed be classed as drilling. Without Hopper, he knew, even that much would have been impossible. The older man – gun-captain now – had sensed his unease and displayed a surprising sensitivity in tendering advice while respecting his authority. Most of the men chosen for the gun-crews had naval experience but none, not even Hopper, had known anything larger than a sixty-eight pounder. But now the shells were three-hundred pounds apiece, larger than any team, however physically strong, could manhandle by themselves. In the time available the only drilling possible was to master loading. That demanded hoisting the charges and the shells from their storage racks by a travelling block on one of the two beams across the turret top, then swinging them across to the muzzles of the retracted guns for ramming.

It wasn't enough, he knew, for neither of the weapons had been fired. Within the close confines of the turret men blundered into each other, tripped and swore. Settling the firing drill and allocating individual roles was a matter of trial and error. Dawlish guessed that his own unspoken fear of a shell slipping from its sling and crushing anybody beneath was shared by all. And this had been while the ship had lain at anchor in a smooth backwater. Accomplishing as much in even a mild seaway would be a nightmare.

Loading of supplies had continued through the afternoon. The bunkers were already full but a lighter came alongside with yet more coal. Seamen stacked the sacks on deck in any space available. Steam had been raised – Dawlish felt something comforting in the smell of coal smoke. The greater part of the Laird's tradesmen left, satisfied, he overheard, with the remuneration and bonuses doled out by Whitby. Much of what had gone undone to complete outfitting would remain so but the engines were ready for sea, and the masts and sails and running rigging too, and the guns were, in theory at least, capable of action also.

The afternoon saw other comings and goings. Bulloch and Whitby had left in the steam launch, had come back an hour later with two portly Belgian officials in frock coats who left again an hour later, smiling smugly.

"They're goddam leeches," Lorance had said when he entered the turret to check progress. "Keeping a sporting house is more decent."

But whatever had been agreed, or at whatever price, there had been no hindrance to the *Galveston's* departure in darkness. The waterway to the sea was closed to navigation in the night hours but a pilot had come aboard. He had boasted of twenty-three years' experience of guiding shipping up and down the Scheldt in any weather, Lorance told Dawlish. Part of his price was that a small ship's boat with a sailing rig be hoisted on board. He would be leaving the ironclad once open sea was reached and he would cover his tracks by sailing directly to Zeebrugge.

There had been a final gathering in the *Galveston's* saloon before Bulloch and Whitby left for the city — they would be returning to The Hague that evening. They stood at one side of the deal table, FitzBaldwin and Lorance at the other, Killigrew, Albemarle and Dawlish with them. Faces grim, a sense of shared but unspoken foreboding.

"I want there to be no misunderstanding, gentlemen," Whitby's voice was level, neutral. "You're here as volunteers. There's still time to withdraw but if you don't —"

FitzBaldwin interrupted. "We're not lawyers here, Whitby, nor diplomats either." He turned to his son. "You want to leave, Al? No! I didn't think so! And you, Mr. Dawlish?"

Only one answer possible, even though Dawlish felt fear gnawing in his stomach. "I'm staying, sir."

"As I am," Killigrew said.

"And no need to ask Lorance or myself," FitzBaldwin said. "We know what we are for eight and forty hours or more. Pirates, buccaneers, outlaws, men of no nation and the possibility of a rope for myself and Lorance even if the other gentlemen might expect leniency."

"Let's get it over with." Lorance looked towards Bulloch. "It's all signed up and watertight, isn't it? Ours tonight and ours again in two months from the day FitzBaldwin accepts her? Under Confederate command then and *Galveston* once more, not some damn Danish name?"

"We've got Mr. Whitby's assurance," Bulloch said. "He's speaking on behalf of a certain august gentleman. And besides, we've got no option, have we?"

"A better reason than most."

Whitby gestured to a canvas-bound package on the table. "The commissions are there. It's weighted. You'll know what to do if you have to, Captain FitzBaldwin." He addressed the others. "It won't be opened until this ship's clear of land and accepted. In the meantime, you all might think of what names you want to go by. And you, Mr. FitzBaldwin, I suggest that you make a different choice to your father's."

The toast was to a happy return, with no mention of a queen or king or prince or princess. As there were no glasses on board, it was drunk in chipped mugs with brandy from FitzBaldwin's flask. Dawlish felt the scene contrived, unreal, wondered suddenly if he should have brought himself to this. He felt no reassurance in Whitby's parting handshake and empty wishes for good luck, nor in Bulloch's either. It struck him that he had made himself a willing pawn for men who cared nothing for him. He had known it all along, he told himself, but he had refused to acknowledge it.

But the die was cast.

They broke up. Bulloch and Whitby left. The sun had already set, the cloud-streaked sky still red and ominous to the south-west.

And the *Galveston* was alive with the last measures for departure.

*

The ironclad nudged downriver at quarter-revolutions, a dark mass that carried no navigation lights other than dim port and starboard lamps. The only sound was of the slow panting of the engines, the low swish of water alongside, the quiet churn of the screws, the occasional instructions from the pilot to the helmsman. Dawlish glanced back from his seat – the bridge was directly behind him and slightly higher. He saw FitzBaldwin and Lorance there as dark shapes against the sky. It must be worse for them than for any other man on board, he thought. The ship was wholly in the hands of a pilot they had only met hours before. They lacked the knowledge of this waterway, winding and narrow in the first hours of passage downstream, to take control of navigation themselves.

No wind. Frost coated every surface. A long plume of smoke drifted astern. Shipping lay anchored at intervals along both sides of the navigation channel, ready for movement upriver or down with the morning's light. From some a watchman called out, surprised by the bulk slipping past, and received no reply. Antwerp lay well astern by now and the flat land on either hand showed no sign of human presence other than an odd point of light. The river had widened slightly, and the sharpest of the turns had been passed. The territory to both north and south was Dutch now, not Belgian. What moonlight there was showed small riverside villages – clusters of housing and lee-boarded sailing barges moored alongside wooden wharves.

Dawlish sensed the tension, the silent fear, among the crews stationed around the guns below him. They must know, as well as he did, that they were unprepared, would be so for days, for weeks perhaps, know too that anything beyond a first salvo would be a chaos of fumbling, delay and worse. They knew nothing of the possibility of a Union frigate lying outside the estuary or of Dutch warships either – that was confidential to officers alone – but the very fact that the Armstrongs were loaded confirmed that there was some possibility of action.

"You'll fire on my order only." Lorance was adamant. "No lanyards on the firing pistols – you'll keep them in your pocket and connect 'em only when I say, and then fast. You understand?"

The prospect frightened Dawlish, and yet it had something of elation in it too. He could imagine the roar, the huge squat iron barrels leaping back up their slides, the choking smoke within the iron drum stinging eyes, while he would strain to discern the consequences through the murk. He realised that he wanted that moment, wanted it intensely. But not yet. Not until the crews had been trained and exercised and trained again, day after exhausting day, in rough seas as well as smooth, until they could function as parts of a single body with himself as brain.

He knew that would never forget this moment, not just for the flat landscapes half-seen in the faint moonlight, or the reflections on the dark waters ahead, or for the half-painful, half-pleasurable, apprehension of danger. It was more – a sudden moment of self-realisation that he recognised as the transition from youth to manhood, that would set the course of his life, and maybe death.

I'm eighteen years old. I saw slaughter and incompetence at the Taku forts when I was scarcely thirteen, as much again there a year later, and horrors at Pekin too. I was terrified, but I did not fall short. I came with credit from fast brutal action when Samuel Caulfield brought the gunboat Foyle sweeping into that anchorage in Colombia. I can be good at this, better than most perhaps, my competence equal or superior, my will and concentration stronger, than so many others of my age. I'm a nobody and I accept that. For now. But not always. Others may try to use me, sometimes will, but my fate will always be in my own hands.

The Scheldt broadened and the navigation channel, marked at intervals by buoys, widened also. Dawlish had studied the charts, had memorised the names of the villages now slipping past, Waarde, Hansweert, Schore to the north, Kloosterzande to the south, some half-hidden by dykes but marked by church towers rising above them. Now a hairpin in the river and the course was just west of south before it shifted over again until the *Galveston* ran south-westwards and the lights of Terneuzen lay directly ahead. Small as it was, it was the largest Dutch town south of the Scheldt. It must have a telegraph connection. Given what Whitby had said about the Dutch willingness to accommodate the Union government, the police there might well be under orders to be on the watch and to report unusual movement. There was no strip of cloud above to shield the moon and, with her hinged bulwarks dropped and her turret exposed, the ironclad could not be mistaken for a merchant steamer. At this very moment some humble constable might be pounding on a post-office door to wake a telegraphist and relay the sighting to Flushing, twelve miles downstream.

Dawlish was numb with cold. He could just make out the voices on the bridge behind him, FitzBaldwin and Lorance pressing the pilot for increased speed. It was four o'clock now, dawn little over two hours ahead, and it was necessary to have reached open sea by full daylight. Not yet, the pilot was saying, broad as the channel now was, the slightest miscalculation, the too-late detection of a buoy, could threaten grounding. Still onwards at quarter-revolutions, but the tide, full earlier, had begun to ebb and the villages now dropped more rapidly astern. The channel widened further.

At last the pilot requested half-revolutions. By now the lights of Flushing were visible to the north-west. As they drew nearer, the dark outlines of shipping moored along the channel edges could be seen, waiting for pilotage upriver in daylight, a long gauntlet that might shelter that gunboat from Hellevoetsluis that Whitby had warned of.

"Mr. Dawlish," Lorance's voice. "Gun-crews standing-to? Lanyards in your pocket?"

"Yes, sir."

"Then rotate the turret, full three-sixty, then back to fore and aft."

It made sense. Noisy as the process would be, it would reveal any chance of jamming. There could yet be time to remedy it before any encounter with the Union frigate that might by now have battered her way at top speed up the English Channel.

Dawlish called down the order. Unaccustomed yet to the drill, men collided with each other in the deep shadows as they moved to grasp the cranks, throw their weight on them, strain for the first tiny movement. Inertia was overcome and momentum built. The rotation was smooth and the oval gun-ports swept over to starboard They were broadside now and still steady as they passed the quarter. For a full thirty-one seconds – Dawlish was counting silently – they were masked by the deckhouse abaft the turret, and then bore on towards open water on the port quarter, past the broadside, heading now towards the barrier provided by the deckhouse ahead.

"Slow down!" Dawlish called.

He wanted to edge the ports slowly towards the dead-ahead, the rotation to end within single degrees of the full three-sixty. Unseen below, Hopper urged the men to haul back on the cranks, to kill momentum, even as he himself spun a wheel to force a friction brake against the drum's perimeter. It was too late – the turret had overshot the desired dead-ahead bearing by five or six degrees before it stilled. It hardly mattered, but there was something of honour at stake and Dawlish called again for the cranks' rotation to be reversed and nudge the turret back until the gun-ports lay each side of the ship's axis.

"Two-minutes, nineteen seconds, sir!"

Pride in the few seconds gain over the first rotation with the guns installed – and that had been at anchor – as Dawlish called back to FitzBaldwin. Yet even as he did, he realised that the men on the bridge had no concern for that at present. A night-glass was clamped to the Lorance's eye, and FitzBaldwin beside him was pointing off the starboard bow and the lookout on the foretop was shouting that a craft was emerging from between moored shipping ahead.

Dawlish could see it. The dark profile outlined against the moon's reflection beyond it was of a small steam craft, an orange glow hovering above the short funnel. Heading out into the channel, then turning to face directly upstream, it was longer and bulkier than any launch, more like a steam pinnace such as larger warships carried. Whoever was in command of her must be insanely brave, for she was holding the centre of the channel even as the ironclad bore straight towards her. A brief flash then, darkness again for an instant, and then a rocket – a powerful one, for its swoosh was audible – shot up almost vertically and exploded in a shower that cast red light over river and shipping.

64

No lessening of the *Galveston's* revolutions, though the pilot shouted for slowing, panic in his voice as his hand reached for the engine-room telegraph.

"Stand away, mister!" Lorance thrust him aside and took the wheel himself. FitzBaldwin grabbed the telegraph and rang for full revolutions, not fewer.

A louder thrash now from the screws. The ironclad surged forward, the pinnace less than two cables ahead and still holding its ground. Another rocket streaked up, another, and another in its wake. The river was bathed in scarlet light and sounds of alarm came from the merchant ships moored to either side, watchmen shouting warnings that brought sleep-befuddled men stumbling on deck.

Dawlish glanced back and in the crimson glare saw cold resolution on FitzBaldwin's face, something perhaps even deadlier on Lorance's. There could be no deviation from this centre-channel course – at this speed a miscalculation of a few degrees could bring the ironclad smashing into anchored shipping or gouging into mudbanks that would lock her fast. Yet still that Dutch pinnace held position dead ahead, her revolutions just high enough to hold her stationary against the ebb tide. Whoever commanded her was a hero or a madman, maybe both.

Two more rockets as the gap narrowed – no doubt that they could be seen from Flushing, perhaps from the estuary opening beyond. The last detonation was almost directly above the *Galveston*, close enough to shower her with falling sparks, just as the pinnace surged forward and steered toward the channel edge. It did so all but too late for, as the ironclad raced past, it was close enough for Dawlish to look down and see the scarlet-lit face of the young officer looking up from the cockpit – his own age and intent perhaps on wining repute by a near-suicidal stand. Waving at the stern in the wind of the ironclad's rush was a small flag striped horizontally in red, white and blue, the ensign of the Dutch navy.

The channel was now at its broadest. The ironclad must be making eight or nine knots, and the ebb lent at least one more, and a high bow wave streamed from her ram. The rockets launched by the pinnace seemed to have brought men on deck on half of the ships at anchor and, as *Galveston* forged past, several launched alarm rockets of their own. A cluster of lights grew stronger off the starboard bow – Flushing, last port before the open sea. The moored shipping was at its densest here, not just coasting craft but tall ships that might have come here across half the world, their masts and yards towering like dark forests.

The young officer in the pinnace had done his work well. A mile ahead, hidden until now by the anchored vessels, a dark shape was slipping out towards the centre of the channel. The outline was unmistakable as that of a gunboat. It might have been the *Foyle* herself, on which Dawlish had served in the West Indies – barque-rigged, a single funnel, two or three thirty-two pounders on each broadside and most likely a single sixty-eight pounder on a turntable abaft the foremast. The yards were bare and she was under steam alone. She foreshortened as her bows swung over into the current. A rocket climbed from her, burst high above the river.

Lorance and FitzBaldwin stood immovable by the wheel, faces bathed in red. Dawlish hesitated to speak – his hand was sweaty as he grasped the lanyards in his pocket – but the set expressions told him enough. At whatever cost, the *Galveston* would run the gauntlet and the threat of her dreadful ram would be her strongest weapon.

A flash ahead. An orange tongue of flame leapt from the gunboat's flank. Smoke billowed and, seconds later, the low boom told of a blank – but a warning nonetheless. Dutch naval forces had seen no action in Europe for three decades and whoever was on the bridge of that gunboat must know that he had acclaim, distinction and the chance of promotion almost in his grasp. But he had to keep his nerve...

... as Lorance kept his as the ironclad held steady on the channel's centre.

No further rockets rose as the gunboat came upstream through the last tendrils of her cannon smoke, all navigation lights burning. The intervening gap was narrowing fast, so fast that Dawlish's view of the gunboat was now masked by the foremast. He shifted his seat to the broad upper rim of the turret and edged across so he could see the oncoming gunboat. Looking back, he saw that Lorance and FitzBaldwin were as immovable as before, iron wills matched against the willingness of the Dutch commander to face destruction.

A cable's separation now, still head-on, the gunboat's weapons no immediate threat as none could bear directly ahead. There was no need of them – if the gunboat held its course, if it forced the *Galveston* to deviate from hers, the ironclad's speed would carry her out of the channel and into the shoals.

The ironclad held her course. The foaming bow-wave piling up and away from her ram must draw the Dutch commander's horrified gaze. Mute but terrified, officers and men must be glancing towards him, realising now the disparity of tonnage, the impossibility of survival of collision, must be praying that –

Almost too late, the gunboat swung over to port. The vessels passed so near that a determined man might have leaped across from one to the other. Dawlish saw relief and anger on the Dutchmen's faces, heard cries of fury and the shout of the commander on the bridge to the crew of a twenty-ponder below him. The weapon roared, leaped back against its restraints, vomited fire and smoke. But no iron – another blank.

Galveston was clear now. She could have given the gunboat four knots had it managed to turn quickly to chase, but it had not done so and was now left far astern. The lights of Flushing slipped past and the buoys marking the channel exit were close ahead. The shorelines, north and south, were opening into a wide funnel to the open sea.

And no sign of any other vessel there. The USS *Conewago* might have left Cherbourg but she had not won the race.

The eastern sky was reddening with the winter dawn as the ironclad responded to the sea's first choppy waves. She drove ten miles out into the English Channel – the world's busiest shipping lane, with traffic in both directions and vessels enough for her to be lost among should the frigate expected from den Helder come to seek her.

Galveston's bows swung over on a course to parallel the Dutch coast.

Towards the North Sea.

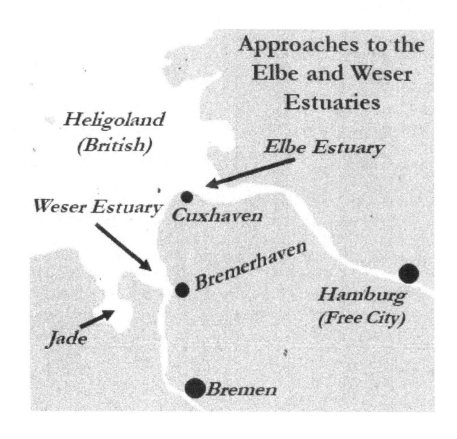

Approaches to the Elbe and Weser Estuaries

Heligoland (British)

Elbe Estuary

Weser Estuary

Cuxhaven

Bremerhaven

Hamburg (Free City)

Jade

Bremen

Chapter 6

She was still the *Galveston*, not yet accepted for two months of Danish service. She had to prove herself fit for that, for three contracted months in which to pay the costs of her completion, for supplies enough to loose her at the end on the world's oceans as a Confederate raider.

The Belgian pilot had been dropped and his single sail was last seen headed south-westwards towards Zeebrugge – an inconsequential place, the man told Dawlish, but easy at which to come ashore. The ironclad drove northwards, ahead of a strong south-westerly, into the central North Sea. It took all the hours of overcast daylight to raise the hinged bulwarks to hide the turret and shelter the open deck. It was backbreaking work, and dangerous too, lifting, one by one, the iron flaps – four-feet square, a half-inch thick and strengthened with vertical flanges. The had been designed for fast dropping – a few blows of a sledgehammer were enough to release the locking pins – but raising them in anything but calm water demanded brutal effort.

Dawlish and his gunners worked along the port side, Albemarle and a similar number along the other, starting forward, moving sternwards. Water and spray washed over the deck-edge as the vessel rolled. Men slipped, fell, would have been torn overboard by the icy water that sometimes surged to knee height had it not been for the lifelines around their waists. Again and again, twenty-four times in all, soaked, as numb as his crew, Dawlish helped lift the hoisting davit into a hole along the deck-edge, connect the lifting strop – a nightmare, since the flap was frequently engulfed – and haul with bleeding hands. When each bulwark section reached the vertical and the locking pins were inserted, he felt a momentary sense of triumph, snuffed out immediately by the need to lift the davit from its hole, manhandle it to the next, begin the same pitiless toil again. There was nothing for it but to endure and show his men that he would spare himself nothing that they must bear themselves.

They secured the last flaps as the short winter afternoon ended. Less water was coming on board now and, as the vessel heeled, most of that which did drained quickly through the freeing ports. But water had been washing around the turret base all day – there was a one-inch gap between it and the deck there – and that worried Dawlish. He sent his crew aft to the boiler room to warm up and dry their saturated clothing before he and Hopper ventured inside the drum. The interior was virtually dry, for the gun-port stoppers had been closed but, when they dropped down through a manhole to the space beneath, they found themselves knee high in water. The roller track, and the rollers themselves, were still far above the surface but they had been drenched and much of the lubricating grease had been washed away. It was hard to know how quickly corrosion might bite but if it did, then jamming would be inevitable. It was essential to pump out the partly flooded compartment, replace the grease and rotate the turret to ensure the lubricant's even distribution.

A long, cold, miserable night lay ahead.

*

The Scheldt lay some two hundred and fifty miles to the south, the coast of Northumbria a hundred and fifty to the west. There was little chance of being sighted by merchant traffic – the time for that would come, but not yet. Most shipping emerging from the Dover Straits branched to parallel the British, Dutch and German coastlines. It was here, close to the southern edge of the rich Dogger Bank fishing ground, where large numbers of sailing craft were visible at any time. With bulwarks now raised, *Galveston's* profile looked little different to that of many merchant steamers. She would not arouse curiosity. It was here that she would loiter for two days in which Lorance must convince FitzBaldwin that she could be accepted for Danish service.

Sails were set just after dawn, an exercise that emphasised the crew's unreadiness, and the furnaces were banked to spare precious coal. The effort brought small reward. Handling under sail proved poor. *Galveston* rolled badly and drifted out of even the mildest turn, slowed by her stationary twin screws.

This was the start of two days of unrelenting exercise, much of the nights too. Half-adequate watches set and trimmed sail, moving by fits and starts towards the established rhymes of a functioning crew. Frustration and small gains, errors and unhandiness, sometimes outright stupidity and resentment, reproof and grudged approval. FitzBaldwin and Lorance, grey with fatigue, as wet through as any of the men, stood watch and watch about to free Killigrew, Albemarle and Dawlish for other duties.

The drill inside the turret proved even more difficult, even more hazardous, as the vessel rolled and pitched, than Dawlish had anticipated. No matter how strongly the crew strained on the rotation cranks, the drum stalled as its weight was thrown on the track's lowest point, then leaped forward a few degrees and sent men sprawling as it climbed again with the roll, then locked momentarily again.

FitzBaldwin and Lorance had come to watch.

"I'm sorry, sir. It'll be impossible to rotate it quickly in anything other than mildly rough conditions." Dawlish felt guilty, sounded apologetic. "It's not like we could do at anchor."

"It's enough that you can swing the turret to bear on the broadside," FitzBaldwin said. "You achieved that much even in this sea."

"Just not fast enough, sir." Dawlish had envisaged the ironclad circling a prey, her turret rotating smoothly to keep the guns locked on it, regardless of attempts at evasion. Impossible, he now knew, in anything but calm water.

"It should be enough if we can get it over and lock it on the port or starboard broadside," Lorance looked to FitzBaldwin. "This ship's damn handy under steam. We'll manoeuvre to bring the guns to bear. It's their crews who'll matter then."

"We can't hope for much more," FitzBaldwin said.

"The guns haven't been fired yet, sir." Dawlish felt uneasy. All effort had gone into loading drill. Until the firing-pistol lanyard could be pulled in earnest it was impossible to imagine what would follow inside the confines of the iron drum.

"We're short, Mr. Dawlish." Lorance gestured to the shells and tin cylinders containing charges secured around the turret's inner wall.

Enough for ten shots from each weapon. Further munitions supplies had been due to arrive in Antwerp from the Armstrong works. *Galveston* had been forced to depart too soon.

"Just one gun then, sir? The men should know what to expect."

"Persistent, aren't you, Mr. Dawlish?"

"Persistent, sir, yes."

"I can't accept her without that much," FitzBaldwin said. "One gun. A blank. Unshotted."

An hour later the turret was locked on the starboard broadside, Dawlish on his seat high on its after edge. Hopper, as gun-captain, sighted down a squat barrel and the crew stood at their designated positions. The ship was rolling, five, six degrees on either side of the vertical. Dawlish gave the order at what he judged to be the summit of the roll. Hopper stepped back and whipped the firing lanyard.

It was even worse inside the cauldron than Dawlish had expected, a thunderclap that deafened, billowing smoke that seared the throat and stung the eyes, the deep rumble of the gun, unseen in the murk, grinding back on its inclined slide. But then, faster than hoped, the smoke rolled up through the turret's open top and cleared and dazed red-eyed men with blackened faces realised that, for all the shock of it, they had survived and would do so again.

Time now to wind the turret forward again, to lock it fore and aft.

Galveston was a step closer to what she must be.

A marauder and a killer.

*

It was March 9th and a fork-tailed ensign, a white cross superimposed on red, proclaimed that the ironclad was no longer the *Galveston*. FitzBaldwin, satisfied, had accepted her. Since midnight she was the *Odin* of the Royal Danish Navy and so she would be for the next two months. An impressive commissioning document on crested parchment, laden with wax seals linked by red and white striped ribbons, attested it. The language was Danish and unintelligible to every officer and seaman on board. The signature at the bottom might indeed have been that of King Christian IX, though Dawlish doubted it. He put on as innocent an expression as he could manage, one of reverence indeed, when he asked FitzBaldwin if it was indeed the monarch's.

"He'll back it if it's ever referred to him. He'll have to," FitzBaldwin said. "But it won't come to that. No need to worry yourself about it."

There were other commissions also, thick paper and slightly blurred printing, with fewer seals but the same signature at the bottom. It was easy to imagine Whitby securing them from some London specialist skilled in production of convincing documents. Blank spaces had been left for entering names. FitzBaldwin made no ceremony of it, even though he was captain now and Lorance his executive officer.

"You've made your choice?" he asked the American.

"Hiram James Custis."

"Kaptejn Custis for now. It's what they call commander," FitzBaldwin wrote it in the blank space and then looked to the others. "And by the way, I'm Kommandör James Merriweather. It sounds grander in Danish but it still means captain."

The commissions would not use Danish names. Since none of them spoke a word of the language, doing so would make these papers look suspicious if they were ever to be examined. English names would have to do. A man might choose to serve a foreign power – the legalities were opaque and arguable. Thousands did – it was well known that the French

Empire had an entire legion of such men fighting in Mexico and the Dutch East Indies Army was heavily dependent on them also. Few, if any, enlisted under anything but a pseudonym.

George Killigrew became Premier-Löjtnant Ernest Cunliffe.

FitzBaldwin turned towards his son and towards Dawlish. "You've had fast promotions, gentlemen," he said. "You're a step above what you can expect next in Her Majesty's Navy. You're Löjtnants now. And you're called?"

"Algernon Herbert Morris, sir." Albemarle said.

"A fine-looking young chap. With a striking resemblance also to somebody I once knew."

And Dawlish would be Ralph William Page. His beloved uncle.

One last document. The man who stood uncomfortably among them had been a foreman of one of the Laird's crews, a mechanic rather than a shipwright. That the engines had performed so faultlessly on the run downriver had been to his credit. Middle-aged, grey and balding, embarrassed by his background and his strong Liverpool accent, he was hesitant when he answered that he was now Michael Nolan.

FitzBaldwin wrote the name on the empty space and handed the paper to him. Ingeniör. A warrant, not a commission. Even with these legal fictions, evidence that would protect them from charges of piracy in the worst event, the conventions must be observed. Engineers were never officers and scarcely ever gentlemen.

"Are we to use those names on board, sir?" Killigrew asked.

"Too damn confusing when we address each other," FitzBaldwin said. "But nothing else to be used in the logs, or anything else you write."

"And the men, sir?"

"All in the books under assumed names."

But whether officers or seamen, Dawlish knew that their numbers were too small. FitzBaldwin and Lorance must have some fifty years of experience between them, Killigrew perhaps fifteen, Albemarle and himself scarcely six apiece. And that was all. In the Royal Navy – in any other navy – this vessel would carry at least another dozen officers and half as many again above than the seventy men of the lower deck. *Odin* was dangerously undermanned by a crew unfamiliar with operation of a sophisticated ship and who had no earlier forged bonds of service.

*

The tiny fortified outcrop of Heligoland, a British possession, merited a wide berth. With Britain ostensibly neutral in the Danish War, at least one Royal Navy warship was known to be patrolling its territorial waters. FitzBaldwin knew not only on her identity, but her commander.

"The *Aurora*," he told Dawlish. "McClintock's commanding her."

"The explorer, sir?" Dawlish was impressed. Francis McClintock was a national hero, knighted for his Arctic expeditions.

"The same. A man worth knowing."

Odin, under steam again, passed ten miles to the south of the island in the clear mid-morning of March 10th. The sea was moderate, the wind falling and the course now directly south towards the waters north of the Jade Bight. There was shipping aplenty visible now, for the estuaries of the Weser, and of the Elbe further east, provided access to Bremen and to Hamburg. Trade flowed to here from every quarter of the globe, much of it in British bottoms, and German manufactures flowed out. Bremen was Prussian but Hamburg was still an independent city state. It didn't matter. Any vessel sailing in or out of either was fair game if it was flying a Prussian ensign.

"I don't give a damn what they're carrying," FitzBaldwin said. "I want them to see one burn, for them to know that we're here and to put the fear of God in them. Keep the rascals in port, damage their huckstering."

The war had so far had no impact on the traffic – information provided by Whitby had told as much. The Danish fleet was concentrated in the Baltic, better employed in supporting the hard-pressed army than raiding commerce or imposing a blockade. For all its power on land, Prussia lacked a serious navy. Its few small gunboats were known to be patrolling approaches to the German North-Sea ports. The Danes had little to fear from them.

FitzBaldwin assented when Dawlish asked to spend an hour in the foretop with a lookout named Crowther. Glad of exposure to clean air, he scanned one distant vessel after another through a telescope, hoping for sight of the black and white of a Prussian ensign. There had been two false hopes so far – they both proved to be British vessels. Now *Odin* was headed to investigate a large four-masted barque some three miles distant and steering for Bremerhaven.

A twenty-seven foot whaler, Royal Navy pattern, had been swung outboard since dawn, ready for dropping, and Albemarle waited by it with its crew and a six-man boarding party. FitzBaldwin and Lorance were scrutinising the barque from the bridge and even from the foretop

74

Dawlish could sense their excitement. He had to quench it. The ensign at the stern was British, the name below it was *Arabella*, the port Bristol. He called down, saw Lorance throw down his cigar in frustration and stamp on it, heard FitzBaldwin's call to the helmsman to bear away and head north. More sails on the horizon there, and drifting smoke.

Cold as he was, but excited by the search, Dawlish was determined to remain where he was until he was ordered down. Below him he could see into the turret – several of the crew cleaning the guns and the remainder unseen in the space beneath, greasing the track and rollers yet again under Hopper's supervision. One of the guns had been loaded earlier, again only with a blank.

Odin was steaming slow racetracks now, five miles eastwards, turning, five westwards, then east again at half-revolutions. Noon passed, and four more disappointments with it – one French, three British, one of them under steam. No sign of Prussian patrols, but several local fishing boats, too small to bother with, though it was welcome that they could see the Danish Ensign at *Odin*'s stern. The word would spread.

At last, success.

"I think we've got one, sir." Crowther handed the telescope to Dawlish and pointed.

The slightest adjustment brought the disc of vision into focus. Three masts, a full-rigged ship under sail and heavily laden, too large for coastal traffic, her hull built for capacity rather than speed, her progress as stately and determined as might have carried her across half the world.

And the Prussian ensign was unmistakable.

Dawlish called down the sighting himself, confirmed that he was sure of it, was ordered down, a man sent aloft to replace him. By the time he reached the deck the *Odin's* bows had swung over on an interception course.

"Mr. Dawlish!" FitzBaldwin, calling from the bridge. "Turret to bear on the starboard broadside!"

"The bulwarks, sir?"

"Mr. Killigrew will see to them. And the lanyard in your pocket, nowhere else for now!"

Dawlish shouted for Hopper to muster the gun-crew, release the friction brake and strain on the cranks. The vessel's roll was less than in previous days and the iron drum crept around easily. He climbed to his perch and from it could see across the top of the bulwarks – all still raised but with a half-dozen men with sledgehammers stationed behind them.

Killigrew was with them and looking up to the bridge for the order to drop.

Close enough now to discern figures on the Prussian ship – what looked like casual interest at first, then alarm growing with the realisation that the *Odin* was cleaving forward on a collision course. The low winter sun flashed on a telescope lens – the captain perhaps – and then the ship's helm was over to swing due north and men scrambled up the shrouds to trim sail even as others hauled the yards around. The execution was slower than the worst a naval vessel might manage – slim profit margins meant that most civilian vessels sailed with inadequate crews.

"Deck there!" Crowther, the lookout, called from the foretop. "*Klara Baumann,* Bremen!"

Ten minutes more. *Odin*, now at reduced revolutions, was on a parallel track a cable's length off the Prussian's port beam and holding the weather gauge. FitzBaldwin ordered an international signal flag run up the halyard, a blue cross on a white background – "Stop carrying out your intentions and watch for my signals"

On the trader's quarterdeck a smartly uniformed man who must be the captain shouted something through a hailing trumpet, the words drowned but the intent obvious. He was damned if he was going to heave-to. He must have seen the signal on *Odin*'s halyard but it had not deterred him.

Dawlish felt a surge of respect, wondered if that man could imagine what was hidden behind the still-raised bulwarks. He hoped that he himself would not be ordered to open fire, even with a blank.

"Mr. Killigrew!" FitzBaldwin shouted from the bridge. "Now!"

Hammering to beat the retention pins free, six of the hinged bulwarks that had been raised with such painful effort arcing down to clank against *Odin's* flank-plating. The turret was unmasked, the gaping muzzles just outside the ports bearing point blank on the trader.

Good sense prevailed.

The *Klara Baumann* hove to, sails flapping, slowing, rocking stationary at last in the swell. *Odin's* whaler dropped, drew alongside the trader. Albemarle yelled for a jacob's ladder to be lowered and, when it was, he was the first of the boarding party to reach the deck. The crew were herded together at the mainmast, cowed by the sight of the rifles. The captain and another officer – also neatly uniformed and probably the mate – were arguing volubly with Albemarle. Unsettled himself, he glanced back towards *Odin*, as if hoping for instructions and seeing only his father standing immovable on the bridge wing and giving none.

Albemarle pointed to the *Odin*, indicated that the Prussians would have to go across. Scarlet-faced, the captain stamped and lost his temper despite the mate's efforts to calm him. That was enough. Albemarle nodded to two of the armed seamen and they frog-marched both to the jacob's ladder. The whaler took them across, leaving the full boarding party on board the barque.

The prisoners already seemed cowed when they were brought on *Odin's* bridge. FitzBaldwin advanced, hand outstretched, but the German captain ignored it. Dawlish could hear only snatches of the exchange. FitzBaldwin regretted circumstances and hard necessities. The Prussian was looking down into the turret, his face drained pale at the sight of the enormous guns. His English was fluent, though heavily accented. His name was Baumann, he said.

"The same as your ship?"

"My wife is Klara." Misery incarnate.

"Part owner, Captain Baumann?" FitzBaldwin sounded embarrassed.

"Fifty percent. My brother twenty-five, my wife's brother the same."

"Other ships, captain?"

"One other. Smaller." He paused. "It's all we have."

He had known that there was a state of war between Prussia and Denmark. He had read the news in Boston before sailing. He had not thought it would mean this.

"What is to me?" he said. "The Danes? Decent fellows, good seamen too. I've nothing against them. They've nothing against me. It's not our quarrel."

Dawlish found it hard to watch. The Prussian looked as if he had been told of the death of a spouse or child. He had realised the full enormity of what had befallen him. His fury had faded. An old man, he looked beaten.

"What cargo?" Lorance asked. No trace of sympathy. He had commanded a Confederate raider before this, had taken prizes.

"Whale oil," Baumann's face told that he realised what that must mean. "One thousand, two hundred and fifty barrels."

Silence. FitzBaldwin had spoken of wanting to destroy prizes, for the word of it to spread. Now the reality was on him. Not just a ship. A family ruined, a decent man crushed. He looked towards Lorance, saw only implacability.

"Your cargo is insured, Captain Baumann?"

"Not for war risk. I never thought…" His hands rose in despair.

"We've got to burn her." Lorance said. "She'll go up like a torch."

FitzBaldwin was avoiding the Prussian's gaze. Dawlish felt himself long for the *Klara Baumann* to be sent safely on her way.

"We'll take your crew off, Captain Baumann." FitzBaldwin said. "They'll be sent ashore safely, all your people, yourself also."

"Why don't you just shoot me, captain?" Baumann's tone was bitter. "You can save me doing it for myself."

*

It took a half-hour and several trips to transport the *Klara's* crew across to the *Odin*. They stepped on board part angry, part bemused, part relieved, and were taken below, clutching their pathetic bundles of belongings. One was carrying a cat. Most appeared to be Germans but there were three Lascars among them and one American. Baumann and his mate were sent back to the *Klara*, under escort, to collect their possessions. On *Odin* they were assigned two empty and incomplete cabins aft – no bunks or other furnishings. The best that could be done for them was to give them a few blankets.

FitzBaldwin must have thought that it was kinder that they would not see their vessel's end for he had them all kept below with a guard on their doors. Only Lorance, of *Odin's* whole complement, officers and men alike, seemed unmoved by the whole squalid business.

"It was foul," Albemarle told Dawlish that evening, long after the blaze had erupted through the open hatch, raced up the tarred rigging, jumped hungrily from each sail to the next above and engulfed the entire ship in a single fiery shroud. The black plume rising from it must have been visible from shore.

"I couldn't look those poor wretches in the face when we took them off. One poor devil asked me if they'd still be paid and I had no answer for him. Do you think they will be, Nick?"

"I doubt it," Dawlish said. "There might be compensation eventually but –" He shrugged. Destitution would have forced most to sign on another ship long before then. They could be half a world away when some bureaucrat in Berlin might approve a begrudged pittance.

Albemarle had been the last to leave the *Klara*.

"I hated it," he said. "Smashing barrels and spilling oil and soaking cotton waste and setting it alight. Blackguard's work. And the worst of

78

it was taking off whatever food there was. As if we were starving beggars. I didn't think it would be like this."

Dawlish had not thought so either and liked it just as little.

But he had accepted the Danish commission, even if it was in his uncle's name, not his own. In honour of Ralph Page he would stand by the commitment.

Regardless.

Chapter 7

Odin steered north as darkness fell. Twenty miles from the faint red glow astern that showed that the *Klara Baumann* was still burning, FitzBaldwin ordered half-revolutions and another series of slow racecourses. Her navigation lights did nothing to distinguish the ironclad from any civilian ship. Other vessels were sighted through the night but no attempt was made to investigate them. Only when dawn was two hours distant did the *Odin* swing over to a south-easterly course that would carry her towards the entrance to the Elbe estuary.

Service on vessels small and large had taught Dawlish not to expect great comfort on a warship. But this was different, worse, far worse, a cold, wet iron shell in which the most basic facilities were lacking. The scramble to get the vessel to sea, to give priority above all else to engines and weapons, had left mess decks bare even of hooks for hanging hammocks or tables or benches for men to sit at to eat. The galley was reliant on what was little better than a domestic cooking range purchased at the last moment in Birkenhead and even the necessary utensils were in short supply. Food was always critical for contented crews but here the tepid slop that passed for stew did little to assuage either hunger or cold. The fresh meat taken on at Antwerp was already gone and an entire crate of canned beef had to be thrown overboard after a sample of a dozen tins showed the contents to be rotten. There was no guarantee that the remaining crates would prove much better. Only the supplies looted from the *Klara Baumann* had eased the situation.

The dropped bulwarks had not been raised – the effort was too great, FitzBaldwin had said, and with luck they'd need to be let down soon again. The consequence was that, even though the sea was moderate, water still came on board. It surged across the deck, sloshed through passageways, found its way down around the turret base and past the rollers to the compartment below. Tired men, wet and cold, slaved hour after hour on handpumps, found no comfort afterwards as they clutched blankets around themselves on beds of sacks on an iron deck.

First light found *Odin* ten miles north-east of the small port of Cuxhaven. The vast sandbanks and mudflats of Nigehörn and Scharhörn lay off the starboard bow, those of Trischen off the port. Together, these obstacles funnelled all traffic into the Elbe estuary through a gap five miles at its widest. There was traffic aplenty here, three vessels under sail sighted in the cold sunlight of a breezy but clear morning and, further to the west, three plumes of black smoke.

Dawlish had been officer of the middle watch, an uneventful one, and the first time for him to have the responsibility on a vessel this size. The three hours' sleep that followed – even in slumber he knew that he was cold – had done little to lessen his fatigue when he found himself summoned to the bridge.

"No need to man the turret yet." Lorance had taken the morning watch and FitzBaldwin was still below. "You've got a good pair of eyes, Mr. Dawlish. I want you on the foretop." He pointed towards the sailing craft – the nearest a brig, was a mile distant, no ensign visible. "We can take one of 'em at any time. But a steamer, that'll impress. Find me one."

As Dawlish climbed, the ironclad swept around to head for the drifting smoke. Crowther – another good pair of eyes – was already at the foretop. Nothing to report, as yet. The steamers were foreshortened, dark rectangles and skeletal masts outlined beneath the dark plumes.

Three disappointments – two British, one Dutch, none Prussian. Unwilling to stray far from the narrow entrance to the estuary, *Odin* began to make slow circles. Several sailing vessels, all neutrals, slipped past and a small Prussian craft, alarmed by the fork-tailed ensign, bore away northwards. FitzBaldwin, now on the bridge with Lorance, chose not to follow.

More smoke to the north-west, two plumes. *Odin's* loiter continued as they drew closer. It was in the middle of the forenoon watch now. FitzBaldwin had stated his intention to move northwards along the Danish coast during the night. If there was to be another prize it must be soon and there were still prisoners to get off.

The first steamer came on, ploughed past, unswerving on her course, undaunted by the warship – for with the starboard bulwarks down and the turret fully exposed, *Odin* was unmistakable for anything else. The *James Faulkner* of Glasgow, confident of the protection of her flag, had something of studied contempt about her as she steered past.

But now the second steamer, three, four miles distant, had noticed something amiss and she was turning away. Her whole port flank was exposed as she settled into a south-westerly course, away from the Elbe estuary that had so clearly been her goal. Dawlish's heart leapt as her ensign sharpened in his lens.

"Deck there!" he called. "Prussian!"

"Sure?" Lorance's bellow.

"Sure, sir! She's running for the Jade!"

Yet darker smoke billowed from the steamer's funnel – stokers must be shovelling like demons there – and a white wave was rising at her bow, speed building.

Dawlish heard the telegraph's ring as FitzBaldwin drove its handle forward for maximum revolutions. Lorance shouted orders for the boarding party, then called to Dawlish to come down, have the turret manned. *Odin's* own speed built up as she swung over, bows aimed at a point a mile ahead of the Prussian and the flag with the blue cross on white once more whipped up the signal halyard.

The chase was short. *Odin* had two knots advantage at the least and the foam above her ram must have seemed a greater threat than any guns as she forged closer. The *Hertha* of Lübeck – six or eight-hundred tons, auxiliary brigantine rig – lost way, stilled, waited.

From his seat above the unneeded guns, Dawlish watched the same grim drama play out as on the previous day. Again the boarding party climbing on board, again the captain brought across. He was so enraged that an armed seaman was called to stand between him and FitzBaldwin. His voice rose to a scream, his face reddened, he seemed on the point of apoplexy. Then suddenly he deflated, hands hanging, face collapsed in misery. *Hertha's* cargo was sugar, loaded at Tibau do Sul. Dawlish remembered the place, a squalid little port on a river estuary in North-East Brazil. He had been there with HMS *Foyle*. It had been the first time he had seen slaves at close quarters. Their passivity as they loaded ships there, their mute and hopeless acceptance of their lot, had depressed him.

The crew was brought across, several black men among them, all frightened, all bewildered by circumstances they could not comprehend, all forced below to join the prisoners of the previous day. Conditions in the cabins they occupied must be appalling now, space, comfort and sanitation lacking. This close to the end of the voyage, the steamer's remaining food supplies were scant, but they were brought across anyway.

The *Hertha's* end was more spectacular than the *Klara Baumann's*. Nolan, *Odin's* engineer, went across to assist Albemarle with the destruction. The furnace was stoked, the safety valve locked down, fires started in the deckhouse forward, in the officers' accommodation aft. Grey smoke was already drifting from the vessel, and the first flames were taking hold, as the whaler stroked back to *Odin* to be hoisted aboard. Full revolutions then, and a turn northwards.

Though she was burning, the *Hertha* was not yet consumed by a single blaze, and Dawlish felt sick apprehension as he watched, fascinated but appalled, by what he knew must happen. The ships were two miles and more apart when the detonation came. The low 'whoomph' of the boiler's bursting washed across the ironclad seconds after the deck abaft *Hertha's* foremast blasted upwards and tore away the funnel. A cloud of steam engulfed her and when it cleared the sag amidships told that her back was broken. The mainmast, its standing rigging ablaze, collapsed. Five minutes more and the hull had parted into two separate drifting blazes. Soon, they too were gone.

Albemarle had expressed it well.

Blackguard's work.

And not a single man on *Odin* had ever before owed a day's allegiance to the Crown of Denmark.

*

Odin took two more prizes that day, small ones. A brig, heavily laden with Norwegian salt fish, blundered down without suspicion from the north. She was detained, boarded, stripped of her crew. The looting was still in progress, the burning not yet commenced, when a second vessel – another Prussian brig, the same cargo – followed on the same course. *Odin* took off the first prize's crew and left her with the boarders, then made for the newcomer. Once more surprise, shocked submission, flapping sails, way lost.

The ironclad drew alongside, lines cast to draw the hulls together. The captain was brought across. His anger collapsed into abject relief and babbled thanks when he learned that his vessel was to be spared. Darkness was coming on as the prisoners were herded over – almost a hundred, outnumbering *Odin's* crew, and likely to have been a danger had they been kept much longer.

The sea was rising and there was rain on the wind. It was a dismal scene – the cowed and miserable crews with their few sad possessions, the cold grey mist of fine rain, the deck washed by ankle-deep water, the groans of the two hulls grinding together. *Odin's* crew seemed scarcely less dejected than the men they ushered across.

FitzBaldwin seemed to have caught something of the mood and tried to end the matter with grace. He had the detained captains brought to the bridge, began to regret the circumstances and hard necessities of war. They listened in silence that was worse than any anger as he wished them a safe return home. None accepted his hand when he reached it out, and one spat as he turned away.

"You're wasting your breath, captain," Dawlish heard Lorance say. "When you rob a man, he'll hate you. There's no help for it."

The ironclad cast off, left the brig under instructions – threat, rather – not to set her sails to head to Cuxhaven for two hours. Back now to the other prize to see the fires set there, the boarders taken off, then *Odin's* screws bit and her bows swung over towards the north-west. Dots of flame winked in the darkness astern, then grew and merged into one. The sails flushed crimson before they too ignited, masts and yards black against the red glow.

Odin forged on. Several navigation lights were visible, though none of her own were lit. Other ships, merchantmen of whatever nation, united by the brotherhood of the sea, would be pulling from their courses and heading for those flames in hope of saving life.

Two days.

Three prizes taken and burned at the gateways of Germany's greatest ports, flames visible perhaps from the coast itself. No sign of Prussian gunboats. Notice served that a powerful Danish warship was on the loose, might reappear at any time, could strangle trade. Prussia did not have a single ironclad to match her and the Austrians, who did, were four-thousand sea-miles away in the Adriatic.

"It isn't what we do that matters," Lorance said. "It's what we threaten."

"But we're not to come back here soon, are we, sir?" Dawlish guessed that there was no intention of a quick return.

"You know what the *Alabama's* done to the Yankees? They don't know where and when she'll turn up next. One ship and only God knows how many chasing her. And it's worse for the Prussians. They know that if or when we do appear there's not a thing they can do about it."

Already insurance rates for Prussian traders would be rising in Bremen and Hamburg, and the most timid underwriters would be refusing any cover. Cargoes would still flow in and out in neutral bottoms but, for now, much of the kingdom's merchant shipping would skulk in port. It had been a cheap and useful, if not glorious, success.

But it had not been *Odin's* main business.

That lay to the north.

*

84

The course shifted northwards at midnight, speed reduced to half-revolutions, keeping well clear of Heligoland. A stiff breeze had raised a choppy sea and occasional squalls of freezing rain. Scudding clouds blotted out the moon and stars. Dawlish supervised setting the tarpaulin cover atop the open turret to keep out the rain, then collapsed into two hours of dreamless sleep before it was time to come on deck again, aching muscles crying for rest, to keep the morning watch. It was still dark and the only lights visible were a few small clusters that indicated fishing craft.

Dawn broke. *Odin's* course was just west of north and she paralleled the sandbanks of the Schleswig coast at a steady eight-knots crawl and a safe ten miles' separation. She sighted other vessels, mostly sailing craft, but made no attempt to close with them. With a large section of the starboard bulwarks still down, water was coming on board with each roll.

This was to be a day of preparation. Cold and wet men, poorly rested on sacking beds, were set to pump partly-flooded spaces, trim bunkers, oil machinery, clean out the cabins – little better than latrines by now – where the prisoners had been kept.

The compartment below the turret was knee-deep in water again and even continuous pumping saw the level drop only slowly. Much of the grease had been washed from the bearing rollers so that the filthy work of lubricating them must begin again. By midday the task – a labour of Sisyphus – had been completed and another round of loading drills commenced.

Earlier training was paying off. Shifting the heavy projectiles would never be easy but the gun-crews coped better with it now. The last loading was reality, not a drill. The silken bags of black powder were extracted from their tin cannisters and rammed home, then the great three-hundred pound bursting shells thrust ahead of them. Wooden tompions closed the muzzles to keep the barrels' bores dry. The twin firing pistols on each gun were removed, tested, confirmed operative and remounted. Their lanyards stayed nestled like coiled adders in Dawlish's pocket. The Armstrongs were ready to discharge their first salvo in anger.

The weary day continued so that by sunset the Danish town of Esbjerg lay, unseen, directly off the starboard beam. It was a substantial place. Essmann had told that Saabye's force had picked up supplies and more troops there as it headed north. The Austrians driving on through ice, mud and slush in its wake would have left a garrison there, Dawlish thought. It was hard to think of them as enemies. He had never met an

Austrian, had only a vague mental image of hussars in exotic uniforms dancing waltzes and fighting duels. He had read of Frederick the Great and Blücher but he knew little about the modern Prussian kingdom. But he himself had already helped wreak havoc on the lives of its private citizens. Ruined families against whom he had no grudge would even now be cursing him and all others on this ship. And worse must surely follow. He had committed himself to killing them, Prussians or Austrians alike, just as they would not hesitate to kill him. He thrust the thought aside — he had given his word and he would stand by it.

Thyborøn was now under ninety miles to the north and would be reached by daybreak.

"Here it is!" FitzBaldwin's finger had stabbed the chart spread on the deal table when he had gathered the officers in the saloon the previous evening. "Here, north of Harboøre — here, you see the place? — that's where Saabye's making his stand."

Dawlish had studied that chart himself, had memorised the outline of the six-mile long peninsula with Harboøre at its south end and the tiny village of Thyborøn at its northmost tip. A half-mile strait there was the entrance to the Limfjord, the labyrinth of waterways, islands and lakes that stretched across northern Jutland from the North Sea coast to the Kattegat in the east.

The Thyborøn peninsula was little more than a mile wide. But it was the two shallow lagoons that lay along its centre that made it easily defensible by a small force. The isthmuses, strips of land to either side of the lagoons, were narrow — along much of their lengths from one hundred yards to two wide — and low too, and devoid of cover.

"There's the key," Colonel Blackwood had said in Somerset — it seemed an aeon ago now — when he had stabbed a finger at the more southerly lagoon.

When Essmann, the Danish major, had arrived at The Priory he had brought a map — poor by British standards — to complement the chart. "An artilleryman's dream," he had called the location.

"With redoubts here, and here," Blackwood's finger had indicated the northern ends of the causeways on either side of the lagoon, "and every available piece of artillery in them, any attacking force would be so bunched that they'll be shredded before they get within a hundred yards of the earthworks."

Friherre Saabye owned the peninsula among much else — his estates were extensive — and was apparently well regarded by his tenant farmers. There would be labour forthcoming, Essmann had said, not just from the immediate area but from land-holdings further north across the Limfjord, from sturdy peasants spurred by patriotic resolve. It had not sounded reasonable in Somerset – Dawlish found it hard to imagine his own tenants showing such enthusiasm. Now as, he stood on *Odin's* exposed bridge in the cold wind and sleet that was driving westwards towards the unseen coast, it seemed wildly optimistic.

He glanced down, saw rivulets running off the turret's tarpaulin canopy. Beneath it lay the two giant Armstrongs.

Their time had all but come.

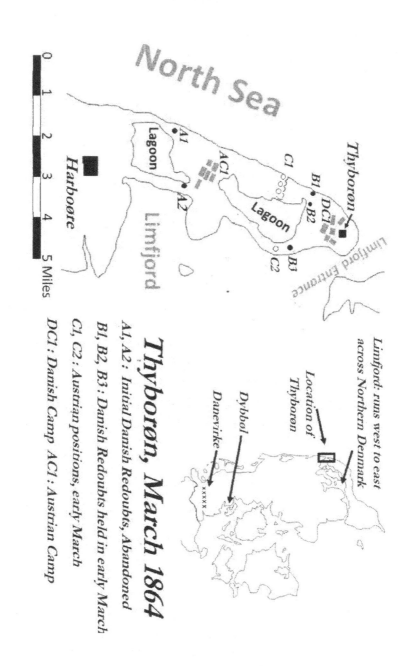

Thyborøn, March 1864

A1, A2 : Initial Danish Redoubts, Abandoned

B1, B2, B3 : Danish Redoubts held in early March

C1, C2 : Austrian positions, early March

DC1 : Danish Camp AC1 : Austrian Camp

North Sea

Thyboron

Limfjord Entrance

Lagoon

Limfjord

Lagoon

Harboøre

0 1 2 3 4 5 Miles

Limfjord: runs west to east across Northern Denmark

Location of Thyboron

Dybbøl

Danevirke

Chapter 8

Odin crept slowly shorewards, the line of dunes ahead still a mile distant, a leadsman forward chanting decreasing depth – still twenty feet beneath the keel, but sudden shallowing was always possible on this sandy coast. The sun was up but only dim light filtered through the angry clouds. The wind had fallen but surf still broke on the beach and rain drifted shorewards, half-obscuring it by a grey curtain.

And no sound of gunfire above the wailing of the wind, no indication that war had come to this desolate spit.

Dawlish, shivering with Crowther at the foretop once again, found the scene disheartening – the glaze of frost on the beach, the wind-lashed coarse grass on the dunes, the dark clumps of seaweed piled along the high-tide mark. During moments of clearer visibility, he could make out the square tower, white and massive, and the red roof of what could only be the church of Harboøre about two miles to the south-east. He hailed the bridge, told what he saw, recognised concern on FitzBaldwin's and Lorance's faces, fear that Saabye's tiny force might have been destroyed already, that this might indeed be a wild goose chase. They consulted between themselves, words inaudible, heads shaking, finally nodding, then called instructions to the quartermaster. The bows swung over for *Odin* to crawl northwards towards the peninsula's rain-blotted tip.

The dunes were lower here, low enough to see over them to the ruffled sheet that must be the more southerly of the two lagoons, and beyond it the slim isthmus that separated it from the Limfjord's dark expanse. The rain was thinning and now Dawlish could see a small hummock looming over the dunes on the nearer strip of land. His heart leapt as he adjusted his glass's focus ever so slightly – this could be one of the redoubts that Essmann and Blackwood had spoken about siting there.

As the image sharpened, he saw that the sides were sloped, the tops flat, the work of human hands rather than of nature. He saw what might have been an embrasure, though with its sides collapsed and no sight of artillery within. It was small, could never have housed more than two weapons. It looked abandoned. He shifted his gaze to the more distant isthmus, to the northerly end where there should have been a redoubt – another from which Blackwood had imagined advancing attackers being shredded – and there also were the makings of an earthwork. It too seemed deserted. If Saabye's gunners had ever occupied them, they were now gone.

A glimpse of movement to the right. A single man on horseback had emerged from cover of a dune at the south end of the nearer causeway. He did not gallop or canter or even trot, but plodded, crouched in dismal endurance of the rain and wind. A little afterwards a wagon appeared, drawn by two horses, and then another and another, a half-dozen more, followed by four teams towing limbers and field cannon. Riders on wagons and horses alike looked swaddled in thick coats as the column toiled up the isthmus's track.

"Danish?" FitzBaldwin's query when Dawlish shouted down the observation.

"I can't see, sir!" and then "No! I can! There's something –"

A knot of horsemen – cavalry by the look of their easy seats and lighter horses – was coming down to meet the advancing wagons. Even at this distance, and regardless of cold and wet, there was a sense of energy and resolution about them. A small flag whipped on a pole held vertically by a leading rider – not fork-tailed like a Danish standard but the black and yellow of the Hapsburg monarchy. It was clear that an Austrian supply train was arriving, artillery with it. That it was headed north confirmed that Saabye must still be making a stand somewhere further up the peninsula. But not at the positions Major Essmann had described as an artilleryman's dream, not where Blackwood had envisaged easy slaughter.

Alarmed by Dawlish's report, FitzBaldwin hauled himself to the foretop. He had brought his own telescope but was panting so much from the climb that he could not focus it immediately.

"It's a supply train, sir," Dawlish said. "They wouldn't be moving north unless –"

"Thank you, Mr. Dawlish." Voice cold, intent clear. Be quiet.

FitzBaldwin swept his telescope back and forth along the isthmus. The Austrian column was at its centre now. It could not be further than two miles distant, some three and a half-thousand yards. The Armstrongs had a range of five.

Dawlish glanced down. The tarpaulin cover had been cleared from the turret and within it he saw the upturned faces of the gun-crews. They had heard his shouted reports, knew that an enemy was in sight, were expecting action. The bulwarks, all of them, on both sides, had been dropped at dawn and the turret had been cranked over to bear on the starboard beam. A single shell falling on that causeway...

"It looks like a damn good target, doesn't it, Mr. Dawlish?" FitzBaldwin said.

"There couldn't be a better one, sir." Heart thumping, apprehension and hope mixed.

"How many ranging shots to find it?"

"Six, seven, sir." Even more perhaps, for *Odin* was rolling gently. And she carried just ten shells for each gun. Only one conclusion, and better to admit it. "Not a good target, sir."

"You're learning, Mr. Dawlish."

Figures appeared on the crest of the dunes above the beach, their movement slow and clumsy in their calf-length greatcoats. Several disappeared again, were back again almost immediately with what must be an officer. The image sharpened in his lens's disc and Dawlish saw a bicorne hat with a feathery black plume, a scarf wrapped around the head beneath, a fair moustache, a telescope raised to meet his own. He must have seen the Danish ensign, perhaps even the twin dark muzzles directed towards him, but he stood immobile, resolute, observing with studied calm. As the ironclad swept past, he snapped his telescope shut and raised his hand in a salute. The gesture had a hint of mockery. Then he and his men disappeared back over the dune. Reports of *Odin's* arrival would spread.

Rain was falling again, drizzle that reduced visibility to a mile or less and blocked view of the peninsula's extremity. The ironclad, at quarter-revolutions, passed the northern end of the lagoon. Fringed along the beach by low dunes, the chart had shown that the low sandy land beyond them extended eastwards for a mile or more towards the now unseen Limfjord.

"Sir." Crowther, the seaman lookout, pointing north-eastwards.

Thin columns of smoke losing themselves in the grey murk, not the rolling flame-shot clouds of a single conflagration, but dozens of small half-hearted smoulderings fighting against the rain.

"Campfires," FitzBaldwin said. "They're here in force"

For now grey tents were revealed beyond the dunes, fewer than the far larger number of what looked like improvised hovels. Men, animals and wagons were moving there and from a pole a flag – Austrian – was standing out stiffly in the breeze. What looked like two companies of infantry were toiling northwards – no sense of attack or urgency, rather of dispirited and chilled men headed back to positions from which they might have been relieved days before. It was all too clear that this was a camp – not a front line – and the Austrians must occupy the whole uninterrupted width of the peninsula at this point. Even if Saabye's Danes were still holding out, they must have abandoned those redoubts glimpsed earlier. The perfect defensive positions that Essmann and Blackwood had put so much faith in were already lost and the Danish position must now be much further north.

The strains of a bugle were all but inaudible on the wind but small knots — officers perhaps — were spilling from a large tent and mounting horses held for them. A half-dozen cantered towards the shore, were lost behind the dunes for a moment, appeared again at the crest and halted in what must be shock and disbelief. Dawlish glanced towards FitzBaldwin — surely even a single shell landing anywhere in that camp must trigger panic, must serve notice that …

"Do you hear anything, Mr. Dawlish? You, Crowther?" FitzBaldwin's attention had passed from the camp, was directed towards the beach far ahead. "Gunfire? Cannon? Small arms?"

"No, sir."

Still nothing, only the sound of the water's wash along the flanks, the slow beat of the engine reverberating through the hull, the wind singing in the rigging.

Fear unspoken that all was already over, Saabye's proud defiance at an end.

The lower, southerly, end of the second lagoon was coming into view. The chart had indicated it to be two miles long on the peninsula's axis, narrow at first but widening further north to a mile across. The strips of land to either side were causeways, the nearer a mile wide in places, the more distant a quarter or third of that and bordering the Limfjord. A track ran north along the centre of that nearer strip. Small columns of men were strung north along it at irregular intervals, none in great haste. But there was artillery also, four six-horse teams pulling what looked like field cannon and followed by wagons.

Odin advanced two miles, parallel to the beach. Rain lessening. The head of the lagoon was visible now. It curved slightly to the west, narrowing the strip behind the beach. And here at last was what was hoped for, two low hummocks, larger, far larger than those seen further south, shadowed gaps in their faces unmistakable as embrasures.

"There, sir! At the western end!" Dawlish could not repress himself.

The flag there, white cross on red, was fork-tailed. Now it could be seen that a low ridge of sand stretched between the two redoubts, that it ran down to the sea on one side, to the lagoon on the other. And there was more. At the head of the further strip, bordering the Limfjord, was a single redoubt, smaller than the others, but with a Danish flag flying proudly above it also.

"Thank God!" Relief in FitzBaldwin's voice. "They're here, the fine fellows! There's hope still!"

The leadsman's cries indicated shallower water. Lorance, on the bridge, directed the bows north-westwards to find greater depth before swinging parallel to the coast again.

The Austrians' full might was now visible. Demilunes of heaped sand, their rears open to the south, stretched like beads on a necklace from beach to lagoon south of the Danish works. Dawlish counted – three, four, five already completed. Men with spades and wheelbarrows swarmed like black ants to complete two more. Four weapons in each, twenty in total – field pieces judging by their size – already in situ, and more, seen earlier, still moving up the peninsula. Small encampments, tents and shelters, lay behind each position, Wagons moved between them, offloading kegs and crates.

"They're in no hurry" FitzBaldwin lowered his glass, was all but talking to himself.

The impression was indeed of patient, steady preparation, of lack of any intention to open bombardment until overwhelming force had been assembled. There would be no infantry assault yet either. Three saps – zig-zag trenches – extended forward towards the Danish redoubts. One had reached half-way. It would go no further for now. Another wall of sand was being thrown up at its end, a small demilune in which infantry might mass before charging forward.

And no gunfire.

Nothing from the Danish line to interrupt the Austrian preparations, nothing from either cannon or rifle. The silence was an ominous indication of munitions in short supply, of necessity to hoard every round until the moment of desperation. On the far side of the lagoon similar Austrian preparations were in hand south of the Danish redoubt there. As in the others, the defenders must already foresee a storm of falling shells and of solid lines of infantry surging towards them. Only the time for it could not be known.

The ironclad was level now with the nearer of the Danish redoubts. Men were rising from within, mounting atop, arms waving, their cheers audible even at this distance. *Odin's* whistle shrilled – down on the bridge Lorance himself was tugging on its line – and crew on deck were themselves waved and cheered back.

"Not so desperate after all, is it, Mr. Dawlish?"

FitzBaldwin pointed towards the small church tower a mile ahead that marked Thyborøn village. And to its east, inside the Limfjord's narrow entrance, rose the masts and yards of another ship.

Blackwood had arrived, and with him the force that must never be called the Alexandra Legion.

*

Dawlish had not imagined it like this. In his mind's eye the *Odin* would have swept along the peninsula, as the gunvessel *Foyle* had swept into a Colombian anchorage two years before. Shells would have roared from her turret, great fountains of earth and flame climbing where they fell, men and horses scattering in panic, the presence of the ironclad enough to deter any assault. The landing of the Alexandra Legion would have been of symbolic value only, enough to ensure prolonged and symbolic defiance of an enemy already cowed in mind by setback.

But the reality was different. He felt humbled by the realisation that he had not foreseen it. Caution and deliberation were what would count here. Not just for the Austrian commander patiently amassing his forces and supplies, but no less for the Danes confined – the word 'trapped' came to mind though he wanted to reject it – at the tip of the peninsula. It applied no less so to *Odin* herself. Massively armed and armoured though she was, she was carrying only shells enough to support an hour's bombardment.

*

Dawlish had never felt so callow, had never been so aware of the gulf of insight and experience that separated him from men like FitzBaldwin when he had been summoned to accompany him to the conference ashore. It was flattering that the captain had brought him rather than his own son, more flattering still that he introduced him as "my gunnery lieutenant." But however valuable his pennyworth might yet be, he was at the meeting only to listen and to learn.

Odin lay now at anchor eastwards of Thyborøn's tip, south of the narrow strait that separated it from the land to the north. Tides surging in from the North Sea scoured the Limfjord's entrance deep and a comfortable four fathoms lay beneath the keel. Close by lay the *Althea*, the grimy eight-hundred ton tramp that had carried Blackwood's force from Newcastle. Boats laden with supplies shuttled between her and the shore. There was no jetty here and Danish peasants stood knee-deep in the frigid waters as they manhandled sacks and boxes from the boats.

The conference was in the wooden single-room village school, the only building of any consequence other than the small church that was now a hospital. The fisherfolk had been evacuated north and their fifty or so small cottages could shelter only part of the Danish force. Tents and improvised huts – most little more than rings of piled sand roofed with driftwood – accommodated the majority. Unshaven men in filthy blue uniforms squatted around small cooking fires and reached out numbed hands towards inadequate warmth. Tethered horses endured with their tails turned to the unrelenting wind. The troops Blackwood had brought had already pitched tents – old patched ones – and were being drilled together for the first time. Everywhere wet cold, the smell of smoke and latrines, coughing, red rimmed eyes, grey faces, misery. Yet everywhere too a sense of patient endurance, of the resolution of men whose lives had always been of hardship, who expected nothing better.

Blackwood was already wearing a Danish greatcoat decorated with what might be a colonel's insignia, the empty left sleeve pinned up. He introduced FitzBaldwin and Dawlish. Friherre Saabye – his English was perfect – was perfunctory in his acknowledgement. He looked as if he had not slept for days or washed for weeks. The half-dozen members of his staff looked no better, other than Major Essmann, who had arrived from Britain with Blackwood. There was a grim determination about them that Dawlish found appealing, an unstated pride too that they had endured an ordeal, had survived it unbeaten, that they would survive as much again.

The schoolroom was Saabye's headquarters – benches pushed to one side, rough tables taken from cottages, a few chairs, piled valises, scuffed despatch boxes, a stove, the smell of sweat and tobacco and woodsmoke. A large handmade map – an impressive piece of work, inked and finely lettered, probably made in parts on a plane table and afterwards glued together – was pinned to what had been the blackboard.

Saabye's summary was brief. He said little of the retreat – it had been bad, very bad, he said, and his officers nodded – but the Austrians had been outpaced by two days. The disappointment had been on reaching the causeways at the southern lagoon. The redoubts the engineers whom he had sent ahead to build with local peasant labour were incomplete.

"But we held them there for three days." Major Stavald, Saabye's artillery officer, spoke with pride.

His gunners had done well in the now-deserted hummocks that Dawlish had seen from the foretop. Two precipitate and ill-conceived assaults by infantry columns had been hurled back by a storm of cannister. While the Austrians were bringing up artillery to precede a third attack with a bombardment – as they should have done originally – the main body of Saabye's troops had continued north towards Thyborøn village. With more peasants brought in by boat from across the Limfjord, they had begun frenzied construction of the redoubts on either side of the northern lagoon. When Austrian cannon had opened sustained fire at dawn in the fourth morning it did so on empty positions. Stavald had withdrawn his guns north in darkness to the new defences that were getting stronger by the day.

Blackwood moved to the map and explained the positions. The Austrian demilunes and the zig-zag saps were well defined but the area below the northerly lagoon, the site of the Austrian camp, was a blank. FitzBaldwin told what had been visible from *Odin's* foretop and a Danish officer began to sketch in each detail in pencil.

The conference ended, for the junior officers at least. A jerk of FitzBaldwin's head indicated that Dawlish should wait outside.

"You would like to smoke a cigar, lieutenant?" The young Dane who had marked the map was standing with a British officer who had come with Blackwood.

Handshakes. Lieutenant Ove Krag, of Denmark's Royal Life Guards, looked two or three years older than Dawlish. Thomas Granville was in his mid- twenties, a lieutenant in the Grenadiers. They seemed easy in each other's company already. Since Granville had arrived on the previous evening, Krag had brought him to see the largest of the redoubts. He would be bringing a company of Alexandra's Own – he did not avoid the term – to take duty there two days from now. Hastily gathered in Newcastle, there had been no time to drill them there, only enough to allocate them to platoons, assign corporals and sergeants, issue weapons and boots and British uniforms hastily dyed dark Danish blue.

"They're just a rag, tag and bob-tail now," Granville said. "But good fellows among them. It'll take a day or two to knock 'em into shape."

"This great ship, Lieutenant Dawlish, what will it be doing?" Krag's English was careful, not fluent. "Friherre Saabye had said nothing to us of this *Odin*. We could not believe it when it appeared today, when he explained. The guns it carries! Will they not turn the tide?"

"I hope so," Dawlish said.

For now there was reason to hope. The *Althea* had brought more from Newcastle than the hundred recruits mustered there. More than the dozen Russian field guns captured at Sevastopol that had lain forgotten in some British depot until Blackwood remembered them and pulled strings. More than rifles and flour and canned beef and medical supplies.

Fifty three-hundred pound shells, hastily forged in the Armstrong works, each filled with a hundred and eighty pounds of black powder and two hundred half-inch iron balls.

They might indeed just turn the tide.

Chapter 9

Saabye's small army was under siege, but under one unlikely to end, as so many had through history, by starvation. No Austrian forces had penetrated north of the Limfjord and supplies flowed in to Thyborøn by water from the lands there. Dawlish saw sacks of flour and sides of bacon, bundles of fire-wood, even a few live cattle, being offloaded from the small sailing craft he had come to see. Only the horses that had dragged the wagons and cannon here were threatened by hunger. Even had twice as many boats had been available, there would still have been too few to carry sufficient fodder. Ribs already showing, at the mercy of the wind on this flat grassless spit, the animals' sufferings had not ended with the retreat.

"Who's paying for these supplies?" Dawlish asked Lieutenant Krag.

"People here trust Friherre Saabye. He looks after his tenants. His family always has. For centuries. They believe his promises."

"They're not being paid in cash?"

"Maybe someday," Krag said. "But it's not important now, not today. We've been invaded." He gestured towards a small gaggle of newly landed peasants who were trudging south towards the redoubts with picks and shovels. Not with enthusiasm, but with doggedness. "You see them? Talk of duchies or treaties or successions or constitutions means nothing to them. They only know that this is their land. That Austrians, people they never knew existed, have brought misery to it."

Dawlish had sensed something of the same about the troops he had seen so far. Stolid, maybe humourless, but with dour resolution on their faces. Most were reservists, he had learned, called back from farm and factory and workshop to the colours little over a month before. The weakest had fallen by the wayside on the retreat north. A few – fewer than he had expected, Krag said – had deserted. Those who had reached here through snow and ice, sleet and mud, hunger and fatigue, had been forged by the retreat into real soldiers.

But Dawlish was paying more attention to the boats. All were open, up to forty feet in length, the larger with two masts. What he sought was smaller still, something shorter, handier, its appearance local enough not to arouse the suspicion that a whaler under sail might do.

"That one," he said at last. It lay close to the shore, and two men – father and son perhaps – were wading from it and carrying open-topped boxes of fish. Twenty feet, maybe less, lugger-rigged, twin masts, one so far forward as to be all but in the bow, that aft little more than a stump.

"You want to speak to them?" Krag said.

"No. Not yet." Better not to draw attention by a foreign newcomer taking interest. "Just make sure that they don't leave. Tell them there'll be a task for them this evening, nothing more. They'll gain from it"

For Dawlish had received his own directions from FitzBaldwin. A plan had been discussed with Saabye, he said, when he emerged from the conference in the school house. Not firm, and dependent on preliminary action that would prove its feasibility.

Action in that small fishing boat this coming night.

*

The tide was falling, the current running seawards from the Limfjord strong, the wind down to little more than a fresh breeze from the southwest when the boat cast off. It was an hour to midnight. The new moon gave almost no light and the stars were all but obliterated by tatters of drifting cloud. The glow of campfires and lanterns pocked the deeper darkness of the land. Fishermen familiar with the waters both outside and inside the fjord, Uffe Østergaard and his son Kristian brought the craft into the open sea in a series of long tacks. Five British gold sovereigns, donated by FitzBaldwin and payable on return, had bought their service. The older man steered, the younger managed the sails.

Dawlish had immediately volunteered for the task when FitzBaldwin shared his plans. He had seen hesitation on Albemarle's face and he put himself forward lest he be beaten to it. That FitzBaldwin accepted without hesitation might have been a bad omen. Another father's son, not his, would run the risk.

When the craft had emerged from the Limfjord mouth she headed west for what the older fisherman estimated to be two miles before swinging south. She ran now parallel to the coast, a faint line of grey marking the waves breaking on the beach. The Danish campfires lay to port and, off the bow, dancing points of lantern light showed movement in redoubts. A slight glow in the sky to the southeast indicated the Austrian camp.

"It's time to move close inshore," Dawlish said to Krag. The lieutenant had come as interpreter.

McRory, the leadsman from the *Odin*, was already stationed at the bow, ready to cast. Kristian, the younger fisherman, was holding his legs

99

to keep him balanced. The half-dozen hastily improvised buoys lay on the boards underfoot, kegs filled with driftwood to ensure buoyancy and daubed with red lead. A mooring line was coiled beneath each and secured to four nine-pound cannon balls in a net at the other end.

The bows were now headed due east, directly towards shore. Dawlish held a small compass as steadily as he could, its face just visible with the aid of a dark lantern. Krag relayed his course corrections to the elder Østergaard. It was impossible to judge the exact distance to the beach, the dots of light against the deeper blackness there no help.

"Now, McRory!"

The lead swung forward and plunged, the line running through the seaman's hands. Tie-marks – leather, calico, serge – at three fathom intervals were telling him by touch alone how much had run out. Now the call – "by the deep eight," something between the seven and ten fathom marks. The boat must be further offshore than estimated. Course unchanged. Another cast, and another, and another, still in excess of seven, and only with the next the first indication of decreasing depth. Seven "by the mark" now and so for the next three casts, then decreasing suddenly – "by the deep five" and "five by the mark" the next sounding. So too for the next three as the bottom levelled. The lights at the redoubts ahead were more than pinpricks now, yet the distance was still impossible to judge.

"By the deep four!"

Somewhere between three and five fathoms. Dawlish held his watch to the dark lantern. Twenty minutes to two. Close to low water. The tide would be turning soon.

Still deep enough but not wise to tempt fortune by venturing further shorewards. *Odin's* draught was fifteen feet but, on this coast of shifting sandbars, FitzBaldwin and Lorance were unwilling to take her into any waters that gave less than a dozen more beneath her keel.

"Five by the mark!"

Time to drop the first buoy. Krag – unused to boats, unsteady even in the gentle pitch – lugged the cannon-ball anchor over the side. The fifty-foot mooring line whipped across the gunwale and Dawlish threw the wooden keg after. The red lead had not fully dried – his hands were sticky from its touch – and he hoped it would not be washed away by the waves. There was no help for that now.

Helm over, the course southwards. The few lights at the Danish redoubts slipped past. McRory still sounded, still chanted, never less than five fathoms. Darkness on the landwards side. They passed the narrow no man's land, and then sighted dancing lanterns again – work in progress to drive the Austrian trenches further forward.

Back in the fjord, work was in progress on the *Odin* also, hurried transfer and storage of supplies from the *Althea*. Hopper, the gun-captain, was supervising filling of the shell racks within the turret. There was insufficient room for all the munitions now available and there was no option but to lash the crates containing the remainder on deck. If all went well, they would not all remain there for long. But there was other work in hand also, and entrusted to Killigrew. He had headed south to the redoubts with Granville, the Grenadier lieutenant. A Danish artillery officer, a Major Stavald who spoke English, accompanied them. For there were howitzers there . . .

The next buoy was dropped, approximately in line, Dawlish judged, with the demi-lunes sheltering the Austrian cannons, a string of cooking-fires behind them. Still southwards, parallel to the beach. The red glow above the enemy's main camp was stronger now.

"By the deep two!" Alarm in McRory's sudden call.

There was a bar here and the next sounding told that it was shallower still, a danger even to this small craft itself should it worsen. Helm over at Dawlish's translated demand, bows headed as close to the south-westerly breeze as possible to claw slowly seawards. Still shallow for what seemed an aeon, four casts of the lead, and then at last the relief of the call of "three by the mark" and deeper still with the next.

Another buoy identified the point where Dawlish had Østergaard swing the boat south again. The Austrian camp lay directly on the port beam now, flickering red reflected on the dozens of trails of smoke rising from its fires. The water depth was nowhere less than five fathoms – but the tide was flooding now and at ebb it would be less. Better to take no chances, not to nudge further inshore, and to drop the next three buoys in line. Wiser to edge out to the west when McRory called slightly shallower depth, to heave an anchor and keg overboard again when five fathoms were called.

The boat had dropped well south of the Austrian camp by now, perhaps even south of the lower lagoon. The few bright dots visible might indicate wagons or guns moving up the causeways but there was still no alarm from shorewards.

One buoy remained. Heading sustained for another ten minutes, depth still satisfactory. Then one last heave over the side and a short claw out to sea again before changing tack and heading north. Two hours in hand, enough to reach the Limfjord mouth before first light.

The Østergaards, father and son, had earned their five sovereigns.

*

Dawlish ate his first satisfying breakfast since leaving Antwerp, fried bacon, even bread with butter and two eggs, luxuries purchased from two peasant women who had brought a boat alongside. Busy as *Odin's* crew had been through the night transferring stores, spirits had been raised, due not only to the food but to the blankets, extra clothing, soap and rum that the *Althea* had brought from Newcastle.

He had sketched the locations of the buoys on a chart as best he could after he returned. FitzBaldwin and Lorance examined the sheet – and him – in detail.

"So you've no idea of the distances from buoys to shore, have you, Mr. Dawlish?" Lorance made it sound like an accusation of dereliction.

"It was dark, sir, and –"

The American ignored him, addressed FitzBaldwin directly. "You think it's good enough?"

"With a good leadsman in the bow – you thought well of that fellow last night, didn't you Dawlish? – and at quarter-revolutions, it's worth a damn good try," FitzBaldwin said.

"As long as we do it soon, I guess," Lorance said. "Even if they aren't spotted, those buoys won't stay there forever. Today's none too early."

"Not without the howitzers," FitzBaldwin said. "No word back from Killigrew yet." He turned to Dawlish. "I'll need your assurance that your guns are ready. You can get some sleep afterwards."

Hopper had done well – new munitions stored, turret bearings greased, the drum rotated through full seven-twenty degrees and lying again fore and aft. The gunners were pleased by their first daily tot of rum. After a full inspection Dawlish dismissed them for rest. Then he went to the boiler room – only harbour pressure maintained there – and had some hot water tapped into a bucket to wash in. He stripped off and soaped himself. The feeling of cleanliness was as joyous as a rebirth. The promise of a sixpence induced a stoker to launder his clothes. Hung here, they would be dry when he woke.

Swaddled in a clean blanket – *Althea's* precious gift – he went to his cabin.

His sleep was dreamless.

"Wake up, Dawlish."

He struggled into consciousness. Granville was shaking his shoulder.

"Saabye's taking Colonel Blackwood and your captain to view the redoubts. They sent me to bring you."

It was early afternoon, and raining, a steady drizzle drifting on the low wind, saturating and chilling. The senior officers had gone ahead and Dawlish followed with Granville and Krag. He felt ashamed to mount the half-starved horse provided, felt reproached by the misery in the great, innocent, uncomprehending eyes.

They plodded south. The tents and shelters lay in regular lines. Individual units created their own small precincts of order, but the impression was still of a large extended slum. It might have been yet worse had there not been sand underfoot. At least there was no mud.

The two redoubts' bulk loomed ahead, their sloped embankment walls complete. A single trench line, sand thrown up in a low ridge before it, linked the separate structures. Fifty yards further back, gangs of troops and peasants were digging a second line.

The sight evoked a memory, one Dawlish wished he could forget, yet knew he never would. Five years before, all but a child, he had been part of a force launched in an ill-conceived assault on Chinese earthworks. He had not seen violent death before then, could never have imagined the horror of torn flesh and shattered bone, of the terror of flame and smoke that erupted from the embrasures, of musket fire that lashed from the walls.

It had been little solace that he had been in the triumphant wave that washed over the same position, with fewer casualties, the following year. And there had been yet worse ahead, in Pekin, the tortured bodies of British prisoners and the vengeance that had followed. He had hardened then, he recognised, hardened when others of his age were still in school, hardened because he knew that the cruel and strong would always oppress the weak, hardened because the alternative to resistance was submission to malevolence.

He glanced across towards Granville. The Grenadier had volunteered because he wanted experience, he had said. Too young to have been in the Crimea, an officer in a fashionable regiment that had been committed to ceremonial duties in Britain ever since, he had never seen a shot fired in anger. Even now there was a hint of the dandy about him and it as easy to imagine him, immaculate, on Horse Guards Parade. Yet he was here, cold and wet, rain on his face, a cigar clamped in his teeth, cheerful in acceptance of discomfort, the brutalities that might lie ahead not yet comprehended.

Dawlish wondered if Krag had looked like this before the withdrawal from the Danevirke. He had let drop, without boastfulness, that his regiment too was socially superior, busy mainly in mounting palace guards in Copenhagen. But he had brought a company of that same regiment north through snow and mud after its captain had been killed, doing well enough to earn a place on Saabye's staff. There was a hint about him of the same mental hardness that Dawlish recognised in himself. The hardness that meant Shrewsbury would never be home again, why father and brother and sister would be beloved strangers.

They dismounted at the entrance of the larger redoubt. On this face the embankment was lower than those on the front and sides, little more than a six-foot ridge. The space within was an irregular pentagon, stretched some seventy yards laterally east to west. The faces towards the enemy formed a shallow vee. Guns on wheeled carriages stood at embrasures with the sides shored up with what looked like driftwood. Crude bombproof shelters for munitions storage had been built into the inner sides. It was easy to imagine them collapsing if even a single shell landed close by. There were other shelters, open-fronted, built against the embankments, comfortless protection in which men who had been stood-down could eat or sleep. The overall impression was of something just short of adequacy, of little more than a hastily thrown-up field fortification.

Saabye was standing on top of the outer wall with Blackwood and FitzBaldwin. Major Stavald was pointing towards the Austrian lines and they were following his finger. FitzBaldwin had a telescope held to his eye, the others, field glasses. He dropped it, turned to speak to Saabye, then noticed the newcomers and motioned to them to come up.

Dawlish was suddenly aware of being fully exposed. The small earthwork at the head of the nearest Austrian trench was not more than four hundred yards distant. Krag had earlier remarked that the Lorentz rifle used by the Austrians was well regarded. A skilled marksman at that trench would have a reasonable hope of hitting anybody atop this earthwork. Saabye and the others must know it too, but were making no attempt to disguise their presence. Further along the wall men were labouring to heighten a parapet, dragging up by rope wheelbarrows laden with sand dug from the ditch at the outer base There must be several dozen men exposed atop the embankment, as many again above the second redoubt, but the Austrians seemed in no hurry to inconvenience them. The workers at their own trenches were no less vulnerable. No fire from either side.

"So you're the young man who's been dumping our cannon balls," Saabye said to Dawlish. The old scar that held his left eye half-open and the rasping voice – he looked feverish – made it uncertain whether he was angry or jocular. "We dragged them all this way for you to throw them in the sea, löjtnant?"

"In a good cause, Friherre" FitzBaldwin said. "A damn good piece of work too." He reached his telescope to Dawlish. "There, see those gun positions?"

Seen head-on, the string of Austrian demilunes running from seashore to lagoon looked more menacing than it had when viewed from *Odin*. It blocked the ground behind it from view and black dots identified muzzles directed north. Waiting.

"That's what we're here for, Dawlish," FitzBaldwin said. "A bloody narrow target from seaward, but we'll do our best."

"Twelve pounder field guns." Cold precision in Stavald's tone. "Seven batteries that we can see. Probably two or three of field howitzers that we can't."

"They're not going to waste their time pounding away and hoping for breaches in these walls. They know damn-well that the sand will deaden solid shot." Blackwood spoke directly to Saabye. "They'll wait until they're confident that they've men enough. There'll be one damn great storm of fire and they'll assault directly after it."

"They'll take losses, heavy losses," Saabye said. "We've cannister enough. They'll break."

Blackwood pointed to the rising earthwork at the head of the nearest of the advancing Austrian trenches. "They'll muster under cover behind that and, when they burst out, they'll have just four hundred yards to cover to get there. Even if we've every gun firing cannister into them, and every rifle blasting, eight out of ten of 'em will be swarming in here."

"Like the Sevastopol Redan?" Saabye's sarcasm was undisguised. He glanced towards Blackwood's empty sleeve. The failed British assault, intended to bring the interminable siege of the Russian fortress to an end, had been a blood-drenched and embarrassing disaster. All Europe knew of it. There was a limit to how much flesh and blood could achieve against direct cannon fire.

Dawlish looked away. The others were doing so also, pretending not to hear. Saabye was clearly exhausted, near the end of his tether, needed help but didn't want advice.

"FitzBaldwin will be giving us a chance to do something about them. Won't you, captain?" Blackwood calm, not rising to the bait.

Dawlish felt a gentle tug on his elbow, turned to see Krag jerking his head towards the redoubt's interior. Granville too was taking the hint. Junior officers should not hear their seniors' disagreements.

They descended, walked behind the embrasures, viewed the twelve-pounder field pieces. Krag introduced the artillery commander, a captain, and translated his account of the problems of getting them here. He was proud that not a single gun had been abandoned even though farm horses had to be requisitioned to replace losses to cold and exhaustion. But he regretted the loss of two of his howitzers and their crews and, of his deputy, not to the Austrians but to Major Stavald's unexplained demand for their removal the previous day. Probe as he did for an explanation, he got none. Only four remained to him, just over half a battery, safely ensconced below the sheltering ramparts.

And unbeknownst to him, the two howitzers he had given up, and their crews and his deputy with them, had a role to play.

Tomorrow.

Chapter 10

Odin slipped out through the Limfjord entrance at high water, two hours before dawn. The sea beyond was calm, the wind slight, the rain light but persistent., and she headed west for five miles before turning south. She was cleared for action. All bulwarks down, turret manned, Armstrongs loaded, shivering lookouts in the fore and maintops.

And Danish howitzers aft.

Dawlish, already chilled and saturated despite an oilskin, was again on his seat above the guns in the open-topped iron drum. It had been rotated to off the starboard bow and locked there. The lanyards were fitted to the firing pistols now and entrusted to Hopper, the gun-captain. There was nothing to do now but wait. In the darkness below him he heard a seaman swearing that he was cold and wet and a fool to be here. Hopper was brutal in his reproof. Silence again. It must be terrible to be down there, Dawlish thought, blocked from all view of the world beyond, dependent on him alone for sight of it. He felt sick, not from the slight roll of the vessel, but from the same fear which had haunted him since that first day at the Chinese forts, fear not just of failure but of loss of nerve. The moment that FitzBaldwin had promised him was imminent, the chance to ensure that his name – a nobody's – might become known, be singled out in some uncertain future from those of others.

Day broke – a grey sky above a grey sea and the land to port hidden by the drifting rain. FitzBaldwin and Lorance were on the bridge, indistinguishable in black oilskins and sou'westers. Further aft, half-hidden by the funnel, Dawlish could see the two howitzers, one before the mainmast, one abaft. Standard Danish twelve-pounders, still on wheeled field carriages, they had been broken down the day before, brought on board in pieces, and reassembled. The cutter and the whaler carried on *Odin's* starboard side had been left behind, and their davits lowered, to clear a line of fire. Short timber ramps had been lashed down behind the howitzers' trails and blocks and tackles rigged to absorb recoil. An open crate of spherical case shot, another of powder charges, and a water-bucket for the sponges lay by each weapon.

Killigrew, who had shown no great energy before, had come to life with the challenge of mounting them. With Krag as translator, he had worked effectively with the Danish artillery lieutenant who had come with his gunners. Now all three officers stood between the howitzers, as

107

silent and apprehensive as the six-man crews for each. Regular troops, faces stolid beneath their leathered-visored kepis, blue greatcoats saturated, they were blowing on cold fingers. The ship's motion had already sent several to vomit over the side. They had once managed three shots in a minute during the retreat, their officer had said, driving off shadowing cavalry before it got within a half-mile of the straggling column's flank. But that had been on solid ground, however slushy and muddy, and not on a slowly rocking and rain-washed deck.

At last the turn to port, the ironclad leaning over as the bows swung towards the unseen coastline. Revolutions dropped to a quarter now, speed a crawl. McRory, the leadsman, was chanting the soundings – still deep enough, ten fathoms and more, to give no concern, yet with every cable eastward the chance was increasing of an unsuspected sand bank. Dawlish's own telescope showed only a grey curtain – no horizon, no sight of land. He glanced over his shoulder and saw the strain on FitzBaldwin's and Lorance's faces as they too searched the murk ahead. The soundings were shallower now – eight fathoms, not immediately alarming – but the promise of less ahead. Albemarle came hurrying to the bridge – he had been responsible for running the patent log astern – and Dawlish just distinguished the words 'eight miles' in his report, the distance run since leaving the Limfjord. *Odin* was now well south of both lagoons.

"By the mark seven!"

Now the helm over, an eight-point sweep to port that carried the ironclad into a northward course parallel to the still-unseen coast. Dawlish felt another fear now, the same, he guessed, that must haunt FitzBaldwin and Lorance also. It was that the beach – perhaps as little as a mile distant – might not be sighted, nor the marker buoys that had been laid at such effort either. Fear that prudence must demand a turn back to open water, that this foray would be futile, a waste of precious coal, an opportunity lost and –

"Deck there!"

The foretop lookout bellowed that he could glimpse land, a thin line of surf, the outline of dunes. Lorance pushed the quartermaster aside and took the wheel. FitzBaldwin was in the bridge wing, eye to glass, calm triumph in his voice as he called to the American. Helm slightly over, bows nudging to starboard and still twenty feet beneath the keel when they edged directly north again.

The rain was slackening, the curtain shredding into individual columns. Between them, Dawlish himself saw land and his heart leapt.

There were the dunes with their dark streaks of grass and, rising above them to the north-east, ghostly in the drizzle, was the massive white tower of the church of Harboøre.

"Dawlish!" FitzBaldwin shouting from the bridge. "Can you rotate the turret in this sea?"

"Yes, sir!" Not easy, but possible.

"I want it bearing closer to the bow, another five degrees, more if possible. And elevation. For three thousand yards – no, make that three and a half."

The elevation angle must be read off the range table supplied by the Armstrong works, supported presumably by test firings on proving grounds. But nobody on *Odin* had seen these guns fired, or knew how reliable these tables were, what corrections must be applied.

"I'm going aloft," FitzBaldwin called. "I'll spot for you myself. Wait for my word – my word mind!"

He had cast off his oilskin so as to climb more easily, but age and girth still told as he hoisted himself to the maintop and crouched there, panting, with the lookout, Crowther. Dawlish shouted instructions down to Hopper to set half of each gun-crew to turning the cranks. The turret lurched as the brake was released and then, as the men strained, crawled slowly anti-clockwise.

Dawlish watched as the muzzle of the weapon on the left crept close to the corner of the deckhouse – too close and the blast would wreck it.

"Hold it!" he called, "Lock it!" when the separation was four feet.

Then the elevation, screw-jacks rotated to give eight and a half degrees, according to the Armstrong tables. The gunners returned to their stations, rain-drenched faces raised in expectation of the order to fire. But that must wait until –

"There's a buoy, sir!" Jubilation in Crowther's yell as he saw it, and no less in FitzBaldwin's down to Lorance at the wheel.

Over now, closer inshore, McRory calling seven fathoms still, Dawlish's eye glued to his own lens, searching for the keg he had dropped two nights since. At last he found it, a wave-lapped red dot, just visible, then lost in the swell, then barely visible again, but mark enough on which to head the bows. It must be the last that he had placed, for the Harboøre church now lay directly east. It was closer inshore than he had expected, five or six cables from the beach.

Lorance pushed the bows over to pass the buoy at a hundred yards separation. McRory's chant confirmed adequate depth as the vessel ploughed north and a little later Crowther called from the foretop that he could see the next buoy. The rain had all but died, and there was a small patch of blue to the west. The more southerly lagoon was slipping past. A train of wagons was strung out along the strip that separated it from the sea, but they were not the target.

Another buoy passed, Lorance's adjustments keeping the ironclad just to seaward. Figures on the low dunes now, glasses tracking *Odin*, close enough in Dawlish's own disc of vision to discern dark grey coats, others brown, red stripes down light blue trouser legs, black shakos. Two men sat still on horseback on the crest, others on foot clustered around them and pointed. Then one rider spurred his mount and disappeared. Alarm was being raised.

The first tents and shelters and smoking fires of the Austrian camp were just visible. Faint bugle calls, men scurrying to form up. The axes of the turret guns were bearing directly on the encampment and the range even to its centre could not be above a mile and a half, well within the Armstrongs' reach. Dawlish was longing now for FitzBaldwin's word, for the moment of release. He looked down into the drum, caught Hopper's questioning gaze, shook his head slowly.

Not yet.

Slow progress now, parallel to the broad isthmus between the northerly lagoon and the seashore. The silence of the *Odin's* guns had indicated that her target lay yet further north. Horsemen were cantering up the track towards the line of Austrian gun positions at the strip's northern end to alert them. Two light artillery pieces followed, almost as fast, sand spraying up from the hooves of their six-horse teams, drivers astride and whipping, limbers and guns bouncing behind, the other gunners somehow holding their seats on them. They were fast and they outpaced the ironclad until they were all but a mile ahead, where they slewed off the track. Men jumped to the ground – the drill was well practised and impressive, the horses unhitched and led behind, guns and limbers uncoupled. Men strained on the wheel spokes to swing the barrels around even as the first charges were thrust through the muzzles and the shells followed.

It was the brave but futile gesture of gunners unaccustomed to moving targets. Orange flashes, billowing smoke, carriages leaping back on the hard sand, the sharp cracks that reached the ironclad moments later. Then a black dot skidded in a feathery plume off the starboard bow before it was lost to sight. A second fell no more effectively fifty yards astern. Again the Austrian crews sponged, loaded, rammed, lifted the trails, slewed the weapons around to bear again. They fired on misjudged elevations when the *Odin* was all but beam on, shells lost once more in running streaks of spray that died fifty yards or more from her flank. It would not have mattered had they reached the hull – no low-trajectory weapon weaker than the ironclad's own monsters could penetrate the teak-backed six-inch iron belt along her sides.

The wind was strengthening and a glance to the south-west showed a dark wall of advancing rain. The line of Austrian gun emplacements was coming into sight, seven hillocks that extended from the foreshore to the lagoon's nearer edge. Protected by their ramparts from fire from the Danish positions to the north, the open-backed demilunes and the guns and men within were fully exposed to attack from the south-west.

"Mr. Dawlish!" FitzBaldwin calling from the foretop. "Your guns! When the first of those positions crosses your line of sight! Then reload like the devil!"

Odin's revolutions had been cut back yet further and she crawled at little over walking pace. Dawlish directed his gaze along the imaginary axis lying between his two guns. It swept across tents and shelters and tarpaulin-covered mounds of supplies, across the pell-mell of running men, across what looked like an entire company forming up on the beach and opening rifle-fire by ranks. He heard the crackle of their fire – and now another company was taking position further on – but his attention was locked regardless on that invisible axis.

Within each barrel, studs on the sides of a three-hundred pound conical-nosed shell were lodged in the bore's spiral rifling to impart spin on discharge. The black powder inside each cylinder was fused to explode after impact, the casing itself designed to shatter into dozens of lethal fragments. Smaller bursting shells than these had torn a Turkish squadron of wooden warships apart at Sinope ten years before. And the Austrians were but flesh and bone ...

The decision was Dawlish's, and his alone. He waited until the line of sight crossed the upper boundary of the lagoon, passed across the furthest of the demilunes. He judged – no! guessed! hoped! – the range to be somewhat over three thousand yards. The ship's roll was minimal but, even then, he waited for it to reach the vertical.

"Fire!"

Two blasts, all but simultaneous. Flame lashed out full twenty feet beyond the turret's gun-ports. All sight ahead blotted by a rolling cloud of choking smoke and then the drum's interior filled with it too. The massive weapons surged back up their slide mountings and the restraining tackles took up the strain. Dawlish felt his breath knocked from him, his ears pounded to deafness for an instant, his eyes stinging in the murk.

"Reload!"

He did not look down – he could rely on Hopper to see to it. The vessel's forward motion was thrusting the smoke aside and the view was clear. The shells were still in the air, perhaps still climbing to the low apex of their flight before starting their plunge, but he could not pick them out, could only hold his gaze on the distant earthwork.

Then failure.

Two great splashes of white water inside the lagoon, a cable's length or more beyond the redoubt, one erupting into a climbing column as the impact detonated the shell, the other sinking harmlessly.

Dawlish's name was being called, Lorance's too. FitzBaldwin's words were indistinct but the intent was obvious from his gestures.

Adjust range. Keep firing. Hold position.

From the bridge Dawlish heard the ring of the telegraphs – Lorance calling for stilling of the engines, perhaps reversal. The *Odin* still glided forward, ever more slowly, and that vital line of sight was moving across the fifth and sixth of the demilunes.

Inside the drum the barrels had been swabbed, new charges driven home, new shells lifted from the racks by chain hoist and hauled across to the muzzles. Aligning the studs in the rifling before ramming home proved most difficult of all but at last Hopper shouted up that the shells had been rammed home. Three minutes at most had passed since the previous discharge.

The elevation had been too high and the warmed barrels would be adding even greater range should it not be reduced. By how much? Dawlish's brain raced. The Armstrong table were clearly useless and only guesswork and gamble could now suffice. He took the plunge.

"Elevation! Six degrees!"

Handwheels spun and the huge barrels dropped. Hopper had checked the pointer on the brass scale, had adjusted with a half-turn more, had moved to the other weapon and had done the same.

"Ready to fire, sir!"

Again the roar, the churning smoke, the rumble of the recoiling cannons. The ironclad's speed was now so low that she did not at once shake free from the acrid cloud enveloping her and Dawlish could not see the target. But FitzBaldwin could, from his vantage above, and he was crying in delight.

"Keep firing, Dawlish!"

The loading drill, so painfully practised, was rewarded as Hopper's men renewed the loading sequence. The smoke cleared and Dawlish could see a plume of smoke rising from behind the fourth and fifth Austrian positions. Not direct hits but close enough to have showered them with glowing fragments, for panicked horses to be now dragging wagons – one was overturned – and men trying to restrain them. And the barrels were well heated now, would add slight range without change of elevation…

Two salvos in quick succession, the spacing perhaps three minutes, perhaps four, for all sense of time was lost in the noise and murk. A brief rent in the fog let Dawlish see the shells of the first pound down just short of the third demilune. Sand fountained up as they landed and an orange flash and smoke followed. The Austrian guns remained untouched but deserted, their crews probably cowering on the far side of the embankments. The second salvo struck – satisfactorily according to FitzBaldwin's call, though Dawlish could not see it. The shells must have still been in the air before the soaking fleeces were thrust into the hot bores and the chain hoists rattled again.

"Mr. Dawlish!" FitzBaldwin's shout. "Crank the turret on to the beam!" He called to Lorance, to increase revolutions, to lay the ship in line with the string of Austrian positions. "And Mr. Lorance! A word to Mr. Killigrew! Time for the howitzers!"

The turret crept slowly clockwise as the gunners strained on the cranks, held it on the beam and locked the brakes. The ironclad had picked up speed – dead-slow ahead. The smoke had cleared enough for Dawlish to see movement on the foreshore. The infantry companies that had opened such ineffectual musketry were stumbling along the beach at the double in an attempt to overhaul *Odin*. Far behind them the two field gun teams that had opened fire before had limbered up and were galloping in pursuit.

Sharp cracks announced the Danish howitzers lashed down close to the mainmast opening fire. Accuracy was impossible but their shells, puny by comparison with those of the Armstrongs, dropped close enough to the men and animals at the Austrian positions to add to the chaos. Two more followed, and the Danes settled into their own practised firing-rhythm.

Odin was almost level with the Austrian line now, the range to the nearest demilune, the first inland from the beach, little over a mile. Exact ranging would be less critical now for there was a good chance that any dropping shell would land close to, or even in, an enemy battery.

"Your guns, Mr. Dawlish!" Relish in FitzBaldwin's cry.

Perhaps better to decrease the range, drop the barrels by a half degree, so as to rake the nearer batteries. Dawlish called down into the drum and Hopper himself made the fine adjustment and shouted back that it was complete. The line of demilunes was foreshortened now and the imaginary axis extending from between the turret's guns was all but aligned with it.

And then the moment.

"Fire!"

One shell ploughed a long furrow of sand before it exploded just behind a battery – it might have been the fifth or sixth. Its companion fell closer and the flash of its explosion was half-hidden by an embankment. It might have fallen between two demilunes, perhaps even inside one of them. *Odin's* Danish howitzers were dropping shells further back. There was no obvious pattern to their impacts – the crews had not mastered the art of firing at the top of the roll – but the haphazardness was in itself an advantage for adding to the chaos.

Despite the rising wind, Lorance held the ironclad all but stationary, grinding the telegraph back and forth to call the engine room for revolutions astern, revolutions ahead. Another salvo from the turret guns, its result unseen by Dawlish but hailed with triumph by FitzBaldwin. Two salvos more. Sensing success, urged on by Dawlish, driven hard by Hopper, the blackened crews inside the drum were slaving to maintain an undiminished rate of fire. Steam boiled from the hot barrels as the sodden fleeces drowned glowing particles left by the last discharges. Time then to lower the elevation again - a full degree, Dawlish risked – before the next double blast.

And this time, not just the by-now familiar detonation of the falling shells, but something deeper, vaster. The flash lit up the rolling wall that blotted Dawlish's vision and the 'whoomph!', long and sustained, identified a much larger explosion. Stored munitions had been set off, perhaps taking with them all within the demilune that sheltered them.

The rain squall spotted earlier now hit, great heavy drops at first and then a frigid downpour driven hard by yet stronger wind. Lorance edged *Odin's* bows a point seaward to counter drift towards the lee shore. Down inside the turret water sizzled as it touched the barrels but the loading drill did not falter.

Another salvo, and another. Almost all the shells and charges stored within the turret had been fired but FitzBaldwin was not calling for slowing. The Austrian batteries were being pulverised, he shouted, they could not take more of it, their guns were being deserted. The Danish howitzers aft barked steadily, hauled around now on their tackles to drop more shells into the chaos behind the demilunes. Dawlish's throat burned, his eyes streamed, his voice rasped when he shouted orders down to Hopper, and yet he felt that there was something almost joyous about the moment, a flush of power, of invincibility. Through gaps in the searing mist he could see that the Austrian infantry on the beach — they were undaunted, game, were still maintaining a useless fusillade. The guns that had chased up behind them had been unlimbered again and were opening hopeless fire at *Odin's* armoured flank. And beyond them, where the Danish shells were falling so randomly, Dawlish saw winking points of light, two in quick succession, and then a third. Other Austrian weapons were coming into play.

White geysers of foam erupted a half-cable length off the ironclad's starboard bow, two close together and the next, an instant later, nearer still. These were not the tracks of low trajectory field-gun shells but all too clearly the plunging fire of howitzers.

"Fire!"

Even as the Armstrongs roared again at Dawlish's command, fear chilled him. Clad all around in iron *Odin* might be, but her decks were only thin metal, little protection for the vitals beneath, and the turret itself was open to the sky.

"Lorance! Slow ahead!"

FitzBaldwin had seen the danger too, had recognised that some skilled Austrian artillery officer had guessed the range, that holding *Odin* stationary was to invite disaster.

"Mr. Dawlish! Hold your fire! Wait for my word!"

The screws bit and the ironclad edged forward. The Danish howitzers aft still barked but from this moving platform they could have no hope of seeking out their counterparts ashore. Three climbing columns marked the drop – astern – of more Austrian shells. Dawlish could now see the front faces of the demilunes, great chunks torn out of several, one all but obliterated. *Odin* was drawing level with the trenches extending from them towards the Danish defences.

"That earthwork, Dawlish!" FitzBaldwin indicated the mound at the head of the nearest, the furthest-advanced, trench. "One salvo only! Then we're done!"

Splashes off the port beam now – the Austrians had shifted aim, were only slightly over on their elevation. The ironclad's course was unchanged, movement her best protection against gunners accustomed to static targets only. But whoever was directing those howitzers was accomplished, was very good indeed …

Now the earthwork lay directly off the beam.

"Fire!"

And with the Armstrongs' roar came something else, a sharper report, a crack, and then an expanding ball of flame somewhere aft. A scorching wave lashed past Dawlish and the ship lurched to starboard. As he whipped around towards the bridge, he saw that Lorance was on his hands and knees. The helmsman was slumped inert by the unmanned wheel. Another body lay in the starboard bridge wing, scarlet-streaked, clothes smouldering. The ventilators before the funnel were twists of shattered metal and coal smoke vomited from a rent in the funnel.

One lucky Austrian howitzer shell had found its mark.

Still under way, still turning, the ironclad's bows were sweeping over towards land and carrying her into the waters that Dawlish knew must be inside the line of soundings he had marked. She was still curving around, must now be well inside the danger area, course almost reversed.

Lorance struggled to his feet, face red-raw, sleeve ripped away to show a bloodied arm. Even as he grasped the wheel and spun it, a great shock reverberated through the ship and all forward motion ceased.

Bows headed south-eastwards, *Odin* was aground.

And at the howitzers' mercy.

Chapter 11

Only the increasing fury of the squall saved the *Odin* – for now at least. The driving rain blanketed her from clear view of the Austrian gunners and their shells fell wide. The screws were still at slow ahead and holding the bows on the sand. Now taking the wind fully on the beam, the ironclad swung slowly, her stern drifting towards the coast.

On the bridge Lorance threw the telegraph handle furiously back and forth to no avail and realised that its cables must have been severed, that he had lost contact with the engine room. Albemarle – he had been aft with the Danish howitzers – ran on to the bridge and hesitated for a moment when he saw the bodies.

"Go below!" Lorance shouted. "Get me full revolutions astern!"

Albemarle disappeared. The ship rolled with the gusts, dull shudders reverberating through the hull as she ground against the sand. FitzBaldwin hurried down from the foretop, joined Lorance on the bridge, controlled fear on their faces. From somewhere aft somebody was screaming, long, piercing cries of agony that ended suddenly. The Danish howitzers, fixed to fire to starboard, were useless, pointing seawards now, and their crews were crouching behind any cover available. Dawlish, ignored in the crisis, stayed at his seat and shouted down to the gunners below him to stay calm. He knew that the squall would pass on in minutes and expose *Odin* again to the Austrian howitzers' fury.

It seemed an aeon since Albemarle had scurried towards the engine room but the screws were still beating at slow ahead. The bows, lodged on the sandbank, were the pivot on which the wind's power was rotating the ship to parallel the beach.

Another roll, and the hull pounded again. Above the dull thump came the sound of a single short explosive crack from somewhere deep within the ship herself. Dawlish, bewildered, but frightened, badly frightened for the first time this day, saw FitzBaldwin and Lorance were looking aft in shock.

"The screw! The port screw!" the American was shouting.

A clanging rang through the ship. The origin could only be the engine room, a machine flailing with its load removed, horrible confirmation of a shaft or connecting-rod sheared. The port screw had smashed down upon the sand and the shock had driven metal beyond its limit.

The clanging died – the steam to the port engine must have been cut off – and the starboard screw stilled also. *Odin* wallowed without power at the mercy of wind and wave, still thumping on the bottom. A wooden hull would have sprung a dozen leaks by now but even iron framing and plating could not stand this indefinitely.

Lorance had gone aft to the engine room, leaving FitzBaldwin alone on the bridge to take the wheel.

"Dawlish!" he shouted. "Can you reload?"

Difficult, all but impossible in this rolling and juddering. But unthinkable not to try.

"Yes, sir! We'll do our damnedst!"

"Good fellow! Double charges in each barrel and a shell besides! It may help to rock her off! You'll have to turn the turret to port."

For the guns were now bearing directly seawards. Any discharge that might help release the ship must be towards the opposite side.

"We'll manage it, sir." Somehow.

"That's the spirit, Dawlish! And when you're done, wait for it! We'll have one chance only! Only fire on my word, and then on the uproll!"

Dawlish swung himself down, landed between the guns, saw fear and confusion on the crews' faces, saw it even on Hopper's.

"It's not too bad, lads!" He forced what he hoped sounded like quiet resolution into his voice. "We're grounded, nothing too bad. We need the guns to help her off." He turned to Hopper, saw that he was not reassured. "It won't be easy. Load 'em one at a time, then wait."

The deck was lurching beneath his feet. Lifting even one of the shells from its rack would be a victory, swinging it across on the chain hoist and aligning the studs a miracle. A three-hundred pound pendulum would oscillate in this confined space, threating to trap and crush all in its path. But it must be done.

"We'd better get moving then, sir," Hopper's tone told that he too recognised it as perhaps impossible. He turned to the gunners. "You heard what Mr. Dawlish said. Slow and steady'll do it."

And now another vibration, the single functioning screw threshing again, now in reverse, and at full power. Dawlish scrambled up the rungs set into the turret's inner wall and reached his seat. He could not see directly aft but a glance towards the shore told him that the vessel had not moved. Worse still, the rain had passed on and was advancing across the peninsula, deluging the Austrians for now but uncloaking *Odin*.

Abaft the funnel he saw Killigrew and Albemarle and a dozen seamen readying launching of the port-side cutter – that to starboard had been left behind to give a clear line of fire for the Danish howitzers. The heavy thirty-four foot boat had been swung out on its davits and drawn back to the deck edge for the crew to enter. They took their places on the thwarts, oars upraised, Killigrew in the sternsheets with the tiller, Albemarle at the bows and an axe and strop of heavy cable at his feet. One look told Dawlish what was intended – to lay out a kedge to supplement the effort of the churning screw.

The cutter dropped, pushed off, was still sheltered in the *Odin's* lee. Oars shipped now, she stroked towards the stern and was lost to Dawlish's sight. There was a kedge stored there – light, a mooring aid only, and the capstan for its cable was a small one. But there was nothing else if the stern was to be dragged out seawards to help give the one functioning screw maximum bite. The cutter must round the stern and approach the starboard quarter to take off the kedge.

Down inside the turret the double charges had been tamped home inside the first barrel. A shell was suspended on the chain hoist, ropes to either side held firm to dull its swings as the travelling block on the transverse beam above was dragged towards the muzzle. Dawlish descended, joined Hopper to see the shell lowered. Dropped link by clinking link on the chain, its base was lodged inside the bore. Brute force rotated it and pushed it back until the rearmost studs found their grooves and it was then rammed home. One gun loaded at the cost of bruises but nothing worse, and one to go.

Sharp cracks, only slightly dulled by the onshore wind, announced the Austrian howitzers opening fire again. This could only be more dangerous than before since *Odin* was now a sitting target. Dawlish climbed back to his seat and looked out to see two columns of water collapsing between ship and shore. And then a whistling, growing in pitch, and a third shell threw up a splash a half-cable seawards. *Odin* had been bracketed. The next Austrian salvos must creep even closer, might even strike.

Lorance had returned from the engine room and was at the stern with a dozen men. They had rigged a davit there and the kedge was being suspended from it, its cable's full length flaked out upon the deck. Bars had already been thrust into the capstan and the cable end secured. Killigrew's cutter had rounded the stern, her crew backing water to hold the pitching craft stern-on to the waves, bows towards *Odin*, waiting for Lorance's call to come alongside.

Down inside the turret drum the second gun was all but ready. It could not be soon enough, for three more Austrian shells dropped, two short, one over, but the over was close enough for its splash to shower the cutter's occupants.

"Loaded, sir!" Hopper called.

"Turn the turret then! Full on the port beam!"

It jerked as the brake was released and seemed frozen even when every man who could lay his hands upon the cranks was straining on them. Then the ship pounded again and, shaken free, the huge cylinder began to move. Each roll threatened to let it slip back again and Hopper was at the brake, locking each incremental gain, loosening again to win the next. Eight or ten degrees at a time, the turret crept around, its ports at last crossing the ship's axis and crawling toward the new heading on the port beam.

The kedge was swinging on a block beneath its davit now. The cutter drew alongside, oars used to fend it off from the ironclad's flank. Albemarle threw up a line from the bow and the cutter was pulled forward until the kedge was just above and ahead of it. Then the most delicate operation of all. The kedge was lowered to hang stationary just above the water. Albemarle hooked the strop above its shank and drew it into the cutter. Ropes were thrust through it and lashed to the empty mast-tabernacle. Once secure, the kedge was lowered gently until it disappeared beneath the surface. The suspension cable fluttered loose in the wind, the kedge's weight carried now by the strop straining under tension across the cutter's gunwale and by the craft's own buoyancy. Albemarle released the shackle securing the lowering line and Killigrew called for the rowers to push away and back water.

Down now by the bow, the cutter fought slowly astern. Each stroke drew out more of the anchor cable that connected it to the ironclad. At fifty yards' separation, Killigrew turned the craft – holding water to port, oars pulling ahead to starboard. With way all but lost, it wallowed in the troughs of wave after wave, the saturated crew pulling at the limit of their strength to fight the cable's drag.

Inside the turret the gun-crews strained with no less effort to gain the last few degrees that would lay the guns directly on the port beam.

"Well done, Dawlish!" FitzBaldwin calling from the bridge. "Ready now for when I –"

The words were lost in the crash of a shell bursting at the base of the mainmast. A hail of fragments lashed out from the blast. They cut down several cowering Danish gunners, upended one of their howitzers, scythed away two of the seamen waiting at the capstan bars at the stern, punched through a ventilator by the funnel. But no fire, and apparently no damage in the engine room, for the starboard screw was still in unchecked reverse. The Danes were dragging their wounded fellows from the wreckage – Dawlish saw that Krag was unharmed, but he was trying to support the artillery lieutenant whose face and torso were blood-drenched. At the stern, Lorance was ordering the wounded men to be laid aside – they would have to wait. The fate of the others, of the entire ship, depended on one thing only now, the kedge and the ability to haul upon it. That knowledge kept every man, however terrified, at the capstan bars and ready to push.

The cutter was still crawling off the starboard quarter, somehow making progress, however slow, against the cable's pull. Every eye on deck was rivetted on it, FitzBaldwin's telescope locked there too, oblivious of the splash of more Austrian shells dropping close. Dawlish watched also, heart-pounding, fearful, yet somehow proud, that it would be on his judgement of the ship's roll that would decide whether the guns' discharge might help break her free. The weapons had been run out, and their muzzles protruded from the ports, directly towards the Austrian demilunes they had so punished before. The elevations were unchanged. Even if the discharges did not free the ship there would be one last rain of destruction on the enemy before their howitzers disembowelled her, as they surely must.

More shells falling close, four in quick succession indicating that the Austrians had brought another howitzer into play, that it was firing on the same azimuth and elevation as the others. If there was a fourth, there might soon perhaps be as fifth, and more still…

An explosion at the bow – somewhere close to the hawse hole. A reverberation shuddered through the ship as the shell smashed against the top of the iron belt. Had it landed two feet closer it might have plunged through the deck but, as it was, the blast was directed outwards and did no more than scour paint.

"Ready Dawlish! Soon now! Soon!" FitzBaldwin calling.

A hundred yards and more off the starboard quarter, Albemarle stood in the cutter's bow with an axe raised above his head. In the sternsheets Killigrew waved acknowledgement of a signal from Lorance at the *Odin's* stern.

Now!

The axe arced down on the strop that held the kedge, biting deep into the gunwale beneath, severing the strands. The cutter's bows leapt as the weight was dropped and the exhausted pulling crew slumped over their oars, their best done, the outcome now in the arms and strength of the men with Lorance at the stern capstan. Their weight flung upon its bars, it rotated fast at first, then slowed as the kedge bit and held on the seafloor sand. Lorance shouted a rhythm and Krag hurried unwounded Danish gunners to lend their strength. A minute passed – the capstan had made but a dozen turns and it seemed to Dawlish that it seemed now almost at a standstill.

And still they strained, feet slipping on the wet planking, a sudden gain, a quarter turn perhaps, a half, and then stationary again until human muscle forced the next few degrees. The howitzer shells still dropped, the whistle of their plunge blood-chilling. Relief soared with awareness of yet another miss, then fear surged back with recognition that the next shell, or the next again, might find its mark.

The cable disappeared from sight fifty yards from the ship. Water streamed from the visible section as the waves dropped before it was engulfed again. It was taut, tauter yet further with each click of the pawls that locked the capstan's gains. The danger was that the kedge might not hold, might tear loose from the sand. The cable was at an angle – some forty-five degrees – to the *Odin's* axis and its tension was divided between dragging the stern seawards and augmenting the full power of the remaining screw. Water churned beneath the counter, the starboard engine at maximum power. Black smoke billowed from the damaged funnel and told of yet more coal being shovelled into the furnace.

A loud rasping roar of metal grinding on sand. A shudder, a jerk that lasted seconds, but confirmation that the bows had shifted. Inches only perhaps, but a shift. Dawlish's eyes were fixed on FitzBaldwin, and he yearned for the signal that must be imminent. The ironclad was rolling only slightly, six or eight degrees to either side of the vertical, and the ideal moment of discharge would be fleeting.

Another explosion abaft the funnel, another Austrian hit. More debris, sudden flame, smoke, but FitzBaldwin's gaze never shifted from the now bar-tight cable and Dawlish's never strayed from FitzBaldwin.

Suddenly, that great rasp again and even before the short jerk ended FitzBaldwin whirled about and shouted.

"Fire, Dawlish!"

The ship was at the limit of a roll to port, was sweeping back up, was approaching the apex too quickly and Dawlish held his silence. Better to wait for recovery from the roll to starboard, until the guns would bear down towards the target. And that roll seemed to be treacle-slow, endless, aeon-long ...

"Hopper!" Dawlish yelled. "On my word! Both barrels together! But only on my word!"

The starboard flank had dipped to the limit, wallowed there an eternity and then began to climb again and quickened. The guns must fire at the top of the roll but two seconds, maybe more, would pass between Dawlish's own cry and the firing pistols' response to Hopper's jerking lanyards.

"Fire!"

An agony of anticipation and then both double-charged Armstrongs roared, bounded up their inclined slides and crashed into their restraining tackles. But more than the rumble of their recoil was something more powerful still, a tremor rippling through the hull, a jerk sternwards that threw Dawlish from his seat, into the smoke-filled drum below him, and knocked others from their feet.

And the ship was still moving, surging astern, her roll a confused thrash. The rasping shudder of iron on sand suddenly died.

Dawlish, bruised, was being dragged to his feet on the turret floor.

"We're free, sir! We did it, sir!" Hopper, forgetting all decorum, was pumping his hand and the smoke-grimed gunners were cheering.

"Belay that!" Dawlish shouted.

He hauled himself up to his seat, looked aft. Wreathed in the anthracite smoke pouring from the half-wrecked funnel – another shell fragment must have torn through it – *Odin* still lurched astern. FitzBaldwin, with only bodies about him on the bridge, had the helm over and the stern was curving out seawards. Cracks from shoreward told of the Austrian howitzers still in action but their shells fell now where the ironclad had lain trapped and that was already a cable distant. Past Killigrew's cutter the *Odin* surged, further out still into deeper water, a full half-mile before FitzBaldwin rang for dead-slow ahead. He brought the vessel around, head into wind, away from land.

"Get your gun-crews on deck, Dawlish," FitzBaldwin shouted. "They're needed aft!"

Needed they were. Some took the place of Lorance's exhausted capstan party to draw in the cable and recover the kedge that had ripped the vessel free. Others laboured to clear the debris of the shattered Danish howitzer – blood and worse was spattered there and hideously wounded men were moaning while others trembled in silent horror. Krag was in shirtsleeves, for he had thrown his own tunic across what had been one of the bodies. Smoke-blackened, eyes red-rimmed, rain and sweat-soaked, voice croaking, he still sounded defiant. The port-side davits had been partly wrecked and the cutter could not be taken up. It had been drawn alongside, its occupants hauled up and set to work, and then strung on a tow astern.

Odin moved ahead, but sluggishly, speed limited not just by having only one engine available, but by the loss of draught in the funnel. When serving on HMS *Foyle* in the West Indies Dawlish had spent much of his free hours in her engine room, an activity most offices despised as beneath them. That experience might be of value now. He suggested as much to FitzBaldwin and was sent below.

"It's bad, sir, very bad," Nolan, the engineer, pointed to the port engine. "It's the con-rod, it couldn't take the shock, did some powerful damage before we could shut the steam off."

It had fractured just short of the crankshaft and had flailed like an enormous whip. Residual steam still leaked through the packing of the stuffing box from which the piston-rod emerged to drive the cross head. Dawlish felt sickened by the sight. Repairs would not suffice. A new connecting-rod – an eight-foot length of accurately machined forged iron – would be needed to bring the engine back in service. There was none on board.

And there was other damage.

"Bits knocked off," Nolan said. "Flying around like birds they was, damn near every gauge shattered an' it's only by the grace of God that nobody was killed." He indicated a section of piping around which a tarpaulin had been wrapped and secured with leather trouser-belts. "Knocked a hole there, one of the bits did, but we closed it off. It won't be too hard to repair that pipe but the con-rod's had it."

"And the engine too, Mr. Nolan?" An unnecessary question. The answer was obvious.

Nolan shrugged. "Without the rod it's dead."

It was raining again when Dawlish came on deck again. In cold wet misery, with blood and vomit on her planking, *Odin* crawled north towards the Limfjord entrance though which she had steamed out with such hope six hours before.

Crippled.

Chapter 12

The *Althea*, the steamer that had brought Blackwood's men, departed for Newcastle with the evening tide. Nolan sailed with her. He had taken the failure of the connecting-rod like a personal affront. He had worked on the construction of *Odin's* engines, had overseen their installation, had cared for them like children. And one had disappointed. Now he was on his way to rebuild trust, to have another rod forged and machined to exact tolerances and to bring it back, all within a week, ten days at most. Dawlish had not heard FitzBaldwin say as much, but he understood that funds, probably close to unlimited, would be forthcoming in Britain to work that miracle. He only knew that Nolan would contact Mr. Elmore Whitby by telegram on arrival in England

"Do you think we'll see him back?" Albemarle asked Dawlish. "The fellow's not fish, flesh nor fowl. He's not a seaman and he's not a naval officer and he's a gentleman only by courtesy. I'd say he's had enough. I don't know how the guv'nor could trust him."

"He'll be back." Dawlish repressed a surge of anger. *Nolan – another nobody.* "That Danish warrant he holds is worth as much to him as your commission or mine to us and he'll treasure it for life. Mr. Nolan's damn good at his work and proud of it too. We wouldn't be here now if he hadn't kept us under power, no matter what."

And 'here' was a point a mile inside the Limfjord mouth where the *Odin* was swinging at anchor. She lay closer to the northern shore than to the southern, well out of range of any howitzer that a zealous Austrian artillery officer might advance and bring to bear. Crippled, barely mobile, she might be for now, but her guns were still potent and Dawlish had worked past midnight with their crews to see the shell racks within the turret replenished.

The wounded had been taken ashore by Albemarle and Krag. It was bad, very bad in the hospital there, a chastened Albemarle had said when he returned and he would not say more. Another boat had brought the dead to be buried on the morrow – without hammocks to sew them in, they were wrapped in blankets through which the blood seeped. Their legacy was a gloom that hung on officers and crew alike, a crew that was now yet further depleted. A half-dozen seamen who had signed on in Birkenhead had thought better of it, and had left on the *Althea*.

"They're better gone. They were expecting another *Alabama*." Lorance was bitter. "Sweeping up unarmed merchantmen and a damn good chance that they'd never encounter a Yankee warship. They didn't count on this."

Nobody had. Killigrew, who had been present, told Dawlish that the mood in the conference in the school house that evening had been sombre.

"A job half-done, Saabye called it. Blackwood was more polite about it, but he said much the same. That we'd given the Austrians a mauling but they'd make up for it in a week. And God knows when we'll be able to do as much again, if we ever can."

"So we're just going to swing at anchor here and do nothing?"

Killigrew shook his head. "Blackwood's going to ask for volunteers tomorrow to go into the redoubts. So many of Saabye's people are sick that he's short of men. FitzBaldwin didn't like it but he agreed in the end. Volunteers only. He was clear about that. And sixpence more for every day in line"

"You'll volunteer, sir?"

"I couldn't hang back," Killigrew said. "Not if any of the men volunteer. And you, Dawlish?"

A sudden memory of the brutal service ashore in China five years before. As bad for the defenders, when they were finally overrun, as for the British and French forces that had suffered so badly during their assaults. A child at war, it had been Dawlish's first experience of combat.

"I couldn't hang back either."

He hoped it sounded nonchalant. The image shimmered in his mind of a seaman who had raised his head above a parapet at Pekin falling back with half of it gone. Better the brief fury of battle at sea than days of privation behind an earthwork in constant danger of unheralded death.

"The captain may not release you," Killigrew said. "You know more by now about that turret and the Armstrongs than anybody else on *Odin*. He won't want to take the chance of losing you."

Dawlish pushed away the unworthy thought that he hoped so too.

And the hope was in vain.

*

It didn't prove as bad as he had feared.

Not for the first two days.

Dawlish and Killigrew and a dozen men from *Odin* joined Granville's company of British ex-regulars in the smaller of the two

126

redoubts on the western isthmus, the one closer to the lagoon. From it they could see the damage wreaked by the Armstrongs on the Austrian demilunes, bite-shaped gaps on their walls' level crests, breaches at several points. It seemed impressive to the naked eye but examination by telescope told that the vast majority of the cannon there were still untouched in their embrasures. Half or more of *Odin's* shells had been expended to scoop craters far from any trench or gun position. Other than the partial demolition of the demilune in which a munitions store had exploded, the sound and fury of the ironclad's shelling had signified nothing.

Dark figures, dozens, were busy with pick and shovel at the Austrian works to repair the damage. The earthwork at the head of the furthest forward of the three advancing saps appeared to be complete and effort was concentrated on advancing the other two. Heads and shoulders dipped and rose and dipped again as spadefuls of sand were thrown up to create a low parapet on either side. Rain was falling, a misty and chilling drizzle, but a band was playing somewhere south of the demilunes, merry waltz-tunes and strident marches – the Radetzky the most frequent – that mocked the discomfort of the troops further forward.

"Why do we let them?" Dawlish said to Granville. The sight of so much unmolested, steady, inexorable work had an air of dread about it.

They were on the redoubt's parapet. It seemed to have become a matter of pride for Granville to stand there, smoking a cigar and waving his cap in greeting to an Austrian officer similarly exposed at the head of the nearest sap. He was just beyond effective rifle range but an accomplished marksman could possibly take him down. A spirit of live and let live seemed to be accepted for now by both sides.

"Why kill one poor devil who's slaving with a spade when there are hundreds to replace him?" Granville said. "And that chap there – see, he's waving back. He's probably a good fellow who'd be a jolly friend if we'd meet him any other way. There's no sense in provoking him just now."

"And that's what we came here for?" Dawlish said.

Granville turned to him, the feigned nonchalance gone. "No, Dawlish. It's like Blackwood says. We came here to kill fellows like that when the time comes. But not yet, not wasting shots we've got so precious few of. We'll kill them in the open when they assault – if we survive the artillery fire they'll bring down on us first – and we'll pray to

God that we'll have shot and shell and canister enough to stop them before they get across these walls."

"And if they do?"

"They'll have as much mercy as when you had when your guns shelled their works. Do you think they'll forget that?"

A routine had been established, each company, whether Danish or British, to spend five days in the redoubts or in the trenches linking them, followed by another five of rest in the scarcely better accommodation at Thyborøn village. Then back into the line again.

Two nights were enough to make Dawlish feel he had been part of this routine forever. He loathed the nervous vigilance and the rounds of sentry inspections in the darkness, the general stand-to in the freezing dawn, the endless pacing on parapets. There was no immediate danger and the worst was the broken sleep on straw in squalid shelters, the stench of the latrines, the smell of unwashed bodies – he knew he must be as bad himself and it disgusted him – and the always-damp clothing and marrow-numbing cold. He strove to ignore the distant false-cheer of the Austrian band striking up in mid-morning, and continuing with few intermissions on until early evening, as dejecting as the mournful Lutheran hymns heard from the burial ground outside Thyborøn's church, now its hospital.

There was food enough but firewood was too scarce to heat it sufficiently. Everywhere was the sound of coughing and the sight of feverish and lousy Danes with flushed faces, infantrymen or gunners already worn down by the sufferings of the retreat. Sieges killed as many by illness as by gunfire and hunger, Blackwood had said when he had reminisced about Sevastopol back in that manor in Somerset.

Now Dawlish was seeing it for himself.

But he knew that he could endure it. Indefinitely, if necessary.

*

It sleeted through much of the third night that Dawlish was in line, freezing the lookouts on the parapets and in the trench linking it to the other redoubt. They were being rotated every hour, the respite just enough to let them warm themselves around a meagre fire. Dawlish had duty. Accompanied by a sergeant, he passed from one sentry to the next to ensure alertness. There was no risk of any sleeping – it was impossible to do so in this cold, sodden, misery – but he doubted that any could remain effectively watchful in the all but absolute darkness.

The bottom of the trench was ankle-deep in water – there was a limit to what even sandy soil could absorb. Dawlish was sloshing through it – feet numb, saturated boots no protection – and returning to the redoubt when he heard low voices ahead. The words were indistinct but for a barked "Yes, sir!" Then other feet sloshing closer.

"That's you, Dawlish?" Colonel Blackwood's voice was unmistakable. "A bloody dirty night for this sort of thing! But as bad for those fellows over there as for us, and that's some consolation."

"Aye, sir. Some consolation." Dawlish raised his voice just enough that the sentry he had just left could hear. "And I'd be surprised if they were standing it was well as our own people."

"That's the spirit! You hear that, Stavald?" Blackwood had turned to the dim figure behind him. It must be the Danish artillery major. Undeterred by the weather, perhaps impelled by it, both men must have ridden from Thyborøn well after midnight.

Blackwood came closer. "Who's that with you, Dawlish? Evenden, is that you? Just like old times, eh?"

"Nothing like so bad, sir." Pride in the sergeant's voice

"Evenden's another sapper, Stavald," Blackwood said to the Dane. "With me at Sevastopol. Right through to the end." He turned again to Dawlish. "How are the walls standing up to this bloody downpour? I thought I'd take a look. Sand's always the devil! Lead on and show me."

Dawlish led them back up the trench and realised that the visit had little to do with subsidence, everything with the troops. Blackwood had a word for each man, encouragement, the odd flat joke, the forced laugh that sounded as if it wasn't, the recollection, in a few cases, of shared duty in the trenches before the Russian fortress a decade before. He stumbled once, pitched on his knees, raised himself with difficulty, uncomplaining, by his single remaining arm while Dawlish wondered if he should help. Better not to, he decided. There was cold calculation in the Colonel's decision to show himself sharing the night's miseries and he respected him for it.

The inspection took two hours, not just the British-manned positions, but the Danish gunners who were roused from their shelters. Afterwards Blackwood shared weak coffee and cigars with the officers by a smouldering fire, his tone just loud enough for enlisted men nearby to overhear. Prospects were bright, he said, reinforcements would be here soon, older Danish reservists mustered in still-unoccupied Northern Jutland, and there was the possibility too of Swedish volunteers. As long as communication could be maintained across the

Limfjord – and *Odin's* presence was the guarantee of that – Thyborøn could hold out for months. But no mention of munitions, nor of supplements to the meagre supplies carried north on the retreat in limbers and wagons. Dawlish suspected that he was not the only one who would have liked to ask the question but did not dare to.

At last Blackwood dashed the dregs in his mug into the fire and threw the cigar butt after them. He wanted a bed, he said, straw would do but he would be grateful if somebody could lend him a blanket. He should be roused at the time of the dawn stand-to. By the time he lay down in an open-fronted shack, somewhat of the gloom of night and cold and darkness had lifted from officers and men alike.

*

The Austrian band was silent this frigid morning – the first time in two weeks according to a Danish officer. Blackwood and Stavald went across to the other redoubt after breakfast and returned through the communications trench two hours later. Both looked concerned. They called Granville to join them, mounted the outer wall and stood on the parapet, telescopes trained on the Austrian works. Dawlish saw heads shaken, Stavald producing a map, Blackwood putting on spectacles to study it more intently, close conversation, pointing.

Then – suddenly – they hurried back down, Granville ahead of the other two and calling for the alarm. Stavald pulled out a writing pad and held it while Blackwood scribbled on it with a pencil gripped in his one hand. He tore the page away, thrust it towards the orderly who had ridden with him from Thyborøn. The man took it, ran back to where the horses had been tethered, vaulted into a saddle and was off.

Dawlish ran up to Granville. "What is it?"

"They don't like what they see. That damn band not playing, work stopped on the saps. They think the attack's coming. They've sent to the camp for reinforcements."

A bugle was sounding and men, some half-dazed with sleep, ran from the shelters to join those already on duty on the fire-steps or in the trenches. Sergeants and corporals shepherded them into their appointed places and yelled at them to keep their heads down. Danish gunners raced to their weapons, hauled them from shelter and into the embrasures, pulled back tarpaulin covers and dragged munition crates from the makeshift stores set into the earthwork's inner slopes.

Dawlish and Evenden were at the extreme left of the forward-facing wall, their full platoon, some thirty men, kneeling below the parapet, a corporal moving along at a crouch, dispensing extra cartridges. With neither cutlass nor pistol, Dawlish was carrying an Enfield rifle like the others. It was a weapon new to him.

"It might be better to fix that spike, sir," Evenden said. "If it comes to the worst, it'll be your best hope."

Fear knotted in his stomach, blood pounding, hands trembling, Dawlish fumbled with the unfamiliar bayonet until it at last clicked in place. He raised his head just enough to see across the parapet and recognised what had caused Blackwood's concern.

The Austrians who had been working so diligently minutes before were nowhere to be seen, neither in the saps nor at the demilunes. And more threatening still than the lack of movement was the silence, the awareness that at any moment now tongues of flame would lash out from the enemy line, that smoke would hide it, that shells would crash into this redoubt for long minutes, maybe even hours, and that then men would pour from those zig-zag trenches that ...

Stop!

Imagination was the friend of fear. Better to cherish the immediate minute and nothing more, better to copy Blackwood's studied calm. The one-armed colonel was standing by a twelve-pounder crew in an embrasure, Stavald with him, both looking out across the no-man's-land, both smoking, the apparent embodiment of quiet confidence.

The single crack was unmistakable as a howitzer's and smoke wisped up from behind the centremost of the demilunes. Dawlish knew that at this moment a shell was climbing close to the vertical, would hover stationary for an instant, would start its whistling plunge. He fought the urge to dip his head below the parapet. That shell would fall where it would fall and he could do nothing to prevent it. Now he could hear its whistle and its approach seemed infinitely slower, and somehow more dreadful, than when similar shells had dropped around the *Odin*.

Relief.

The shell impacted on the open ground a hundred yards or so ahead, in line with this redoubt's centre, he judged, the spattering of wet sand thrown up by the detonation an anti-climax. On the distant demilune he could see figures now, glasses no doubt trained on the point of fall, hurried discussions on elevation correction. For another round would come...

And when it did, a full two minutes later, it fell just beyond the rear wall of the redoubt, no injury inflicted there either. But that Austrian gunner must know now that the earthwork was bracketed, that a slight adjustment of angle and allowance for the heating barrel must surely drop the next round into the interior.

Only a nine or twelve-pound shell, Dawlish told himself, a puny thing compared with a naval weapon's, but the memory of the torn remains of the Danish gunners on *Odin's* deck would not be swept aside. *Dear God…*

Another sharp bark, the smoke wafting up again above the Austrian embankment, the silent climb, the apogee, the fall, the whistle loudening through a long aeon. He glanced to where Blackwood and Stavald stood – still, unmoving. Around the field gun in the embrasure before them the Danish gunners were no less impassive at their stations. It was the same fear of showing fear that kept them there, Dawlish guessed, the fear he felt himself, he and the men crouched to either side of him along the fire-step.

The shell gouged a crater on the inner side of the rear wall, its flash and roar more frightening than the sand and fragments that blasted from it and found no victim. But the enemy gunners had both azimuth and elevation correct. More would come.

He raised his head above the parapet, could see the figures atop the distant demilune, could imagine the exultation there. And suddenly another movement flickered in the corner of his vision – there, at the earthwork at the head of the nearest trench. A head briefly exposed, as quickly withdrawn, evidence perhaps of troops crowded there and waiting for the moment of release. And if…

Three reports, close enough to be all but one only. Another salvo on the way. To his left one of the men was praying in a loud whisper, the words rushing in a babble. Sergeant Evenden was shouting for him to hold his tongue, his words suddenly cut off in the triple blasts, two inside and one without the redoubt's open centre.

This time, blood was drawn. An explosion on the sloped rear of the forward-facing wall smashed fragments into the backs of men crouched on the fire-step above. A scream of agony was cut off by the next round falling between two unoccupied shelters in the centre, ripping through canvas and setting it alight and hurling boxes and cooking pots and shredded blankets up and out with the fragments of shattered shell.

The wait for the next to come seemed endless, broken only by Blackwood's shouted command, relayed by Granville, to stay behind cover, to hold fire, and by the moans of the wounded men. Dawlish glanced towards them – they were on the wall that angled to that on which he was himself. A half-crater had been scooped in the fire-step. Two men were being pulled from it, one limp but gasping, the other thrashing and crying out even as two others half-cradled, half-restrained him. There was a glimpse of scarlet, of a ripped uniform, of what might have been the white of exposed bone. He looked away quickly.

Three more shells, one only within the redoubt's centre – and it did no more than throw up a harmless shower of sand, for it did not explode – and the others dropping to no effect behind the rear wall. To the north the first dark columns of Danish reinforcements were hastening from Thyborøn but were not close enough yet to be under threat.

Then long suspense.

And nothing more. No plunging shells, no field guns opening from the demilunes, no human torrents erupting from the zig-zags. It would all come, but not today.

Movement at the right along the fire-step, Blackwood and Stavald hurrying this way, no crouching, heads and shoulders defiantly above parapet level. Dawlish rose to meet them and saluted.

"Somewhat of a damp squib, Dawlish" Blackwood said. "The blackguards want to put the fear of God in us, to bloody-well exhaust us with alarms. They won't waste much more powder and ball than's needed to keep us on our toes. They're not much more flush with supplies of them than we are."

"There'll be more of this," Stavald said. "No warning. Anytime, day or night and –"

The Radetzky burst into life from behind the line of demilunes.

"That bloody march again!" Blackwood said. "Back to business as usual then!"

He took up the glasses hanging around his neck, leaned against the parapet and began to scrutinise the saps. Even with his own naked eye Dawlish could see that activity had resumed there, not massing before assault, but picks and shovels wielded by unseen men and sand showering out on to the flanking ridges. The saps' steady advance had resumed. Only occasionally did a head and shoulders appear, some officer surveying the ground ahead and deciding whether to order another abrupt zig or zag.

"Sergeant Evenden!" Blackwood called without lowering his glasses.

"Yes, sir!"

"You've got that fellow Eltham with you? A bloody good shoot if I remember. Still good?"

"As murderous as ever, I'd wager, sir."

"Fetch him."

Eltham, thirty-five, forty years perhaps, looked consumptive. Civilian life could not have treated him well but it was hard to imagine him as ever being a formidable soldier. He seemed very pleased that Blackwood had remembered him.

"D'ye see there, Eltham?" Blackwood indicated the head of the nearest sap. "A thousand yards, I'd say."

A long pause, Eltham's scrutiny intense. At last he said "Nearer nine hundred, sir."

"You could manage it?"

"Couldn't count on it, sir. It'd need a lot of luck. Never seen this here rifle until a fortnight back an' there's never been no chance to check the sight."

Infantry units trained on targets out to six-hundred yards – the three spiral grooves in the Enfield's barrel made it possible. Accuracy fell fast away above that and only men qualified as marksmen could hope to hit up to nine-hundred or more. The nearest Austrian was at, or beyond, extreme range.

"Nothing to lose, Eltham," Blackwood said. "Nothing to lose."

Dawlish watched with fascination as the man took off his greatcoat and wrapped it tight with his webbing belt. He laid it on the parapet and settled himself along the slope of the embankment, wriggling for a full half-minute until he found comfort. Then, with absence of all haste, he drew up the rifle, laid it on the coat, drew it to his shoulder and clicked back the hammer. Only now did he flip up the back-sight and begin his aim, pausing, adjusting the sight in microscopic steps, concentrating, adjusting yet again until at last he was satisfied.

Austrian heads and shoulders were still showing intermittently at the trench. Eltham might be holding them in his aim but, if so, no move of his showed it. He was still, dead still, frozen in immobility, his barrel not perceptively wavering.

A minute must have passed, perhaps more, no sound other than the distant Austrian band. Dawlish shifted his gaze towards the trench. Somebody had climbed out for an instant to retrieve a spade that had slipped from his grasp on the upthrow. A living man – flesh, blood, family, hopes, fears, ambitions. There was a murderously personal quality about Eltham's aiming, one man focussed to the exclusion of all else on the destruction of another. Dawlish found himself relieved as he saw the Austrian slide in safety back down into the trench, spade held up in modest triumph, perhaps laughing with his fellows. And spared.

Another head, another shoulder, the impression of field-glasses raised and held, an officer most probably, studying the redoubt with calculated bravado.

The shot.

Arms flying up, then dropping, head and shoulders cast back into the trench below by the half-inch and more Boxer round.

Eltham had had his luck.

And the time of live and let live was ended.

Chapter 13

The Austrians might indeed have been short of powder and ball, but what they did have they used well. Twice or three times a day, as much again in the hours of darkness, single howitzer shells dropped in, or around, each of the redoubts, even in the third, isolated one, on the inner isthmus, that between the lagoon and the Limfjord. Casualties were few, two dead in the first three days after the irregular bombardment began, and others wounded – one hideously – by fragments.

The fall of shot was random within a radius of some fifty yards and many did no more that blast craters in the level sand ahead or behind the redoubts. But the intent was not damage or injury, but rather to wear down the spirits of the defenders by uncertainty, by forcing stand-to, by drawing cold and exhausted men from uneasy sleep to reinforce those on watch and wait for an assault that never came.

"I hate that band," Granville said to Dawlish. "I'd horse-whip the blackguard who conducts it if I could lay hands on him."

The Radetzky March, jaunty, confident and triumphant, was sounding again from the Austrian positions. It was as much a weapon as the howitzers themselves, sometimes presaging the fall of only a single round – none fell without its accompaniment. Most times it did no more than bring the defenders to futile and exhausting alert.

"I'd whip him with you," Dawlish said. "He ruined our rest again, what we had of it."

His platoon had been relieved at two o'clock. There had been perhaps an hour of unsatisfactory sleep, blanket-wrapped and freezing in the squalid shelters, before the band struck up. It brought him and his men to the fire-steps to double the numbers there and they had remained until well after daybreak. No shell had fallen, but it had not needed to. Now, in late morning, with scarcely two hours' rest snatched before the guard was changed, Dawlish's weary platoon was on duty on the fire-step again. So too was that which had just been relieved but hastily called back. The latest rendition of the Radetzky March had seen to that.

It had been played for twenty minutes already, sometimes breaking off, sometimes replaced with some cloying waltz, but each time it returned, heralded by a long roll of drums. Now it was in full vigour.

Granville and Dawlish had been studying the Austrian trenches, crouched below the parapet, barely peeping over. Since Eltham's lucky aim several Austrian marksmen had tried to match his kill. Without success so far, but long shots had thrown up spurts of sand from the crest and one had ricocheted off the iron tyre of a nine-pounder in an embrasure. No standing exposed now, no brazen smoking of cigars, no chivalrous waves to gallant enemies.

"They've come just about as far as they'll come," Granville said.

Like that at the head of the most distant sap, earthworks were rising at those of the two other zig-zags, locations for troops to mass in just before assault.

"God! I do so hate this!" Granville, crouching by Dawlish was keeping his voice down lest the men nearby hear. "But only another day and –"

The band had fallen silent.

A howitzer's crack. A shell was climbing.

Then the whistle, the long agony of wait. It made it no easier that this had happened before.

Sergeant Evenden shouted to the men to lie down and others caught in the centre of the redoubt scurried for shelter. Dawlish thrust his face against the sand before him – *My eyes! Not my eyes, Dear God!* – and his stomach was knotted and his buttocks clenched. A small cold internal voice was telling him that the chance of him being hit was small, yet the fear was still there.

Then the explosion, somewhere behind. He looked around, saw a smoking crater in the slope of the low rear wall.

No harm done.

None except to the nerves of the dozens within the redoubt.

The Radetzky resumed.

*

They were relieved during the night by stolid Danish infantry bundled in greatcoats and scarves. The eastern sky was brightening as Granville's column plodded back into the Thyborøn camp. There was accommodation for them in fisherfolk's wooden cottages, already empty of furniture – long since sacrificed to cooking fires – and strewn with straw stamped flat by the most recent occupants. But before rest there was sizzling bacon, and even bread that had been fresh the day before. Granville produced coffee for Dawlish, Killigrew and himself from his private store. Afterwards Dawlish a found a pump. Despite the cold, he stripped to the waist and scoured himself as clean as he could. He washed his face – filthier than he had imagined – but did not shave. Few of the officers were doing so either, he noted, their beards worn with pride like the veterans of the Crimea. It pleased him to think of his sister Susan's reaction – surprise and pride mixed – when she would see him bearded on his return.

There was nowhere to sleep but on floors, bodies closely packed. Dawlish found a corner for himself – he wanted the men to see him share their discomfort. He drew his blanket around him and rested his head on the haversack he had acquired. He drifted into sleep to the accompaniment of half-heard snatches of the men's foulmouthed grumbling about the miseries of recent days. But there was humour too, and pride that they had borne themselves well, and acceptance that they would be back in the redoubt in a few days. A few had been at Sevastopol, several at Delhi, and two at Pekin. Those who had not been were assured that this present was nothing compared to what had been experienced there. And the money was good, most admitted. Better than starvation, one said.

The respite was brief, one day only. Two new redoubts – big ones – were under construction just south of Thyborøn village. All troops out of the line, Danish and British alike, and supplemented by peasant labour brought across the Limfjord, were as busy with pick and shovels as the Austrians had been seen to be in the south.

"It's the last ditch," Granville said. "Blackwood doesn't think we can hold the other positions for long."

He and Dawlish and their people – they were unhappy about it, had not volunteered to be navvies – were assigned to work on the eastern redoubt. Its left flank lay directly on the Limfjord shore, a mirror image of its counterpart bordering the seashore to the west.

"Why's that not straight?" Dawlish pointed to the new trench. That linking the redoubts to the south had been so. "Why the extra labour?"

"You see how its's bowed back towards the village? You see how it's jagged with fire bays?" Granville said. "You see the ground ahead of it and the redoubts on either flank? Blackwood's plan. It'll be a slaughter ground for our Austrian friends if they get ever this far."

"You think they will?" It was hard to accept that the existing redoubts could be over-run.

"They might," Granville said. "It may come to that. Blackwood thinks so, and he knows that he's talking about."

Dawlish did not like the work and hungered for *Odin's* sparse comfort and familiar routines. It was a relief when he and Killigrew received a message from FitzBaldwin the following day to rejoin her and to bring with them the men she had contributed. A whaler awaited them at the foreshore – the ironclad lay nearer to the fjord's northern bank. Small Danish craft were still delivering food and firewood. A half-dozen cattle, too exhausted to protest, had been towed behind boats across the fjord's narrow neck by ropes tied around their horns. Now the wretched creatures were being goaded ashore through the shallows.

A small paddle-steamer was moored close inshore, the name *Hulde* at her bows. It was the first such vessel Dawlish had seen since arrival. Passengers were disembarking into boats alongside.

"Where's she from?" Dawlish asked the coxswain.

"A place called Aalborg, sir. It's a town up there." He motioned towards the north-east.

About seventy miles, Dawlish remembered from his earlier study of maps, the largest town on the Limfjord and presumably still in Danish hands. The steamer had navigated a tortuous sequence of channels and lakes to get here and must have held close to the northern shore during the last approach so as to stay out of Austrian range.

"Let's take a look," Killigrew said. "Take us over."

The whaler circled her, a typical small ferry for carrying passengers and limited freight on inland waters. Her gay livery – dark blue hull, white deckhouse, ochre funnel – was at variance with the rough utility of the other craft about. A boatload of passengers had just pulled away, reservists, most in dark uniforms, but clean and unrumpled, like visitors intruding from another and more comfortable world.

"There are ladies too, by God!" Killigrew said.

Eight or ten were waiting by the paddle-box. A stout woman was being handed – with difficulty, for her long skirts hampered her – into a boat tethered below. A flustered man in civilian clothes was complicating the process and arguing with a grim-faced middle-aged lady who frowned down from the deck. Dawlish caught the rhythm of French in their exchanges, but it was too far off to make out the words. As the whaler swept past, he saw that the women's cloaks and dresses, though well cut, seemed of some heavy material, serge perhaps. Identical black bonnets hinted at something like a uniform.

"Who are they?" Dawlish asked the coxswain.

"Beggin' your pardon, sir. Don't know. A bit like fish out of water, I'd say."

And they did. All had a look of delicacy. None had the weathered complexions of the peasant women who waded to and from the moored boats in the frigid water to carry produce ashore, skirts hoisted above their knees. Already several of the newcomers – and some were young – were looking towards Thyborøn with what might be misgiving, as if full reality was dawning on them. Their presence seemed as incongruous as the small steamer itself.

"Whoever they are, there are one or two fine fillies among them." Killigrew nudged Dawlish and spoke in an undertone as he raised his cap in salute. None of the women – ladies, by the look of them – responded.

"They must be mad to come here," Dawlish said. They reminded him of similar groups handing pamphlets about temperance to drunken seamen in Portsmouth public houses. "Some charitable committee, I'd say. They'll be back on that steamer as soon as it leaves."

Odin's funnel had been patched and the other damage repaired as far as possible. The surviving Danish howitzer had been removed – it could be of greater value in one of the redoubts. A faint whiff of coal smoke told that one of the boilers was being maintained at minimal pressure.

FitzBaldwin gathered all the officers in his quarters. Blackwood was present and, by the state of his uniform, looked as if he had spent the night in another visit to the redoubts and trenches. Major Stavald was representing Saabye.

"Bad news, gentlemen," FitzBaldwin said. "Bad news, but you'd better hear it. There's a telegram. From Mr. Nolan."

It was two days old, come with the steamer from Aalborg. Despite the interruptions of war, Europe's telegraph network had brought it by some circuitous route from Newcastle to Copenhagen and from there to Aalborg. That last section could be cut at any time if the Austrian drive continued north.

"The connecting-rod's going to take longer than expected, Nolan says. Another week at least, longer maybe. There's a steam hammer broken down at the Armstrong works and the forging's only half complete."

"What did I tell you, Nick?" Albemarle whispered. "We've seen the last of the fellow."

"You can do nothing in the meantime, Kommandör Merriweather? Like the nothing you've done in the last week." Bitter resentment in Stavald's use of FitzBaldwin's alias. "You have two engines, I believe? One of them unharmed and still two great guns at your disposal?"

"I can't risk this ship without two engines, major." FitzBaldwin's voice calm, even understanding. "She's Friherre Saabye's last reserve."

"We can't risk taking her out to sea," Lorance said. "She's damn near unmanageable on one engine. We were lucky to get her back in here through the mouth. It'd be madness to try it again."

"The general isn't asking you to bombard from the sea," Stavald said. "You don't need to leave the Limfjord."

"Have you any idea of just how shallow it is? Just how damn little we know about the shoals?" Lorance's voice was rising. "There's no decent chart of it. This ship's not some light paddler that can navigate across this country with impunity!"

"Gentlemen!" FitzBaldwin held up his hand. "Enough!"

"No!" Lorance's face was flushing. "You've got sixty days' use of this ship. That was the deal and you've had damn near twenty of 'em already. All reasonable risks accepted – that was the agreement! But not sheer stupidity, not the *Galveston* – excuse me, the *Odin* – thrown away! I've gone along with this farce of commissions and aliases until now, and I'll continue if it's rational, but I'm still first and foremost an officer of the Confederate States! That's my loyalty!"

Stavald was trembling, was about to speak, but FitzBaldwin was ahead of him.

"Gentlemen! We're friends and allies!" Forced joviality in his voice. "Major Stavald – engines or not, we're here to take the war to the enemy! Colonel Blackwood and I have some ideas about that. You'll like 'em when you hear them! But you've something to tell the gentlemen, Stavald! Good news you've told me already about what arrived in the despatches today. About Denmark's other battle." He looked around to the others but the words were for Stavald to hear. "Something damn impressive, damn heroic, gentlemen, an example to us all!"

The despatches from Copenhagen had confirmed that the greater part of the Danish army was holding the Dybbøl position in the southeast. Massive Prussian forces had gathered before it but the Danish earthworks had been strengthened and, though under steady artillery fire, had not yet been assaulted.

"And best of all, there's a Danish ironclad harassing the Prussian flanks from the sea," FitzBaldwin said.

"The *Rolf Krake.*" Stavald glared at Lorance. "The only one like her our navy has. Two turrets, not one! No fear of howitzers, no complaints about engines! The enemy has no way of stopping her."

"Or of stopping the rest of the Danish fleet either." FitzBaldwin said. "It's blockading Prussia's Baltic ports very, very effectively."

"And the Austrians?" Lorance asked.

"Half-way up Jutland already, right up the centre," Stavald said. "There's almost nothing to stop them. They could have Aalborg any time they like. But they've stopped that advance for now. They're shifting all they can across to support their forces here."

"Can you be sure?"

"No," Stavald said. "But there are Danish landowners and peasants and villagers who're risking their lives to get reports to Copenhagen and to Aalborg – there's still a small garrison there. And no matter where the information's coming from it's always the same. The Austrians are rushing artillery forward. Heavier than we've seen here yet. Fortress artillery, siege guns, heavy mortars. Probably taken from Austria itself. They've brought them as far forward as they can by rail and they're requisitioning every strong farm or brewery horse they can find. They're using them in relays to keep the heaviest guns coming forward four and twenty hours a day."

"The Limfjord fishermen have been a godsend," FitzBaldwin said. "Your friends the Østergaards, Dawlish, and more like them. They've been going in close to keep an eye on things for us. Even at night they've seen movement north from Harboøre."

"The Austrians want Thyborøn at any cost," Blackwood said. "If the Dybbøl position falls then that'll be the end of it and it's Prussia that'll have the glory of this war. Austria can't afford that. It must have a victory to balance Dybbøl if it's going to hold its head high in Europe."

He moved to a scuttle, threw it open. The prospect was as dismal as ever, a new wall of rain drifting across the spit beneath a leaden sky.

"That's our ally, gentlemen," he said. "General Winter's last throw. Cold, sleet, hail, slush and mud. Roads a quagmire, wheels sunk to their axels, exhausted men, horses dropping in their traces. God knows how long it'll last but while it does the new artillery will be arriving only in dribs and drabs. If we believe these Østergaard fellows, then the first of the big 'uns reached the Austrian camp yesterday."

"It's while they're still in dribs and drabs that we can hit them hardest," FitzBaldwin said.

"Tomorrow night will be ideal," Blackwood said. "The moon will still be damn near full but if the sky doesn't clear it'll hardly signify."

FitzBaldwin laid his arm on Stavald's shoulder.

"You'll like what we have in mind," he said

And when the Danish major heard it, he did.

*

142

But two other messages had come through also, ones that did not concern the Danes. They were shared with *Odin's* officers in FitzBaldwin's cabin.

"Word from Mr. Whitby. About that American frigate, the –"

Lorance cut FitzBaldwin off. "Not American, captain! Union!"

"Very well, Union, if you wish! The *Conewago*. She's still in European waters. She put in once at Hull, later at Dundee."

"And word from one of Bulloch's agents that she's been sighted off Bergen," Lorance said. "She's not leaving the North Sea. She's waiting for us."

"But she's neutral in this Danish war, sir," Killigrew said. "She's surely not –"

"But she damn-well won't be neutral after May the ninth," Lorance said. "Not when *Odin* will be *Galveston* once more."

It was hard to look him in the eye. Not FitzBaldwin, not Killigrew, not Albemarle nor Dawlish, would remain on board then.

Unless Bulloch found them elsewhere by then, Lorance would not have a single officer.

*

Late afternoon, the light already fading, rain fine as a mist.

The Østergaards' boat approached the shore, the father at the tiller, the son balancing in the bows, holding up two large fish by their tails.

"Lækker fisk! Billig!" he shouted.

A small Austrian patrol had fired a single rifle-shot above their heads, but that had been for form's sake only. Now the half-dozen muffled troops were beckoning to them to approach close. The surreptitious trade had gone on for weeks – the Østergaards were not the only Danish fishermen who crept across the Limfjord to secure higher prices while the demand held up. Several other craft had been seen already this afternoon.

The sail had been dropped and Dawlish and Krag each pulled an oar. Wet through, hands numb, both were dressed in coarse clothing borrowed from the Østergaards. It smelled strongly of fish and might indeed have never been washed. Krag looked convincing as an impoverished fisherman and Dawlish had been assured that he did also.

"You're a deaf mute, Dawlish. An idiot too," Krag whispered. For the fifth time. "Don't forget it!"

The vast Austrian camp lay ahead, stretching toward the North Sea shore beneath a pall of campfire smoke. Several off-duty soldiers had joined the patrol on the beach and had also indicated interest in buying.

"Billig! Billig! Mest lækre fisk i Danmark! Frisk! Fanget i morges!" Kristian Østergaard called as if from a market stall.

The language was close enough to German for the message to be clear and what looked to be a sergeant beckoned them closer in. The boat stroked forward and the bows ground on sand. Dawlish rose and used the oar as a pole to hold it steady while Krag dragged a basket of fish forward. Kristian had dropped into the water – he was barefoot, trouser-legs rolled up and it came to his knees, but the cold did not appear to bother him. He took the basket from Krag, lugged it towards the beach and started negotiations.

It was the first time Dawlish had seen Austrians so close. They looked not unlike the Danes, he thought, or British either, simple men far from home with no air of malevolence about them. It struck him for the first time – and was instantly ashamed that he had not felt it sooner – that he had no quarrel with these people, no right to rain death on them. That he should not be here.

But I've given my word. A fool maybe, but I've given my word.

The Austrians might have taken the whole basketful without payment, but they seemed to be honest people. Kristian was selling the fish in ones and twos and accepting coins. Brief laughter when Krag made some joke in German, shouted assurances from Uffe Østergaard in the sternsheets that he would be back tomorrow with more lækre fisk.

Dawlish had turned on the thwart and had adopted a vacant expression as he looked southwards. The strip that separated the fjord from the southerly lagoon stretched off into the wet mist.

Basket empty, peaceful credentials confirmed, Kristian put his shoulder against the bows and shoved the craft free. Krag pulled him on board, then joined Dawlish at the oars. They backed water and then the sail was raised again to head further south along the beach.

They stayed close inshore, passed the abandoned redoubt at the head of the isthmus, almost in line with the northern end of the lower lagoon. It had been thrown up when Saabye's force had staggered to the end of its retreat.

"A waste of time and effort." Krag spoke with bitterness. "Weak, but we knew it, just like that over on the western side. But they bought time for completing the stronger positions further north."

Another foot patrol was traipsing along the beach just south of the abandoned redoubt. Kristian Østergaard repeated his pantomime with the fish. A waving arm beckoned them to come close. The southern lagoon lay unseen to the west across low dunes but the track along the isthmus was visible a hundred yards from the shore. A column was labouring up it with a dozen guns – two nine-pounder batteries – and as many wagons, the horses as exhausted as the single companies of infantry before and behind. An orderly on horseback left the column, pushed through the patrol on the beach, drew the beast alongside the boat, with water to its knees, and paid an exorbitant asking price for an entire basket. He laughed with Krag over each other's German.

Dawlish, standing to anchor the craft with his oar, studied the deserted redoubt and committed what he saw to memory. It lay on the far side of the track, its sand walls little more than sloped ridges six or eight feet high, the tops already scoured by wind erosion. Two south-facing gaps with collapsed sides marked what had been embrasures. The position was unoccupied as inessential to the Austrians.

The boat pulled out amid expressions of mutual goodwill. It was dusk now.

"He let drop that they've been nine days on the road," Krag said when they were far out. "Forced marches all the way. It's like Stavald said. When one team of horses is worn out, another takes over. These men would welcome even one day's rest in camp."

"And the redoubt," Dawlish said. "What do you think of it?"

Krag shrugged. "Possible," he said. "But perhaps madness."

The south-west wind had strengthened as the Østergaard's boat broad-reached towards the single distant red light that marked where the *Odin* swung. They had again been worth a promised five sovereigns. Nobody spoke. Numb, hungry, wet and shivering, Dawlish longed for hot food.

But only after Blackwood and FitzBaldwin had his report.

He was sure he knew how they'd react to it.

Chapter 14

It might be a fool's errand, exposure without gain. All depended on the Austrians, on whether an insane determination to match Prussian zeal was indeed keeping heavy artillery straining northwards even through the hours of darkness.

The night of March 25th was as overcast as Blackwood had hoped, an almost uniform blanket of cloud and intermittent rain blocking the full moon's light. The boats — *Odin's* cutter and two whalers, and the two large lifeboats belonging to the *Hulde* paddle steamer from Aalborg — crawled southwards, down the centre of the Limfjord.

Dawlish and Killigrew sat in the sternsheets of the whaler that led the straggling column and navigated by a hand-held compass. They crouched down on the bottom boards at intervals to read it by the brief illumination of a dark lantern. A strip of white canvas draped around the stern provided the only mark for the next craft in line to follow. That carried a similar strip, and so in turn to the last craft of all. There was no way of knowing if any had gone astray. Absolute silence was being enforced, the only noise the low creak of oars on rowlocks, of the strokes on the calm water.

The pulling crews came from *Odin* and from the Danish troops. Between them the boats carried almost a hundred men. The cutter, the largest craft, was packed with a half-platoon of Danish grenadiers and a handful of gunners who had proved their mettle on the retreat. More Danes followed in the paddler's life boats to make up the two-platoon force that Krag commanded. Granville's platoon, the men from Blackwood's force with whom Dawlish had served in the redoubt, and supplemented by volunteers from *Odin*, were in the whalers.

Midnight passed. The peninsula lay to the west, a low black strip dividing the lighter darkness of sky and water and dotted with the flickers of Austrian campfires.

"No sign of life on the isthmus." Killigrew's voice a whisper.

That could be good news or bad. There were no lights on the dark strip south of the Austrian encampment. That meant no movement, no trundling cannon, no supply train on the track. Good for assisting a stealthy landing, bad if that landing would be in vain, necessitating taking the force off before daylight with no harm inflicted. The men's spirit was at a peak tonight. This was the Danes' first chance of retaliation since they had left the Danevirke over a month before. That spirit could not be expected to be so ardent again should tonight prove an anti-climax.

Five minutes more. The campfire lights lay well off the starboard quarter now and the southern lagoon was directly on the beam. And still no lights on the track. A few pinpricks in the south marked the village of Harboøre.

"I think it's time now, sir," Dawlish said to Killigrew. That he had been this far south before, albeit in daylight with the Østergaards, made him an authority.

Hesitation, and then Killigrew said "I'll take your word for it, Dawlish."

The order was passed to the whaler astern that carried Granville and the other half of his platoon. It helped that light rain had drifted in from the west and deadened the low call yet further. Granville's confirmation and the relay of the instruction to the lifeboats and cutter further astern were almost inaudible. A full minute passed, the whalers stroking onwards, before Krag's acknowledgement came back. His three craft would be turning to a north-west heading. Towards the abandoned redoubt.

A little later it was time for the whalers also to part company. Granville's swung directly westwards, Killigrew's to the south-west. One towards the centre of the isthmus, the other to the point a half-mile further south, where it joined the land north of Harboøre.

Dawlish was frightened and guessed that so too was every man in every craft. The plan was complex, the force divided, the value of surprise perhaps overestimated, the chance of failure high. And all based on the assumption that the advance of the Austrian heavy artillery would not be halted by this night's wet misery of rain.

The undulating crest of low dunes ahead now blotted out the lights of Harboøre. The whaler moved forward in short leaps, backing water between to halt so ears could strain for any hint of a patrol moving along the beach, stroking forward when there was none.

At last, sand rasped beneath the bow, onward motion stilled. Two seamen slipped from the bows – Dawlish heard their gasps as the cold hit them. Dragging hard, aided by the rowers now poling with the oars, they brought the whaler a few yards further. All assigned to land now slipped over the side – water to the knees shot chill upwards. Half headed directly towards the dunes with Killigrew, the remainder stayed with Dawlish to pass ammunition boxes with rope-handles to the beach by a human chain.

He followed with the last of them and the lightened whaler pushed off and disappeared back into the night, there to wait. He carried a rifle, bayonet not yet fixed. Lorance's Colt revolver was in a holster at his side, a dozen reloads in a greatcoat pocket.

"Here, son. You're welcome to borrow it," the American had said. "Handier than anything longer if things get too close. Just be sure you get it back to me."

Killigrew's group – eight and himself – were already crouched behind the nearest dune. Neither it, not those stretching on either side rose higher than six feet. Dawlish's men brought the boxes forward – the lids had been levered off before departure and were secured now only by a few nails, ready to be loosened by a single twist of a bayonet.

"No alarm from up there," Killigrew nodded northwards. "Krag must be ashore by now. He's managed it, the fine fellow!"

That would have been the most difficult landing of all. Two planks were to drop from the cutter's bows to form a ramp. The Austrian four-pounder that had been captured on the retreat was to run down it into the shallows and be manhandled up the beach. The greater part of the infantry was to head directly to the empty redoubt to guard against any force coming south from the Austrian camp to investigate. The remainder would follow, dragging the four-pounder, lugging its shells and charges. Then they would return to the cutter for something yet more important before it stood out again to wait in the darkness.

Within ten minutes of running ashore Krag would make the abandoned redoubt a small fortress manned by almost sixty men. Their rifles and the four-pounder would cover the track leading south from the camp. Not a position that could be held for long, if at all, but one where the small Danish force could lurk undetected until the time for action came. If it would.

"The track's clear," Killigrew said. It was barely visible, some thirty yards ahead of the dune-crest below which he and Dawlish crouched. "Granville must be ashore too."

No sound of trundling wheels, of weary feet or hooves, no lights. Nothing northwards, to where Granville's group must by now be hidden in the dunes half-way up the isthmus. Southwards, only the few lights of Harboøre two miles distant.

Dawlish sensed that Killigrew was haunted now by the same unspoken fear that was growing in himself. That this was the wrong night, that nothing was coming, that this was indeed a wild-goose chase.

"Get your people under cover there, Dawlish." Killigrew pointed beyond the track. "Keep a bloody good look out. And no matter what happens, nothing without my signal."

Seven *Odin* seamen with him, Dawlish flitted across the rutted track, two carrying a box of rifle ammunition between them. Low dunes there, little more than small ridges half-covered with coarse grass. They threw themselves down beneath its cover, the lagoon level behind them, the track fifty yards before. Only now, when the wait began and stillness was essential, did the reality of the cold strike. Greatcoats sodden with rain, trousers and boots soaked since the shallows, limbs growing numb, teeth chattering, drowsiness threatening.

And this was only the beginning.

*

An hour passed, maybe longer. It was impossible to risk a match to read a watch. Nothing to be done but to endure the chill, to stretch and flex muscles without standing, to blow on fingers and to check that the men on either side had not drifted into torpor.

And then a hand tugging on Dawlish's left sleeve.

"Sir."

Crowther, always the keen-eyed lookout, was nodding northwards. Dawlish could see nothing but the muffled tread of hooves on damp sand was unmistakable. It came closer. Tall, indistinct shapes were just visible, sharpening as they approached, men on horseback, two abreast. Not trotting, not cantering, no hint of haste, no suggestion of alarm, just endurance of an unwelcome duty. They could only have come south from the Austrian camp, past the redoubt where Krag's troops hid, past the dunes where Granville's men were disposed on either side of the track. They had detected nothing because they had expected nothing to be there, because they had patrolled along here a dozen times before, because cold and wet and unrelieved routine had sapped alertness.

They were passing now. Dawlish had waved his men down below the crest but he allowed himself a single glimpse. Twelve riders slumped over their pommels, reins loose, horses' heads drooped in mute endurance. It was a patrol in name only, minds focussed on a respite that might lie ahead at Harboøre, time for hands to warm and clothes to steam around a fire, time for a mouthful of coffee. Now, for the third time since leaving their camp, they were unaware that their saddles could be emptied in seconds. They trudged on, were lost in the night. No acknowledgement from Killigrew on the far side of the track. He too had kept his men under cover.

The waiting continued. The light rain fell, stopped, began again. Behind Dawlish's hidden group lay the level surface of the lagoon. A mile across it, wholly lost in the darkness, lay the western isthmus. Dim lights, lanterns most likely, showed there at intervals and low, indistinct sounds indicated movement. There might well be a supply column toiling on through the night towards the Austrian camp but it was on the wrong isthmus for ambush.

It was hard to keep track of time. It might have been three o'clock, perhaps later. The south-eastern sky had not yet shown the first faint glow of dawn – the signal for withdrawal – and might not for hours more.

Suddenly the Radetzky March sounded from the north. It must be a torment for the Austrians in camp there, Dawlish realised, no less than for the Danes standing-to in the redoubts and waiting in fear for shells to fall. He waited to hear the crack of howitzers but none came. The music crashed to a finale – still no firing – and then began again. And again. He hated the tune by now, hated it all the more when three howitzers finally barked in quick succession, hated it most of all when it began again after them. The bandsmen must be exhausted, must be cursing whichever senior officer had dreamed up this assault on nerves and slumber. But it was a good sign, he told himself. It was still a routine night in the Austrian camp with no suspicion of –

"Sir!" Crowther's voice low, insistent. "Lights, sir!"

He was pointing south, towards Harboøre. And there were indeed more lights, not just dim static glows in a few windows, but closer, dancing spots seen for a moment, disappearing just as quickly, then seen again. They could only be lanterns carried by men moving between objects that alternately exposed and shielded them.

Dawlish moved at a crouch between his men. All rifles loaded and ready, spare rounds and cartridges to hand. Absolute stillness, heads down, waiting for his word. If there was indeed an enemy column it must be allowed to pass. On the far side of the track Killigrew would be giving similar orders.

The Radetzky ended at last. No sound as yet from the south but the lanterns seemed to be drawing closer. Dawlish forced himself to breathe slowly, to still the fear that he might not rise to the moment when it came, might fail the humble men about him.

A familiar sound, and close, plodding hooves on damp sand. An unseen man coughing, no lights, no lanterns. The dim shapes of approaching horsemen were just discernible through the curtain of rain and darkness. Closer now, and they looked like the same riders seen before, each lost in his own world of cold, wet wretchedness. They must have been sent south to meet those nearing lanterns, to guide them to the track along this isthmus and not that on the other.

They passed, were lost in the drizzle, were heading towards the point where Granville's force flanked the track. There too they would be let pass, unsuspecting and unmolested until they reached the redoubt sheltering Krag's men.

Nearing sounds – a man crying out in anger, a whip cracking, a horse whinnying in protest, the tread of hooves, the creak of wheels. Now a lantern rising, held up, lowered, then gone.

The onset was slow, but inexorable. But at last vague shapes were resolving themselves into horses, a pair, heads bent and straining, others behind, great heavy beasts with vast hooves in a team of eight, a blurred mass behind them. A horseman rode alongside, shouted in an angry voice – for more haste, perhaps – and then wheeled around and disappeared back down the column. Closer again, progress snail-slow, then halting altogether. Laboured breathing of the animals, more shouting, lanterns bouncing as men ran forward from behind.

The load was trapped in the ruts, the lead horses hardly thirty yards from Dawlish. More shouts, as if men were being set to put shoulders to wheels. Whips beat down on the patient beasts, followed by the sounds of gasping effort and the loud urges of a single voice that seemed on the edge of hysteria. And no movement.

A pause. Men and horses caught their breaths, enjoyed their moment of respite. Then the shouted command began again, and the same brutal concentration of effort until at last the exhausted horses heaved forward and regained momentum as the men gave a weak cheer.

Oblivious of the watchers in the dunes to either side, the team lurched on. The load was visible at last, a huge piece of fortress artillery, its barrel carried high above its carriage so it could clear a parapet. The wheels were a full six feet in diameter, the spokes metal, not wood, the flat steel tyres twelve inches wide or more. It would have been a big weapon on a ship – close to a sixty-eight pounder, Dawlish guessed – but it was a monster on land.

It trundled past at half walking pace, threatened to get stuck again, was saved by men throwing timber balks beneath the wheels and straining on the spokes and shoving from behind. An officer on horseback lost his temper, his voice shrill as he ranged back and forth and gained nothing other than sullen compliance. At last the cannon crawled on northwards and the night and rain closed behind it.

Nothing followed for another five minutes and then the previous scene all but repeated itself, another monster grinding forward, and after that another, and another, four in total. Besides the gun teams, a full company, infantry perhaps, must be solely occupied in supplementing the horse's brute strength to keep the weapons moving. None seemed armed – their packs and rifles must be loaded in the half-dozen two-horse wagons following.

The first of the guns must have passed Granville's positions and still there was no alarm. Now Dawlish saw heavy wagons pass also, eight, ten, twelve great wains, four horses in the traces, crates and barrels stacked inside their beds. Twenty men on horseback followed, no more alert than those who had passed some twenty minutes before.

That was the end of the column.

All had gone as well as had been hoped and there was indeed a target tonight. There was nothing to do now but to wait, still wet, still numbed and conscious that the true test was yet to come.

*

A rifle-volley from the north, a single crash, and then a steady ripple of shots and the distant shrieks of terrified horses.

The Austrian riders at the head of the column had reached Krag's redoubt and almost forty of his grenadiers were pouring fire into them at point-blank range. Men would be spinning from their saddles, some dead perhaps before they hit the ground and wounded horses would be plunging and rearing as the surviving riders dragged their heads around to spur back down the track.

The firing died – what remained of the horsemen must be racing to warn the advancing column. Then another sharp bark, a brief stab of flame in the darkness, and an instant later a larger flash and a duller boom part-way down the isthmus. The captured Austrian four-pounder that Krag had landed was in action now and firing directly down the track. Shouting there, sounds of panicked horses and then Krag's weapon blasted again, three rounds within the minute, puny in physical effect – if any – but devastating in their power to trigger shock and confusion.

Then another rifle-volley, this time closer. Granville's men were opening fire, and sustaining it, on the centre of the column. The Austrian infantry who had been pushing on spokes to keep the cannon rolling, and whose weapons had been stacked in the wagons following, must be milling there, dying, scurrying for cover. The rifle-fire was a fast staccato now. Granville's platoon must be on its feet, shooting, loading, ramming their muzzle-loading Enfields and firing again individually.

Krag's four-pounder blasted again, giving notice that escape northwards to the Austrian camp was blocked. But it was from that camp that the danger to Krag's group must come. The sudden noise must have come as a surprise but there would be experienced officers in that camp, battle-hardened in the war in Italy five years before, and they could be relied upon for fast decisions. Already a cavalry picquet might be rushing to investigate. The Danish rifles in the redoubt might see to it but infantry must surely follow, and field-artillery also. Krag would be lucky if his tenure of the small redoubt lasted half-an-hour.

Now the drum-beat of galloping hooves coming closer.

From the darkness across the track from Dawlish, Killigrew shouted "Up, lads! Fire only on my word, on my word, mind you!"

Dawlish brought his own men on their feet, yelled the same command to hold fire for now. The rain had died, the sky was marginally lighter, enough to show a knot of cavalry pounding down the track, the rear-guard seen a half-hour since now heading back towards Harboøre to alert whatever forces might be there. They were close, very close, fifty yards and closer by the second.

"Fire!"

Killigrew's cry was lost in the volley and Dawlish's an instant later brought another eight rifles into play. The leading horses were down, riders catapulted over their heads, some to lie still, others to stagger to their feet to be smashed down by the Enfields' terrible Boxer rounds. Horses crashed from behind into the chaos, screamed as the fire lashed them, plunged and threw off riders, struggled free and galloped back up the track. Rifles smashed down unhorsed men who blundered in shocked indecision. An officer on a rearing horse shouted some hopeless command before a round tore him from his saddle. A single beast, its rider crouched along his neck, broke from the mass and, untouched, disappeared towards Harboøre.

Dawlish fired with the others as fast as he could reload. The fear that had troubled him was gone, his hands steady, no past or future, only this furious present of ear-shattering noise and spitting flame. Maimed horses were trying to rise on broken legs and a man stumbled towards him, what might be a sabre clutched in his hand. Dawlish was in the action of reloading, thrusting the ramrod home as he saw terror on the face — an older man, dark moustachioed, fatherly in some other life — and he knew that he must kill him. Something like pity surged through him as he swung his rifle up but even as he squeezed his trigger a shot was blasted from his left and threw the Austrian down. Shouts from his right — two of his men were pounding a wriggling body on the ground with rifle butts. Angry English swearing drowned what must be pleas for mercy in frantic German that was suddenly cut off.

Killigrew shouted to hold fire, reload if necessary, move north, keep to either side of the track. The firing ahead — Granville's force — was as furious as ever, the sounds of panic louder, no hint of organised resistance to what must be local slaughter.

Then — more ominous, a single crash of rifle-fire from the north, a concentrated volley, a pause — twenty seconds perhaps, and in it the sharp bark of Krag's four-pounder — and then another great crash. The few individual shots that followed petered out. Some force had thrust south from the Austrian camp to investigate, had not anticipated a presence in the redoubt, had been thrown back. Krag was holding firm. For now.

Dawlish and his men advanced at a fast pace, Killigrew and his group just discernible to their right. Tongues of flame stabbed in the darkness ahead, Granville's fury unrestrained. A horse moaned in agony in the middle of the track and tried to rise on broken forelegs, its rider splayed lifeless before it. Furtive movement in front and to the left, two dark figures crossing the dunes towards the lagoon, freezing as they saw the advancing men, throwing up their arms and babbling.

"Leave them!" Dawlish shouted as a seaman by his side — Crowther — raised his rifle. "Keep moving."

For the real work was ahead. Granville's gunfire had not slackened and fresh volleys were crashing from Krag's redoubt and his four-pounder was firing — northwards now — as quickly as its team could reload. Some force was thrusting south from the Austrian camp and now that the initial shock was past it was likely to outnumber — and certainly outgun — the Danes in the earthwork.

"In line!" Killigrew shouted, "In line! Wait for my word."

A crowd rushed towards them, fugitives from Granville's hail, a mob intent only on escape, some dragging wounded comrades.

Dawlish too yelled for his men to form a line, to drop to one knee, take aim, to wait for his command. Men with empty weapons were still standing, ramming in cartridge and ball, then dropping to join the others closer to the ground.

The clustered mass of fugitives saw too late the line before them in the dark. They scattered to run for illusory cover as Killigrew called "Fire!" and Dawlish echoed him. A ragged fusillade then, men felled, those behind stumbling over them, any who could turning to flee back as they had come or to disappear across the dunes towards the isthmus's dark shores.

"Fix bayonets!" Killigrew's shout. "Forward in open line!"

No time to reload, better to maintain momentum, to thrust on to join Granville's force. The firing there had died down – Dawlish guessed that many of the Austrians were now cowering with upraised arms and that a new work of destruction was beginning. He hesitated to fix his bayonet – he knew he was not skilled enough in its use – but he pulled out Lorance's Colt, identical in weight and balance to the weapon he had been familiar with when on the gunvessel *Foyle*. He took it in his right hand, carried the Enfield in his left and kept pace with the others in the line.

Krag's force was still holding and his small artillery piece was still in action. But there was other artillery fire too, louder, flashes silhouetting the outline of the redoubt's sloped walls. The rifle-fire was heavier than before, rapid staccato, as if the Austrians too had brought infantry forward as well as light artillery.

The advance was at the double now, bayonets outstretched, past the wounded on the road, ignoring the dark shapes – caught between two fires – that still darted for cover. Dawlish saw a rocket climbing ahead, a yellow tail of sparks and then a red starburst that was reflected on the calm surface of the Limfjord.

It was Krag's signal that he was starting his withdrawal, notice to the cutter that had brought his force to stand in to the shallows. And pre-agreed notice too for the whalers to come in for Granville's and Killigrew's forces.

Dawlish and his group had reached the Austrian wagons. Some were still on the track, horses dead in their traces while others, unwounded, struggled for release. A few vehicles had pulled to the side, had attempted to turn back, had become stuck or had overturned. Bodies slumped in death between them. Other Austrians, unarmed or slightly wounded, were dragging more badly injured fellows out into the darkness under

Granville's troops' armed supervision. Others of his force moved between the wagons, climbing up to smash bottles of lamp-oil they had brought with them over canvas tilts and tarpaulins. Barrels of powder were being broken open beneath the huge wains identified as holding shells.

Killigrew and Dawlish found Granville, face blackened by powder as their own must be, savage triumph in his eyes.

"Get your men to the shore – the whalers are waiting," he said. "Any wounded? No? That's good! There's not much time now." He gestured northwards towards Krag's position. The rifle-fire had lessened, might only be Austrian now, shots fired at shadows, but several light field guns were firing at the redoubt, a likely prelude to an infantry assault. A few of Krag's men must still be offering token resistance – the four-pounder still barked – before they flitted towards the cutter and lifeboats.

"The guns?" Killigrew asked.

"Spiked," Granville said, "and powder kegs and shells stacked underneath. Now hurry!"

Killigrew and Dawlish gathered their men, threaded their way between the wagons – the smell of lamp-oil was powerful. The sky had lightened ever so little. The outlines of the whalers were just discernible against the Limfjord's deep grey expanse.

A figure – Austrian by his uniform – lurched from under a wagon, more than half-hidden by the shadows, almost close enough to touch. Too late Dawlish saw the arm rising with a pistol and the jet of flame, heard the blast, felt Killigrew tumbling at his side and crying out. Without thinking he swung his own revolver up. For all the horror of the moment a small calm internal voice was telling him to cock the hammer back, thrust the pistol forward toward the man's midriff, feel it sink against soft flesh. He squeezed the trigger, heard the blast, felt the man before him convulse and fall. Crowther and two others leaped to his side and beat their rifle-butts on his head.

Killigrew was hurt, badly hurt. Blood already soaked through the left thigh of his trousers and the leg below flopped at an impossible angle. "It's not bad, it's not bad," he babbled, face already draining, voice trembling in shock, the full pain not yet biting.

Dawlish reached for his bayonet and ripped the cloth away. Somebody produced a box of lucifers. Three failed to ignite but the fourth spluttered into life. Even in this poor light Dawlish could see the white of bone within the red crater and the blood spurting on to his own hands. The sight and feel all but paralysed him.

"Here, sir. A tourniquet. Quick, sir." A seaman was ripping his own neckcloth loose, was thrusting it towards him. He jerked his ramrod from his Enfield's retaining bands. "This too, sir. Fast now, fast!"

Lucifers, lit one from the other, gave light enough to work. Dawlish passed the cloth around the thigh – Killigrew's moan was chilling as they lifted him – and knotted it. The seaman thrust the ramrod through the loop and began to twist. The blood flow weakened, stopped, but Dawlish now saw that flesh alone held the leg together.

Now the nightmare of carrying Killigrew to the whaler, chaired by seamen on either side, another behind to hold him upright. Strips of torn clothing lashed his leg along a rifle to hold it straight. His head had fallen forward but he was alive, still moaning, shaking himself for a moment and gasping "It's not bad! It's nothing."

Through the shallows to the free-floating whaler. They lifted him across and he was laid on the bottom boards aft, quieter now. Dawlish, water to his knees, counted his men in, was then dragged aboard himself. The whaler backed water, swung about, stroked fast away into the brightening gloom.

The second whaler, Granville's, pushed away also and fear of what was brewing added power to its strokes. Flames flickered over the wagons, weak at first, then bursting into sheets and roaring upwards as the canvas was consumed and the wood beneath took fire.

A dull "whoomph!" and an expanding incandescent ball marked the first explosion of a powder keg. Now another and another detonation, flame and smoke rolling over the jumbled vehicles and drawing piercing screams from the trapped horses.

Dawlish watched, sickened with the knowledge that worse was to follow. A wall of flame was blazing along the centre of the isthmus, still climbing higher, still reaching out to either side to engulf what was not yet consumed, its mirror image crimson on the water's surface. The great fortress guns stood outlined stark against the red inferno, still intact. Now a massive explosion threw up debris as the first of the shell-laden wains succumbed. In the north too were explosions, powder kegs left with long slow-burning matches when Krag and the last defenders escaped from the redoubt. In the ghastly light now flickering over the Limfjord, the cutter and the lifeboats that were now well out from shore.

Then the last and largest detonations, the cannon barrels themselves torn from their mountings, hot fragments of shattered shell casings arcing out beyond the beach, dark objects that the mind recoiled from identifying ripped skywards through the flames.

The five boats drew together a mile offshore. Exhausted men slumped on bottom boards or thwarts while the officers held a brief conference. Krag – three dead, two wounded, one badly. Granville – one dead, three wounded but only lightly. Dawlish spoke for Killigrew, the only casualty of the southmost party. No sense of victory, no elation, only exhaustion, cold and raging thirst. And something vague but strong, amazement that it was all over, that it happened at all, that they were still here.

The sky was brightening, a cold watery light that showed dark smoke drifting above the few last flickering fires on the isthmus.

Time to start the pull north.

Chapter 15

Dawlish had wanted to know nothing of the hospital. His own imagination and Albemarle's shocked hints had been deterrence enough. Now he had no choice.

Killigrew was still alive, but unconscious, as the whaler pulled up the Limfjord. His drained face was already corpselike, his moans weak, his skin cold to Dawlish's touch when he adjusted the greatcoats piled on him to keep him warm. The old seaman who had overseen positioning of the tourniquet was concerned.

"Better to loosen it now and then, sir," he said, "The blood must flow a little, sir – he'll surely mortify if it don't. Seen it as Sevastopol I did, sir. Saved a good shipmate, loosening did."

So they had loosened it, two turns of the ramrod, and the blood did flow, five or six seconds before they twisted it tight again. And each time Killigrew's groans grew fainter and his face paler and Dawlish wondered if he was killing him.

The boats did not return directly to *Odin* but ran instead into the shallows on the Thyborøn shore. Men jumped out to drag them closer in and a messenger was sent sprinting towards the white clapboard church. He was back minutes later, a dozen soldiers following behind with stretchers – invalids themselves by their looks, unfit for service in the redoubts. A hatless civilian hurried with them, his well-cut frock coat streaked with what might be dried blood, a leather bag in hand, his pince-nez bouncing on a cord as he blundered forward. Dawlish recognised him – he had been with the ladies disembarking from the paddle steamer *Hulde*. Two of them were struggling to keep pace with him, their skirts drawn up to reveal their ankles. They were volunteers, Krage had told him – "Like your Miss Nightingale" – and there were Swiss and Swedish among them as well as Danes.

The civilian – apparently a doctor – had problems making himself understood as Killigrew was lifted from the sternsheets. His English was broken but his French intonation was unmistakable.

"I'll translate, sir," Dawlish been fluent in French since his time as a boy in Pau.

"Merci, monsieur." Relief on the doctor's face.

His instructions were few but they eased Killigrew's transfer. A glimpse of the shattered leg made Dawlish turn his face away and he was ashamed of it. He sloshed behind the bearers as they headed for the beach. The ladies were waiting there, one the stern middle-aged woman he had seen on the *Hulde*, the other younger, in her early thirties perhaps. The impression of delicacy was gone – both looked exhausted and the once-white-aprons worn over their dark dresses were soiled. The doctor left to supervise the removal of Krag's wounded from the cutter but the older woman had taken over. She had no English either and, by all appearances, even less Danish, but she too spoke French in what Dawlish recognised as a Swiss accent. He translated for her. She looked at Killigrew's wound – it did not seem to shock her – and adjusted the tourniquet. As she did, she snapped orders at the younger woman to pour out laudanum on a spoon. Killigrew took it as if in a trance.

The sad procession headed for the church at a pace which, however slow, was fast enough to draw gasps of pain from the wounded man. Even from a distance Dawlish could see that a huge red cross had been painted on the church's nearest wall and, as they grew closer, he saw a smaller one above the door.

"C'est la Croix-Rouge, monsieur."

He turned, saw that the younger woman was keeping pace and must have sensed his surprise.

"C'est quoi, madame?"

"It's a symbol. It's that ... that a wounded man is not an enemy."

Her words came in a rush. She seemed comfortable in French but her accent was not Swiss. There was a tremor in her voice, more than fatigue, Dawlish thought, rather horror suppressed, fear too that it should be suspected. He knew the feeling.

"You're a nurse, madame?"

"Just a helper."

They were at the church door but the stench hit them five yards before it. A thick-set man in a filthy uniform was standing there and beckoning them to hurry. He might have been florid faced before but now his features sagged and the red-rimmed eyes behind the thick spectacles looked dead. He ignored the grim-faced lady and shouted in Danish to the bearers to get the stretcher inside. He must be Hartling, the army surgeon, Dawlish realised, a name he had heard spoken of with awe, even if he had not seen him before.

The pews were gone and the floor was packed wall to wall with crude beds that must have been taken from the village houses. There were sixty or more and only the narrowest of passages allowed movement between them. Each was occupied, some double-occupied, foot to head, coarse blankets covering them, no sheets, some men sleeping, others awake but fevered, a few babbling or moaning or coughing. Orderlies, and several volunteer nurses, were busy among them, many looking exhausted, some close to collapse. A single wood stove at the centre was insufficient to heat the cold, damp air and the floorboards underfoot were slippery with liquid filth. Dawlish found himself brought close to nausea but fought to choke it back.

A curtain of blankets closed off the far end of the church and towards it the stretcher was carried, Hartling leading the way and shouting for orderlies to join him. Killigrew had revived enough to realise where he was. There was new fear in his eyes and he was mumbling what could be a protest. Dawlish reached out and took his hand. It was cold and he wanted at that moment for something of his own warmth, his own vitality, to flow across to him.

"There," he said, "there, there, sir." The words, useless, meaningless, but he could think of no others. "It'll all be well, sir. You're in good hands."

He knew at once what must come when the blankets were parted for the stretcher to pass. Two benches, improvised from pews, waist height, no blankets, bare wood, an orderly washing fresh blood from one, a human hand projecting from a pail beneath. Small tables with trays on top, dread implements set out in neat rows on one, jumbled and blood-streaked on the other.

Killigrew was laid on the cleaner of the benches. His head was twisting in mute protest. Dawlish still held his hand, still whispered empty reassurances. His eyes kept drifting to the rectangular saw on the tray, the scalpels, the bowls, the reel of thread with a needle stuck in it, the pile of discoloured napkins, the rolled bandages.

The older woman moved to hold Killigrew's head but Hartling drove her away with a snarl, then called for an orderly to come forward. The man had a brown bottle in his hand, was already pouring liquid from it on to a thickly folded towel. The smell was unfamiliar, but strong, enough to blot out the stench.

"He'll feel nothing, monsieur." The younger woman's voice was low. She must have sensed Dawlish's fear and horror. "I've seen it before."

Hartling held Killigrew's head himself and the orderly thrust the towel over his nose and mouth and kept it there. Dawlish saw the eyes glaze, the body relax. He still held the hand but it was limp now. Two other orderlies were holding the shoulders down now and two more were at the feet. Another was cutting away Killigrew's sodden trouser leg, untwisting the tourniquet. Blood gushed, was caught in a bowl.

Dawlish was afraid now that he would faint. He had heard of such operations, heard of them boasted of and even joked about. He had known that such a day might well come but the reality was more terrible than he had imagined. He locked his gaze now on Killigrew's face, determined to see nothing else until it was over. He sensed that the woman was still at his side but a bellow from Hartling drove her away. Dawlish glanced towards him, saw the anger on surgeon's features fade. He was suddenly calm, all expression lost as he turned to the orderly holding the tray of tools behind him.

It was fast, faster than Dawlish had imagined. The pad was removed from Killigrew's face, was saturated once more, was pressed again upon it at a word from Hartling. The temptation to turn and look was almost irresistible. The clink of metal. Curt commands, cold, as if routine, part of a familiar drill. And then the worst, a sound to be remembered in nightmares, the saw's bite on bone. Killigrew's hand trembled in Dawlish's, but his face showed no consciousness of pain. Hartling was calling for other instruments and a thump told of something heavy being dropped into a pail.

Other voices, blankets parting, another stretcher being carried in, the Swiss doctor leading. The body on the stretcher – the soiled uniform indicated that it must be one of Krag's men – was lifted across to the still-bloody second bench. The doctor threw on a stained apron and sorted through the jumbled instruments left from some previous operation. Another woman entered and he shouted at her in French – where had she been? – and his voice had an edge of panic in it. Before he looked away Dawlish saw a pad thrust against the Danish soldier's face and an orderly cutting his clothing away.

Hartling stepped back from Killigrew and sighed in what might have been either relief or satisfaction.

"Löjtnant," he said, then repeated himself before Dawlish realised that he was being addressed.

The surgeon was nodding to him. "Godt," he said. He smiled as he wiped his bloody hands on the sides of his coat. "Det gik godt. En stærk ung mand. Han vil leve."

It sounded reassuring. Dawlish dared to look towards the orderlies crouched over the leg. He caught sight of blood, white flesh, black criss-crossed stitching, and the stump that ended little short of Killigrew's groin in the instant before a white cloth hid it and the bandaging began.

Hartling had crossed to the other bench, was crouched above the body there with the Swiss doctor, seemed to be probing within the torso. They were arguing, voices subdued, in what seemed to be German.

Killigrew was still unconscious. The pad was held to his face as intervals as the remainder of his clothing was cut away. Dawlish helped roll and shift him. Yet deeper pity filled him as he pulled off the right boot and the stocking beneath, saw the uninjured white foot – something perfect, he realised, a miracle, a thing of beauty – and no counterpart to match it, now or ever again. When the body was fully naked an orderly began to wash it with a rag and warm soapy water from a bucket.

"You can dry your friend with this, monsieur." The young woman was by him with a dry grey towel.

Beyond her, Hartling and the Swiss doctor had stood back from the other bench, one gesturing to the orderlies to take the body away, the other shaking his head as if in despairing frustration.

Dawlish was shocked, embarrassed, that a woman should be exposed to a man's naked body. He took the towel, mumbled thanks, avoided her eyes. He began to dry Killigrew's arm, holding the wrist up in his left hand. There was a pulse, however weak. The older lady was here now with a nightshirt, coarse linen but clean. It was necessary to prop Killigrew up to get it over his head, to lift the body to slide it underneath and then pull it down. Only when Killigrew was fully clothed did Dawlish turn to the girl.

"Thank you, madame."

"Not madame. Mademoiselle."

He found himself blushing. Other than his sister and some officers' wives he knew no other women. She was older than Susan, he realised, by six or eight years perhaps. Light blond hair showed beneath a white cap and, tired and pallid as she was, she seemed beautiful to him. And she had courage. He felt ashamed that she should see him so shaken.

The older lady was calling her away to assist with moving Killigrew. As she turned, he saw the left side of her face for the first time. A huge port-wine stain covered it from ear to chin. He looked away, embarrassed, realised that she had noticed his reaction. She must be used to it, but that would make it no easier.

They carried Killigrew back out through the blanket-curtains into the foulness of the church beyond. A man was lifted from a bed to free it. Straw protruded from the stained mattress on which they set him down, a packed sack beneath his head. A chair from which the back had been knocked off and the legs cut short was positioned over the stump to keep the blankets off it. A pauper in the most wretched British workhouse would have more comfort.

"We can give him better rest than this on board our ship, madame," Dawlish said in French to the older lady.

"Have you a doctor on that ship? No? I thought not."

Beneath the anger in her voice Dawlish sensed weary sadness.

"It may kill him if we move him," she said. "The worst is yet to come for him." Her voice softened. "Go back to your ship, young man. You need rest yourself. We'll do all for him that we can."

He did not argue. Krag and Granville had arrived with the other wounded, had no time to talk. Only when he emerged into the fresh air outside did he realise that he had not ask either woman her name.

A column of smoke still drifted skywards to the south. And the Radetzky March was playing once again.

*

"It bought a week, ten days at best," FitzBaldwin said. "Not much, but maybe just enough for Nolan to get the connecting rod here."

He was in his cabin, Lorance with him. Dawlish had finished his account of the night's raid. It seemed remote already, like a half-remembered dream.

"A damn great pity about poor Killigrew," Lorance said. "We were shorthanded before but now —" He lifted his hands in exasperation.

"We'll manage," FitzBaldwin turned to Dawlish. "As long as you don't get yourself knocked out too. Blackwood wants as many as we can spare for now in the redoubts. You'll replace Killigrew there."

"When, sir?"

"As soon as possible. The Danes are starting to come down like flies. Saabye and Blackwood are worried. It's typhus. Only a few cases so far, but it never stops at that."

Typhus. That one word chilled. When it struck, it killed not hundreds, but thousands, devastated close-packed populations, halved the strength of armies, feasted on misery and deprivation. Nobody knew what caused it, even less how to prevent it. Only the strongest survived.

"Perhaps those Swiss volunteers..." Dawlish began.

"Well-meaning busybodies! Hartling doesn't think much of them, I hear. Thinks they'll be falling over each other to accompany the wounded back to Aalborg when that *Hulde* starts back tomorrow and that'll be the last we see of 'em."

Dawlish knew that he should have spoken up, should have defended them. That doctor, however despairing, would not be leaving, nor that older lady either. Perhaps not even that younger woman with the –. He stopped the thought. She was more, much more, than her disfigurement. But he was too tired to speak, was fighting the urge to sleep. FitzBaldwin had recognised that.

"You haven't done badly, Dawlish," he said. "All our people did damn-well."

And, for all Dawlish's exhaustion, sleep did not come easily, nor did it bring rest when it did. The memory of Killigrew's ordeal saw to that.

*

They did not go directly to the forward redoubts for the next two days, but laboured instead on the new defences south of the village. Boredom, and the promise of an extra shilling a day, led another half-dozen of *Odin's* crew to assist Granville's British ex-regulars. Even to an inexpert eye, the two new redoubts and the trench line between them showed the influence of a professional. Blackwood was everywhere, assessing slopes, siting embrasures for optimum lines of fire, supervising construction of robust bomb-proof shelters. Noting Dawlish's interest, he took pains to instruct him in the basics of fortification.

"There's no better weapon than the spade," he said. "Dig a trench or throw up a rampart and one man armed even with an old Brown Bess is worth three times as many charging him. Enfilade them and he's worth as many more again. That's the trick!"

He pointed southwards with his single arm. The existing Danish redoubts there were a half-mile distant and the ground was open, with but the slightest undulation. Only the low dunes close to the sea and along the Limfjord beaches offered a modicum of cover.

"See what any attacker would have to cross? God help them!"

But Dawlish had seen worse, would never forget it. Five years before, when he was not yet fourteen. Not sand, but five-hundred yards of soft mud before the walls of the Taku forts, mud that had hindered advance, had held men trapped to be lashed by gunfire and rockets, had swallowed the wounded. The stupidity of a naval commander – a courageous and decent man, but stupid – had launched an unplanned assault on the Chinese defences. It had cost hundreds of casualties. Dawlish's childhood had ended that day and he had learned that courage alone was never enough. War was a science and it must be his study. Not just for his career alone – and he knew now that the navy would be his vocation always – but for the men whom he would command. And whom he would himself serve.

The weather was better now, with sunshine and only occasional showers. The little vegetation around Thyborøn showed signs of spring. It was still cold, but the squalid chill of damp clothing was past for now. The Austrians had made no move – the Danish redoubts were still double-manned in anticipation of an assault that would avenge the destruction of the recent raid. Only the Radetzky, sporadic by both night and day, sometimes heralded brief howitzer shelling, as often not. It hardly mattered which – nerves were frayed and rest destroyed in either case and a reminder was served of Austrian vengeance pending.

And all the while the *Odin* swung at anchor. Too ungainly with her single working shaft to manoeuvre inside the Limfjord, or exit to the sea with any assurance of getting back inside safely, her fearsome guns were useless.

Only Nolan's return with a new connecting rod could change that.

Chapter 16

Dawlish visited Killigrew as often as he could. He had recognised him as a competent officer before but there had been no personal bond of respect or affection such as he felt towards FitzBaldwin. But now, sitting with him in the foetid church, Killigrew's life seemed very precious to him. The reality of the amputation had dawned on the wounded man, recognition of what his future might be little less a torment than the pain itself. He was feverish now and not always coherent. It was hard to know what to say to him. No subject, least of all the raid, interested him and he refused Dawlish's offer to take down a letter. It would kill his parents, he said, his sisters too. He would write himself when he was better.

And that would be never.

Dawlish forced himself to stay, to hold Killigrew's shoulders, to try to lend him strength when the older Swiss lady –her name was Madame Racine – changed the dressing. She must have previous experience, for she showed no sign of revulsion as she cut away the bandages and pad. The Swiss doctor, Venel, stood behind her and let her work without advice or interruption.

The stump was exposed. The orderly who thrust the soiled bandages into a sack was too slow to hide the blood and pus. Killigrew saw them and thrashed his head from side to side and moaned. And there was another smell now, a whiff only, but more foul, more putrid than any other in this dreadful place. Doctor Venel bent over the stump, looked closely, sniffed and probed. He looked up towards Madame Racine. Their eyes meet and his head shook ever so slightly. No need to say the word.

Gangrene.

*

The *Hulde* left for Aalborg and took some forty sick and wounded with her. Killigrew was not among them – the amputation had been far above the knee, Doctor Venel told Dawlish, and the chance of a haemorrhage was high, enough to kill him. Several of the volunteer nurses were gone but the young woman who called herself a helper had not. Dawlish realised that it pleased him that she hadn't, for he had half-expected it, but would have been disappointed if she had. There was something heroic about her, a willingness to take on what others would shirk, despite the ridicule her blotched face must so often evoke. He saw her busy when he visited Killigrew. Her tasks were menial – changing bedding, feeding patients too weak to feed themselves, washing bodies, fetching and carrying for Madame Racine – but that did not seem to deter her. He raised his hand to his cap brim when they passed but did not speak because he did not know how to begin.

It came easily in the end, on the night before he would go back to the redoubts with Granville's company. He had come to see Killigrew and he found her by him, giving him laudanum for a spoon.

"Could you please hold up his head, monsieur? It's easier that way."

"You're looking well, sir," Dawlish said as he did. "You're looking a lot better."

Killigrew wasn't. In the dim candlelight his sunken face was ashen. The gangrenous smell was stronger now and he must have noticed it himself, must know its meaning. It was merciful that the laudanum was carrying him into drowsiness.

"You'll stay with him for a while, monsieur?".

In a rush Dawlish said "If you could stay too, mademoiselle. I think you are a great comfort to him. If there's no other work for now. . ."

"A few minutes." She smiled. "As long as Madame Racine doesn't come. She doesn't allow us to talk to men, not unless they're sick." She gestured to the beds around. Since the paddle steamer had departed, half were empty. "It's easier here now. Even Madame can rest a little."

"Madame is Swiss, I understand," Dawlish wanted the talk to continue.

"Not Swiss. I'm Swedish."

"But you speak French well, mademoiselle."

"As you do, monsieur. The language of civilisation, my tutor told me."

Killigrew had drifted into sleep.

She was handsome rather than beautiful, Dawlish thought, but it was her calm confidence that impressed. Squalid as the surroundings were, plain her dress and soiled her apron, she had a dignity that appealed. One day he would marry a woman like this, he thought, even if –

Even if she had some disadvantage that others would hold against her. And if I had the courage to face that disapproval.

"I don't know your name, monsieur."

"Dawlish," he began, then stopped himself. "No, Page." The alias he should use. "Löjtnant Page. Of the Royal Danish Navy."

168

She began to laugh. "Just as my brother Arvid is Kaptajn Gustaf Gustafsson," she said. "Of the Royal Danish Army. All the Swedish officers who have volunteered use different names."

"But Sweden's neutral."

"So is England, löjtnant. But you're here."

"Is your brother?"

He wasn't. He had gone with a dozen other officers to Copenhagen and she knew no more. They must be facing the Prussians at Dybbøl by now, Dawlish thought.

"Your name isn't Gustafsson then," he said.

"Blomqvist. Eleonora Blomqvist."

It was easy talking to her, as easy even as it had been with Clothilde in Pau. But that recollection was painful now. The news he had of her still haunted him. The Reverend Augustus Lyall's report might just be salacious gossip, but there could yet be truth in it ...

"You volunteered too?" He wanted to blot out thought of Clothilde. For now. "Like your brother?"

She had, for a Swedish group of nurses. To support the handful of officers who had been outraged by the Prussian and Austrian invasion of Denmark and had felt compelled to assist. Her father, a colonel himself, had opposed her volunteering.

"But I talked him around," she said. "He gave in. He always did with me. He imagined that I'd be safe in a hospital in Copenhagen."

When the group she was with reached there, it had joined a Swiss delegation that had already arrived. La Croix Rouge.

"So that's the red cross on the church?" Dawlish said.

It was a new idea, she said. The words came in a torrent. More than an idea, an ideal. International, neutral, no wounded man an enemy. It was the horrors of the war in Italy five years before that had inspired it. A Swiss businessman had seen the aftermath of Solferino, had done what he could for the wounded, had realised that it was too little. He had afterwards imagined an organisation, well-equipped, well-funded, competent medical personnel willing to go wherever needed and make no distinction between sides. Like here. And it would grow, she said, the red cross on a white ground respected and protected by friend and foe alike in every conflict.

Over her shoulder Dawlish could see orderlies casting dim light on the beds as they passed between, pausing here and there to make some groaning wretch more comfortable. He could hear the coughing and the babbles of delirium, could smell the human waste and Killigrew's gangrene. He had heard what had happened that day behind the blanket curtains. Another amputation, a Danish private who had been too slow to take cover when an Austrian howitzer had barked, who had died on the bench.

This was reality.

He could not tell her that her Croix Rouge vision was utopian, naïve. Easy to send a few well-meaning – and valuable – volunteers like Doctor Venel, like Madame Racine, like this woman herself and the few others who remained. Impossible to imagine them in any greater numbers or staying the course through long campaigns. It was the Surgeon-Major Hartling and his orderlies, soldiers as much as any man who carried a weapon, who had carried the burden through history, always would.

"There's typhus," he said. "Aren't you afraid?"

"I'm terrified," she said. "It's bad. Two more dead today."

"But you're staying?"

"If my brother Arvid is like your friend at this moment, then I hope's there's somebody like me with him. I hope she'd stay also."

Dawlish motioned towards Killigrew. He kept his voice low. "He's going to die, isn't he?"

"Doctor Venel has no hope. Madame either. In a few days. No longer than a week."

It seemed a terrible way to go. Then a sudden memory of the Austrian who had shot him. His end had been brutal but swift and Dawlish felt no pangs of regret for his own part in it. An easier death than Killigrew's. It would have been better if he had died then too.

Somebody was crying out in a far corner, not pain, but raving, shouts of inchoate terror. Lamps bobbed towards him in the partial darkness, orderlies hurrying towards him.

"I must go now."

Eleonora Blomqvist stood up and went to join them.

And Dawlish too must go. He needed rest. Two hours before dawn he would be marching with Granville's company towards the same redoubt as before.

*

But rest was not to be immediate. Dawlish found himself summoned with Granville, and a dozen Danish officers to gather in the simple schoolhouse that was Saabye's command post. Other than Krag, few of the Danes spoke English but that did not disguise the foreboding

170

hanging over all waiting for the commander to appear. No conference like this had been called previously for the officers who were due to take their troops into the redoubts in the early hours. A few oil lamps cast vast shadows on the walls and the air was thick with tobacco smoke and the reek of unwashed clothing.

Major Stavald, the senior officer present, called them to attention as Saabye entered. He looked a decade older than when Dawlish had seen him before. Blackwood followed – the only man here who was smiling. He saw Granville and Dawlish and came over to stand with them once Saabye had stood the group easy.

"Raring to go, both of you, I'll wager," Blackwood said. "Come over here, join us," he called to Krag. "You're damn nearly an honorary Englishman and we'll need an interpreter."

Saabye was brief.

The crisis was all but upon them, Krag translated. There was news from the south, news just arrived. Saabye beckoned to Major Essmann to come forward from behind him, a surprise, since he had not been seen at Thyborøn for days. His greatcoat hung open and was spattered with mud, his boots too, and he looked exhausted. A nod from Saabye told him to speak.

Essmann had ridden in a single day from Aalborg, along the northern shore of the Limfjord. He had been there, and further south, gathering information on enemy movements. Estimates of enemy numbers – some unreliable perhaps, but most in general agreement – were flowing in from peasants and townspeople in areas already occupied by the invaders. Despatches were still arriving by water from Copenhagen – the Danish Navy controlled the waters along Jutland's eastern coast. A cheer, silenced by a glare from Saabye, at news that the army at Dybbøl was still holding out. The fortifications there had been strengthened yet further, that there was every expectation of resisting the massive Prussian assault that must be inevitable. But that was not the news that had precipitated the day-long ride that had ended just an hour since.

"The Prussians," Krag translated in an undertone. "More reinforcements arriving from Germany, but they're all not joining the forces at Dybbøl. Some coming north to reinforce the Austrians here, reinforce them whether they like it or not."

The listeners were stirring, looking one to another, dismay apparent.

"Hvor mange?" A Danish infantry major broke protocol, spoke out of turn, spoke for them all. "How many?"

171

Saabye did not reprove him and motioned to Essmann to answer.

"An infantry brigade, marching fast. Two troops of cavalry for reconnaissance. And artillery. Six batteries at the least, maybe more. Possibly another brigade to follow."

Dawlish felt a thrill of fear, hoped he was disguising it, saw from the faces around this that he was not alone.

"The Austrians won't want to share a victory here." Saabye was speaking now, Krag's interpretation a whisper. "They'll want to have taken Thyborøn themselves before the Prussians get here." He paused then answered the question that hung above them all. "The first of them in five days, six at the most."

So an assault must be imminent. Perhaps in the morning, certainly in the day thereafter, or after that again. But before the Prussians arrived, as if coming to rescue an ally incapable of completing the task alone. Prestige mattered.

Then the measures. The advanced redoubts and trenches to be manned as before, but with heightened vigilance. All other Danish forces to be held in reserve at high readiness to be directed where needed. The new defences – not complete, not even halfway so – would only be fallen back upon should the Austrians break through.

Word had gone to the Danish towns that lay north of the Limfjord. All able-bodied troops had already been stripped from the garrisons there to reinforce the Dybbøl defences and only the older and infirm remained. Now they, and all available munitions, cannister especially, were to be sent to Aalborg. The *Hulde*, the paddler that had carried wounded there, would tow these reinforcements and supplies back here on barges. No mention of how soon.

This was the moment for which the *Odin* was here, to scourge the Austrian gun positions, to scour the no-man's land across which their assault would storm. Dawlish longed now to be back inside her iron drum, the great three-hundred pounders heaving back on their slides, the fall of shot spotted through the acrid fog. He wanted Hopper and the crews below him, sponging the smoking barrels, swinging the next rounds over on the chain hoists, ramming them home, firing again. And again. And again.

That was how he had imagined it would be. But instead, the crippled *Odin's* contribution would be himself and a handful of seamen crouching on a fire-step, rifles in hand.

Saabye finished, a brief speech only, voice low but steady. They had come this far together, he said, had outpaced their pursuers, had repulsed them on the first arrival at this spit of land. Their resolution had given the Austrians pause, had compelled them to wait, to force them to build up their forces and supplies before attacking. They had not been broken by band-concerts and howitzer fire. They had defied Austrian fury before. They would do so again. There would be no surrender.

The words were heard in silence, some heads nodding in agreement. At the end, Major Essmann stepped forward to lead the cheering, three for Denmark, three for its king, as many again for the defenders of Dybbøl. The village pastor – an old man who had been untiring with his comfort of the wounded – led a prayer. Then what might have been a Lutheran hymn, or perhaps the national anthem itself – Dawlish knew neither, could not distinguish, but felt moved by it nonetheless.

"Fine stuff in its way," Blackwood said to him as the singing ended. "There'll be something of the same over there with our Austrian friends, God with them as much as with us. It won't make a damn of difference." He dropped his voice. "If you haven't emptied your bowels today, do it before you march. Not heroic but bloody practical. You'll thank me when their bombardment starts."

Four hours later, Granville's company marched south. The redoubts before them were dark hummocks, silhouetted against a sky lightened by the glow of the Austrian campfires. Fear knotted Dawlish's stomach. Killigrew's tragedy had shaken him and he might now expect the same or worse for himself. He remembered the expression on Eleonora Blomqvist's blighted face when she had been at the bedside. Pity. He would never want that, least of all from a woman.

He marched on. His concern in the coming days must be for the men whom destitution had driven to accept this service.

The Radetzky was blaring yet again.

*

Granville's company was assigned to the middle of the three redoubts, that flanked by the western shore of the lagoon. Krag was with it, responsible for liaison with the two Danish companies already there. Two hours before dawn they relieved units that had spent five days on duty here and that were going back for rest – and as reserves. These men had laboured hard. The shelters built into the walls were deeper now, shored up by planks stripped from huts and by small tree-trunks brought from across the Limfjord. Entrances were shielded by embankments. Shallow square pits, ten yards to a side and no deeper than a foot, had been dug in the redoubt's open centre, sand piled in ridges along their edges, to catch falling shells, prevent them bouncing further before bursting. Every advantage had been taken of the delay caused by Austrians' reluctance to assault before they had assembled sufficient force.

Now the waiting.

Dawlish stood on the fire-step with Krag and peered out into the darkness and strained his ears for sounds of movement. The head of the nearest Austrian sap was about eight-hundred yards distant but could not be seen. It had not advanced further since he had last been here. Now it was protected by a long sand ridge that lay across it like the bar of an inverted T. Sixty yards long or more, there must be a trench behind and in it a storming force would muster. A few voices could be heard from there at intervals – they might have been brief questions, shorter answers, inspections of guards perhaps. Nothing to indicate troops massed there in great numbers. It was from the more distant demi-lunes that the initial threat would come, the line of flashes that would signal the opening bombardment. There had been no howitzer fire in the night, not even when the Radetzky had fallen silent. That had happened before and might signify nothing.

Dawn now, grey light in the south-east. All forces in the redoubts stood-to, a thin line along the fire-steps but the greater number gathered below them in the shelter of the embankments. Cannon, loaded with solid shot, lay ready to be pushed into the embrasures. No rain, but the wind was bitter and every man must be as chilled as Dawlish.

An hour passed. Increasing brightness showed strained faces, pinched by cold and fear, lips moving in silent prayers, glances avoided, each man in his own hell of apprehension. Faint bugle calls sounded from the Austrian camp but gave no impression of urgency.

This might be the day of my death, Dawlish thought, Thursday, March 31st, not yet nineteen. If it must come, let it be quick, not mutilation, not impalement on a bayonet. His mind shied from the image of the news reaching Shrewsbury. He prayed, asked for courage to endure what might come without disgracing himself, found that even at this moment the prospect of what lay beyond life held no fear. Only the possible agony of departure did. It was a relief to move among the troops with Sergeant Evenden, check weapons that had been checked a dozen times before, speak bland words of encouragement to men older than himself.

Another hour, no Austrian movement. And slowly, realisation that the assault might not come that day.

But it would come.

Chapter 17

The day passed slowly, apprehension never fading even though there was no obvious movement of Austrian troops up into the saps. The cold wind did not relent but the rain held off. Men on the fire-steps shivered and dreamed of relief, those stood-down snatched comfortless sleep in the shelters. Soup was brewed, bacon fried, rough bread brought from Thyborøn. Dawlish felt fear each time he looked so briefly southwards over the parapet – in the last week an Austrian marksman had killed two unwary Danes who had showed their heads above it. Saabye and Blackwood exhibited no less caution when they came to view the enemy positions, inspect the men, pass on through the communication trench to the western redoubt.

Noon came and went. The chance of an attack this day diminished by the hour but could not be discounted. The line of Austrian embankments and demi-lunes hid movements behind them. There was activity there nonetheless, frequent bugle calls, a prolonged concert that might have accompanied a large troop parade and inspection, distant singing, a thousand voices, maybe more, raised in some hymn or anthem. This had not happened before.

Granville relieved Dawlish – he filled Killigrew's role now and had responsibility for the eastern face of the redoubt, that which slanted towards the lagoon. Years of standing watch, when anything more than three and a half hours of continuous sleep was a luxury, guaranteed slumber on a straw bed in a corner of a shelter. When Dawlish awoke, he was cold to numbness and could feel lice burrowing between his flesh and clothing.

It was late afternoon now, light fading, and there would be a stand-to until full darkness. There would be no assault this late, he knew, but that made it more likely that it should come the next morning. He looked north towards Thyborøn, across the low rear wall of the redoubt. The new defences were incomplete, almost a mile distant, the interval devoid of cover. Smoke drifted above them from the cooking fires of the Danish reserves in the huts and tents beyond. Better they be there than in the redoubts when the bombardment – the inevitable bombardment – would begin.

In the Limfjord, opposite Thyborøn, he could see the *Odin's* dark bulk. The great guns that he himself should be bringing into action were lying useless at this time of crisis. He looked eastward, across the grey waters of the lagoon. The third redoubt lay between it and the wind-ruffled fjord. It had been subjected to the least howitzer fire and no Austrian sap approached it. The assault would come on the west side of the lagoon.

Southwards, he could imagine the Austrians behind their own sand embankments, many feeling the same trepidation that he felt himself. For weeks they had seen the line of Danish defences, had known that the time must come when they would advance against them, had concealed the fear that fear itself might unman them when the moment came. If it was to be on the morrow – All Fools' Day – they must know it by now. Tonight, there might be confession of sins, for they were Catholics, and masses, private prayer, letters, regrets, handshakes ending old quarrels, feigned bravado, bombastic exhortations, rings and watches labelled to be left behind, names scribbled on pieces of paper and pinned to collars, weapons checked and checked again.

For many the long night ahead would be their last.

Mine too perhaps. And not for my country.

But he had put a signature to a document. An alias, not his own name, but that did not matter. It pledged his word. Even if he could, he would not betray that.

*

Stand-to an hour before the cold, clear dawn. One man in ten on the firing steps, crouched, head down, the greater number below them at the base of the wall. Gunners ready to push their weapons from cover and into the embrasures.

The sun climbed as a red ball above the Limfjord. Long shadows cast, frost sparkling in the early light. Silence broken only by the cries of seagulls. Long minutes passed, fifteen, twenty, an eternity.

Then a bugle call and a single red rocket soared from the Austrian camp. A howitzer crack, another following almost instantly, and then another and another, settling down into a steady drum beat. Their shells were in the air, were at their apogee, were plunging down. Men shrunk against the sand embankments – they would have burrowed if they could – and threw arms across their faces. Each howitzer, Dawlish knew, had already been ranged on these redoubts when the Radetzky had so often sounded. Successive elevation corrections had ensured reasonable certainty of landing shells inside.

"Into the shelters!" Granville yelled to Dawlish, "Get 'em under cover!"

The drill had been agreed, rehearsed several times, the greater part of the men to be sent into the shelters once the likely howitzer bombardment erupted. Only the men on the fire-step would remain and lie prone, pray that no shell drop directly on them, rise only at intervals to watch the Austrian lines.

Now the first impacts. A crash, a flash, a fountain of sand rising some fifty yards outside the redoubt and then another over to the right, square on the communication trench, yet more towards the other redoubt.

Dawlish was on the fire-step, Krag with him, Sergeant Evenden down at the base of the wall, bellowing for the men there to take cover. They were funnelling into the shelter entrance as a shell pounded down on the central space. Dawlish saw it bounce – a black cylinder – but the low walls of the square pit into which it had fallen stopped it. Its explosion hurled up sand and fragments, but none that reached the crowded men. Now another, and another – an impact on the wall's crest over to Dawlish's left, a few safely captured and contained within the shallow pits, several falling short before the walls, then one that exploded close to the few men not yet inside the shelter, cutting down several.

"Get down, lie down!" Dawlish was flat himself as he shouted at a panicked seaman who had leapt to his feet, thrown down his rifle and was hurling himself down the slope from the fire-step.

Sergeant Evenden met the fleeing man below. He swung up his rifle-butt, caught him on the chest and sent him sprawling, then grabbed him by the collar and hauled him with him back up the slope. He picked up the man's rifle and thrust it back into his hands.

"Keep your bloody head down until you're needed," he shouted, then scurried towards Dawlish.

"Damn near all safely under cover, sir," he said. "Wellard's done for – a bloody great splinter – 'an Holmbury 'an Porter are down but it won't kill 'em."

"The gunners?" The most important of all for what was to come.

"First into the shelters."

Grey smoke was drifting across the centre of the redoubt and shells still fell there, their effect limited by the pits. The Danish companies that manned the far wall were also under cover, all but the men lying on the fire-step. Some rounds were still falling short, gouging craters in the open ground, and a few had bitten into the walls. Dawlish, head cradled in his arm, could feel the shudders of the impacts. His fingers were locked into the sand and his mind screamed for this to stop. He was trembling, felt that his bladder was about to burst, prayed that he would not break.

An impact close enough now for the falling shell to shower sand upon him in the instant before it exploded. A hot wind blasted past him, ripping his breath away, and the ground lurched beneath him. Dazed, he rose on his knees, could hear screaming through the smoke on his right, saw others no less stunned rising also. He was up now and running at a crouch towards the choking cloud. Krag and Evenden were at his side and they dragged others to their feet. The screaming was cut short, but another voice was babbling in pain and terror.

A shallow bite had been torn from the parapet. The two men behind – one clearly dead, the other's torso bloodied and blackened, his face burned – had taken the full force of the detonation. Dawlish recoiled, felt powerless in the face of hideous injury, felt sour vomit rising in his throat. He choked it back, knelt by the injured man, looked into the despair-filled eyes, knew he could not save him, could not assuage his pain.

I will not yield.

"Sergeant Evenden! Two men to get him into shelter! And the rest of you! Lie down!"

He was on his feet again, his head exposed to any sharpshooter at the Austrian sap, his whole body to any hot fragment blasted from a shell impact within the redoubt. His terror was not gone but he knew that he could and would control it. He lay against the undamaged parapet above the fire-step, looked south. A haze hung over the enemy gun positions, smoke billowing up from behind them with each howitzer bark. The high-angle weapons were hidden from sight but black snouts jutted from each embrasure in the demilunes, the low-trajectory field guns waiting for their turn. And worse perhaps, other fortress artillery like the handful destroyed in the night raid.

The fire on this redoubt was slackening. Single shells dropped in its centre, others fell short. One must have plunged on a shelter dug into the far wall. Frantic Danes swarmed there. They tore away shattered planking, dug with spades or with their hands, dragged out bodies from it, some of them staggering to their feet to join the effort, others cast lifeless aside. Behind one of the embrasures, gunners emerging from a shelter had found their piece fallen over, its carriage shattered.

The Austrian fury had shifted from the other redoubt also and was concentrated on the linking trench – a more difficult target, because it was so narrow. Eruptions of flame-shot sand rose before and behind it but except for a single smoking crater no shot had as yet fallen inside. Danish infantry manned it and the shelters built into its walls had nothing like the strength of those in the redoubts.

But now there were other sounds, distant bugle calls just audible between the howitzer's crashes. Dark masses were moving in the gaps between the demi-lunes. They were coming into the open, funnelling towards the saps, disappearing from sight behind the flanking embankments as they entered them.

"A damn hot business, Dawlish." Granville was at his side now. "The men are holding?"

"Well enough, sir."

Granville nodded towards the saps. "We won't be welcoming those fellows for another half-hour."

"Should we man the firing step? Get every man up?"

"Too soon! Keep 'em in the shelters. Our friends'll be pounding us first with their field guns, blast breaches if they can and —"

He stopped, pointed. Another red rocket soaring above the Austrian line. "That's it," he said, "That's the start!"

Orange dots flashed along the demilunes and the reports followed, deeper than the howitzers' continuing barks. Now the first rounds landed — solid spherical shot that thumped into the redoubt walls or fell short, flinging up long plumes of sand as they bounced. The roar grew to be continuous, the slowing drumfire of the tiring howitzer-crews overlain by the field pieces and the yet deeper, but more infrequent, crash of larger weapons. The redoubt walls shuddered under the hail. A few rounds skimmed over the parapet or ripped through its crest, but the majority seemed to be either falling short or burying themselves uselessly in the wall's inclined outer face.

Dawlish saw Granville, crouched beneath the parapet to his right, beckoning to him. Krag was there too, head bare, uniform singed and torn, blood on one side of his face but appearing not to notice it. He must have been close to a shell burst, had been lucky to have survived it.

"Krag's been to the Danish commander here — damned if I can remember his name," Granville said. "Poulsen, Colonel Poulsen, that's it, yes, thank you, Krag. Poulson's had a message from Friherre Saabye."

"He's bringing reserves forward," Krag said. "He's sending only two companies into here, into the other redoubt too. They'll be here in ten minutes. They're coming at the double. Saabye's going to keep the others further back." He motioned northwards. Dark blocks of men were emerging already from between the half-completed new defences.

"We'll have to hold with what we have until those companies get here," Granville said. "God knows how long this pounding's going to last. But when it ends the Austrians will be pouring from their saps. Poulson wants every man who can hold a rifle on the fire-steps when they do."

"And hold fire," Krag said. "It'll be on Colonel Poulsen's order only. A bugle call. Then rapid fire, sustained. They'll be close by then. Kill them while they're still on open ground. No bayonets fixed unless they start getting to the walls."

No let-up in the Austrian fire – it was well concentrated and what had seemed ineffective at first was now starting to tell. Tremors ran though the redoubt wall as solid shot and explosive shell smashed into it. Small rivulets of sand cascaded down its faces and at several points shallow gaps had been torn by repeated impacts. The sloped embankments would not collapse as a masonry wall would do, but with time – and sufficient munition reserves – whole sections might be reduced to low mounds across which attackers could surge.

Only a handful of men were on the fire-step now, the remainder sent down to take cover. But for a single man, killed instantly by a ball tearing through the parapet crest, there had been no further losses on this length of wall. It was worse at the nearest embrasure – a lucky shell had entered, had exploded just beyond, had scythed down half a Danish gun team and dismounted their field piece as they were pushing it back into deeper cover.

The first of the Danish reserves arrived, panting and stumbling through the gap in the low rear wall. They carried nothing but weapons, ammunition and small haversacks, no blankets, no encumbering greatcoats. Colonel Poulsen and two other officers met them, directed the first company to crouch at the base of the walls on the western flank – there was no room for them in the shelters. Even as they deployed, a ball came bounding across the nearest wall and tore a path through them. No explosion, but a half-dozen men down, two with enough life left to be dragged to cover, the others dead. Granville sent Krag down to meet the second company, bring them to the eastern sector. Fighting to recover breath after their advance at the double, they found no space in the shelters.

Krag brought their commander up to meet Granville. Introductions as formal as in a society salon even though they were cowering behind a shuddering embankment and shouting to be heard. Kaptajn Marius Lauring, 22nd Infantry Regiment, had a livid, half-healed, scar on his left cheek. His patched tunic was a private's, his officer's insignia clumsily sewn on. It was easy to imagine him standing firm in some rear-guard action on the retreat, a man unbeaten. Quick discussion. One of Lauring's lieutenants was to be posted on the fire-step for now, ready to call for support when needed.

And the shelling continued.

Dawlish's forced himself to move from man to man along the fire-step, mouthing encouragement to ears as deafened as his own. On each face he recognised the same unspoken fear that was close to mastering himself and yet also the same determination not to yield. Poverty, even destitution, had driven these men here but they had survived as bad or worse at Sevastopol or Delhi. While they could endure this, then he could also.

He forced himself to look above the parapet. In the instant before he ducked again – almost too late, as sand blasted from an impact below and to the left – he saw the bayonet tips jiggling above the embankment at the sap head. Austrian troops were shifting into position there, pushing past each other, packing perhaps three or four deep in the narrow trench, waiting for the signal that would send them scrambling up and over. It must be the same at the two other sap heads, men in fear, knowing that their deaths might lie only yards ahead on the open ground.

Time had lost meaning. It was impossible to guess how long this storm had lasted – it might have been minutes only, could well have been an hour. The walls were crumbling under the repeated blows, the sharp angles of slope and parapet blunted, the once-smooth crest now gap-toothed.

Then the end, felt rather than heard through half-deafened ears.

The bombardment died, the tremors too with the few last individual shots. Dawlish lurched to his feet and saw Austrians spilling over the sap-head embankment. He turned, shouted down to Evenden to get the shelters cleared, men on the fire-step. Other officers along the wall yelled similar commands. The Danes who had been in shelters boiled from them, sergeants urging them up the inner slopes. The gunners were trundling the field pieces from cover. They heaved on the wheel-spokes, slewed them around into the embrasures and rammed charges and balls down the barrels while still moving.

Sergeant Evenden drove the British volunteers up the inner slope and Dawlish, on the fire-step, directed them to line the easternmost section of wall. To the right, the newly arrived Danish infantry were clambering up and stringing out behind the parapet. Orders were shouted in English and Danish to keep crouched in cover, rifles loaded and ready, ammunition pouches open.

"Hold your fire! Wait for the command!" Granville's order, echoed by Dawlish. Krag and Lauring were calling in Danish, the intent no different.

The Austrians, still eight hundred yards distant, were coming forward at a fast-march pace, flags flying, bayonets fixed, not a single unbroken line but distinct companies three and four lines deep. Their flanks extended as they came on, the ranks behind moving out towards the units at either end. To their rear, more were emerging from cover, not just from the sap-heads but from the trench behind. No cheers, but steady drum beats, and in the southern distance the Radetzky's strains loudened as another band, and another, took up the tune. They still poured from all three saps, already forming into two main blocks, the larger heading towards the western redoubt, a gap – two hundred yards or more – between them.

Dawlish watched in dread and fascination. The advance was no longer just a mass, for individuals in it were discernible, dark grey coats, blue trousers, white cross-belts, faces as bearded and grimed as those around him. Officers strode out in front, swords drawn, white gloves, the hint of gold on epaulettes or shakoes. The levelled bayonets told there would be one volley from them, one only, for their rifles, like the Enfield that Dawlish carried himself, were muzzle-loaders. Standing still to load and ram them in the open ground would be suicidal. If they were to take the redoubts it must be at the point of the bayonet.

Granville called for Eltham, the consumptive marksman. He thrust his field glasses to him, pointed. "Take a look, that officer, you see him?"

A portly man, already tired, plodding ten yards ahead of his troops, scorning to look either to the right or to the left, eyes locked on the redoubt.

"Could you take him, Eltham?"

A nod. "A good chance, sir."

"Do it."

Eltham moved slowly. He wedged himself against the parapet, sling wrapped around his arm to hold the rifle steady, took aim.

"Here, Dawlish." Granville handed him the glasses.

The magnification was low, little more than a lady might need in an opera house, but enough to show the worn features and grey beard and whiskers. The shako, topped at the front by golden knob and circled with two bands of gleaming braid, carried a large crest in front. The face, though set, had a hint of kindliness about it. It would be easy to imagine this man as a popular commander, stern but understanding, a loving grandfather too. He was still breathing – was puffing with unaccustomed exertion – but he must know that death might well be only steps away.

As it was.

A click, Eltham drawing back his rifle's hammer.

Dawlish could not drag his gaze away. He had nothing against this man, could not hate him, yet knew that he would act just as Eltham did had he got the skill. Necessity demanded it.

It seemed for a moment as if the Austrian was looking directly into his eyes. The bark of Eltham's rifle, the brief roll of smoke, the whiff of sulphur, the shot perfect. The wound was low in the neck, blood spouting, hands clawing at it as the body twisted and fell, mouth locked open in horrified surprise.

Krag was shouting in anger.

"Colonel Poulsen's orders aren't changed, Granville! Hold fire! Wait for the bugle."

An order for the rifles, not the guns.

For a single field-piece was blasting from the centremost embrasure, was leaping back in recoil even as its sisters opened also.

And the first gaps were torn in the Austrian ranks.

This was the Danish artillery's moment.

Chapter 18

The Danes were firing solid shot and their aiming was low and deadly. Lanes were ploughed through the Austrian ranks, men scythed down, those untouched to either side flinching sideways. Some balls fell short, bounced, leaped on at head or waist height to cut their own swathes. The Danish guns blasted from the embrasures of both redoubts, the angled faces allowing concentration on the centre of the advancing line, the other walls showering fire on the extremities. The gunners had hit their stride and had settled into the lethal rhythm learned in days of peace.

The Austrians still came on, their pace unchanged, no hint of hesitation, a march but not yet a charge. Many of the officers and men might well have been blooded in Italy five years before when they had faced the French and Piedmontese in the slaughters at Magenta and Solferino. Now they showed no less resolution, aware, despite all the present scourging, that a dash forward too soon would exhaust them long before they could reach the ramparts ahead. Better to suffer now, better to endure, if the assault's climax was to be at full fury.

Another line was forming behind, troops scrambling from the saps, forming into ranks, lurching forward. From yet further back, from between the now-silent demilunes, dark blocks of men emerged into the open, flags flying, drums beating.

A wall of smoke now churned along the redoubt walls, half-obscuring the enemy advance, as the Danish field guns roared and leaped back in their embrasures. Yet more gaps were ripped through the Austrian line but, each time, men to either side moved over to fill them, to keep that line unbroken. The wounded – worse still, the maimed, for roundshot sheared limbs away – lay where they had fallen as ranks pressed on. Crouched, faces down like men struggling through a heavy rainstorm, the initial march pace was now an often-wavering trudge. The line was no longer straight but undulating as whole sections stopped, stunned by the Danish guns' fury, then shambled forward again as officers and sergeants reasserted control.

For Dawlish, still holding Granville's glasses, the advancing line was no anonymous mass. He saw faces briefly raised, then dropped again – some set in resolution, others flushed with terror, all enduring. Vomit ran down some fronts, and more than one wept and babbled in impotent protest, but they were carried forward nonetheless by the greater horde. Their bayonet points promised merciless retribution should they ever get this far and he longed for the moment of Colonel Poulson's call for rifle volleys. The nearest Austrians were little over three-hundred yards away now, within effective range of the best shots and soon be close enough for the average.

The Danish guns were ceasing fire one by one. The vast silence that was broken only by shouted commands endured a minute only but, in it, still-greater lethality was being thrust into hot barrels that steamed from their sponging. The smoke before the embrasures had thinned to drifting strands and revealed to the oncoming Austrians the horror that now awaited them.

Cannister.

Thin-walled tin cylinders, packed with half-inch balls, nestled now in the cannon bores, turning them into giant shotguns. The gunners lowered their elevations, stood back, waited for the command, faces turned to Colonel Poulsen. He had mounted the parapet and stood there erect, sword in hand, in open defiance of the attackers.

"Åben ild!"

His cry was drowned by the roar of a dozen cannons opening as one, followed instants later by a similar dreadful salvo from the western redoubt. Caught in the fans of flying iron, men were smashed down along great sections of the Austrian line. And yet that line, halting, thrown back in places, was somehow reforming and stumbling forward again. Bugles sounded, officers out in front turned toward the troops following, raised swords in white-gloved hands, and called for the charge. Their troops shambled into a run, rifles held low, bayonets outstretched, many yelling.

The next wave of cannister hit them, the elevation fractionally lower so that the balls were ricocheting before them, flattening the cone of death. The first line was ruptured in two places and that following moved up at a trot to fill it, but it still rolled on.

"Ready, lads! Any moment now!" Dawlish shouted.

Danish reinforcements and British volunteers were intermingled along this section of fire-step, still crouched below the parapet, rifles held white-knuckled. Only Dawlish was peering over. The closest attackers were two-hundred yards away, bunching now into a more solid mass that was headed directly for this face of the redoubt. A yet-worse hail was lashing into them now, for the Danish gunners were double-shotting, thrusting in roundshot first, then cannister, and depressing the barrels below the horizontal. Impacting in showers of sand scarcely a hundred yards beyond the redoubt wall, the skipping balls, great and small alike, tore down ever larger numbers.

The advance was no longer a coherent whole, rather small groups racing forward but with the second line some fifty yards behind still largely intact and yet more following further back.

And then the longed-for command, Krag shouting the translation, Granville bellowing it in English, Dawlish echoing it.

"Choose your targets! Rapid fire!"

All along the fire-step men rose to their feet, rifles raised, first isolated shots and then a ripple along the whole length. Dawlish forced calm upon himself, took careful aim at a swarthy hatless man with rage on his face who might have been a corporal, for he was dragging a laggard with him. First pressure taken on the trigger, then a gentle squeeze and the butt's kick into the shoulder – and the realisation that he had missed. But others were falling on the Austrian front, not just to another shower of cannister and shot, but to the rifles too. Along the fire-step men more adept than Dawlish rammed new rounds down their barrels and even as he struggled to match their pace they were firing again.

The foremost Austrians were now close enough for some to be sheltered from the arcs of the embrasured cannon and it was rifle-fire alone that now lashed them. Some were dropping to one knee, aiming up to fire at their tormentors' exposed heads and shoulders above the redoubt parapet. It was a stupid decision, the chances of success minimal, of surviving standing to reload even less, their rounds to be better spared for combat inside the redoubt itself should they get so far. Several were cast down and left behind by the onrush.

Pressed forward by the men behind, the advance funnelled towards the low gap pounded in the redoubt's parapet by the Austrian bombardment. Several of the Danish guns had been pushed out a yard or two in front of their embrasures to increase their arcs so that their canister could ravage the attackers' flanks. An Austrian officer had gathered a small group, was ordering them to their knees to take aim on the gunners even as a new fan of iron scoured them away. But others, no less undaunted, was hanging back, edging just outside the Danish cannons' lines of fire, shooting as they knelt, bobbing up to load and ram, dropping again to aim. Gunners pitched down and were dragged back inside the embrasures. Granville shouted for fire to be directed on these attackers but few took heed of him – the terrible Austrian bayonets were now but tens of yards away and each man on the fire-step had eyes for them alone.

Over to his right Dawlish saw that a fieldpiece now stood crewless before its embrasure, a body slumped over the trail, others strewn on the ground to either side. A wedge of Austrians was driving towards it.

They will be inside in less than a minute. A frenzy of close-quarter slaughter such as I survived in the second storming of the Taku Forts. And no quarter.

He had lost count of the number of times he had fired – his fingers searching in his ammunition pouch detected only a few cartridges left. The first Austrians had reached the base of the wall, and a few were already scrambling up the incline. The range was point blank and they were dying there, half-hidden by the swirling, choking gunsmoke. Some fell back but yet more were crowding forward and preventing all retreat.

"Fix bayonets!"

Granville's cry, reinforced by Sergeant Evenden running along the fire-step and shouting to men intent only on firing and reloading and firing again. It was the order that signified desperation – ramming new rounds was possible with the bayonets fixed but was slower, much slower.

A handful of Austrians reached the parapet to Dawlish's left, were hurled back, but more stumbled up the sand embankment behind them. Dawlish fumbled to snap his bayonet into its latch as a man to his right shouted "Here, sir! Here they come!" He swung around to see faces rise above the parapet crest. The men there were blasting their last rounds – no possibility of reloading now – then lunged upwards with their bayonets as the first Austrians came across.

And then the melee on the fire-step, three, four, five defenders down, others shrinking back to either side, parrying the attackers with bayonet and rifle butt. From one side Granville, from the other Dawlish and Evenden, rushed men forward to support them. A few had managed to reload. Now they thrust their rifles over the shoulders of the foremost defenders and fired point-blank into the heaving mass of Austrians still crowding on the crest and jumping down on to the fire-step. Several had been carried across by their own momentum and tumbled down the inner slope. As their regained their feet, bewildered and isolated, fire from the Danes above stuck them down.

Granville's men pressed forward, stabbing and flailing, driving the Austrians back against the hedge of bayonets that stood firm with Dawlish and Evenden. From further back on the fire-step to either side rifle-fire poured into more attackers clambering up the slope. Panting and exhausted, many were on hands and knees as they dragged their rifles with them.

The fire-step was clear, bodies heaped on it, some still moving, groaning, writhing underfoot. Butts pounded on pleading faces, bayonets driven into throats, fresh corpses flung, limbs flailing like rag dolls, down the inner slope. The parapet was a barrier again and the Austrian heads and shoulders that emerged above it were meeting point-blank fire and driving bayonets. Along the flanks of the attacking wedge on the outer slope, attackers were falling to the rifles along the fire-step.

The assault died, at one moment an enfeebled but still determined thrust to reach the parapet again, an instant later a wavering, then a stop, and then a torrent that surged back down the wall's incline. No bugles, no yells of command, only the shouts of panicked men stumbling and tumbling. At the wall's base a few heroes tried to stem the flood, but the majority streamed past them, some dragging wounded with them.

An officer – an older man, grey-bearded, bare-headed, face blackened with powder – stood there, revolver in one hand, sword in his other. Undaunted in defeat, magnificent in defiance, he was joined by two sergeants. Fugitives halted, formed with him despite the fire that tore several down but, by some miracle, left him untouched. Then he turned westwards and led a growing column to join the assault now threatening to break through there.

For there the Austrians had reached the embrasure where the Danish gun-crew had been killed. Despite the fire poured down upon them from the fire-steps to either side, the attackers pressed forward, regardless of casualties. Numbers alone carried them onward, packed too close to use their weapons until they spilled into the redoubt's open interior beyond. Already, some who had entered rushed up the inner wall towards the fire-step, intent on clearing it of Danes on one side of the embrasure. An officer led them, flourishing a sword, but he was shot down before he reached the step. The men following gained it and drove at the Danes there with levelled bayonets.

Now more and more Austrians flooded through the embrasure, turning to scramble up the inner wall to join the battle on fire-step. Another group sprinted along the wall's base towards the next embrasure to take the gun there from the rear. Their charge was halted by rifle-fire from above and some threw themselves down behind any cover they could find, shelter entrances, water butts, stacked crates. Across the redoubt's open interior Granville's and Dawlish's people had turned to fire on them.

Every defender on the walls was now firing inward. Driven by corporals and sergeants, men were scuttling between the riflemen with open ammunition boxes, throwing down handfuls of cartridges beside them. More Austrians still arrived but on the far side of the redoubt a Danish crew had dragged their fieldpiece back from its embrasure and were straining on its wheel-spokes to slew it around. The Austrian impetus was slowing, but some troops were climbing up the inner wall to join their comrades who had gained the fire-step and were now hemmed in by Danes on either side.

A roar — the field-gun dragged from its position now hurled roundshot across the open interior towards the close-packed Austrians emerging from the opposite embrasure. It smashed a channel through them, killing and maiming and halting the advance in horrified shock. Dazed, reeling, the survivors were flailed by rifle-fire as the gunners sponged and loaded — solid ball again, for cannister would not discriminate friend from foe. The Austrians edged back into the body-strewn embrasure — not yet in panic, but close to it.

That came with the next roundshot that ploughed through them.

They broke, surged back, oblivious of the efforts of officers and sergeants to halt them, their wounded abandoned, their flight a headlong rout. Up on the fire-step the survivors of the Austrians who had reached it were throwing down their weapons, hands raised in surrender and despair. Down in the open centre others were doing likewise, a few too late.

The Danish rifle-fire from the walls was directed outward again and the guns opened with cannister once more. No regular Austrian lines now, no cohesion, no coordination between units, only ragged groups falling back towards the safety of their saps. At several points, determined men turned to make a stand as fugitives streamed past, but at last they too fell back. The retreating attackers were too dispersed, too far off by now for cannister, so the Danes were firing solid ball again to shear down the isolated groups that still held briefly firm.

Rifle-fire was now wasted and Granville was shouting for it to cease. Dawlish felt his energy drain, his limbs weak. He was exhausted. His rifle was hot to the touch and only now did he realise that his shaking hands were bleeding, skinned in the constantly reloading. His bayonet was blood-smeared but he had no recollection of how that had come about and the time just past — minutes? an hour? hours? — were a blur. His mouth was dry, his thirst a fire. Only the Danes were still firing, peasant faces that had seemed so stolid, and often so kindly, now set in savage intent to exact retribution for invasion. Krag – he looked like a coalminer – was shouting for them too to cease fire, kicking one man, dragging a rifle from another to get compliance.

And the firing died.

Not just from this redoubt, but from its counterpart to the west. Dawlish's world had contracted to yards only as he had battled for survival. Only now did he gain the first inkling of the full magnitude of the repulse. The greatest killing had not been here but in the centre-ground between the redoubts. The Austrian assaults on both positions had been to clear the flanks for a thrust towards the trench line that linked them. Even when those attacks had failed, that central drive was launched – a demented, unforgivable decision by the Austrian commander. Danish guns blasted cannister on the enemy thrust from either side. Breached though the trench was in several places, the steady volley-fire of the mass of reserves that Saabye had brought up behind it stopped any Austrian breakthrough.

But full understanding of that victory must wait. Now the aftermath, the search for living wounded among the dead, the revulsion at hideous wounds, the pity that all but paralysed. Bodies slumped on the fire-steps – Danish or Austrian or British, it made no difference, for all seemed equal now. Some moaned, some begged or wept, some lay in the lethargy of near-death, eyes dull and uncomprehending. Austrian prisoners had already been set to drag their comrades' corpses from the clogged embrasure or to roll them down from the parapets on to the ground outside. They would have to bury their own dead.

Out on the intervening ground small groups – walking wounded, three or four men carrying or supporting others – still retreated. Some brandished once-white shirts or handkerchiefs to signal that they had disarmed themselves, were no longer a threat. Others crouched by prostrate bodies, moving from one to the next in search of life.

Two more Danish companies arrived, released from uncommitted reserves. They took position on the fire-steps, freeing the troops who had borne the brunt to care for their fellows. There were seven British dead on Dawlish's section of the wall – Eltham, the marksman, among them, belly slashed open, entrails spilled, face ground by a boot. Nine had been wounded, five badly. The Austrians were many more.

After his first urge to nausea Dawlish found that he could distance himself from the horror. He improvised and twisted tourniquets, helped strap a shattered leg to a rifle for a splint, pushed a bundled handkerchief into a bleeding wound without flinching. It would come back to him later, he knew, wakening in terror in comfortable beds in darkened rooms, but for now he did not recoil. One by one, the stricken bodies were eased on to blankets and carried down with rough kindness.

In the redoubt's interior the wounded were laid in a line, friend and foe intermixed. A dozen of Surgeon-Major Hartling's orderlies had arrived – he himself had gone to the other redoubt with as many more. They staunched bleeding, bandaged where they could, gave laudanum, shook their heads over some. They had brought five farm carts and into their straw-strewn beds they loaded as many as they could of those who seemed to have some hope of survival. The remainder must wait. Some of the wounded were already crying out in pain as the unsprung carts jolted into their journey back to the church at Thyborøn.

The carts were back an hour later, and an hour after that again, departing each time with their loads of suffering. It was mid-afternoon now and a misty-rain was drifting in from the south-west, adding chill to the general misery. The remaining wounded had been brought into the shelters. The disarmed Austrian prisoners had been driven out to return to their lines – here, they would be liabilities, useless mouths.

Granville's batman had somehow brewed coffee and Dawlish was sharing it when Krag appeared.

"They're showing a white flag." He looked weary but jubilant.

"They're surrendering?" It sounded too good to be true.

"No. But they know they're beaten for now. They'll want a truce."

They mounted the wall to watch.

Out on no-man's land an Austrian rider was advancing, a bed-sheet drooping from an upright lance. He threaded his way between the bodies, ignored slumped shapes that came to pleading life and cried out to him. Some Danes on the fire-step cheered in derision. He halted a hundred yards ahead of the western redoubts. A wait, five, ten minutes.

"Friherre Saabye's thinking about it," Krag said. "If it were my decision, I'd let the whole lot of them rot out there. Nobody invited them here."

A white flag waved at last from the Danish rampart. Soon afterwards a single figure emerged on foot through an embrasure.

"Löjtnant Harmsen," Krag was watching through his glasses. "I know him. Good fellow." He laughed. "Saabye's rubbing in the salt. That Austrian's a major at the least. He won't be happy talking to a junior officer but he's got no option."

It took another hour to agree a truce. The Austrian returned to his lines, came back with another officer. Major Stavald met them as

Saabye's representative. Salutes, discussion, shaking heads, cold formality, agreement reached only when the light was failing and a light wind rising. The terms were harsh. A truce of thirty hours, beginning at six o'clock.

Through the night lanterns would bob in no-man's land, living sorted from dead by their feeble light, Austrian carts coming out to pick up the wounded. The burials would have to wait until morning. There would be little joy in looking down to see unarmed Austrians dragging bodies from below the redoubt walls, piling them like lumber into wagons, bringing them back to tumble in long trenches for priests to intone prayers over before the filling.

And if Thyborøn was to fall, it would not now be to the Austrians alone. That glory had escaped them.

For the Prussians would be here soon.

Chapter 19

FitzBaldwin recalled Dawlish and the other volunteers from her crew to the *Odin* two days later. The truce had ended, and the Austrian dead and wounded had been recovered, but there was no gunfire from either side, only a sullen and weary recognition of stalemate. For now.

"Nothing from Nolan," FitzBaldwin said. "For all we know he might be on the way here already with the connecting rod. We're not even sure if a telegram could still get through to Copenhagen, much less the message reach here."

"Once it's here it'll be installed in a day at most," Lorance was present also. "All else to be ready ahead for that. Your guns, Dawlish, most of all, your crews exercised, the turret turning smooth as cream."

Hanging unspoken, but palpable, was recognition – shame – that the *Odin* had lain impotent at the very moment for which she had come here. Caution, concern about her limited handiness with a single screw, fear of another grounding, had kept her safe inside the Limfjord. The Austrian assault might have been broken long before it could have reached the redoubts' walls had the ironclad been free to range along the shore and pour devastation from her Armstrongs.

The price of that caution was being emphasised by the mournful singing from the shore, the Lutheran hymns accompanying the Danish burials. They would not be the last. The church was full to overflowing with wounded and many would not survive. The *Hulde* paddle-steamer, due from Aalborg with supplies and reinforcements, was their only hope, the chance of evacuation to a well-equipped hospital there.

Odin was a paradise compared with the accommodation ashore. Dawlish had brought the volunteers who had come back with him straight to the boiler room. There they stripped off to have their clothing scalded with a steam hose to kill the lice and to wash themselves in warm water. He was shocked by the livid patches on the bodies of the men, even more when he realised that he was no different himself, that he had so quickly come to endure – if never accept – the torment of itch. It was a joy, a luxury, to pull on clean clothing.

Turret maintenance and exercises filled the day. He felt comfort in the routine obligations and duties, the small decisions, the solution of minor problems. Cold, cheerless and always damp, the *Odin* might be, but she offered hot food, an opportunity to wash, prospect of sleep in a cot. Other than for minor injuries, the volunteers from the crew who had joined the fighting ashore had come through unscathed and he sensed a pride among them for it. Bad as it had been, he felt the same himself. He had come through. He had not disgraced himself.

FitzBaldwin called for him that evening. "I'm going ashore. A conference with Friherre Saabye. You're not needed at it but you could come and visit poor Killigrew. The word about him isn't good. Not good at all."

It was dark when they came ashore. The sky was all but cloudless and the waning moon cast cold, silver light. Danish guards waited to escort FitzBaldwin to the headquarters at the school. Dawlish continued on alone to the church. He passed the lines of tents and improvised shelters, half-lit by the glows of dozens of meagre cooking fires. Small clusters of Danish troops crouched around them, some smoking, few talking, the overall impression one of morose stoicism.

A few lanterns lit up the ground around the church. Several peasants were standing with shovels beside a pit, the dug-up earth piled up beside it, waiting to fill it in again. Two orderlies upended a basket into it – there had been more amputations. Beyond, the new graves stretched back into the darkness, low mounds that had still not settled. Wood was too precious here for crosses to mark them. The stench was strong even before Dawlish reached the church door and he had to step aside to allow a stretcher to be carried out, the face of the body on it covered by a blanket.

He had steeled himself to enter. This hospital had seemed dreadful to him before, but he was still unprepared what it had now become. In the flickering lamplight it was impossible to discern any individual beds, only a sea of bodies, some still, some moving restlessly, some groaning, a few raving in the gloom. Orderlies and nurses were busy among them but none took any notice of him as he picked his own way towards the place where he had last seen Killigrew. He found what he thought was it. Three men lay in the bed there, head to heel. One might already be dead, another close to it and the third was stirring weakly, sweat gleaming on his face, his left arm truncated and bandaged above what had been the elbow. And a whiff of gangrene. He became aware of Dawlish's presence.

"Drei kleine Kinder." The words almost inaudible, German, not Danish. An Austrian, abandoned inside the redoubt. "Eine liebe Frau und drei kleine Kinder…"

The voice trailed off in infinite regret, eyes glistening.

Dawlish felt pity well up inside him. He could find no word, felt powerless, inadequate. He turned away, struck a lucifer, in its light scanned other nearby faces, saw no sign of Killigrew. He struck another, and another, shuffling aside with difficulty in the narrow space between the beds as a Danish orderly pushed past and swore at him. Despair was rising in him when he felt a pluck on his elbow.

"You're looking for your friend, monsieur?" The words French.

He turned. It was the senior Swiss nurse, Madame Racine. He feared to ask the obvious question. She answered it anyway.

"He's still with us. I'll bring you to him." Slack-featured, eyes red-rimmed, she looked a decade older than when he had last seen her.

Killigrew's bed stood alone in a corner, curtained off with blankets brought across from the *Odin*. He had no lantern by him but Madame Racine's showed that he was propped up to a half-sitting posture, hands limp before him, head lolling. He smiled weakly when he recognised Dawlish and he murmured something incomprehensible.

"You're looking better, sir, you're looking a lot better," Dawlish said, the words inane, but he could think of nothing else. He reached out, took the dying man's hand, felt it weak and warm. He did not want to let go of it.

"You can stay with him for a while," Madame Racine spoke of him as if he was already absent. "Not long, but he'll be glad of it." She left.

The decline had been fast and Killigrew was worse than Dawlish had expected. The smell of gangrene pervaded the entire church, but it was strongest here, all but smothering the odour of laudanum.

Killigrew was trying to speak, his voice almost inaudible when Dawlish dropped his ear close.

"You're a good fellow, Dawlish." He lapsed into silence, as if the effort had exhausted him.

An orderly pushed through the curtain, put down a wooden box for Dawlish to sit on – Madame Racine must have asked for it.

He had come prepared, had brought a pencil and notebook in case Killigrew wanted to dictate a letter. He saw now that he was past that. The mind behind the dull eyes was already distancing itself from life, had already slipped beyond sadness and regret, was close to the final departure. In China Dawlish had seen others die, a few fully conscious to the last, taking solace in prayer, or weeping, or raging against Providence. But this was different, a slow but steady ebbing for which no words of consolation could have meaning. Nothing could be done but sit and hold that limp hand and hope that it gave some slight comfort.

He could not guess how much time had passed, for Madame Racine had taken the lantern away. Beyond the blanket curtain were the low sounds of suffering, broken at random intervals by shrieks or raving, by orderlies calling to each other, by the noise of rushing feet. Killigrew tried to talk twice more but the words were unintelligible and he lapsed back into silence as Dawlish told him yes, it was all good, sleep now. Here, in this foetid darkness, he felt that he was on the brink of a great abyss. Pressure of a hand alone would not save Killigrew from it. He knew that he should be praying at this moment, but he could not.

The curtain twitched and dim light leaked in. In it, Dawlish saw the features of the Swede, Eleonora Blomqvist. She too had aged since he had last seen her, a worn middle-aged woman rather than the younger one whose image he had carried in admiration with him. The port-wine stain – that injustice of Fate – made her seem older still. He stood and invited her to sit.

"Madame Racine wouldn't allow it."

"But you'll stay a while?"

She would. But not for long

They drifted into whispered conversation.

"We could hear the cannon from here," she said. "We knew what would come here for us. It must be very terrible to fight, löjtnant."

"Not as bad as here. It's finished, it ends … but here…" He sought for words. "What you do here… I couldn't." He recognised in her a fortitude that was beyond him.

"One gets used to it."

"Can you speak German?".

"Why?" The question seemed to surprise her.

"There's an Austrian here, he's lost an arm, he's in despair and …" He could not bring himself to admit his own inadequacy, that the misery of it had driven him away.

"There are nine Austrians here," she said, "bad cases, too bad to move. Their people know they're here, that they're being looked after."

"How do they know?"

"Doctor Venel went across. Under a Croix Rouge flag. He was very fearful, we all were, in case the Austrians didn't understand it. But he went anyway."

"They knew what the flag was?"

"And the whole world will know it soon too," she said. "That a wounded man is not an enemy." Then suddenly, without warning, she began to weep.

It must have been pent up for days, Dawlish recognised, the same despair he felt in himself in the presence of this suffering. She had averted her face, was hiding it with her apron, and her shoulders were trembling. He wanted to reach out to hold her – he would have held his sister Susan in such a moment – but reticence prevented him.

She collected herself, dropped the apron, turned back to face him.

"I'm sorry, löjtnant. I keep thinking of my brother. That he might be like…" She gestured towards Killigrew. His eyes were closed but he was still breathing. Just.

"That Austrian, the one who lost his arm…" Dawlish was still troubled by the man's desolation. "Can somebody…"

"Most of the Swiss ladies speak German. They do their best. For him, for all of them." She pulled the curtain aside. "I can't stay longer."

He saw that she was embarrassed by what she might think her own weakness.

"I'm glad you're here," he said. "You, all of you –"

The report of a single cannon froze him. Long seconds and them the crack of an exploding shell.

And not far off. Then shouting and alarm outside even as that unseen gun blasted again.

For the first time, Thyborøn village itself was under fire.

*

The camp was in uproar, men rushing from huts and tents, some already forming up in their units under resolute officers and sergeants, others still blundering in confusion. Peasant labourers stumbled in confusion through the partial darkness and tripped over tent stays. Tethered horses plunged and whinnied. Cattle already doomed to slaughter on the morrow lowed in uncomprehending distress. Two shells only, then a third, had fallen to the west, but at no single point. Outlined against the moonlit sky, three thin billows of smoke told as much.

Dawlish pushed his way through the throng towards the school house. FitzBaldwin was there and he thought only to join him. Suddenly a flash – from the west, not from the south – and the boom followed. Then the explosion, somewhere beyond the fishermen's huts over towards the North Sea beach.

No doubt now. The fire was coming from the sea – it was essential to know more. He turned westwards, ran between tents, dodged past men in his path. The low dunes blocked the sea from his view but as he reached the first, and ran up, he knew already – and feared – what he would see.

He halted, out of breath, at the top. Out on the dark waters before him the faint moonlight showed only the slightest ruffling by a steady breeze, the horizon clearly defined against the sky above. Before he could take it all in, he saw a flash, flame jetting from a single weapon, the ship that carried it illuminated for a flickering moment before darkness enveloped it again. The report rolled past him – he recognised it for a twenty or twenty-four pounder. The shell impacted somewhere to his right on open ground, but even had it reached the huts the effect would have been slight. That vessel might trigger panic but could inflict no significant damage.

Another flicker, slightly further south – a second ship. Its shell dropped in shallow water fifty yards from the beach, its explosion flinging up a white fountain steaked with sand. The two vessels were too far out to land their shells any further inland. They might be creating confusion in the camp, might be ruining sleep, but for now they were a nuisance, not a threat.

Sounds behind, hoofbeats. He looked back, saw four horses halting. Three riders threw themselves off and hurried up the dune while the fourth held the beasts.

"It's you, Dawlish!"

It was FitzBaldwin, winded. Saabye and Major Stavald followed.

"Two of 'em, sir," Dawlish said, "They're –"

The roar of both vessels firing simultaneously drowned his words. One shell impacted on a dune-face to the right and the other must have shaved over, for it burst on the open ground just beyond. Both futile.

"Who are they?" Saabye shouted. "They can't be Austrians? Not yet! Are they Prussians?"

"Damn bold fellows, whoever they are" Something like admiration in FitzBaldwin's voice. "I'd thank you for your glasses, Friherre." He took them, pushed them to Dawlish. "You've keener sight than me. Tell me what you see when they fire again."

The next flash confirmed what Dawlish had surmised from what he had seen already.

"It's a gunboat, sir! Small, three masts, single funnel and –"

"Prussian, by God!" FitzBaldwin said. They've eight or ten like that, damned puny vessels."

"Puny, Captain FitzBaldwin?" Saabye said. "But slightly more useful than your *Odin!*" He turned to Stavald, spoke in Danish.

The major ran down the dune, mounted, disappeared.

"You're wasting your time, Friherre, if you're having artillery sent up here," FitzBaldwin sounded stung to bitterness. "It's better needed in your redoubts. Those fellows won't stand inshore any closer to be a problem."

Dawlish stepped back a few paces. He sensed the edge of hysteria in both voices and did not want to be a witness of two fine men in conflict.

"And you're sure they're not Austrian, captain?" Saabye said.

"They won't send anything that small, not so far from the Adriatic." FitzBaldwin's tone was conciliatory. "They're Prussians, all right, probably up here from the Weser or Elbe approaches. That's why they're confident in shallow water, and in darkness too. They're used to channels and shoals and sandbanks and they'll take no risks."

The gunboats had fallen silent, had headed out westwards into deeper water, dark shapes now barely visible.

"And the *Odin*, captain? How long more?" No sarcasm now in Saabye's tone, but something like weariness.

"It can't be long. A week at worst, not more."

"I'm getting tired of hearing that."

Other officers, Danes, arrived. FitzBaldwin excused himself.

"Come with me, Dawlish." At the bottom of the dune he left his borrowed horse with the orderly. "Let's walk. Better for talking."

They skirted the tents. The hummocks of the half-completed new defences lay to their right. From beyond there came the distant strains of the Radetzky for the first time since the failed Austrian assault. Grudged Austrian praise for Prussian daring and a mocking reminder to the Danes that their ordeal had not ended.

"There's bad news, Dawlish – that's why Friherre Saabye called the conference tonight. A messenger got through from Aalborg – he must have ridden his mount to death because the news is scarcely two days old."

"The Prussians, sir?"

"The Austrians. Two damn great frigates of their Levant squadron already on their way and a heavier force is readying to leave their base at Pola."

"Pola, sir?"

"On the Adriatic, close to Venice. Powerful vessels too, but they can't be here for another three or four weeks. It's the Levant frigates that count. They should be here by early May – the *Schwarzenberg* and the *Radetzky*. No wonder they're playing that bloody march again."

"How can we be sure, sir?"

FitzBaldwin laughed. "British consuls, Royal Navy vessels. We may be neutral but that's no impediment, not when a certain royal personage is keen to please his wife and spite his mother and his sister. Word was telegraphed through to Copenhagen. There's still a connection from there to Aalborg, though God knows for how much longer. A single troop of Austrian dragoons could cut it at any time."

They stepped aside as two nine-pound howitzers and their limbers passed. The horses dragging them looked emaciated, wretched.

"Damn stupid, pulling them from the redoubts," FitzBaldwin said. "Even if the Prussians come back in daylight there'll be no chance of hitting 'em. Wasted powder and shot and nothing more."

"These Austrian frigates, sir?"

"Powerful, good steamers too, I hear, not armoured Our people at Malta think highly of their commander, a chap called von Tegetthoff."

"So they're nothing like the *Odin*, sir?"

A sudden vision of glory, the twin Armstrongs, under Dawlish's own control, smashing one frigate to matchwood while the ironclad bore down upon the other, foam boiling over her ram. The prospect that had tempted him in Somerset seemed at last within reach. He was glad that he was here.

"Steady, Dawlish. *Odin's* still a cripple and there's still no word from Nolan."

"But it can't be long, sir, he might already be on the way and –"

"And if he is, then those two damn Prussian gunboats will be waiting. You think they're here to keep the garrison awake of nights? No! British merchant ensign or no, they'll stop and search Nolan's ship. She'll be carrying shell and charges too. War contraband, fair game. They'll be within their rights to turn her back and if she tries to run then their twenty-fours won't seem so puny anymore."

They had almost reached the Limfjord shore. Dawlish fancied that he could smell the church over to the left and wondered if Killigrew's ordeal there was not already at an end. Ahead, the *Odin* lay like some brooding, sullen, impotent monster.

Waiting for a single forged iron rod to bring her to deadly life.

Chapter 20

Two horsemen set out just after midnight to ride ninety miles eastward to Aalborg along the land north of the Limfjord. One was Krag, the other an artillery lieutenant with a reputation as daring rider. They were to follow different routes and authorised to commandeer remounts at any point on the way. Given the state of roads and tracks in the aftermath of a wet winter, it was unlikely that either could reach the telegraph office at their destination before evening. Saabye had not hesitated to allocate them – FitzBaldwin had swallowed his pride despite earlier bad-tempered exchanges and had gone to see him. The case he made was irrefutable – there was no option if *Odin* was to play the part she could.

FitzBaldwin had set Dawlish to encrypting the messages the riders carried – the keywords had been agreed before leaving Britain, one per sentence. He opened a copy of Scott's Ivanhoe that had been selected for providing them – first words of eight letters or more on successive pages. It was an exact duplicate of a volume held by Mr. Elmore Whitby back in Britain. Dawlish found satisfaction in the work – he was adept, for his uncle had taught him the Playfair system when he was a boy. It had been a game between them, the only one the dying consumptive had any strength left to play in his final months. This present task felt like an act of homage.

He went ashore to see the horsemen depart. Neither knew the content of the messages, only that they must get through and stand over the telegraphists as they tapped them out without delay. The telegraph line might be cut at any time – it was remiss of the Austrians not to have done so, indeed not to have taken Aalborg already. Whatever the final outcome might be at Thyborøn, Saabye's decision to hold it had proved correct, drawing forces away the Austrian thrust north through central Denmark. Vienna had placed prestige higher than strategic necessity.

But there were risks other than the telegraph being cut.

So many other 'ifs', Dawlish thought, as the riders cantered into the night. If shoes were not cast, if falls on rutted tracks were not to break the riders' necks, if fresh remounts could not be found. And the greatest 'if' of all. If Nolan and the SS *Althea* and the precious connecting rod had already departed from Newcastle.

It was a gamble, but there was no alternative. Not with a powerful Austrian squadron on the way and *Odin* still crippled.

For the presence of those puny Prussian gunboats off the Limfjord entrance had tipped the scales.

The *Althea* could not be let venture close to the Danish coast. The *Odin,* half-crippled or not, must meet her at sea.

*

The paddler *Hulde* arrived in late morning, two days after leaving Aalborg, her speed a crawl due to the two barges that strained on tows astern. She hugged the northern shore, safe from the token Austrian howitzer rounds that dropped five hundred yards short, and moored close inshore at Thyborøn. Some eight hundred men, gunners as well as infantry, packed the vessel and one of the barges. The greater part were reservists called back to the colours and they were all but the last effective Danish forces left north of the Limfjord. Now they were being ferried ashore and artillery – antiquated field guns by the looks of them, equipment of second-line units – was being lowered into waiting fishing boats from the second barge. Piled crates and kegs waited their turn, probably the last munitions Thyborøn would ever receive. Northern Denmark was being left all but defenceless to save Thyborøn.

Until Krag or his comrade returned there was nothing more to be done than to hold *Odin* in readiness. If lack of power on one shaft had not cut down both speed and handling, the ironclad had never been better prepared for action. All other damage had been repaired. The challenge was now to keep the crew usefully occupied, not just with drills alone – Dawlish's Armstrong crews most of all – but with maintenance. *Odin* had arrived here streaked with rust, for there had been little painting done before her hurried departure from the Laird's yard, but now metal had been scoured clean and brushed with the last, meagre, stores of red lead and paint. In the Royal Navy's livery of black hull, white upperworks and ochre masts, funnel and ventilators she would have looked magnificent. Now, black where paint supplies allowed, blotched with red where they did not, she seemed somehow both bizarre and sinister. The single operative engine had been oiled and greased to perfection, the shaft turned slowly under power each day to guarantee lubrication.

Dawlish went ashore in the evening. The typhus cases would stay in Thyborøn but the *Hulde* would carry wounded back to Aalborg on the morrow. He hoped – a vain hope, he suspected, but his mind rebelled against the alternative – that Killigrew might go with them. The church was as foetid as ever but more brightly lit with lanterns than was usual and there was a greater sense of bustle as patients were readied for the move. Surgeon-Major Hartling was passing between the beds to select those whom travel might not kill. He paused at each, bent to look closer, nodding or shaking his head to the orderly following him with a ledger. Doctor Venel was doing the same and Madame Racine was noting his verdicts. Nobody took any notice of Dawlish.

He sought out Killigrew's bed, slipped between the hanging blankets that screened it. Two men occupied it now, one still, perhaps in death, the other looking up with pleading eyes and struggling to speak.

"He died an hour ago at least." Madame Racine had seen him and had followed. A cold statement of fact, a voice long since too tired for pity. "Mademoiselle Blomqvist found him when she came to clean him."

"Where is he now?" Dawlish had hardly known Killigrew, had had no opportunity to warm to him before his wounding, and yet he felt bereft.

"He's outside – there's a small shed. You want to take the body?"

The question was unexpected, shocking, business-like.

"I'd like to see him first."

Fleeting images of a formal burial, an ensign on a coffin, seamen drawn up in ranks, FitzBaldwin reading the service from the Book of Common Prayer, dust to dust, ashes to assets, our dear brother departed. And it must be soon, before news came from Aalborg.

Madame Racine had already left. He went outside, found the shed. It must once have housed the sexton's implements, picks and shovels, tools for repairing the picket fence around the burial ground, but it had been extended with planks torn from demolished huts. It was unlit and there was no door. He should have borrowed a lantern but instead he struck a lucifer. Five long bundles on the floor. Bare feet protruded – ivory white – from beneath single blankets and jute sacks covered the heads. The shadows danced, the flame died and he had to strike another as he drew the sacks away, then pulled them back again over unknown faces. Killigrew was the fourth. There was no sense that this had ever been the man whom he had known. Corpses were always like that.

He went back inside, saw Eleonora Blomqvist helping a patient sit up while an older woman – a Swiss – changed a dressing. He waited until they were finished before he approached.

"We're busy," she said. "I can't talk now."

The Swiss was glaring at him. He ignored her.

"Lieutenant Killigrew, it was you who found him, Mademoiselle?"

"He wouldn't have felt anything. He'd just have drifted off"

204

When he had first met her, he had sensed suppressed horror. She sounded past that now, her voice, like Madame Racine's, too tired for pity.

"There's so much to do tonight," she said. "You should leave now. You can do no good here"

He went back to the *Odin*. A coffin of sorts must be constructed and a grave dug tonight to allow burial in the morning.

When Krag, exhausted but resolute, might already be drumming back from Aalborg.

*

A whistle blast announced the *Hulde's* departure while FitzBaldwin was reading the service. Men from the *Odin* lined one side of the grave, Blackwood and Granville and several of their men on the other. No Royal Navy ensign was available to cover the crude casket. The British mercantile colours under which *Odin* had escaped from Birkenhead had to do instead.

The grave was filled – the sound of the first shovelful of sand hitting wood was chilling – but no tears sprung to Dawlish's eyes. The desolation he felt was wider, deeper too, than regret for a single man, however great his sufferings. This was the tragedy that all were at last doomed to, and some vain hunger for advancement had hastened it for Killigrew. As it might do for himself. The bargain that FitzBaldwin had offered the dead young officer could not have been much different to that which he himself had made.

Back on the *Odin*, FitzBaldwin told him to climb with a telescope to the foretop and report. Two, three miles outside the Limfjord exit, far out of range to damage or be damaged, the Prussian gunboats loitered. There was a third there now.

More than enough to deny the ironclad her connecting-rod.

*

Rain returned that afternoon, wide grey columns that drifted in from the south-west under a gentle breeze. The overcast above offered no likelihood of it clearing soon. It brought misery to the soldiers and peasants shovelling sand at the new defences but it pleased FitzBaldwin.

"Two or three more days of this, that's all we need," he said. "Krag must be back by then. It surely can't take even that long."

The night passed, decks washed by an intermittent drizzle. Albemarle and Dawlish stood watches in turn, a melancholy occupation since there was little more to do than check lookouts. During the dry intervals, Dawlish fancied that the glow on the clouds above the Austrian camp was brighter than it had been before. He wondered if there were more campfires, if it indicated that the first Prussians had arrived and, if they had, how long before the next assault.

Daylight came, cheerless as the night itself had been. Lookouts in the fore and maintops shivered in oilskins, telescopes trained not only on the Prussian gunboats cruising two or three miles offshore but on the roads on the north side of the Limfjord, searching for sight of galloping horsemen. A whaler waited by the shore, ready to bring the longed-for arrival across.

And they waited in vain all day.

Precious coal was devoted to raising boiler pressure – not yet ready for sea, but enough not to over-stress the furnace firebricks when more would be shovelled in. Another turret drill – essential as it was, Dawlish sensed that the gun-crews were as sick of these endless exercises as he was himself. FitzBaldwin and Lorance paced restlessly and failed to look nonchalant as they scanned with their own glasses. From the south came sounds of Austrian howitzers, individual shots, perhaps for ranging, and once the muffled sound of music, the resented but jaunty Radetzky.

Dawlish was on deck when the whaler's hail came through the rain and darkness two hours before midnight. He sent a seaman to alert FitzBaldwin and Lorance as the craft drew alongside.

Krag had to be lifted on board. Even on deck a man had to support him. Exhausted, wet, mud-spattered, trembling, his voice was a whisper.

"There's a reply."

FitzBaldwin arrived, collarless.

"Get him to the wardroom. Fast! And bring him coffee, beef tea, something hot. Brandy too."

Dawlish steadied Krag as they went aft. Lorance and Albemarle had arrived too, and the word was spreading among the crew. They knew nothing of the import of Krag's mission but it was clear that something urgent and important was afoot.

They laid him on a bench. His numbed fingers fumbled with the buttons of his tunic, failed to open them. Dawlish did so instead and found the package nestling there and handed it to FitzBaldwin.

He ripped the protective cover open to find a single envelope. Within, a half-dozen sheets, telegram forms, strips pasted to them. He thrust them to Dawlish.

"Decipher 'em! Quickly."

He took them to his cabin, transcribed them quickly to a notebook, laid Ivanhoe beside it and got to work. It took him ten minutes, pulse increasing as he did. For Aalborg was indeed still linked by telegraph. The coded message that had flashed by overhead wire and undersea cable from there to Copenhagen on to Sweden, and through to Britain, had indeed reached Elmore Whitby in time. He had contacted Nolan immediately – the SS *Althea* was close to departure from Newcastle. The connecting-rod was already loaded. The last of the newly-manufactured three-hundred pounder shells from the Armstrong factory were on the quayside.

The *Althea* had received her new instructions in time.

And she was now headed towards a patch of sea 55° 11' North, 2° 59' East, where she was unlikely to encounter anything but fishermen casting their nets on the Dogger Bank.

*

High water, essential for safe navigation through the Limfjord mouth on one screw, would be just after three o'clock. Four hours for readiness – little enough to be done, for *Odin* had been prepared for this for days past. FitzBaldwin went ashore with Krag for consultation with Saabye and Blackwood. Small parties of Danish troops moved along each side of the fjord's mouth to ignite the lanterns that had been positioned previously on posts at hundred-yard intervals. Drizzle blocked view from the ship of all but the half-dozen nearest, but the pinpricks of light assured that the boundaries of the path seawards from beyond them were also marked.

Dawlish and his gunners manned the turret, stripped away the tarpaulin cover, loaded both Armstrongs, checked rotation, then waited, chilled by the mist of rain. Looking aft, he saw the shimmering orange glow above the funnel telling of boilers all but lifting their safety valves. All other lights had been extinguished. Forward, the leadsmen's platforms had been rigged on either side of the bows and Albemarle stood with the capstan party, ready to draw in the anchor cables. The only night-glass on board was in the foretop, the other lookouts equipped with telescopes only. FitzBaldwin and Lorance were on the bridge, smoking endless cigars, exchanging brief conversation.

And silence.

A stilling at last of the low gurgle of the incoming tide along the flank, the ironclad drifting to a new heading under the influence of the weak breeze alone. High water.

Then the order, the capstan creaking, gasps of effort from those thrusting on its bars, feet slipping on the wet unplanked iron deck, telegraph ringing on the bridge for dead-slow ahead, rung back for stop as the screw began to churn and the ship edged forward. Now the anchor breaking free, hauled in, screw biting again.

Dead-slow ahead – a slightly crabwise motion countered by Lorance, who had taken the wheel himself. The leadmen's cries began, alternately from port and starboard. The bows nudged towards the centre of dark half-mile expanse lying between the dots of light along the shores.

Down the centre of the channel, the course slightly sinuous, the asymmetric thrust of the starboard screw pushing the bows over to port, Lorance correcting constantly. The first lanterns were dropping astern, new ones emerging through the misty rain. The ironclad was crawling at some three knots but the progress was steady and the leadsmen were chanting depth enough for three fathoms under the keel. Now came the first hints of the ebb beginning, speed quickening. No call as yet from the tops, no indication of a Prussian gunboat close outside the entrance – only a madman would venture close inshore in such rain and darkness but one might well be present further out.

The lanterns to either side had drawn closer and the *Odin* was gliding through the narrowest stretch of the Limfjord's mouth, no sound but the leadsmen's reports, the swish of water alongside, the steady throb of the starboard engine, the slow beating of the screw, the odd half-audible exchange between FitzBaldwin and Lorance.

We're going to make it out.

Dawlish was on his seat, head above the turret rim, counting the lanterns – sixteen had been placed on land to port and one more to starboard, and already thirteen had been passed on either side. He could almost feel the gaze of the gunners beneath him, every face upturned, eager for information. The rain had grown heavier, visibility reduced yet further, only the closest pair of lights discernible.

The ironclad crawled on, snaking slightly as Lorance fought the bows' wandering urge. More lanterns passed, just two remaining, then

208

onwards steadily until they too dropped astern and the wide expanse of the North Sea lay in the darkness beyond.

A mile, another, and then a turn – a wobbling four points to port until the bows headed directly westwards to gain as much sea room as possible before turning again. Every eye in the tops and on deck was straining to identify any sign of the Prussian gunboats but there was no sighting of a faint funnel glow or of a dark mass emerging suddenly from the murk. *Odin's* engine was at half-revolutions, enough to deliver six knots, and the hull had settled into a gentle pitch and roll in a moderate swell from south-west.

Dawlish glanced towards land, saw none, felt cleansed, freed from the squalid realities of Thyborøn under siege. This was the element he felt happiest in, that would be the mainspring of his life.

As it might have been Killigrew's.

First light was now but an hour away. *Odin* had ploughed ten miles west, and the sky was clearing. Time soon to alter course to west-south-west.

Towards the Dogger Bank.

Chapter 21

Dawn broke on a calm sea, visibility seldom more than two miles, rain squalls drifting lazily north-westwards. Hands to breakfast, normal watches resumed, everywhere a sense of triumph mixed with relief. Released from the turret, Dawlish sent its rain-soaked crew in relays to the engine room to warm and dry themselves, did so last of all himself. By now, some lookout on a Prussian gunboat venturing close inshore must have discovered *Odin's* absence but confusion must now reign as to her destination. Speculation might be raging that she was heading towards the Jade and the Elbe estuary to resume prize-taking.

Now came brutal labour, raising and locking the hinged bulwarks that had been dropped during the escape to give the turret its full field of fire. It was late afternoon before all were in position, hiding the turret and providing protection against water surging across the decks should worse weather be encountered – as was likely. Seen from a distance, *Odin's* profile was, once more, not unlike that of a tramp steamer. Only close by, would the wicked forward curve of her ram reveal her for what she was.

Steady half-revolutions through the day, conditions unchanged, rain, and sometimes mist, invaluable cloaks even though they forced navigation by dead-reckoning. Only four times were other ships sighted – two small trading brigs, a huge barquentine most likely laden with Finnish timber, a steamer identifiable by her grime, even at a distance, as a collier. None passed close, nor showed curiosity, disappearing on unchanged courses into the murk.

On through the night. Dawlish took over the middle watch and during it the wind began to rise, waves with it, so that when he handed over to Albemarle at four-o'clock there was every prospect of worse to come.

As it did. Not a full storm but by mid-morning the sea was piling up, foam stripping from breaking waves and running from them, wind-blown, in long streaks. *Odin* ploughed directly into this sea, her pitch considerable, the forecastle on occasion plunging under, rising again through the white surge, dropping again. Water flowed over the decks, sought any pathway below, flowed out through the bulwarks' freeing ports with each roll, penetrated, to Dawlish's concern, through the narrow gap between turret-edge and deck. He set the gun-crews bailing below the turret, first with buckets, then with a hand pump. The scum of grease on the sloshing surface confirmed the roller bearings being washed clean – new lubrication would be needed once this weather had passed.

It was now that the lack of a second screw was worst felt, bows falling off to port, the helmsman fighting them, sometimes regaining heading too late to prevent a vicious corkscrew roll. Lorance had taken the forenoon watch but he seemed elated rather than otherwise when Dawlish replaced him at midday.

"I love this ship," he said. "One screw or two, the Union's got nothing like her." His face was wet with spray, rain running down from his sou'wester, dripping from his long oilskin. "And this," he waved towards the sea ahead, "it's a man's life, couldn't ask for more. You relish it too, Mr. Dawlish?"

"I do, sir." Dawlish knew that, for all the discomfort, this moment satisfied him, suspected that others like it always would.

Lorance made no move to go below. Dawlish sensed that something was unsaid, but coming. At last the American gestured towards the port bridge wing. "A word with you, son. Over there."

They braced themselves against the rails, out of hearing of the helmsman and the seamen by him.

"She's *Odin* for less than another four weeks," Lorance said. "Prussians or Austrians or the devil himself notwithstanding, she's *Galveston* on the ninth of May. That's the deal and Captain FitzBaldwin will be gentleman enough to honour it. We'll sail her into a neutral port, British or Norwegian as the situation suits, and the captain and whoever wants to go with him will leave."

He paused. Dawlish guessed what was coming.

"The question is if you'll want to leave too," Lorance said. "You know the guns, you did well ashore, you'll never get a chance like this again. And money in it too if that's what you want, though I doubt it."

"Hopper can take my place and I've heard him say he'll be glad to remain."

"I'm not talking about Hopper. A good man, but I don't just need a turret captain. The *Althea's* bringing another man to replace you as gunnery officer. But I need watchkeeping officers who can navigate and you've all the makings of a good one. And a fighter too."

"I couldn't –"

Lorance cut him off. "It wouldn't spoil your British prospects. Bulloch will see to it so that fellow Whitby can get it squared. You wouldn't be the only one. You know how many half-pay British captains

211

are running the blockade into Charleston and Wilmington and God knows where else besides? Do you think your Admiralty doesn't know it, nor your government either? Nobody's going to lose their commission or spoil their prospects, not when they've been sailing under aliases and gaining damn valuable experience."

"It's not that," Dawlish said.

A memory was strong within him. The smell in the empty hold of a vessel that HMS *Foyle* had run down off Brazil some sixteen months before. He had been part of the boarding party. Splintered wood had shown where chains and fetters had been ripped free and cast overboard during the chase. No hard evidence remained that slaves had previously been carried – there had been none on board at the time, for she had been Africa-bound. Human ordure had soaked into the timbers with every crossing, its stench a foetid legacy, but testimony which no court would recognise. The slaver had gone free.

"No, sir. It's not that. Not that at all."

"What is it then, son?"

It was hard, almost impossible, to answer. He liked Lorance, admired him even – his professionalism, his calm courage, his willingness to serve under an equal and give his loyalty. A leader, not a driver. Hard to imagine a whip in his hand.

"It's the cause, isn't it" Lorance said. "The Confederacy?"

Dawlish nodded. Not just that squalid slaver. Reading *Uncle Tom's Cabin* as a boy of nine, half-fascinated, half-horrified, weeping over it with his sister and his nurse. His father, a man of no little coarseness, first mocking them for sentimentality, then reading it himself, being no less outraged than they.

"Do you own slaves yourself, sir?" He had to ask it.

"No. No, Mr. Dawlish, I don't hold slaves and I don't hold with slavery. Not me, not my father nor my brother. Preachers both, they've stood their ground against it, warned that it would bring God's judgement down upon us. And it has."

"But you're fighting for –"

"For the rights of Virginia, of another dozen states. Rights that in time will allow us to bring that evil to an end in a way our people can accept. Not foisted on us by Yankee abolitionists who want to know nothing of the practicalities or of our way of life." His voice had been rising. Now he checked himself. "We're proud people, Mr. Dawlish, too proud to be dictated to."

"It can't be right, sir."

Lorance lifted his hands in a gesture that conveyed something like despair. "You don't see it, son, do you? So damn few over here do, even if they're ready to do deals with Jim Bulloch when it makes money for them or when it suits a royal prince"

"No, sir." It pained Dawlish to say it. "I don't see it."

"I'll leave you to your watch then. No need to mention anything to FitzBaldwin." No hint of bitterness in Lorance's voice as he turned away. "The offer stands. Think about it."

"I'll think about it, sir."

And Dawlish knew he wouldn't.

*

Late afternoon, still overcast, high seas, patches of rain.

Dead reckoning indicated that *Odin* had reached the point of rendezvous with the *Althea* but the error accumulated through battle with wind and wave might well be one of miles. The presence of fishing boats – too intent on their own struggles to take much heed of *Odin* – was confirmation that the Dogger Bank lay beneath. But of *Althea* there was no sign, though she should have reached here long before now. With visibility so limited, she might well be just a few miles away, searching too, the blind seeking the blind as the long spring evening died into darkness. There was nothing for it but to decrease revolutions, breast the waves and wait for dawn.

They found each other soon after first light. They drew close – a cable's length – and held position.

"That's Nolan waving." FitzBaldwin's telescope was trained on *Althea's* bridge as his son took a whaler across. He passed it to Lorance. "I suspect that those are the fellows you need?" They were crowded along the flank and several had climbed rigging and ventilators for a better view. Volunteers – mercenaries – to augment *Odin's* crew for a month and take *Galveston* raiding on the world's oceans thereafter.

"Looks like enough of them. Bulloch's been busy." Lorance was scanning them. "Let's hope he's chosen well."

The whaler had reached the *Althea's* side, was plunging and rising eight or ten feet with every wave. It failed twice to draw alongside in time to allow Albemarle to jump at the moment of crest. He succeeded on the third attempt, grasping the Jacob's ladder and hauling himself up as the whaler dropped below him and stood off. Dawlish was glad that he had not been assigned the duty. Such transfers always frightened him and he hoped that it did not show when they were unavoidable.

He was standing close to FitzBaldwin and Lorance and recognised concern in their voices.

"Too bloody rough to risk it. They'll rip each other apart if we bring them alongside," FitzBaldwin said.

"Just the connecting-rod? The whaler can take it, Nolan too. All's ready for them in the engine room."

"We just can't risk it. We'll wait. This weather can't last, not at this time of year. Another day at most."

Albemarle was back, cold and soaked and carrying an oil-skin package. His father disappeared below with it. Ten minutes later he sent for Dawlish.

"More deciphering for you."

Only two of the documents received had been encrypted, those whose contents should not be known had the *Althea* been intercepted. Mr. Elmore Whitby was taking no chances when an august personage's involvement was concerned. Dawlish worked fast, brought the full messages to FitzBaldwin within the hour. The first was a surprise, a message originating in Copenhagen and relayed by Whitby.

"Three Danish vessels coming from the east coast." FitzBaldwin handed the sheet to Lorance.

"Powerful?"

"Two of 'em steam frigates, *Jylland* and *Niels Juel*. To blockade the Jade and the Elbe and lure those Austrian frigates there, keep 'em away from the Baltic. Until the Danes get there to relieve us, we're to blockade with *Odin*."

"How long?"

"Four or five days."

"It's madness," Lorance said. "With the Prussians on the way there, shouldn't we be at Thyborøn?"

"No choice about it. Saabye must take his chances."

"Any news of the Austrian ships?"

The second decrypt had carried reports from Malta.

"Sighted off Messina a week ago," FitzBaldwin said "Time aplenty to give us an unhindered blockade before they reach the North Sea. They won't be here before early May."

"Anything more of that Yankee frigate?"

"Nothing."

Hanging unspoken was the awareness that from midnight on May 8th *Odin* would be *Galveston*. The Southern Confederacy had no quarrel with Austria or Prussia, no commitment to Denmark, and had a war of its own to fight.

Less than four weeks to go.

*

The near-gale blew itself out in the night and by morning the sea, though still choppy, was calm enough to drop *Odin's* starboard bulwarks and drape rope fenders over the side. The *Althea* edged in close, lines were cast, and the two vessels drew together. Continuous attention to rudders and revolutions must now keep them bow-on to the diminishing sea.

The connecting-rod was first across, eight-feet in length and wrapped in sacking, wooden planks strapped along it for protection. It swung across from *Althea's* foresail yard and was lowered close to the hatch above *Odin's* engine room. Suspended then by block and tackle from a temporary shear-legs, improvised from spare topsail yards, it inched down into the passageway between the engines. Only then was the protection stripped away to reveal the mirror-smooth iron rod and the bronzed bearings at either end. For all its mass, it was a thing of beauty, forged, machined and polished with the precision of a delicate watch.

Nolan had brought three artificers with him, two from a Newcastle shipyard, another with a dozen years in the navy. Bulloch's gold had tempted them to Confederate service, just as it had enticed fifty-three more seamen volunteers. Down in the engine room, Nolan's crew, newcomers and old hands alike, began the cautious work of installing the connecting-rod, positioning first the great split-bearing on the engine's cross-head. Slow, cautious, meticulous work stretched ahead to complete the link to the propeller shaft. Beside them, the starboard engine rotated slowly and held the vessel bow on to the unseen waves.

Dawlish saw none of it. He had been set to organising the newly arrived seamen, recording names, assessing experience, allocating them to watches. Now, for the first time, *Odin* was close to the manning level she had always needed. The majority of the newcomers were British – merchant seamen, a few with whaling experience, many ex-Royal Navy – but there were French and Dutch and Swedes also, even a single black Jamaican. They stowed their gear – for many, just pitiable bundles – and were sent back on deck to assist in stores transfer.

And not just seamen either, but two officers also, a taciturn Dutchman of forty and an American scarcely older than Dawlish. He saw them only from a distance as they supervised stores transfer from the *Althea*.

She had come heavily laden, not just with extra shells and charges for the Armstrongs, and tons of coal in sacks, but with crate upon crate of tinned food, bottled lime juice and medicines. There was rough work garb for the crews, blankets and boots and oilskins, and cans of whale oil for the lights and lanterns, kegs of grease for the engine room, coiled rope, spare canvas, timber. *Odin* might avail of these supplies for a few weeks but they were *Galveston's* stores. She should have set out from Birkenhead provisioned like this for her raiding voyage had she not been forced to make a fast escape. Bulloch must have already received part-payment for *Odin's* services, Dawlish thought, enough to stock this ship for months at sea.

The ships lurched and rolled and ground against each other even in the improved weather conditions, mangling fenders, scouring iron flank on iron flank. Every item brought across was a triumph as men strained on ropes and blocks squealed and loads were swung over and dumped on *Odin's* deck. Toes and fingers were crushed and bruised as stores were shifted and brought below, Dawlish and Albemarle keeping tally. Replacement shells and charges were hoisted into the turret and the bunkers were filled to overflowing, the remaining coal stacked in sacks on the open deck, arranged to give the Armstrongs the widest possible arc of fire.

Visibility remained good – too good – all through the day, clear to the horizon, enough to show distant sails or smudges of smoke from hull-down steamers. None deviated to investigate but several curious fishing boats did draw near. One, from Grimsby, was summoned alongside and cod and haddock purchased. Transfer of stores went on into late evening and only as light faded did FitzBaldwin order the vessels apart for the night.

Dawlish snatched a brief meal in the wardroom, reading as he did one of the British newspapers the *Althea* had brought. A correspondent with the Prussians marvelled at scale of the Danish defences at Dybbøl, even more at the power of the sustained Prussian bombardment, the imminence of a mass assault that must surely carry the positions and end the war. It was madness for the Danes not to have sued already for an armistice. And no mention of Thyborøn. There was no newspaperman there and therefore it did not exist.

216

"May I join you, sir?"

The young American. He was holding out his hand.

"Welborne, Travis Welborne. Lieutenant, Confederate States Navy."

Dawlish introduced himself in his own name, mentioned his alias also.

"You command the turret, I gather," Welborne said. "I understand that I'm to replace you when you leave. I'll value learning from you, sir, I surely will."

"You're a gunnery officer yourself?"

Welborne laughed. "Better say a gun-captain, never much more. Only a midshipman in the federal navy when we seceded. And river service ever since. Fighting Yankee tyranny with whatever we could put together. Railroad rails for armour, timberclads, any gun we could get our hands on. Poor men's ships. Nothing like this *Galveston*."

She was *Odin* still, but Dawlish did not correct him.

"You're a smoking man, sir?" Welborne searched inside his tunic, produced two large cigars. "Prime Havanas, sir, picked 'em up on my way through."

He had escaped from Mobile on a blockade runner, had spent a week in Cuba, had taken passage to Cadiz and on to Britain to meet Bulloch. Other Confederate officers were following, he said, not just to join this ironclad, should they arrive in time, but any other commerce raiders that could be financed. The *Alabama* – last heard of taking American prizes off Malacca – had shown the way.

"We'll hit the Yankees where it hurts them most," he said. "In their pocket books, their coffers, the only damn things that worry them."

Dawlish sensed a vehemence that was absent in Lorance but he liked the easy manner, the self-confidence, sensed that this could be a good comrade. And for that reason, he would not probe this man's stance on slavery, would not want to hear support for it. Better not to know and to concentrate on business instead.

"You'd like to see the turret and the Armstrongs?"

Welborne would.

*

Work in the engine room continued through the night. Dawlish, when he came off the morning watch, went below to see progress.

"Almost ready, sir." Nolan looked exhausted but proud. "All in place, all tightened up, ready to try a revolution."

But not under steam, not yet. Instead, jacks pushed on the crank of the port propeller shaft, edging it around a few degrees, were reset to thrust again, repeating the process until a full three-sixty had been achieved. Dawlish watched in fascination, impressed, as he always was, by the exactitude of machining, the precise fit of parts, the crosshead inching down and up again as the shaft rotated. And most of all by Nolan's expertise and pride, the skill of a man who would never have been granted entry to a British wardroom and not to be made welcome there if he had.

"I think Captain FitzBaldwin would like to see this," Nolan was satisfied by a second smooth rotation.

FitzBaldwin came, Lorance with him. They demanded a third rotation with the jacks. The shaft crept around, no hint of binding.

"You might want to open the steam valve yourself, captain," Nolan said, "A quarter turn, slowly."

"The honour's yours, Mr. Nolan," FitzBaldwin said.

The engineer cracked it open. A low hiss of steam, the piston creeping down, crosshead gliding on its guides, the propeller shaft shifting into slow rotation.

Odin was ready for war.

Chapter 22

Last stores taken on board, *Odin* headed east-south-east in mid-afternoon over a calm sea, leaving the *Althea* to return to Newcastle. Heligoland lay some two hundred miles ahead and at the current speed – seven knots, economical for coal – she would be off the Jade Bight in thirty hours.

Dawlish did not relish what lay ahead. Action against the Austrians had not troubled his conscience – brutal it might have been, but it matched armed men against armed men, and both sides accepted the risks. But there had been something squalid – blackguards' work indeed – about the interception and looting and burning of merchant shipping. It seemed an assault against civilians without means of defence, a ruin of livelihoods. He did not share his concern with the American, Welborne, for whom he had had a second seat mounted on the turret's inner rim. They would sit side-by-side, master and pupil, when it next went into action. Welborne had already made himself familiar with the guns. Now he hungered to use them. For him, the prospect of months of raiding lay ahead. He had not encountered its reality yet and Dawlish wondered if in time he too would feel about it as he did himself.

The Dutch officer, van der Horst, had taken Killigrew's place and had already stood a watch. He had ignored Dawlish's greeting in the wardroom at breakfast. His face, above a dark greying beard with no moustache to accompany it, looked set in permanent disapproval. When he turned his head, Dawlish saw that his right ear was missing, the area around it a livid, hairless scar.

"What do you know about him?" Dawlish asked Welborne.

"An officer, Dutch navy. Mr. Bulloch warned me never to allude to his face. A gun exploded and several fellows were killed and he was found at fault. It's unclear if he was dismissed or if he resigned. He needs money for a wife and God knows how large a brood."

"Did he talk to you on the *Althea*?"

"Not a word. Whenever I saw him, he was reading a great big black bible."

"Lively company to go raiding around the world with," Dawlish said. "You'll have lots of fun in the wardroom."

"Crews are easy to find, Bulloch says. Officers are harder. He's got to take what he can."

The *Odin* was entering frequented shipping lanes again, was sighting both sail and steam, but did not close to investigate. The rearing hummock of tiny British-held Heligoland lay to the east when the late evening sun dropped against a red sky in the west. Engines throttled back, the ironclad would cruise slow racecourse circuits until dawn, and ignore the now more-frequent lights that passed in the dark.

Early morning, north of the Jade, saw the first capture. A small Prussian-flagged steamer blundered from a haze over a calm sea. *Odin* surged alongside. A single rifle shot in the air was enough to ensure instant compliance with the order to heave to. A whaler went across and Albemarle boarded with four men. No resistance, the captain and crew stupefied by their sudden misfortune. The whaler came back with information. The *Ludwig Wermuth* of Lübeck, three-hundred tons, bound for Hamburg with a cargo of jute sacking from Dundee. FitzBaldwin's decision was to take off the crew and burn her.

All over in an hour. The crew – three officers and eight men – filing on board and taken below, the captain too stunned to complain. The deckhouse set alight, coal fed into the furnace, safety valve screwed down, Albemarle the last man to leave the drifting vessel. First smoke, then flames, and the *Odin* already three miles south when the report of the boiler's rupture reached her.

"It seems too easy." Welborne had watched in fascination.

"It is," Dawlish said. "It's remembering it afterwards that's hard." He was glad he did not have to deal with the captives face-to-face as Albemarle had to do.

"A darned sight easier than the Yazoo or Mississippi," Welborne said. "No Yankees trying to shoot your head off. I won't complain."

He volunteered to join the next boarding party but he had to wait. The vessels encountered through the rest of the day were neutral and FitzBaldwin had no intention of stopping them to investigate whether they carried stores of war. Diplomatic complications must be avoided. It was enough that *Odin's* presence be known, that Prussian-flagged trade would not leave port, that Berlin would importune Vienna for its frigates to be directed to break the blockade. And to divert them from confrontation with the Danish warships supporting resistance to the Prussians at Dybbøl. Destruction of a few more unsuspecting vessels heading to or from Bremerhaven or Hamburg could only make Berlin's demands more difficult to resist.

Two more prizes the following day – a topsail schooner carrying oranges from Spain and a large brig with uncured hides from the

Argentine. No resistance, only an anti-climax for Welborne when he boarded with Albemarle, no triumph in herding the crews back to *Odin*, enduring the shouted protests of a captain who had left Quequén before outbreak of war and had known nothing of it until now. Fires again, flames racing up tarred rigging and engulfing flapping sails, blazing hulls drifting away with the light wind, billowing smoke columns visible for miles. As was intended.

More neutrals. *Odin* came close and, satisfied of their identities, drew away again. They passed on unhindered, but with what Dawlish sensed was something like disdain. He felt the same within himself.

He stood the first watch that night, eight to twelve, cruising repeated slow tracks east to west and back again twelve miles south of Heligoland, well clear of the shoals to the south. The sea was calm, the sky clear but dark due to the new moon. The engines were turning smoothly and, as he paced the bridge, he felt a surge of pride that this iron beast had been entrusted to him for four hours. That feeling ended when he remembered that three dozen men were locked in squalid confinement below. There were those among them, merchant officers, who would not hesitate to risk their own lives and vessels to aid fellow-mariners in distress, men who had attained modest prosperity through years of hardship. It had pained him to see their humiliation and despoilment, and it had worried him to see the seamen with their few wretched belongings. That they had their lives, that they would be placed aboard some new capture and let go free, was no consolation. He felt soiled by this work, depressed that there was more of it to come.

As it would on the morrow.

*

Odin turned eastwards at sunrise, towards the approaches to the Elbe estuary, a promising hunting ground for shipping heading for Hamburg. They had taken prizes here before but, rather than venturing closer inshore, it was better to loiter north of Cuxhaven and remain just outside the sandbanks and mudflats bordering the narrowing channel that led to the great port. Five vessels were investigated before midday, all neutral.

"Deck there!" Crowther, again at the foretop, arm extended towards the south-east. "A brig. Maybe a Prussian ensign."

Dawlish was sent up to join him. He followed Crowther's finger — it was brig indeed, six or seven miles distant and headed northwards. He took the glass. The ensign drooping at the stern might well be Prussian — he could be no more sure of it than Crowther.

"You're not certain?" FitzBaldwin questioned him when he came down. "But worth trying, maybe?"

"Yes, sir."

FitzBaldwin turned to Lorance. "What do you think? At the very worst she's neutral."

"If she's Prussian she's either got a damned stupid captain or a damned brave one. He must have heard of our presence before slipping out of Hamburg. He's banking on us still being off the Jade."

"We'll try her," FitzBaldwin said.

An interception course now, three-quarters revolutions — no need to waste coal. Thirty minutes would bring *Odin* alongside.

And soon after, another call from Crowther. No doubt of it. A Prussian ensign. A legitimate quarry. The brig was hardly moving, ghosting on the lightest of breezes.

Two more vessels in sight — another under sail and a dark smoke plume drifting from a funnel just visible above the southern horizon.

"Both trying to slip out from Hamburg before we got here," FitzBaldwin was pleased. "All to the good if they're Prussian."

If they were, then sight of *Odin* must have given no alarm for they were still coming on. Her hinged bulwarks were still raised and from a distance her lines were still those of a merchantman.

"That fellow's piling on the coal." FitzBaldwin was studying the steamer that had emerged above the horizon. He passed his glass to Dawlish. "What do you make of it?"

The smoke was thicker, darker than before, no longer drifting upwards but falling in heavy billows that half-engulfed the hull. Too-hastily fed, the furnace could not immediately cope with the added fuel. Soot and embers must be showering from the funnel.

"She's seen us, sir," Dawlish said. "No doubt of it. And she's pressing on hard."

Crowther shouted again from the foretop, pointed southwards. Another steamer, a mile to westward of the first and further distant. That plume was dark also, another fast-fed furnace, another fore-shortened hull.

All glasses on the bridge focussed on her. Impossible to count the masts, for she was head-on, but the yards were bare of sails, and the smoke spilled from a long, thin, ochre funnel. A white wave piled beneath her bowsprit. No doubt of her intentions. This second vessel was also driving towards *Odin*. Only one conclusion was possible.

Prussian gunboats.

"They're madmen," Lorance said. "It's suicide to engage us."

"They know damn-well that it is. Brave fellows." Admiration in FitzBaldwin's tone. "They're making a matter of honour of it and we'll oblige them." He turned to a seaman. "Rouse Mr. van der Horst." The Dutchman was sleeping after standing the morning watch. "My compliments, and ask him to join us."

Lorance himself took the wheel. *Odin* swung into a sixteen-point turn, as if turning away, half-revolutions called for to slow her and draw the gunboats on. All hands to their stations now.

FitzBaldwin spoke to van der Horst. "Have the bulwarks dropped."

"All, sir?"

"All, and smart about it, port and starboard. I want maximum turret arcs. Rifles in the fore and maintops, four each, my son one of 'em – he's a good shot. Everybody under cover once the bulwarks are down and the fire hoses laid out." He turned to Dawlish. "Man the turret and load. Bursting shell in both guns, then train on the starboard beam."

"What will the range be, sir?" Hitting land targets had proved difficult, moving ones immeasurably more so.

"As bloody near point-blank as we can make it. Fire on my word only, but the exact moment is yours. Just before the peak of the roll. If you're in doubt, hold fire, wait for the next roll."

The bulwarks were clanging down as the gun-crews entered the turret. Welborne took his seat next to Dawlish at the rim and below them Hopper supervised the loading – fast and easy in these calm conditions. Then the turret was rotated to bear on the starboard beam, brakes locked, the weapons run out. FitzBaldwin could be heard shouting down the voice-pipe to Nolan in the engine room to build pressure, stand by for full revolutions. Albemarle was in the foretop with three seamen – two of them had been with Dawlish in the redoubt during the Austrian attack, stalwart men. Telescope to eye, Albemarle called down reports on the gunboats' positions. The bridge and superstructure abaft the turret made it impossible for Dawlish to see them. They had drawn abreast, he heard, three cables between them, were still ploughing on a mile and a half astern. They must have attained maximum speed – eight or nine knots – and were steadily overhauling *Odin*.

Ironclad or gunboat, none could yet bring a weapon to bear since what they mounted could not fire directly ahead. Minutes more – the separation closing. Dawlish glanced back, saw FitzBaldwin and Lorance on the bridge and looking astern, calculating the moment for turning. No sign of van der Horst – he must be aft, ready to take over steering from the emergency position there in the event of a hit on the bridge.

The telegraph bell rang – FitzBaldwin's order for full speed. Down in the engine room Nolan would be opening the steam throttles slowly and watching the revolution counters and smoothing the increase. A minute passed, but now the building of the vessel's speed was palpable as the throb of the beating pistons rippled through the hull and water climbed up the ram and broke free in a high vee of bow-wave. On *Odin* ran, speed still mounting, until the screws' churn settled at a steady rhythm.

"How fast now?" Welborne broke the silence – though he should not.

"Maybe ten knots," Dawlish said. *Odin* had never run trials over a measured mile but the shipyard had promised as much.

Another minute and then FitzBaldwin's order to the helmsman. The wheel spun. Long seconds passed before the rudder gained effect and the bows swung over to starboard and heeled in the broad curve of a sixteen-point turn. Dawlish saw the easternmost of the gunboats sweep into view as the ironclad lay briefly beam on to them. Less than a mile distant and still coming on. And, far astern of them, another smoke plume, a third unit hurrying in their wake.

Odin sustained her turn, straightened, drove south on a track that would carry her just east of the two foremost gunboats. Dawlish could see them just off the starboard bow, their flanks increasingly exposed as the ironclad ploughed towards them. The first Prussian must have slowed to allow the second to draw level two or three cables off her port beam but now the foam beneath their bowsprits indicated that they were both at full speed again. A mile behind, the third gunboat was forging on with no less resolution.

"Mr. Dawlish!" FitzBaldwin's shout. "Hold fire, mind you! Only on my word, no matter what!"

The first gunboat was almost fully masked by the superstructure ahead of the turret, but along its side Dawlish could see the Prussian's bows. *Odin* was rushing at her on a collision course at a combined closing speed of close to twenty knots. It flashed on Dawlish's mind that warships had never engaged at such speeds in all history.

"We're going to ram!" Welborne's yell was jubilant. "We're saving Confederate shells!"

The Prussian captain had recognised that too. The gunboat's helm was over and she was swinging to port. Dawlish could see her forepart – jutting bowsprit and foremast, a crew standing by a pivot-mounted cannon abaft it, a sixty-eight pounder or something close to it.

He shouted down. "Hopper! Get the men down! Brace yourselves! Lie down if you can!" He gripped the sides of his seat, fearful of being thrown from it but fascinated, almost hypnotised, by what seemed inevitable.

The gunboat was just off the starboard bow and he could see yet more of her now – men on the bridge, funnel, ventilators. At this moment, at this range, *Odin's* Armstrongs could have blasted this vessel apart, had the turret been angled forty-five degrees ahead of the beam. Rifle-fire crackled from Albemarle's men in the foretop. A Prussian gunner threw up his arms and pitched down in the very moment that the weapon he served roared. Flame blasted from the muzzle and an instant later came an explosion somewhere aft on *Odin,* the shock reverberating through her even to the turret itself.

And then contact.

Not the brutal impact of the sharp ram, not the cleaving smash through the frail gunboat's side that *Odin* had driven for, but a long scrape, flank against flank, abaft the Prussian's funnel. Hull ground on hull as the ironclad tore at bulwarks, ripped their planking away. It lasted seconds and felt like an aeon. Dawlish saw faces frozen in shock on the gunboat's deck, a broadside-mounted cannon aft bucking against its tackles and breaking free, a boat swung out aft shattering to fragments, standing rigging parting and whipping, the mizzenmast tottering.

A cry from *Odin's* foretop, a rifleman shaken from his perch, limbs flailing in the long second before the dreadful smash on the forecastle. Two seamen there dashed to him from cover, recoiled – nothing to be done – and ran back.

The grinding ended. The gunboat was left somewhere astern. Dawlish could not see her, but he did see smoke pouring from somewhere abaft *Odin's* funnel, a flicker of flame, van der Horst and a small group dragging a hose. The Prussian shell had struck high above the armour, must have detonated somewhere within the superstructure.

Odin's helm was over again, FitzBaldwin carrying her into a broad sweep to starboard that would bring her back to finish the stricken gunboat. As the turn increased Dawlish could see her on the starboard beam. She was still under way – only just – but her mizzenmast was down and a tangle of spars and rigging trailed astern like a vast sea anchor. Men were clustered at the counter, hacking the wreckage free. The vessel was an almost stationary target.

"Look, Dawlish!" Welborne was grabbing his elbow, and pointing over the port quarter.

There was the second gunboat, coming on with a bone in her teeth to pass aft of *Odin* and towards her crippled sister. And a mile astern of her, still closing, was the third.

"They're madmen" Dawlish's remembered Lorance's words.

Slow at their best and wooden-hulled, outgunned, incapable of penetrating *Odin's* armour and at the mercy of her ram, speed and manoeuvrability, the Prussian gunboats were not flinching.

"Mr. Dawlish!" FitzBaldwin called. "Full broadside on my word! Wait for it!"

The crippled Prussian was listing to starboard and she still dragged wreckage astern. *Odin's* curve would cross her bows and sweep over to run parallel to her damaged flank. Now the second gunboat came into view on the ironclad's starboard quarter, but still too far behind to interpose herself to defend her sister.

"The fire's out." Welborne was looking aft. "We can't be badly hurt."

Dawlish had no ears for him. Nothing counted but the target vessel. She now lay on *Odin's* beam, bow on, foreshortened, two cables separation, incapable of firing ahead. But in another minute the ironclad would pass into the arc of her pivot-mounted cannon. It had done damage enough before and the Prussian gunners must be thirsting to do as much again, even if it was in their last minutes of life.

Lorance, at the helm, pulled *Odin* out of the turn, straightened, then nudged slightly over until her course, though opposite, was parallel to the gunboat's. They would pass close, fifty yards only, for she was now part hidden from Dawlish's view by the superstructure ahead.

Yet nearer. The Prussian captain was now trying to turn away to port, the gunboat lurching slowly over – too slowly to escape but enough to unmask the pivot cannon. From the foretop Albemarle and his remaining riflemen were opening fire on the gun-crew. For an instant Dawlish saw the dark circle of the weapon's mouth, as if directed straight at himself, and then, an instant after, the blast of flame that smashed a shell against *Odin's* armoured hull just level with the bridge. It shattered – no harm done.

"Your guns, Dawlish!" FitzBaldwin's longed-for order.

The sea was calm, *Odin* rock-steady in her straight run, no pitch, no roll. Now the turret was slipping past Prussian's bowsprit, then level with the foremast. Abaft it, yellow-gunsmoke still wreathed around the cannon. The gunners there were reloading despite Albemarle's hail and one dropped as a shot took him down. Dawlish's gaze was fixed on the funnel. Clustered below it were the boiler and engine rooms, sheltered by nothing more than six-inches of oak. His target, seconds away.

Then the seconds that saved the Prussian.

FitzBaldwin realised, too late, that the gunboat's wallowing turn had dragged the wrecked mizzen and tangle of rigging astern of her directly into *Odin's* path. Lorance threw the helm over to avoid it. The rudder gripped just enough to push the bows two or three points to port, the hull heeling from the vertical, towards the gunboat.

And in that instant Dawlish called "Fire!" as the funnel that had so fixated him swept past.

In the iron drum below him Hopper whipped back the firing lanyards. The Armstrongs roared, their report deafening, their smoke choking.

But no secondary explosion, no blast to tear the wooden gunboat apart.

Odin's heel had been enough to save her. The Armstrongs' shells had plunged beneath – and past – the Prussian's keel.

My moment. My failure.

Chapter 23

"Reload!"

Odin forged on, leaving the Prussian gunboat on her starboard quarter. Within the turret the smoke had cleared and the gun-crews were already sponging the smoking barrels, hoisting charges and shells from their racks and swinging them across on tackles from the beams above.

"Missed! We goddamn missed!" Welborne had risen in his seat to stare back. "And she's cut the wreckage loose!"

But the crippled gunboat was no longer *Odin's* concern. Another quarry lay all but directly ahead. Along the side of the forward superstructure Dawlish could just see the second Prussian, that which had been hastening to her sister's aid. By now her captain had thought better of it and she had turned away, was running south-westwards.

Odin had the speed advantage and Dawlish felt hope soar. Another chance.

Rumbling from beneath him as the reloaded Armstrongs ran down their slides again to jut their muzzles through the open ports.

"Ready one! Ready two!" Hopper's confirmation.

Dawlish turned, relayed it to the bridge. Lorance at the helm there, controlled fury on his face, FitzBaldwin standing by him, telescope locked on the fleeing Prussian.

"Deck there!" Albemarle calling from the foretop. "Buoys ahead! Big 'uns! A line of 'em! Scarce visible! Eight or ten cables ahead!"

"Shallow water?" His father shouting back.

"Maybe!"

"And that fellow's heading for them!" Dawlish could barely hear Lorance's words to FitzBaldwin. "A sandbank?"

"He's no fool. He knows these waters. He'll go where we can't. He's leading us on."

"Hold course?"

A pause. Then FitzBaldwin said, "Hold course, for now. We'll run him down short of 'em." Now he called to Dawlish. "I'm coming in close, like before! Turret still on starboard beam! But drop the guns a fraction!! Hold 'em barely depressed!"

Dawlish's orders to Hopper. Each geared handwheel spun in turn, creeping the barrels down to just below horizontal.

"Look there!" Welborne plucked Dawlish's elbow and gestured southwards, off the port bow.

A half-mile distant the third Prussian gunboat was swinging off her northerly course and towards her sister. Her broad beam and the white foam churning on either flank told she was a paddle-steamer. Her captain must know that her thrashing wheels made her even more vulnerable than the two others but that was not deterring him. Another madman, intent on death or glory. The turn was unmasking a weapon that must be mounted abaft the paddler's foremast for there was a sudden, tiny, stab of flame there, then billowing smoke that half-hid the paddle-box. The report identified something punier than the other gunboats' armament. A ball dropped two cables off the ironclad's port quarter, raced on in a skidding plume of spray before sinking. Even had it reached her armoured side it would have shattered – a peashooter could scarcely do less.

Yet even so, the paddler was still coming on, her turn still held to carry her parallel to the gunboat now scarcely two cables ahead of *Odin*. She had only distraction to offer, but her captain was intent on delivering it, regardless of cost.

Dawlish tore his gaze from her, concentrated on the escaping gunboat, just visible along the angled side of superstructure before the turret. Foam boiled beneath her counter and she could bring no weapon to bear. The nearest buoy – impossible to spot from the turret, could now be little more than a half-mile ahead and *Odin* would be level with her in scant seconds more.

"She's turning!" Albemarle, in the foretop, was the first to spot the gunboat's lurch to starboard.

Her helm was hard over now, a tight curve that would carry her northwards just short of the buoys – the captain had shirked a turn to port that would have carried her across *Odin's* bows and towards the nearing paddler.

Even before FitzBaldwin shouted for it, Lorance was spinning the wheel over and the ironclad's momentum swung her also over to starboard. Her radius of turn was tighter and the Prussian's lay outside it. Now Lorance eased the turn, straightening, cutting across the chord of the gunboat's arc, driving ahead on an interception course. The enemy's side was exposed now, her dropped bulwarks forward revealing a pivot-mounted cannon similar to her sister's, gunners slewing it around to bear on the onward-rushing *Odin*.

"Ramming! All down!" FitzBaldwin was bracing himself against the bridge rail.

Two seamen dropped to their knees on either side of Lorance and grabbed his legs to steady him. Dawlish called down into the turret, hooked one arm over its rim and grasped his seat frame with the other, Welborne following suit. Below them, Hopper and the gunners were crouched against the turret wall closest to the bow.

The Prussian cannon blasted – too soon, for its shell must have all but shaved past *Odin's* bow and dropped in a racing line of spray a cable's length to starboard. Albemarle and his riflemen in the tops opened fire again but the Prussian gun-crew, undeterred, were sponging, heaving another shell into the muzzle and ramming like men possessed.

Collision now but half a minute away, the gunboat still drove on in a hope to cross the *Odin's* course and then, just in time, the Prussian captain recognised that it was in vain. Helm thrown over, the vessel's bows nudged to port, a turn to take her on a parallel course to the ironclad's.

It was enough to save her.

Still heeling over in her turn, no longer beam-on to *Odin*, the gunboat's bowsprit alone lay before the ironclad in the moment of impact. Dawlish saw it sweeping like a scythe low over *Odin's* bow and shearing through her forward stays, then crashing against the foremast just above deck level. It shattered and fell, dragging a tangle of whipping cordage with it, gunboat's and ironclad's inextricable. He ducked as fragments flew past him and he saw another figure tumbling from the foretop. A cry from beside him alerted to him to Welborne being thrown forward from his seat and down between the guns below

Odin hurtled on. As the Prussian slid past, Dawlish glimpsed the rent torn at her bow where the bowsprit had wrenched free – damage above the waterline only, no hindrance to this steamer. For this brief instant the enemy was human – crew flung down by the shock now struggling to their feet, the helmsman on the open bridge hunched over the wheel, yet keeping control, an officer stumbling forward to survey the damage, the gun-crew trying to swing their heavy weapon, a seaman standing in the main shrouds and screaming abuse.

Then she was gone, still lurching away to port, still holding her turn, blocked from Dawlish's sight by the superstructure aft. Ramming had failed again – what seemed so devastating a tactic on paper, or deadly on a stationary target, was proving futile. FitzBaldwin and Lorance had recognised that also, for they were swinging *Odin* across to starboard. On that beam were trained the turret's guns. Straightening from a sixteen-point turn would carry the ironclad again on a course paralleling – and overtaking – the escaping Prussian. It would be the Armstrongs' moment again.

Down inside the turret, Hopper had the gunners on their feet. Welborne there too, bruised and winded and no worse for his fall. Van der Horst was leading men forward to cut free the remnants of stays trailing over the sides from the wreckage on the foredeck. The man who had been thrown from the foretop was not dead but his cries were piteous as they tried to lift him.

And, on the bridge, FitzBaldwin and Lorance stood, unmoved, silent, grim-faced.

The turn was half-completed, Dawlish's view clear southwards. He saw the damaged Prussian ahead – loss of her bowsprit had not cost her speed. She had drawn out of her turn, was running directly south. Just west of her, he at last spotted one of the buoys that had previously been visible only from the foretop. The gunboat must be running just clear of a shoal. Her captain must know these waters well, must have approached as close as he dared, must guess that his own vessel's draught was shallower than *Odin's,* that the ironclad could not risk venturing further over to run alongside. Powerful as the Armstrongs were, they could not now be used at point-blank range and every yard of separation would reduce their chance of hitting a moving target.

But there was another Prussian, the paddle steamer that was beating directly westwards as if to block *Odin's* own run south. Weakest of all three gunboats, she too was ploughing towards death or glory. A flash near her bow, and a splash well short of the ironclad, confirmed her hopeless determination.

"Mr. Dawlish! Increase elevation!" FitzBaldwin was not specific – he could not be, for there were no proven range-tables for the guns. "We'll try to give you two cables."

My decision, mine alone.

Mind racing, Dawlish realised that this must be a gambler's throw. And then decision.

"Mr. Hopper! Two degrees above horizontal! Two degrees, I say! Elevate 'em!"

The twin barrels rose as *Odin* pulled from her turn to plough south. His view directly ahead blocked by the forward superstructure, Dawlish could see the paddler off the port bow, froth churning at her flank as she drove on to cross the ironclad's path. Off the starboard bow, the other gunboat was still running south, close to the submerged sandbank.

The paddle gunboat was all but dead ahead – a half-cable – and again her weapon barked in useless but magnificent defiance that sent a shell skimming far off *Odin*'s flank. The Prussian captain might be set on glorious death for his ship, and for himself, but he would be denied it, for Lorance was edging the ironclad's bows ever so slightly to port to avoid collision. In seconds more, *Odin* would pass directly astern of the paddler and for one fleeting moment the great Armstrongs would bear along her axis. It was the position that captains had dreamed of for two centuries, the opportunity to disembowel the enemy, smashing through from stern to bow. It had decided countless ship-to-ship duels. Dawlish too had dreamed of it since his first childhood reading of Nelson's glory days ...

"Captain FitzBaldwin!"

He dared – it was insubordinate – to twist around and shout to the bridge, arm extended towards the paddle gunboat, his face a plea.

But FitzBaldwin shook his head. His quarry was unchanged. Laying *Odin* alongside the damaged Prussian, slowing to match her speed, allowing long seconds for gauging the ideal moment for firing, was a better bet than a brief instant of opportunity when crossing the paddler's wake.

And now *Odin* was indeed passing through the line of froth left by that paddle-gunboat, some twenty yards – no more – between the pointed ram and rounded stern. She was a pathetic thing, an insufficient guardian for an approach to a great port, little different to a Thames pleasure steamer. But as she receded, Prussian ensign streaming, foam churning beneath her paddle boxes, a gun-crew clustered by a cannon aft, Dawlish recognised magnificence of courage. That puny weapon blasted – it could not miss – and its solid shot shattered into fragments on *Odin*'s side-armour.

The damaged gunboat was off the starboard beam now – two cables – and *Odin* was overtaking. There was no escape now, for there was another buoy just west of the Prussian, and further on another, clear warning of shallows. Turning to starboard would risk grounding, turning to port would lay her open to impalement on the ironclad's ram.

Ringing on *Odin*'s bridge as FitzBaldwin pulled back the telegraph handle to call for three-quarters revolutions, slowing her as she drew level with her quarry.

"Your guns!"

"Hopper!" Dawlish called down into the turret. "On my word!"

The Prussian might have been the *Foyle*, the gunboat he had served on, the same long graceful hull, the single screw churning beneath the counter. Here also three masts and a thin funnel, a single port aft for a broadside cannon, bulwarks dropped forward to reveal the pivot-mounted gun abaft the foremast.

And oaken planking that offered no more protection against *Odin's* guns than a sheet of card.

The ironclad was now almost level with the gunboat, speed all but matched so that the gain was at a slow and steady creep.

Two cables range, as near as dammit, two degrees elevation. And two Armstrongs, two separate chances…

"Hopper!"

"Sir?"

"Each gun only on my word! Individual fire!"

Bows level now with the gunboat's stern, flame blasting from her single broadside weapon, another solid shot smashing into *Odin* somewhere near the hawsepipe, black shards fanning from the impact.

Odin crept on, speed scarcely greater than her prey's. The Prussian was still a living ship, helmsman at her wheel, engineer and stokers below, gunners by their weapons and officers on the bridge-wing. One was raising his cap in salute – he must know what was unavoidable but there was no irony in the gesture.

A roar, the pivot-mounted weapon vomiting flame and thick grey smoke and a shell – not solid shot – that exploded an instant later somewhere aft on *Odin*. Dawlish ignored it. His eyes were locked on the gunboats funnel. Any moment now…

"Fire one!"

The crashing, the Armstrong surging back, the long spear of flame stabbing out beyond the muzzle.

And in the instant before the rolling smoke blocked vision, sight of a rent torn in the Prussian's hull just abaft the funnel.

"Fire two!"

The second cannon, already blinded, blasting into the billowing murk even as another flash told of her sister's shell bursting somewhere deep inside the gunboat.

Odin thrust on through her own gunsmoke. Dawlish's view was clear again and, in the moment before the second shell burst, he saw white steam gushing and flames licking inside the now-huge breach blasted by the first's explosion. But it was that second detonation that tore the Prussian asunder, rupturing her boiler, showering wreckage skywards, breaking her back. Steam and black coal-smoke and glowing embers erupted around the collapsing funnel. The foremast still stood vertical but the main and mizzen were toppling to port, twisting the hull with them. Bow and stern rose as the centre sank – water streaming from the keel forward as it climbed, the propeller's last feeble revolution dying aft. Men spilled into the water, striking out for pieces of floating wreckage, but others still clung on the hull's remnant. Now came the sound – loud, tortured, squealing – as metal rent and sundered and the bow section tore itself free from that aft. They drifted apart, that forward slipping down as if along an inclined plane, all that had been aft of the funnel rolling over as it sank. The deck, already half-submerged, stood vertical for an instant, flailing bodies dropping across it. Then the main and mizzen masts were crashing against the surface and throwing up cascades of spray. The shattered after section settled, great bubbles of air venting around it, and it grounded at last so that its starboard flank lay just above water. What remained of the hull forward had hit bottom already. It had settled all but horizontal, forecastle clear of the surface, foremast canted but still standing.

Odin swept around in a wide turn back north.

"Mr. Dawlish. Turret to port beam!" FitzBaldwin wanted the paddle steamer now.

Dawlish tore his gaze from the horror in the water – there seemed already to be fewer heads among the flotsam, though a few were swimming back to climb on to the exposed wreckage. He yelled down into the turret to set the gun-crews to the cranks, felt the great drum begin to rotate, gather speed, set into a smooth slew – over a hundred and eighty degrees, so that the Armstrongs bore directly on the port beam. Brakes locked, and then the practised haste of loading, charges and shells rammed home, and the huge weapons dropping down their slides again to extend their muzzles through their ports.

The ironclad was headed north again and the gunboat's remains were dropping away off the port quarter, stark warnings of the shallowness of the water there. But off the port bow the paddle-steamer was visible, a mile distant or more to the west. Her thrashing wheels allowed a shallower-draughted hull than any screw-propelled vessel and now they were carrying her over shoals and sandbanks where *Odin* could follow. She was curving to the south, then over eastwards to approach her wrecked sister.

She was out of range for now but *Odin* could circle back and blast her also to fragments should she close to rescue survivors. The guns were loaded, success assured. Dawlish's mind recoiled from the prospect. It would be butchery. And still, he knew that, if the order came, he would obey it.

I gave my word and I must stand by it, but I gave it too easily.

But FitzBaldwin's decision saved him. *Odin's* course was northwards, heading back out into the safety of deeper water. She disregarded the first gunboat to have been damaged, now two or three miles off the starboard bow, and crawling north-eastwards towards the coast.

"Let her go. We've been hurt enough," Dawlish heard Lorance say, "and damn little to show for it."

"Not a single vessel will dare put out from Hamburg after this." FitzBaldwin sounded like a man striving to convince himself – and failing.

Time now to count the cost.

*

Two dead – the second man lost from the foretop had died. The enemy's shattered bowsprit and the tangle of parted cordage on *Odin's* forecastle were easily heaved overboard, new foremast stays run and tensioned. The shell that had penetrated the unarmoured superstructure aft had exploded in the wardroom, then empty. The resulting fire had consumed furniture alone and would have been worse if wooden panelling had been installed – a valuable lesson. The flames that had gushed up through the skylight had been easily extinguished by van der Horst's hose party. The shots that shattered on the armoured flank had done no more than scour paintwork.

An hour later *Odin* overhauled the brig which had been sighted before the action. The breeze had freshened and she was heading north-west towards Heligoland, perhaps to seek the protection of its neutral waters. Hope of escape extinguished, she hove to. Welborne led a boarding party. The *Adolf Seehofer* of Rostock was headed for far-off Brazil, her cargo enamel ware, cutlery and glass. She could keep her cargo but would have to take the prisoners. Her captain was first relived that he would not lose his ship, was then indignant that her voyage must be interrupted to land the captives. He screamed in a paroxysm that gained him nothing.

The crews taken from the other victims were herded out on *Odin's* deck, pitiful, half-blinded by the light, clasping what little they possessed, amazed at their deliverance. Shut in a closed compartment, bewildered by the gunfire, terrified by the reverberations of the shot striking the armour, their ordeal had been a terrible one. It took three trips with the whaler to get them all across.

Now north again. Dawlish was glad it was over. It seemed a squalid victory.

Blackguard's work.

And for the Prussian navy, puny as it was, even negligible, a day of glory.

Chapter 24

Odin loitered one more day – an uneventful one, with only neutral shipping sighted – off the Elbe estuary. Dawlish realised that he was not the only one to whom triumph had brought little pride. The mood among officers and crew alike was subdued, not helped by the burial service FitzBaldwin read for the men who had hurtled from the foretop. Both had served with him a decade before, had fallen on hard times since, had been grateful for the chance to join *Odin*. Now they lay on planks beneath foreign flags, canvas-wrapped bundles, with fire-bars at their feet, until FitzBaldwin's nod to their comrades sent them sliding overboard.

They've had that much. Most of those Prussians probably won't have even that.

The lookouts scanned the horizon for sight of the expected Danish force that would relieve *Odin*. Seas continued moderate, though the sky was overcast, visibility sometimes restricted by occasional showers and mist patches. Dawlish sensed that neither FitzBaldwin nor Lorance wanted to be here, nor did they relish being put at direct Danish disposal. The bargain agreed for the ironclad had related to support of Blackwood's Alexandra Legion at Thyborøn and it was likely that every day spent on blockade was one in which Prussian strength was growing there. By sunset there was no sign of the Danes – they should have been here by now. *Odin* settled back into her old west-east-west patrol off Heligoland through the night but no navigation lights were spotted.

When Dawlish came on deck at four o'clock to take the morning watch it was still dark. The wind had died, the sea had calmed and the sunrise, an hour later, was glorious. He felt joy at the sight, as he always did, an impression of a world reborn, and he hoped that this day would bring no more captures.

"Deck there!"

The foretop lookout was pointing north.

"Smoke, sir!"

It was invisible to the naked eye and even when Dawlish saw it through a telescope it seemed like the slightest stain against a clear sky. But it was darkening, strengthening, as he watched, even though the ship causing it was hull down below the horizon.

He waited ten minutes before having FitzBaldwin alerted. In that time masts and yards swam into his disk of vision, strong and heavy by their look, sails furled. Thick black smoke billowed, drifted skywards.

There was no doubt that this vessel was driving fast south, had probably spotted *Odin* herself, was undeterred by the sight.

The hull was visible, foreshortened, when FitzBaldwin reached the bridge. It was larger than an average trader and impossible to spot her ensign.

"It could be one of the Danish ships, sir."

"Damn strange that there's only one of them, if she is. There were to be three." FitzBaldwin had taken the telescope. "But yes, she looks like a warship. A frigate, maybe,"

"Do the Prussians have anything like that, sir?"

"No. But the Austrians do." FitzBaldwin turned to a seaman. "My compliments to Mr. Lorance, Mr. van der Horst too. I want to see them here."

And they also were baffled.

"If she's Austrian, she must have flown here," Lorance said. "If that report from Malta was correct, she'd be lucky to be somewhere north of Spain by now."

"She must be as uncertain as we are," FitzBaldwin said. "What does she see? Another steamer, bow on. Maybe a civilian. She can't see the turret. We have the advantage."

No chances taken. All hands to their stations, the turret manned and cranked on to the port beam, the Armstrongs already loaded, Dawlish and Welborne on their seats again. The bulwarks had not been raised since the action with the gunboats, so the field of fire was maximum. Albemarle's marksmen in the tops. *Odin's* course remained unchanged, the other vessel's also. In minutes they would be passing port to port. Point blank, if neither captain faltered.

And FitzBaldwin would not – the steady course confirmed that. The stranger was almost certainly wooden-hulled, unarmoured, carried at most a pair of bow-chasers for fire ahead, had all her others guns on the broadside. And none of them likely to penetrate the iron that clad *Odin's* flanks. A single discharge of the Armstrongs, when level with the other's funnel, would be enough to disembowel her.

"Deck there!" Albemarle himself calling down. "The ensign! I think it's –"

"Union!" Lorance had seen it too. "It's the *Conewago!*"

And neutral – for now.

At FitzBaldwin's call the wheel was spinning, bows lurching to starboard, straightening again into a parallel but opposite course. A single cable would separate the ships as they passed.

Dawlish could see her clearly now, a slim black flush-decked hull, graceful clipper bows and long jutting bowsprit, hinged bulwarks dropped abaft the foremast, abaft the mainmast too, open gun-ports further aft, smoke rolling from the ochre funnel. Officers on the bridge had telescopes upraised and focussed on *Odin's* white-cross-on-red, fork-tailed, Danish ensign.

"The *Conewago.*" Lorance's words to FitzBaldwin were barely audible. "I served on her. Second Lieutenant, two years." He moved alone towards *Odin's* port bridge-wing. FitzBaldwin made to follow, then paused, understanding.

The ships were cleaving past each other now. Wooden-hulled and unarmoured the USS *Conewago* might be, but the two massive pivot-mounted guns on her centre-line were little less powerful than *Odin's* Armstrongs. The muzzles of the great bottle-shaped barrels – ten-inches bore or more – were trained over on the beam. Their crews stood by them, firing lanyards in the gun-captain's hands, the young gunnery officers by them looking up toward the bridge and waiting for the signal to fire.

None came.

A single American officer – the captain, no doubt of it – stood in the bridge wing, hand raised to cap-brim in salute.

And Lorance saluted back.

Both men held their stances as the vessels passed, dropped their arms only when stern slipped past stern. Lorance remained in silence on the wing for a long five minutes, then walked back to FitzBaldwin.

"Joel Cutler," he said. "With me in Annapolis, Class of '54. To China and Japan together. A damn fine officer." He paused. "And my friend."

"Until the ninth of May?"

"Forever. Even if we have to kill each other."

Conewago receded southwards, course unchanged. *Odin* continued north.

For there were two more smudges – but not three – on the horizon.

*

Two Danes, the large frigate *Niels Juel.* and the corvette *Hejmdal.* Signals exchanged, honours observed. *Odin* and *Niels Juel* hove to and the corvette held course to the south. FitzBaldwin crossed to confer with the Danish commodore.

Though he had held a nominal commission from the crown of Denmark for almost two months, this was the first time that Dawlish had seen a Danish ship. She was all but new, he had heard, and yet, but for a squat funnel announcing steam to supplement her sails, she would not have surprised Nelson when he turned a blind eye at Copenhagen over six decades before.

"Damned hard to imagine her lasting five minutes against anything like *Galveston*." Welborne was watching with Dawlish. "The Yankees have dozens like her. Let's have at 'em, say I."

Ship-rigged, with towering masts and yards, two dozen gun-ports running in a long row along each flank, her wooden hull striped black and white from bow to stern and with a gilded figurehead beneath her bowsprit, the *Niels Juel* was built to fight in line, broadside to broadside.

"The Austrians who're coming won't look much different," Dawlish said. "They'll be well-matched enough."

And yet the *Niels Juel* impressed him. Salt-streaked, paint faded, weather-beaten, there was an air of determination about her, of efficiency about her crew. Studying them through his glass, Dawlish sensed the same stolid resolution he had seen on the faces of the troops onshore.

"Tough looking fellows," Welborne said.

"There's not a man of them knows what brought this war about." Dawlish had himself failed to understand the dynastic complexities, much less remember them. "But, right or wrong, their country's been invaded and they're damned if they'll swallow it."

"So you know how we feel, Dawlish, when Union armies violate our Southern homes? When they threaten our womenfolk? When the Union navy blockades our harbours? And do worse! Destroy our peculiar institution, beggar us?"

Dawlish recognised the same vehemence in Welborne's tone that he had heard before, not just an urge to settle scores, but something like a loathing that would know no bounds. It repelled him. Men fought men on land. At sea ships fought ships.

"That God-damn Union *Conewago!*" Venom in Welborne's voice. "I'm praying to the Good Lord himself for the day she'll lie plumb in *Galveston's* sights! And fillet her like that Prussian gunboat, the bitch!"

"You think you'll find her?"

"She'll find us. Bulloch told me that the Yankees have a lot more agents in Europe than we do. Not just informants. They've got their consuls and their embassies. They know damn-well about the deal, that this ship's *Galveston* after May the eighth! They know we'll be at Thyborøn until then. They'll be waiting for us – there or where we'll be taking on more crew and more supplies."

The transfer back to Confederate service had seemed so far in the future that until now Dawlish had not given it much thought. He had assumed that it would happen either at sea – a rendezvous with a steamer chartered by Bulloch – or in some neutral port. With more recruits, officers and men for the reborn raider *Galveston*. FitzBaldwin and Albemarle and himself, and any crew unwilling to continue, would all be set ashore to make their own way back to Britain. It would be a decorous affair, he imagined, handshakes, expressions of mutual regard, hopes of meeting in happier times.

But the presence of the *Conewago* changed everything. The fact that she had remained two months in European waters implied relentless determination to eliminate the *Galveston*. The Union could not afford to have another *Alabama* loose on the world's oceans.

"Did Mr. Bulloch mention anything about where the transfer will take place?" Dawlish said.

Welborne laughed. "You think he'd share that with me? Lorance and FitzBaldwin know – but they'll be damned if they tell any of us. They'd be fools to."

FitzBaldwin was returning from the *Niels Juel*. Responsibility for the blockade had been exchanged. Even as his whaler pulled away, the frigate was churning south on the heels of her consort. He gathered his officers in his saloon cabin. The news from the Danish commodore, Suenson, was not good.

"The Danes are just hanging on at Dybbøl but it can't be for much longer," he said. "The Prussians are bombarding day and night and they bloody nearly stormed the positions a week ago. Without the *Rolfe Krake* – that Danish ironclad – hitting their flank, they'd have succeeded."

"How soon does Suenson think they'll try again?" Lorance said.

"It could be any day. It's hard to see how the Danes can withstand another assault. Not with the numbers the Prussians have already and not with reserves and artillery still pouring in from Germany."

"There was to be a third Danish ship coming to blockade the Jade and Elbe," Lorance said. "Where is she?"

"The *Jylland*. Engine trouble. She's on her way. The Danes are keeping the rest of their ships in the Baltic, blockading the Prussian coast. All with wooden hulls, no help for Dybbøl. The *Rolf Krake's* the only vessel they can risk exposing to the Prussian guns onshore."

"And Thyborøn?" Lorance's tone neutral.

He's counting the days, Dawlish thought. *It's not his war. He doesn't want this ship risked before the ninth of May.*

"Thyborøn's still holding out, and the Prussian forces have been reaching there too. And every man and cannon of theirs who is, isn't at Dybbøl. That's why Thyborøn still matters."

Where *Odin* was heading once more.

*

Dawn found *Odin* three miles west from the Limfjord entrance. The sky was clear, the sea calm, the coast a long beach-fringed streak. Distant gunfire had sounded in the last hour of darkness, two or three reports at a time, the same Austrian harassing fire that had been in progress for weeks. Sunrise was greeted with the faint strains of the Radetzky. It was at least confirmation that Saabye's force still held out.

A single Prussian gunboat beat away north-westwards when she spotted *Odin*. She too might have been harassing in the night. No sign however of the second such craft that had been here before. She might well have been that which *Odin* had dismembered.

"Join me, Mr. Dawlish. You too, Mr. Welborne." FitzBaldwin pointed towards the foretop.

They were ahead of him, made as if not to notice his gasping breath when he arrived. *Odin* had turned south again, was running parallel to the beach, a full mile and a half out from it, avoiding any danger of grounding. The Austrian demi-lunes lay on the port beam. Dawlish had already surveyed them and he handed the telescope to FitzBaldwin.

"Two more since we left and a third under construction, sir. But see over there, on the far side of the lagoon."

Close to the head of the far isthmus, that bounded by the Limfjord, lay the third and easternmost of the Danish redoubts. It was the smallest and had been faced by an even smaller Austrian counterpart. The Austrians had mounted no attack there, had concentrated on breaking through at the two redoubts further west. But now that eastern enemy position had grown, looked higher, more massive.

"It's damn-near stretching all the way across from shore to shore." FitzBaldwin had rested the telescope on Dawlish's shoulder. "Professional work too, and still building. Guns in place."

"Do you see the flag, sir?"

"Prussian, by God! They're here and they're not worried by a narrow front."

And further back, along that isthmus, more artillery moving north.

"If they're like those fellows on the gunboats, then God help the Danes," FitzBaldwin said.

"We could hit them from the east, sir" Welborne gestured towards the Limfjord. "We're going in there, aren't we?"

"Shallow," FitzBaldwin said. "Shallow and unsounded. Dawlish can tell you about it. We can't venture in too far from the entrance."

Odin was level with the enemy camp now. It too had grown, long regular lines of tents on the eastern, Limfjord side, wagons parked in rows, horses tethered, campfires, companies paraded for inspection. This new part was the Prussian encampment. The Austrians' looked untidy by comparison.

"There must be twice as many men as before we left, sir," Dawlish said.

"All to the good. If they're here then they're not at Dybbøl. That's why Saabye's holding here. And we're back to support him."

*

Dawlish and Welborne remained in the foretop as *Odin* crept through the fjord entrance. Thyborøn looked even more squalid than before. Most of the huts had disappeared, their wood consumed in campfires or as trench-shoring. Improvised shelters, little better than scrapes roofed over with whatever came to hand, had replaced them. The few tents looked grey and weather-beaten. Only the school and the church had been spared destruction. A funeral service was in progress in the burial ground – five blanket-covered bodies, a pastor in a surplice, an officer and half-a-dozen men to show respect – and a little further on a work-party was busy with yet more graves, some digging, some filling. The small wooden crosses that Dawlish had seen before were gone – for kindling, perhaps – and only low mounds, some large enough to accommodate several bodies together, marked final resting-places. A few wretched cattle awaited slaughter nearby. Boats were moored at the foreshore – supplies were still reaching Thyborøn from the north. Even at this distance, there was a faint scent of human waste, of too many men occupying too small an area.

"What's that?" Welborne pointed towards the red crosses that stood out stark on the church's whitewashed sides.

Dawlish told him. He repeated the phrase that he had heard Eleonora Blomqvist use, that a wounded man is not an enemy.

Welborne laughed. "They're Swiss and Swedes, you say? It's not their fight, is it? It's not their country that's been invaded, is it? It's damn easy to talk like that when they've nothing against the wounded man."

"I don't think it would make a difference to them."

Not just to Doctor Venel or Madame Racine or Eleonora Blomqvist, Dawlish thought. It didn't make a difference to Surgeon-Major Hartling either. That dying Austrian in his hospital was no worse treated than any of the Danish wounded. Amidst the filth there was nobility.

"You haven't learned to hate yet, Dawlish," Welborne said. "If you'd been in Mississippi, the Yankee locusts would have taught you fast."

But Dawlish barely heard him, his own attention fixed on the new defences that Blackwood had laid out directly south of the village. They had been a row of low hummocks when he had seen them last. Troops and peasant labourers were still swarming over them, but they were higher, more massive, now. They crossed the peninsula tip like a curved bow, anchored by redoubts close to each shoreline. The trench-line linking them was fronted with low breastworks. Not yet complete, but almost. Beyond them to the south, almost a mile distant, lay the existing defences that had withstood one assault already.

And in between, open ground that stretched from the Limfjord shore to the North Sea beach.

As Blackwood had wanted, as he had convinced Saabye.

Odin pressed on and dropped anchor where she had lain before, well out of range of enemy gunfire.

April the twentieth.

Just eighteen days more in Danish service.

Chapter 25

FitzBaldwin went onshore, on arrival, to see Saabye. He looked concerned when he returned and he closeted himself with Lorance. A half-hour later Dawlish was called in. He was surprised to find no other officers present. FitzBaldwin invited him to sit down.

"They want bombardments," he said. "Not the Austrian positions, like before, but the new Prussian works."

"Madness," Lorance said. "A useless waste of powder and shot."

"What do you think, Dawlish?" FitzBaldwin said. "You and your crews know your Armstrongs better now and you've seen the situation from both land and sea."

Wait. Think. This was why we came here, but...

"We're not accurate enough, sir. We couldn't hit those Austrian demi-lunes before, even when we were close inshore –"

"And when we grounded and lost an engine," Lorance said. "I'm damned if you're going to risk the *Galveston* like that again, FitzBaldwin."

FitzBaldwin ignored him "Your opinion, Mr. Dawlish?"

"If we could have brought the guns to bear when the Austrians attacked, accuracy wouldn't have mattered. There were crowds of 'em, masses, impossible to miss. They'd have broken long before they reached the redoubts."

"Only if we'd been close inshore." Ice in Lorance's voice.

"We're not going to take her close inshore along the sea-coast," FitzBaldwin held up his hand as if weary of an argument long decided. "That's settled Lorance, I agree to it. No bombardment from the sea. But from the Limfjord, that could be something else."

"Too damn shallow, too damn unpredictable. It's never been sounded. It's just as much a risk, maybe greater."

"We're not going to settle that now," FitzBaldwin said. "Before we do anything we need to know more about those Prussians." He turned to Dawlish. "Report to Colonel Blackwood in the morning. My compliments, and tell him I want you to see that new redoubt. I'll thank you for your report by midday."

*

Blackwood was welcoming and he provided a horse for Dawlish to ride with him to the easternmost Danish redoubt. Both mounts were miserable creatures, for supplies of oats were meagre.

"Winter's over," Blackwood said, "but little's left from last year's harvests north of the fjord. Not just for the horses. We'll all be tightening our belts soon."

"Those new graves, sir." Dawlish gestured to them as they rode past the churchyard. "I thought there'd been no fighting recently."

"Typhus."

"How bad, sir?"

"Worse than when you were here before, much worse. Eight or ten deaths a day last week, even higher now".

And the most recently arrived Danish reserves – the last scourings from the remaining garrisons in the country's north – were being whittled away just as quickly as the first units to have reached here with Saabye.

"The Croix Rouge people. Are they still here, sir?"

"They haven't left," Blackwood said. "Hartling would be lost without them. Brave people. Two of them died, I understand. Typhus. Both women."

Dawlish hesitated to ask if they had been Swiss or Swedish. He feared the answer, did not want to think of Eleonora Blomqvist dying in squalor. He would find out, he promised himself, but not now.

They rode out through one of the three gaps in the breastworks fronting the trench that linked Blackwood's three new redoubts. Each entrance – a twenty-yard passage running parallel to the trench line and shielded on its far side by another sand breastwork – was flanked by what were virtually small redoubts in themselves. Low embankments projecting from alternate sides within the passage precluded any direct rush through. Rough knife-rest barriers constructed from driftwood lay along the walls, ready to be pulled out to block the gaps.

Dawlish glanced back as they emerged on to the open ground. From behind, from either flank, embrasures gaped at him, black barrels in each. Every gun that had reached here with the last reinforcements seemed to have been mounted here, not in the older redoubts further forward. Blackwood's siting of the new defences had been masterly. There was no point ahead on the open ground extending from the Limfjord to the North Sea that was not covered from two directions, some from three.

Work had finished on the new defences but now the troops and peasants who had laboured on them had been reallocated to the three older redoubts to the south. From this distance they looked like dark swarms of busy ants, busy with pick, shovel and wheelbarrow. They seemed to be destroying, not building.

"What are they doing, sir?" Dawlish was baffled.

"Undoing work that shouldn't have been done in the first place," Blackwood said. "They're levelling the rear walls. They're making demi-lunes of the redoubts. A bloody unpleasant shock for the enemy if they ever take 'em."

"I've heard no shelling, sir, since getting back."

"It'll come, and the assaults with it. They're still building up stocks. They're short of men, they'll need artillery to make up for them. A handful of Austrian units have arrived – I'd be surprised if they've been enough to replace their losses in their big attack."

It was the Prussians who were arriving in greater numbers and concentrating on enlarging their redoubt on the Limfjord shore. Reaching here was easier for them now, for these spring days were warm and dry, the roads more passable than before. But no rail line ran along this desolate North Sea coast and the nearest point of contact with the railway system that extended back into Germany was eighty miles to the south. Marching the Prussian infantry here and hauling the guns – some of them heavy siege pieces – was still a slow and brutal task.

Granville and the British volunteers were with the Danes who manned the redoubt that faced the Prussians. Situated at the head of the eastern isthmus, a thousand yards of bare sand separated it from the Prussian position. The rear walls had been reduced to hummocks, height dropping with each shovelful cast into a barrow. Much of the sand was still being used to cover new shelters built against the forward-facing walls. Most of the timber taken from Thyborøn's houses must have ended as shoring and roofing for these shelters – as it must also be at the two other Danish positions to the west.

"They've got at least eight heavy siege pieces there." Granville pointed to the line of northern-facing embrasures of the Prussian redoubt. Screened with rope curtains, it was impossible to know what lay behind. "Field gun too, and God knows what they've got further back."

"How do you know?" Dawlish asked.

"Our friend Krag's been out watching from fishing boats at night. The Prussians move nothing by day."

Trenches, fronted by sand breastworks, stretched on either side of the great redoubt, linked it to two smaller positions further forward, on the fjord and lagoon shores. The barely adequate position constructed by the Austrians had been converted into a fortress. Blackwood had a worthy match in the Prussian engineer who had driven the transformation in so short a time.

"This is where the real attack will come," Blackwood said. "The Austrians will do their best, but it'll be little better than before. Their men know now what to expect and they'll hang back as much as they can. But these fellows," – he towards the Prussians – "they're the ones that matter. They've scarcely slept since they've got here and they've worked like Trojans. They won't budge until they've shells enough to smother this position, or think they have. It'll be only after that when they'll send their infantry across."

Dawlish hardly heard him. He was looking from the Prussian emplacement back towards the *Odin*, safe at her mooring far up the fjord, then back again. He realised what Saabye must have demanded, what Blackwood and Granville must be thinking now. On this fine spring morning, when the tranquil waters gave no hint of what lay beneath, it must seem simple – bring the ironclad south and pound the Prussian position from its rear. The Dane's *Rolf Krake*, armed and armoured like *Odin*, had done something similar at Dybbøl.

There was no alternative to confronting Blackwood with the unwelcome truth.

"I don't know if we could bring the *Odin* this far south, sir. Not without –" He checked himself just before he said the word 'grounding'. Never give up too soon. "Not without sounding, sir. That's what I'll report to Captain FitzBaldwin."

And that was what he did, however much Lorance might dislike it.

*

The Østergaards, father and son, could not be found. The money earned on their night reconnaissances was burning holes in their pockets. They had last been seen drinking heavily in their village on the northern side of the fjord. Lieutenant Krag sent two of their neighbours, who shipped farm produce across, to find them. It did not matter if they did not turn up until the morrow. In the meantime, there were small buoys to be fashioned from driftwood, difficult to notice if the single strip of red paint they bore was not being looked for.

Dawlish got permission to go ashore in the evening, ostensibly for discussions with Krag. There was little to discuss – it was already agreed that the Danish officer would again act as translator during sounding expeditions with the Østergaards – but Dawlish sought him out anyway to avoid having lied. The shelter that Krag shared with three other officers was as miserable as the others that had replaced the houses torn down for their wood. Even with the blanket that closed the entrance pulled aside, the interior was foetid and Dawlish was glad that he was not invited to enter. They stood outside to talk. Two other young Danish officers joined them. Both had limited English and all were eager to know more of *Odin's* encounter with the gunboats. As he spoke, Dawlish noticed that all three were scratching themselves at intervals. They seemed unconscious of doing so, had accommodated to being lice-ridden. He remembered how degraded he had felt when he had been infested himself. These men had gone beyond that.

He finished his account. "Brave fellows, all of them," he said. He remembered with pity – and a degree of shame – the Prussian seamen spilling into the water from the dismembered gunboat.

"I hope every one of them drowned," one of the Danes said. The others nodded agreement.

"They were seamen like –" Dawlish began but he stopped himself.

He had wanted to say that ships fought ships, not men. But it was not his country that had been invaded. He sensed the same cold hatred in these men – likeable, decent, honourable men – that he had in Welborne also. In the soldiers they commanded, uneducated peasants, most of them, who knew of nothing but the brutality of labour and the humiliations of poverty, that hatred must be even stronger. This war would have begun with clean uniforms, polished leather, gleaming brass, kit inspections, groomed horses, jingling spurs. Now officers and men alike were filthy and lousy, had reverted already half-way to barbarism, and the horses' ribs had all but broken through their flanks. But they were still enduring, were not beaten.

Not my country, not my fight. And yet…

Denmark was not in the right in the dynastic and diplomatic complexities that had led to this conflict – Krag had told Dawlish as much before now and had said the Saabye probably felt the same. But that seemed irrelevant now that large alien armies had brought misery and bereavement to thousands, a punishment infinitely disproportionate to the offence. For Krag, for Saabye, for the humblest soldier on this barren peninsula, there was more at stake than arcane legal subtleties. They were fighting for hearth and home, for a notion of honour too that few could enunciate but most must feel.

And he was suddenly glad that he was with them.

Right or wrong.

*

Light was fading as he walked to the church. Every effort had been made to give order to the encampment. Nothing could disguise the reek of latrines or the grime and unshaven faces of the troops cooking over meagre fires. Fresh water was valuable, since there were only a few wells, and there was none to spare for washing. Another enemy assault was all but imminent and many of these men were living their last days in filth.

There was worse at the church. It was no longer large enough to accommodate all its patients and two large tents now adjoined it. Dawlish held back – the very word 'Typhus' terrified him. Even as he stood there, two orderlies carried out another body. They looked worn-out but one made some remark and the other laughed when they emerged after leaving it in the shed where Killigrew had awaited burial. The orderlies' humour in the face of such suffering, crude as it might be, was somehow touching. They had been two months here, had seen agonies and deaths innumerable, were exposed to contagion themselves on a daily basis. Feeling reproved by their defiance of Fate, Dawlish entered the church.

That he knew what to expect made it no easier. The bodies were more closely packed, the moans and gasps and quiet babblings no less pitiful than before. This was a place in which to die, not recover.

"Lieutenant – my apologies, I don't know your name." A man's voice, speaking French.

Dawlish turned, saw Doctor Venel. He introduced himself.

"You shouldn't come here," Venel said. "It's dangerous. Not just for yourself. You can carry typhus back to your ship."

Dawlish knew it, and felt foolish.

"I heard that two of your people died."

"Madame Racine. A noble woman, I believe you met her."

It was impossible to imagine. She had been calm strength and competence personified, never smiling, never showing revulsion either.

"She is a great loss at this time, we miss her badly. And a young Swedish lady." Venel held up his hands in a gesture of powerlessness. "Typhus respects neither age nor worth and it kills quickly. That's why you should go now."

"A Swedish lady?" It was hard, very hard, to ask.

"Mademoiselle Boström. Poor girl, she had no training but she did her best." Venel pointed to the door. "Now you must go, lieutenant. You can do no good here, but much harm for your friends on that ship if you carry the infection back."

"And Mademoiselle Blomqvist, is she still —"

"There is the door, lieutenant."

He went outside and waited in the shadows to watch comings and goings between church and tents. She might not be here at this time and might be resting. One of the remaining wooden houses had been allocated to the medical staff and he kept that in view also. He was unsure how long he could afford to wait but, as each ten minutes passed, he promised himself that he would allow just ten more. To his right lay the burial ground – Madame Racine, stiff and dignified, as unsparing of herself as she had been of others, lay there among humble Danish peasant soldiers. That Swedish girl who had done her best was there too, perhaps one of the fine fillies whom Killigrew had admired. She might have tended to him later, had perhaps choked down revulsion as his dressings were changed, had done her best. Now they lay yards apart, strangers forever in alien soil.

At last he saw her. She was coming from the house with another young woman and carrying a lantern that cast a flickering light on their faces and on their white aprons. He advanced to meet them.

"Löjtnant Page." She had remembered his name but showed no pleasure in recognition.

"I trust I see you well, mademoiselle."

Now that he had seen her, he was not sure what to say, wondered even why he was here.

"Nobody's well here, löjtnant."

"I'm sad to learn about Madame Racine. And your Swedish friend."

"Thank you, löjtnant." Her tone was dead. She might be forty years older since he had last seen her. The port-wine stain seemed little worse than the other signs of ageing "Now we've got work to do." She made to move past him.

"Mademoiselle has received bad news," The other woman, by her accent, was Swiss. "It's no time for talk, löjtnant. She has her grief."

Eleonora Blomqvist turned to Dawlish.

"My brother," she said. Her eyes were filling. "Friherre Saabye sent for me. He had a message from Copenhagen. He was very kind. I knew what it was even before he told me, I could see it in his face. That Arvid had died at a place called Dybbøl." Her voice had begun to tremble.

"He would have known nothing, they said. A single bullet in the heart. He didn't suffer."

He could see that she knew better. Families were always told that, or something like it. He knew that, if he rose in the service, he too might have to write such lies someday.

"I'm sorry." Words failed.

"It will kill my father. He had such hopes of Arvid."

"Are you going back then, mademoiselle?"

"My place is here. Good night, löjtnant."

"Good night, mademoiselle."

And he returned to *Odin*.

*

The first sounding expedition was on the following night. The Østergaards, when found, demanded a higher a price than before

"They're worth the six sovereigns a night," FitzBaldwin said. "More than worth it." The skies were clear and the full moon over the calm fjord would increase the risk of detection.

They set off just before midnight. All active fishing boats were working close to the northern shore. Ever since the raid on the supply column moving up the isthmus, first the Austrians, and later the Prussians, had opened fire on any boat that had approached too near. The Østergaards' craft would stand out stark and solitary on the silvery waters.

"Get as far south of the Prussian redoubt as you can," FitzBaldwin said. "They won't be expecting you this first night. Don't venture closer in than two cables. If you find anything less than five fathoms then move out further."

The slightest of south-westerly breezes carried them down the centre of the fjord – it should be deepest there. The lights of the Thyborøn camp and the pinpricks in the Danish redoubts slid past a mile to starboard. There was still depth enough. Mc Rory, the leadsman in the bow, was calling seven fathoms, then eight, then seven again. Dawlish crouched behind him with the buoys and anchors and Krag helped him lug the first overboard a mile south of *Odin's* mooring. The elder Østergaard was at the tiller and the younger tended the sails.

They were level with the Prussian redoubt, then past it, and off the starboard bow they could see the lights of the enemy camp. There was still depth enough – six fathoms – here at the centre. Getting *Odin* in position here would indeed allow her to take the Prussian positions under fire from the rear. But not with any accuracy. The poor results of the bombardment of the Austrian demi-lunes from the sea — annoyance rather than destruction — had testified to that. It was essential to get in closer.

On for another half-mile, depth ranging between six and seven — still satisfactory. Another buoy dropped to mark the point for turning south-west. The breeze was against them, and too weak to allow tacking with any chance of speedy progress. Kristian Østergaard lowered the sail. Dawlish and Krag shipped oars and began to pull — tiring work, for the boat was heavy. McRory was still calling six fathoms and they were getting closer to the shore. Six fathoms, and another buoy, and still creeping in. The beach could not be more than two cables ahead, the irregular profile of the dunes visible against the bright sky behind.

McRory called "By the deep four!" — less than five fathoms. The bed must be shelving steeply here.

The bows swept around to head back to deeper water as Krag relayed Dawlish's instruction. Six fathoms again, another buoy, then moving north, parallel to the shore, repeated shallow soundings at intervals, necessitating pulling further out. The rear of the Prussian redoubt was off the port bow now, lanterns visible there.

Then suddenly a rifle shot from shore, and a voice shouting and then a rattle of further fire. Cool reason told Dawlish that the danger was minimal, however well the boat was silhouetted against the moonlit water — the range could not be less than three cables, six-hundred yards — but his heart pounded and his mouth was suddenly dry nonetheless. He yelled for Uffe Østergaard to steer out before the breeze, for his son Kristian to raise the sails, for McRory to help him.

More firing, muzzle-flashes, even brief shouts that sounded triumphant when some Prussian private thought he had scored a hit. Gaff raised, boom swung out, the breeze was catching, the boat speeding up enough for Dawlish and Krag to rest exhausted on their oars.

It was a good start, enough to prove that the Prussians could be menaced. But more buoys would be needed in this area if *Odin* was to be risked.

That was work for the next night.

Chapter 26

The next night was more fraught. The single string of buoys laid down already did not constitute a channel that *Odin* could navigate with safety. Finding six fathoms and more along that line might well have been luck and it was impossible to know how close it might be to shallows on either side. Another string was essential, as parallel to the first as possible, and nearer to the shore. In just semi-darkness, and with minimal landmarks and no method of measuring distance, establishing it could only be a matter of touch, go and judgement. And after the last night's alarms, the Prussians must guess that something of the like was intended.

The Østergaards' boat crept south past the Danish redoubt, a half-cable closer inshore, Dawlish judged, than it had the night before. Lights bobbed at the Prussian position. From *Odin's* tops, more artillery had been sighted moving into it during the day. Much further south, yet another column of marching troops, interspersed with wagons, had been spotted approaching the Prussian camp. A calm, more ominous than any harassing fire, had lain over the peninsula all day, a promise of strength building, of fury waiting to be unleashed. The Radetzky had still been heard at intervals but it seemed to lack the mocking confidence of its earlier performances. No music sounded from the Prussian positions.

The moon was brighter this night but shreds of cloud drifted across it, leaving broad but shifting dark patches across the fjord. The lightest of breezes blew from the east. Under oars alone, but ready to hoist sail, the boat crawled southwards, rowlocks well-greased and wrapped in rags. The plop of each cast of McRory's lead seemed loud enough to rouse even the most inattentive of Prussian guards, but no alarm was raised. Dawlish glanced north-eastwards and glimpsed the faint glow above the funnel of *Odin's* steam launch as it kept pace. He had not asked for it – it was FitzBaldwin's idea.

Nine buoys had been dropped by now and the Prussian redoubt was just abaft the starboard beam. The craft's course snaked to port when less than five fathoms was encountered, moved south then into deeper water, then probed inshore again and repeated the process. And still no alarm was raised.

Then a sudden crash of rifle-fire, not from the black silhouette of the dunes to starboard but from off the port bow, brief tongues of orange stabbing in the half-darkness. There was a boat there, three hundred yards away but driving forward, moonlight flashing from the water that spilled from its beating oars. Frozen for an instant, then realising that only flight could be a saviour, Dawlish yelled for the helm to be thrown over. Even as he did a rocket whooshed up from the dunes and exploded overhead to suffuse the fjord's rippled surface with scarlet light.

"Keep pulling ahead!" Dawlish shouted to Krag as he himself backed water to assist the helm and drive the bows north-eastwards. The younger Østergaard was already hauling the gaff aloft, McRory straining with him. More rifle-fire rattled, ineffective for now but likely to gain accuracy as the separation decreased.

Another rocket – more light – and the Prussian-manned boat was closer now – a squat heavy craft confiscated from some fisherman. Two or three men, rifles raised, were trying to keep their balance between the rowers, two or more of them to a side. But now the Østergaards' boat was headed north-east and Dawlish stroked ahead again in unison with Krag, and the breeze caught the raised sail. The craft heeled slightly as she speeded up and began to draw away. The last sparks of the rocket were falling and the Prussians were still sustaining rapid fire – more rapid than might be expected from such a handful.

Breech-loaders, Dawlish realised. He had read of them, had never seen one. Only the Prussians had them in any numbers. Faster to load than any conventional rifle, even in a rocking boat.

Panting, Dawlish and Krag slumped over their oars. The Prussian craft was dropping away astern, its rifles falling into silence.

Another rocket soared from the black outline of the dunes, followed by a second even before it burst at its apogee. Now flame stabbed from the dark shore and an instant after came a sharp crack of a light cannon. In the light of the rockets' blazing fragments, a plume of spray showed a ball skidding along the water's surface some twenty yards to port. Even as the plume died another weapon opened – light horse-artillery by their reports, four or six-pounders. The second ball dropped far ahead and raised a brief column of foam. Alerted by the previous night's intrusion, the Prussians were all too well prepared for a repeat.

Even without Dawlish's prompting, Uffe Østergaard was shifting the tiller over, then back, and so again, but never so much as to lose wind or speed in a shifting course that would distract the gunners' aims. More reports now. A third weapon had come into play, and then a fourth. As the range opened. the trajectories were no longer low and the balls were plunging to throw up fountains of spray, one close enough to shower down inside the boat. Dawlish was frightened now – they all were, he saw it on their faces – and the worst was the inability to reply in any way. Yet more light guns had opened fire – the Prussians must have ranged an entire battery along the isthmus south of their redoubt in expectation of this incursion. The chance of any single aimed shot hitting its moving target was negligible but numbers mattered, however random the fall of shot. Foam was erupting ahead, on either flank, once close astern, crimson in the light of bursting rockets.

"There, sir!" McRory shouted from the bow and pointed.

Odin's steam launch was advancing towards the falling shot, course undeviating, sparks spilling from her brass funnel, a man crouched in the bows, others standing in the small cockpit aft. A geyser boiled up off her bow, showering her as she forged on, rocking with the expanding ripples. At thirty yards' separation, Dawlish saw her speeding past – eight knots was her maximum in calm water and she must be making that much now. Van der Horst had taken the helm himself and now, as calmly as if at a summer regatta, he was bringing the craft creaming over in a wide half-turn through the fleeing boat's wake and continuing on to draw alongside. The man at the bow was Welborne, yelling to stand-by to catch a rope. The launch's speed dropped to keep pace and then the line came flying over. It fell inside the boat, Krag grabbed it and Kristian Østergaard whipped the end in a clove hitch around the mast.

The launch surged forward, the line tightened, the boat's bows dipped, then lifted, as she followed in the wake.

It was slow, but faster than under sail, enough to clear the zone of danger, to leave the enemy's last, useless, falling shots astern. Independent of wind, the launch ran parallel to the shore, past the Prussian redoubt, past the no-man's land that separated it from the Danish earthwork to the north, back past that also, and so into safety.

A deliverance, not a victory.

The waters south-east of the Prussian redoubt had not been sounded, nor would they now be either.

A battery – maybe less – of Prussian horse-artillery had seen to that.

*

Further surveying was impossible and without more sounding *Odin* could manoeuvre no further south than the no-man's land. Dawlish sensed that the failure had pleased Lorance, that he had no stomach for risking the ironclad scant days before she would revert to being *Galveston*. For FitzBaldwin it was more difficult. It was he who would have to explain to Saabye that the Prussian redoubt could not be attacked from the rear. It would be harder still to argue that bombardment of its forward face would yield little, would be as much a waste of shot as *Odin's* attack on the Austrian demi-lunes had been.

"The guv'nor isn't happy," Albemarle told Dawlish after his father had returned from the meeting ashore. "I can see it, I know him. He won't show it, not openly, won't admit it. But he knows that he promised too much."

"He thinks that?"

"Don't you, Nick?"

"There's still time."

He knew that he was saying it only because he did not want to admit the truth. *Odin* had fired his blood since he had first seen her drawings, as she must have fired FitzBaldwin's also. So much had been expected of the ironclad's huge Armstrongs, of her thick side-armour, of her fearsome ram. And every encounter with the enemy had been a disappointment. The Armstrongs' accuracy had been overestimated. The armour had availed nothing when Austrian howitzers had exposed the vulnerability of the unprotected upper-works. Ramming had proved too difficult a manoeuvre in practice. The only success had been the point-blank destruction of a weakly-armed wooden gunboat and the capture of a few prizes – blackguard's work – that an armed despatch vessel could have achieved just as capably.

That sense of failure seemed to lie heavy on *Odin's* entire complement. The sounding expeditions in the fjord had indicated a likelihood of action and, for all that most might view it with trepidation, it was preferable to confinement on a ship that swung impotently at anchor. Typhus still raged in the Danish camps and redoubts and only for the most pressing reasons were members of the crew allowed ashore. FitzBaldwin, obliged to attend meetings with Saabye and Blackwood, was probably the most at risk of all on board.

Each day now brought expectation of a Prussian and Austrian attack. Howitzer fire had resumed again by night, spasmodic, unpredictable, enough to deprive the defenders of the forward redoubts of sleep after they had scurried into their shelters. Fishermen standing-off well clear of the Prussian-dominated shore observed further reinforcements – infantry, not artillery. It was impossible to gauge overall numbers, since much of the movement was by night, but it was clear that the inevitable assault would commence with numbers that would vastly outweigh the Danish defenders.

Dawlish was counting the days now – as everybody aboard the ironclad must be – and wondering if that assault would come before she sailed away on the morning of May 9th. Bulloch had driven a hard bargain for the Southern Confederacy, and FitzBaldwin's honour was at stake in seeing it complied with to the letter. Most of the men on board had already decided to remain when the transfer of command would come – they might never have a chance to earn such money again. And yet, from overhearing them, Dawlish sensed that they too wished for the assault to come before they left, for something perhaps akin to victory. They too had their honour

Odin's daily round of drills and duties went on without remission on the assumption – a vain one, Dawlish realised – that exhaustion allowed little time to brood. He had lost count of loading and training exercises with the Armstrongs, of the constant inspection and greasing of shafts and gears and rollers that were already lubricated to perfection. He was glad that Welborne plunged into the drills with such zeal – he was already speaking of the Armstrongs as his guns. Down in the boiler and engine rooms, and on decks washed and washed again though no speck of dirt remained, and as sails were shaken out and furled again, as brass was polished and bulkheads painted, other men were kept no less busy – and were hating it.

It was all the worse for the cat-calls and mockery from the local craft that still ferried supplies into Thyborøn – worse because there was some truth to them. Dawlish had picked up enough Danish to understand the gibes that implied that *Odin* and her crew were holding back, were moored in safe impotence well back out of range of enemy fire, were uncaring of the sacrifices and dangers onshore. Knowing what he did of conditions in the camp and redoubts – and of that dreadful hospital – he felt something of guilt that here on the ship he was free from lice, had warm water, tapped from the boiler, in which to wash, clean clothing, a cot to sleep in, a dry blanket to keep him warm.

The contrast struck most painfully when the *Hulde* paddle steamer arrived from Aalborg. The town was still in Danish hands – if a single company of aged reservists could so be called. The enemy had higher priorities for their forces than taking it. Its value for Denmark now lay in its hospital and it was to bring wounded there – not typhus cases, so great was the fear of spreading it – that the *Hulde* had returned. For there were wounded now again, victims of the nightly howitzer shelling, of undetected Prussian sharpshooters who waited with such patience to put a single shot into a head carelessly raised above Danish parapets and who killed more often than they maimed.

Dawlish watched as the wounded were hoisted aboard the steamer. Doctor Venel was busy supervising the hospital orderlies handling the stretchers. There was no sign of Eleonora Blomqvist or of any of the other nurses – they must be remaining. Afterwards he was surprised to see Venel having himself rowed across. FitzBaldwin, alerted, met him as he came aboard. Despite the outward courtesy, Venel, potential typhus carrier, would not be invited to the captain's cabin. A seaman approached Dawlish. Captain FitzBaldwin's compliments, and would he join him.

Neither man knew anything of the other's language other than a few trivial salutations and observations. These had run out and captain and doctor were standing now in embarrassed silence.

"You speak French, don't you Dawlish? Good fellow. Translate for me. The doctor wants something and I'm damned if I can understand a word of it."

Venel's words came in a torrent. The steamer's captain had told him that he had arrived here only by hugging the fjord's northern shore. Prussian guns were now reaching out into the centre. And the passage was narrower further east, and what if the Prussians brought guns there too? It would be a massacre, wounded unable to save themselves, horror inexpressible…

"What's he saying?" FitzBaldwin was impatient. When Dawlish translated, he said. "I can't see what we can do about it. Tell him we regret it but we can't help."

Dawlish began to explain but Venel interrupted.

"La Croix Rouge," he said. "The Prussians aren't barbarians, they know of it, they'll respect it., they'll give safe passage. But we need paint, monsieur, red paint and white and we have not got it."

FitzBaldwin laughed when he heard it. "He's a damned optimistic fellow, this Switzer. But tell him we've paint and he's welcome, and he can have men for laying it on too."

Another way of keeping the crew busy, and one they liked, welcome for its novelty. When the *Hulde* beat back east the following day, great square white patches had been painted ahead and abaft of her paddle boxes. The squares bore red crosses from which the paint ran down like blood in half-dried streaks.

And Dawlish hoped that the Prussians did indeed know of La Croix Rouge.

*

More days passed in impotent frustration, of waiting for an assault that did not come.

Then, at last, alarm.

Red rockets climbed into the night sky from the Prussian positions and a hail of howitzer fire dropped on the Danish redoubts. Amid the booms and detonations, bugle calls sounded in Thyborøn, rousing men from their shelters to hasty mustering. *Odin* too came to readiness – all hands to their stations, husbanded coal shovelled into her banked furnaces, anchor party at the bows, the turret manned, Dawlish on his seat, van der Horst supervising laying out of hoses, FitzBaldwin and Lorance on the bridge.

Now the waiting.

Sky overcast, fjord surface dark, two hours more to raise full steam, three hours to sunrise and to sufficient light for *Odin* to manoeuvre to provide support.

The howitzers fell silent. Thousands of Prussian voices were cheering as one, words indistinguishable but the sense of confidence was unmistakable. Then a brass band blared into life and the voices rose to join it in a slow, thundering anthem. Three times it was repeated, then followed by what sounded as solemn as a hymn, that too repeated, then more cheering. In the brief pauses there came from further westwards the strains of an Austrian band pounding out a no-less ponderous paean.

The sun rose, and at intervals the bands played again and there was yet more singing. It was a celebration, not a prelude to attack, though the Danes stood-to in their defences until midday, and *Odin* remained ready for action.

It could mean only one thing, one that all hesitated to speak of.

Confirmation came a day later. Dawlish was keeping the forenoon watch when he saw a commotion on the northern shore. Intrigued, he focussed a glass on it. Two horsemen were drawing rein at the landing where supplies were shipped across to Thyborøn. They must have come from Aalborg. Officers by their uniforms, as dust-grimed as their mounts, they were demanding to be taken over. He watched them as they crossed, saw them spring ashore as the craft grounded. A word from one sent a guard sprinting towards Saabye's headquarters and they shambled in pursuit, their exhaustion as obvious as that of their horses. Even before they reached half-way, two other officers met them, accepted satchels from them and hurried back to the school ahead of them.

Ten minutes later a request arrived for FitzBaldwin to go over. He was back a half-hour later and he called the officers to his cabin.

"Dybbøl," he said. "It's fallen."

Silence.

By all reports previously received it had sounded impregnable, the strongest entrenched position ever seen in Europe. It had withstood earlier bombardments, had hurled back assaults. Krag had told Dawlish that besieging it would bleed the Prussians dry, force negotiation. Dybbøl had all but been the war.

"What happened?" Lorance asked at last.

FitzBaldwin shrugged. "The inevitable. Days of heavy shelling – the Prussians built up vast stocks before they began. And then a massive assault along the entire line three days ago. Fierce resistance, counterattacks, redoubts falling, breakthroughs. Serious losses. Collapse."

"Surrender?"

"No. The Danes are still in the fight – stout fellows that they are. What's left of them fell back across their pontoon bridge to Sønderborg. It's on an island, Als. They're safe enough for now – there's four hundred yards of open water between them and the positions they've just lost."

"What does Friherre Saabye say about it?"

"That attack's imminent here. Maybe tomorrow, not later than the day after. The Prussians can afford now to release troops from their forces at Dybbøl. They'll need another day or so to get moving – they took heavy losses too but they'll be here in eight or ten days. The commanders here, Prussian and Austrian alike, will want their victory without them. They won't want to share the glory."

Seventeen hours later, the storm broke.

Chapter 27

Dawlish was in his cot – he had stood the first watch – when the rumble woke him. He had struggled into his clothes even before a seaman came to rouse him. His watch told him that it was three o'clock, still two hours to sunrise. He felt mixed trepidation and relief – the wait was over and he was prepared. The ship was coming alive and bleary-eyed men were rushing to their stations. He reached the bridge, found FitzBaldwin there already, Lorance and van der Horst joining. They stood transfixed for a moment by the sight and sound.

To the south, across the entire isthmus, flashes rippled along the enemy lines, their reports merging into a single rumble that rose and fell in waves. At the now open-backed Danish redoubts, orange detonations showed that the howitzer shells were falling there like hail. Most of the defenders must have already reached the shelters, must be praying that the layers of wood and sand above would save them. It must be worst of all for those posted on the parapets, watching for first signs of an infantry assault.

FitzBaldwin's order was simple.

"Man the turret."

The Armstrongs were already loaded, the hinged bulwarks dropped, the gun-crews ready for this moment. Dawlish climbed to his seat below the rim and Welborne joined him. It would be a half-hour yet before the boilers were at full pressure – already half-way there for two days, they wanted little stoking – and until then the ironclad would remain immobile. Time enough to rotate the turret through a full three-sixty, grease the recoil-slides, check elevation gearing.

The artillery-fire continued unabated. The sun rose to show a dark pall of smoke lying over the redoubts of both sides and drifting over the intervening no-man's land. Rope curtains still shielded the Prussian embrasures – the fire was still from howitzers hidden from direct view by the redoubt's sloped walls. Infantry might also be massed there, brought up the isthmus from the Prussian camp during darkness. Lookouts in the foretop reported a huge explosion in the most westward of the Danish positions – a magazine hit and a fire raging there. In the Thyborøn camp bugles sounded as men spilled from their shelters, formed into units, moved south to wait behind Blackwood's new defences.

A boat stroked out to *Odin* – Krag was coming aboard. Brought to the bridge, he handed over a note to FitzBaldwin, gestured southwards. Dawlish could not hear their voices but the errand seemed unnecessary. What must follow had been agreed with Saabye and Blackwood days before, had been translated into detailed orders for *Odin* and her guns.

The anchor party strained on the capstan as a few churns of the screws urged the ironclad forward to help lifting. Released, she began her slow crawl down the fjord. FitzBaldwin called for the turret guns to be laid on to the Prussian position and to be inched over to keep bearing on it as the ship advanced.

And then yet-louder, deeper, blasts, long flames reaching out from the forward face of the Prussian redoubt. The embrasures were unshielded now and six, eight, ten large cannons, large enough to be fortress artillery, dragged here by superhuman effort, fired almost as one to smash shells into the Danish ramparts. A pause – the gunners reloading – and from the west came the reports of the Austrian artillery opening from their demi-lunes. Then the fastest gun-crew had its piece in action again, and a second followed close behind, and again a line of flame flashed through the rolling smoke that now hid the embrasures. Plumes of sand were showering up from the sloped Danish walls.

The devastation that the Austrians had rained on the redoubt where he had survived the earlier attack had been nothing to this, Dawlish realised. Even as the Prussians' great fortress weapons tore great craters in the ramparts – gaps through which infantry must surely storm – the howitzer fire did not slacken. It plunged down behind the ramparts and made any movement outside the shelters there suicidal. Embrasures had also been unmasked in the two smaller Prussian works further forward and lighter weapons there – field guns, five, six batteries – were adding their own unrelenting hail.

Odin crept south at quarter-revolutions, well inside the buoyed area and with McRory as leadsman on the starboard bow calling the depth. Dawlish's gaze was fixed on an imagined axis running between the Armstrong barrels and called down instructions to the men on the cranks below to hold it on the centre of the enemy redoubt. The fjord's calmness – all but mirror-still this fresh spring morning – allowed the gearing to inch the turret around with a smoothness that would have been impossible on the open sea. Welborne was estimating range – still too great to allow engagement but closing steadily. FitzBaldwin was on the bridge and Lorance, beside him, was at the helm. Far aft, van der Horst stood at a secondary steering position and had a party ready with axes, crowbars and hoses to cope with any damage. Up in the foretop, Albemarle and Crowther scanned with telescopes to detect the buoys.

The open area between the new and the old Danish defences was slipping past two cables to starboard. Occasional overshoots by the Prussian howitzers dropped there – *Odin* had entered their range even if she had not yet become their target.

As she must…

The Danish redoubt was all but invisible through smoke and upthrown sand. Showered by the howitzers, gouged by the heavy fortress artillery, it was hard to imagine anybody surviving within. And yet Confederate troops had withstood as much at Vicksburg, on the Mississippi, Welborne had told Dawlish with pride, had emerged to repel two great Union assaults. Even simple buried shelters had withstood heavy fire and it had been starvation, not storm or bombardment, that had ended the siege there.

"Dawlish!" FitzBaldwin calling from the bridge. "Your guns now! Two salvos – two only. And over the redoubt, over, I say!"

The rolling fog of smoke that obscured the Prussian position was broad on the starboard bow.

"Range!" Dawlish yelled to Welborne.

"Four cables!"

A guess, and close enough to Dawlish's of four and a half. The lack of reliable range-tables made elevation selection nothing other than a guess. The guns were at two degrees, enough, he hoped to graze the redoubt's crest, enough to drop the shells far behind it where Prussian infantry might be massed, awaiting orders to assault. If wrong, there would be no time for correction. He found his hand trembling. At this moment, he was *Odin*.

He looked down, saw Hopper, face turned up to him and with the firing lanyards in his hands. Two men stood at each crank, ready to realign the aim.

"Mr. Hopper! Two degrees more to starboard!"

Men straining on the cranks, the turret creeping over.

"Lock it, Mr. Hopper!"

Confirmation.

"Stand by, Mr. Hopper! On my word!"

"Buoy ahead! Three cables and a half!" Albemarle calling from the foretop to the bridge. It must be the furthest south of the markers that Dawlish had dropped. *Odin* must turn away before it.

"Fire now!"

A double thunderclap, the Armstrongs heaving back, choking smoke swirling in the drum and rising to obscure Dawlish's view. Through it he saw a single flash — greater than any blasting from the Prussian guns — and an instant later the crash of the exploding shell.

One, one shell only, too low to clear the redoubt crest, had torn a gash in the wall below it. But there was a second shell...

And detonation far beyond told that it had indeed shaved over the Prussian earthwork, had dropped three or four hundred yard behind, ploughing a furrow perhaps through waiting companies of grim Prussian grenadiers ...

Now the endless drills paid off — guns sponged, loaded, rammed and run out in a time inconceivable weeks before.

"Turret, back five degrees starboard!"

Aiming to the east of the redoubt, the target now the ground to its south.

"Ready, Sir!"

"Fire!"

Both shells were still in the air as Lorance flung the helm over. The buoy was still a half-cable ahead as the ironclad began its ponderous swing towards the Limfjord's centre.

Two explosions, flame and smoke rising like geysers. Impossible to know the damage — there might be none, not material at least — but notice had been served that Prussian forces held in readiness behind the redoubt were not immune.

Odin heeled over in a half-circle turn, left it as her bows headed again northwards toward the fjord entrance. Suddenly a column of spray was climbing off the port quarter, and another, equally harmless, ten seconds later. Some Prussian battery commander was hauling his howitzers around to bear on the retreating vessel. Too late. She was already passing out of range — and gunners trained to lob shells into static targets could rely on chance only for success against a moving one. But even a single shell plunging down on the unarmoured decks could wreak havoc, could kill the iron ship should that shell find the boiler. And *Odin* must return...

Still forging northwards, leadsmen still chanting, guns reloaded. Albemarle shouted down from the top that the Austrian shelling had also not diminished, that the two western Danish redoubts were still being pounded and not retaliating.

Another sixteen-point turn now to run back south on the same path as before. Difficult as it was to hear FitzBaldwin's shouted commands above the anger of the enemy guns, Dawlish welcomed them, saw their logic. Confident now of the depth within the buoyed area, FitzBaldwin had ordered increased revolutions and in the calm water the ship was still rock-steady. Her Armstrongs' elevation wound up one degree, the turret was edged over on Dawlish's instructions, holding aim once more on the end of the redoubt closer to the shore.

Now passing the tortured Danish position again.

"Your guns, Mr. Dawlish!"

Again the roar, the smoke, the recoiling monsters, this salvo at longer range, hoping to drop closer to the rear of the Prussian redoubt.

And success – Albemarle was confirming it from his high perch, troops scattering there as the three-hundred pound shells exploded in their midst.

Now the controlled rush of reloading, men straining on the cranks to edge the turret bearing over.

"Drop elevation one degree!" – another guess.

The next salvo, and then two more in rapid succession. All shells but one cleared the Prussian rampart to burst beyond and that one alone buried itself to the side of an embrasure, smothering the gun within it with sand as it detonated.

Odin had pulled out again into another half-circle turn and into the area on which the Prussian howitzers could bear. Splashes began to rise within the turn – too far off and too closely grouped to be of danger, for wider dispersion would have been more dangerous. FitzBaldwin rang for half-revolutions and Lorance guided the vessel into a wide turn to port that carried her back north.

Into safe water.

Unmoored, held on engines alone, *Odin* hovered off Thyborøn, an air of mixed relief and triumph as black-faced men with smoke-rasped throats slaked their thirst from buckets carried around. Five salvos, ten shells gone, as many charges. It was time to hoist up more from the magazine, replenish the storage racks inside the turret.

For it was only seven o'clock.

The day's work had just begun.

*

Odin waited.

And waited. A message carried across from Saabye had requested that. Dawlish, summoned to the bridge, was told why. The Prussian and

266

Austrian artillery supplies were not unlimited and the firing had lasted for three hours by now, must soon be lessening. The assault was imminent. There would be better targets for the Armstrongs than the forces hidden behind the Prussian redoubt. Dawlish received permission for the gun-crews to rest on the deck outside the turret once the racks within had been refilled – it had been brutal labour. The sun was shining and some fell asleep.

The first slackening of the fire came soon after nine o'clock, at first from the Austrians to the west, soon thereafter from the Prussians too. All hands to their stations again on *Odin*, turret cranked over to the starboard beam. FitzBaldwin brought her crawling down to hover just north above the battered Danish position.

A half-hour passed, the bombardment dying to individual shots from the enemy redoubts, the howitzers sheltered behind them falling wholly silent. A few figures – Dawlish fancied that he recognised Granville and Evenden – had emerged from shelter and on to the fire-steps of the Danish earthwork. They were looking south, heads rising above the parapet for seconds only before dropping again. Their dilemma must be a terrible one, whether to call the defenders to the ramparts and to drag the guns from their shelters and into the embrasures, and risk another pounding, or to keep in shelter and risk being overrun.

Long minutes, the near-silence as full of dread as had been the fury of the guns. The smoke of the falling shells had drifted clear of the Danish redoubt to show great bites gnawed from the sloped walls – at one point a broad gap almost to ground level where an embrasure had been. Craters and unexploded howitzer shells littered the interior. What had been left of the rear wall that Blackwood had had demolished was all but beaten flat.

Then the storm.

It was the last paroxysm of the Prussian guns, unseen howitzers blasting together, the heavy guns in the embrasures vomiting flame through what grew into a line of rolling smoke. It lasted two minutes, lashing the Danish works, driving the few men on the fires-steps there to cower and burrow.

Then silence, abrupt, seconds only before the shrill of whistles, a band somewhere behind the Prussian redoubt launching into a blaring march, cheering men, with bayonets levelled, emerging through the smoke. They funnelled out, formed into long lines, three, four, five, yet more following, the slightest gaps between what must be individual units, not shoulder-to-shoulder but each man a pace apart from those on either side. They came on steadily – a fast tempo, but not yet at the double or at a run. With a thousand yards to cover, they should not arrive exhausted at the start of the final charge. Blue-uniformed, only their round brimless caps made them look different to the Danish infantry. At many points single officers on horseback rode out in front, swords drawn, and close behind them followed colour parties with standards upraised.

"Your guns, Mr. Dawlish"

FitzBaldwin was ringing for quarter-revolutions and the ironclad settled into her own steady advance. Dawlish's orders for what now lay ahead had been made clear during the long wait.

Men were rushing from the Danish shelters, dazzled by the light, then scrambling up on to the fire-steps. The gunners were dragging their pieces from their own shelters to the embrasures – few remained intact and in places open gaps in the ramparts must suffice. From further back, from the new defences south of Thyborøn, distant bugles called. From them were emerging the first reinforcements for the redoubts – fresh troops, not dazed by the shelling.

The foremost Prussians had advanced two hundred yards and, far in their rear, three separate bands were keeping pace, all beating out the same march but not achieving full unison. As they ended and began again, the strains of the inevitable Radetzky, no less discordant, could be heard in snatches from the west. The Austrians had started their own assault.

Odin was level with the Danish position and still edging ahead, revolutions reduced to the lowest churn. And still gunfire, neither rifle nor cannon, as the Danes waited for the range to close. The Prussians must know that a hurricane must soon be unleashed. There was something magnificent about their advance, unhurried and remorseless as a flowing tide, something arrogant too in its apparent contempt for what confronted it.

From the west, came the first roar of Danish cannon, opening on the approaching Austrians. It must be solid shot, Dawlish thought, as when he himself had stood in defence of one of the redoubts there, round balls that would bounce and leap and rip long lanes through the attacking infantry.

But the Armstrongs would do much worse…

Now the Danish guns erupted into life from the half-wrecked redoubt, past which the ironclad had just slipped. The range still too great for canister and they too were firing roundshot. Black dots were throwing up sprays of sand ahead of the Prussian ranks, then bounding on and scything gaps through them. The advance did not slacken, nor did it speed up, was no less steady than before.

Odin was level with the centre of the no man's land now and FitzBaldwin was telegraphing to the engine room for dead-slow astern to kill her forward momentum. The imaginary line between the Armstrong barrels was bisecting the open ground and the leading Prussians had not yet reached it. Dawlish had ordered the elevations set to a half-degree to limit the range – another guess.

His hands trembled. Hurling shells at unseen men beyond the redoubt had not seemed dreadful but sight of the advancing ranks was suddenly horrible. They were living, breathing beings like himself, mastering their fear but terrified nonetheless, sons, fathers, brothers, many with but minutes to live. He could feel no hatred for them, only pity.

But he had pledged his honour…

"Mr. Hopper! On my word!"

A horseman – his sword was raised – had passed the invisible line, so too the colour party following him, and now the first full rank was also all but across.

Wait. The small voice in Dawlish's mind *Wait…*

Seen end-on from *Odin*, the lines of Prussian troops snaked across the isthmus from fjord to lagoon in a long sinuous curve, some units slightly ahead, some lagging, the bands, encumbered by their instruments, now far behind.

"Fire!"

The shells hit the ground two hundred yards inland from the shore, ploughed forward, throwing up plumes of sand. They smashed down dozens along the advancing ranks, bodies flung up in their passage, and then the plumes collapsed and flame-shot explosions blasted out fragments to cut down yet more men ahead and behind. A smoking gap lay at the centre of the advance, but it still continued, ranks yet untouched striding between, and past, the dead and wounded.

Odin was all but stationary, held on engines alone. Within the turret the gunners had loaded and again the barrels slipped down their slides and the muzzles ran out through the ports. Hopper was yelling up that they were ready.

"Fire!"

More carnage, another swathe of death and a circle of scorched sand littered with bodies and wounded men tottering to their feet, bewildered, ignored by the fresh ranks marching on through them from behind.

Lashed on their front by the Danish fire, by *Odin's* on their flank, the Prussians advanced, pace unchanged, colours high, bands still blaring. The greater part had passed the Armstrongs' invisible line by now and Dawlish had the turret wound round ten degrees abaft the beam before they opened again. And again.

Only three hundred yards now separated the Prussian leaders from the Danes. Rifle-fire rippled from the fire-steps and grew into a sustained rattle as reinforcements, flooding in from the north, joined the defenders. Above the din the Prussian bugles were sounding and they were lumbering into a run. The Danish guns were firing cannister now, great fans of screaming balls that flailed down wide breaks in the leading Prussian ranks. *Odin's* fire – Dawlish counted salvos, seven, eight – was now smashing obliquely along the Prussian rear. He saw a band blasted apart – brass instruments flashing briefly in the sun – and riderless horses racing in panicked flight, wounded men staggering to their feet, falling again, and still bodies strewn across the wide expanse of furrowed and cratered sand.

The Prussians' charge had carried them almost to the foot of the sloped walls, close enough in places to be sheltered from cannister-fire from the embrasures. Danes were packed shoulder to shoulder on the fire-steps and shooting down point-blank. Prussians had dropped to one knee, were firing up, were feeding rounds, even from the crouch, into their wonderful breech-loaders, firing again to keep Danish heads down while their comrades clambered up the slopes. Behind them, the Prussian ranks had compressed into a single dark mass that still ground forward, stepping across dead and wounded.

Now the crisis, the first Prussians on the crests, met with bayonets and rifle-fire. The few Danish embrasures that could still bring guns to bear were still pouring canister. Yet more reinforcements from Thyborøn – panting from their at-the-double dash – were crowding up on to the fire-steps and adding their own volleys.

The Armstrongs had fallen silent – there was as much chance now of driving shells into the redoubt as into the Prussian rear. Smoke cleared from the turret's interior and the gun-crews, exhausted now, reloaded, then slumped at their stations. Dawlish, eyes smarting, throat parched, saw the fury on the smoke-wreathed ramparts. He had experienced it himself, now all but felt it. The slopes were paved with bodies and men still stumbled up as the unrelenting Danish rifle-fire added to piles.

And then the incredible.

The Prussians were falling back, not in panic, but in something like order, small groups turning back at intervals and dropping to one knee to direct fire on the Danes who had climbed on to the rampart crests and were cheering. The Danish guns were still showering merciless cannister, strewing the ground with yet more dead and wounded. In places colours still waved in defiant pride above units that had re-established cohesion, men beaten but not defeated.

"Mr. Dawlish! What are you waiting for?" Anger in FitzBaldwin's shout.

Dawlish had been all but hypnotised by the sight of the retreat, by the dark heaps littering the open sands, by the smoking furrows and craters his own shells had torn, by the limping wounded dragging others with them, by dignity in the aftermath of bloody failure.

But not yet an aftermath...

"Dawlish! Your guns, man, your guns!"

Two last salvos, the storage racks emptied.

Massacre.

He knew already that he would regret it until the end of his life.

Chapter 28

Odin moved back north, out of range of any Prussian howitzers that had enough shells left to threaten her. The Danish artillery and rifle-fire had died. There was silence also over to the west, where the Austrians had suffered their second repulse across the same ground as before. It was soon clear that there would be no further assaults that day and the ironclad returned to her old mooring opposite Thyborøn. Boats crossed back and forth, Krag carrying messages to and from Saabye and Blackwood.

Dawlish felt exhaustion, as much of the spirit as of the body, sensed that others did also. Men released at last from turret and engine-room slumped in sleep on deck in whatever shadow they could find. Dawlish feared reprimand when he was summoned to FitzBaldwin's cabin. His moment of hesitation must seem unforgivable.

"Bloody well done, Dawlish!" FitzBaldwin had either forgotten, or had decided to ignore it.

"It was Mr. Hopper, sir, and the men. And Mr. Welborne too." The only answer possible, the only one too that FitzBaldwin would expect.

"There's a truce starting at three o'clock." It was after two now. "For recovering wounded. It's to last until midnight. Granville and his people were in the thick of it this morning."

"They were wonderful, sir. Heroic."

"They'll have wounded. Blackwood says that the hospital can't cope. It'll kill more than it can save. He's asked me to take onboard as many of the less serious cases as possible – no amputations, nothing needing surgery. I know you get on well with Granville. I want you to go across, see what we can do."

Dawlish took a half-dozen men, none from the turret-crew, and crossed over. Even before he reached the church, he saw a line of carts stationary before it, those at the head being unloaded, those behind waiting. There were not stretchers enough – most of the wounded were being manhandled, some crying out as they were lifted, and laid in rows in the open. Danish orderlies moved between them, doing what they could to make them comfortable. Emptied, each cart turned south again. The church interior and the hospital tents had been already full with typhus victims. Now they were being overwhelmed.

He told his men to help with the unloading – one had vomited already at the sight of one wretch carried in a blanket. He was close to doing so himself. One of the Swiss women was helping orderlies ease a body off the ground and on to a stretcher – no sign of external injury but with blood bubbling from the mouth with each gasping breath. She stood back, jerked her head, sent the men into the church with it, then moved down the row with two more orderlies following. She bent over each victim, looked closely, reached out to touch the wounds, shook her head, passed on to the next. At last she nodded and the orderlies eased the body on a stretcher and headed for the church. Dawlish recognised her – she had been with Eleonora Blomqvist when he had last seen her. She was not a doctor, possibly not even a trained nurse, but at this moment her judgement was better than nothing. Her apron, dress and hands were blood-stained.

Dawlish approached her, spoke in French.

"I need to speak with Surgeon Major Hartling, or Doctor Venel."

"They're too busy." She motioned towards the church. They must be at work behind the blanket curtain at the far end.

"Are there English wounded here?"

She shrugged. "English, Danish, Prussian, Austrian – it doesn't make much difference now, does it, Monsieur? Search for yourself. I'm busy too." She turned away.

He walked along the rows, horror and pity mixed, choked back nausea, tried, but failed, to be deaf to the moans and cries, forced himself to look into every face, however disfigured or contorted.

Recognition at last. The name came to him, Coulter, ex-fusilier – Sevastopol, drink, destitution, glad of the chance to be here. Granville had spoken well of him. Fragments of a torn shirt were wrapped around his throat, blood seeping through, eyes locked open. He must have died only minutes before.

Another further on, conscious but in pain, his leg still bound to a rifle as Killigrew's had been. He was a corporal, Burgess. He spoke in gasps – he had been wounded when the first Prussians had reached the parapet. A few empty reassurances before Dawlish left him.

One more British volunteer found, name forgotten, if ever known – a head wound, unconscious. Death would be merciful.

Dawlish went back to the Swiss lady. She was still moving along the rows. He saw that she wanted to be rid of him. The other members of the Croix Rouge group were at the redoubts, she said, and no, she didn't know to which one Mademoiselle Blomqvist had gone.

He marched his men south to the redoubt that *Odin* had defended, marvelling, as they passed through them, how much stronger the new defences seemed. All still untouched, their canon silent while the battle had raged to the south. Down across the open ground – far longer than the no-man's land the Prussians had stormed across with such futile courage. Individual carts were still moving north with their cargoes of misery and Dawlish did not stop them to enquire if they were carrying British. Anybody in them would be too seriously injured to be tended to on the ironclad.

The state of the redoubt was even worse than it had looked from *Odin*, walls little more than hummocks, shelters collapsed, canon smashed from their mountings. But it had held, if only just, and a flagpole had been re-erected and a Danish flag drooped from it.

Blackwood and Granville were unmistakable as they stood on a parapet, looking south with field glasses. Dawlish joined them.

Congratulations, handshakes, forced humour. Granville's left arm was in a sling and his face was pale and drawn, but he said nothing of it. At the outer base of the wall, under protection of white flags, Prussians were dragging bodies back and laying them in rows. They looked no different to the Danes – nor to the British either – and they broke silence only when they found a sign of life. Out in the no-man's land, stretcher parties moved between the bodies, turning some over, leaving them, passing on to the next, then hurrying some back to the ambulance wagons that were carrying wounded rearwards. It looked efficient, well organised.

Dawlish hoped that Blackwood would not pass him his glasses – he did not want to see more closely. It was impossible not to feel pity. The carnage at the Taku forts in China had horrified but had not saddened. The enemy there had cut off heads, had mounted them on stakes, had done far worse to prisoners. His heart had hardened then, fourteen-year old that he was. But he had heard of nothing such about the Prussians, or the Austrians either. They seemed not unlike himself, braver too perhaps.

"They shot their bolt too soon," Blackwood seemed sobered also. "Too bloody confident, too damn eager to finish the job before more forces got here from Dybbøl, or anybody more senior with them to take over command. Too bloody-well obsessed with glory, too damn-well concerned to show the Austrians what's what. The fellow who ordered this deserves to be strung up."

Dawlish told why he was there. Granville noticed him looking at his own injured arm, gestured for him to ignore it.

"You remember Evenden, Dawlish? The sergeant?"

He did.

"Killed outright, bayonet in the neck. A good man. Four others dead and six wounded."

Dawlish held back from telling that one of those wounded was already dead at the church, and a second close to it. Granville had enough to deal with already.

They went down together to where the last of the wounded were being set on carts. The only medical personnel were two Swiss nurses, applying dressings, spooning laudanum. Mademoiselle Blomqvist was at one of the other redoubts, they said. The only cases they could recommend being taken to the *Odin* were badly concussed from blows to the head. That counted as minor injury, though when Dawlish saw them, he suspected that one might never have his full wits again. Blackwood had ridden here from Thyborøn and he insisted that both men be put astride his mount, one clutching the other, a seaman steadying them on either side and a third leading. He walked back with Dawlish.

"They'd have succeeded if it hadn't been for the ironclad," he said. "The Austrians hadn't got a chance but the Prussians could have broken through. It was a close-run thing."

Just short of the new defences Blackwood stopped, turned and gestured to the low ridges that were what remained of the southern redoubts. Before the bombardment started the rear walls had been levelled at his command. The front walls were gapped, crests undulating.

"They'll come again," he said. "They won't give up. It's not in the Prussian nature. And this time we'll be even better prepared for them."

Dawlish did not remind him that it was April 29th.

In ten days, *Odin* would be *Galveston*.

And gone.

*

The Prussians swallowed their pride and requested a twenty-four-hour extension of the truce. Saabye refused, demanded that it end at six in the evening, well before sundown, and not at midnight. He was in a position, for once, to set the terms. Recovery of the wounded continued through the night and next morning the turn of the dead commenced. Work parties loaded bodies on wagons, two and three deep, scooped others into blankets – *Odin's* shells had been brutal – and trudged back to the Prussian lines. In late afternoon, somewhere behind the defences, the burials must have begun, marked by a band's solemn dirges that were interspersed with no less mournful singing. In Thyborøn too there were burials, marked by dreary Lutheran hymns.

The truce ended – officers meeting half-way in no-man's land to confirm that terms had been honoured, stiff salutes, bugles sounding as they rode back to the lines. And then silence as dusk came on.

Odin crept south, engines at dead-slow, turret manned, Armstrongs loaded, leadsman in the bows, an hour before midnight. It was full moon, the sky but lightly striped with cloud, a zephyr rather than a breeze, the fjord unrippled. Lorance, at the helm, was confident of these waters now, was familiar with the landmarks. The ironclad began to crawl slow racetracks, down the centre of the fjord, then back again, never further south than the Danish redoubt, out of range of any Prussian howitzers with shells remaining, but close enough to move in fast to bring the Prussians defences under fire.

If need be…

Dawlish had sensed tension between FitzBaldwin and Lorance, cold formality in tone but underlying mutual respect, affection even, preventing open anger. Welborne had noticed it too.

"The magazine's half-empty," he had said to Dawlish. "Lorance is entitled to be concerned."

"But you're expecting to be resupplied?"

At the location that only Lorance and FitzBaldwin knew, where not only munitions but Confederate officers and mercenary volunteers would be waiting.

"Resupply? Only if Union agents haven't tumbled to what Bulloch has afoot. And if they have, then every Union diplomat in Europe will be screaming for ports to be closed to us."

The shells, the charges, every sack of coal and bite of food on board, the payment of the crew, had been bought by funds managed by Mr. Elmore Whitby, secretary of a certain august personage's wife. They had purchased two months' use of the ironclad. Dawlish did not know the terms of the agreement – he wondered if there was anything in writing, if it was a gentlemen's agreement only– but it must allow for return to Confederate service with some minimum of supplies and munitions on board. And that minimum must now be close, might even have been reached. The Armstrongs would only speak again *in extremis…*

From his seat above the guns, Dawlish could see the undamaged profile of the Prussian redoubt against the bright sky and, to the south, the winking lights of the Prussian camp. The mood must be sombre there, recognition of failure and futility, awareness of loss not only of lives but of reputations, of careers ruined by poor judgement and heedless lust for glory.

Odin remained silent as she churned over the moonlit waters. On the enemy ramparts, eyes must be rivetted on her dark mass, gravid with menace as she was. Their fear must be of the moment when she might steam in close to give clear notice that the truce was indeed at an end.

An hour passed, and another.

Dawlish was in on the secret, the other officers too, yet even they could not detect from this ship any indication of what must by now have started. Danish guns were being hand-hauled north from the redoubts on well-greased axels, their embrasures left veiled with sacking. Wagons would follow with remaining supplies, dragged by teams of men rather than horses to ensure silence. One by one, by whole companies, troops would leave their positions and pad north across the sand towards Thyborøn's new defences, until at last only a few platoons remained in the trenches and redoubts, until it would be their turn too to leave just before dawn. Behind them would remain positions immediately useless to the enemy, no more than southward facing walls and bastions that had been gouged almost to destruction by artillery fire, shelters deliberately collapsed by frantic labour in the recent hours. The demolition ordered by Blackwood in anticipation of this moment had reduced the north-facing walls to low ridges.

Silence reigned on *Odin* too, her crew tense in expectation of orders that never came, her lookouts and officers vigilant for the first sign of Prussian alarm. As the ironclad turned and turned and turned again through her long vigil, Dawlish had the turret cranked over each time to bear south of the enemy redoubt, barrels elevated for maximum range. Clear as the night was, it was cold, and he longed for dawn.

The sky was brightening in the east when Thyborøn's church bell tolled, five chimes only, but enough to confirm that the withdrawal was complete. The last Danish forces were now inside the new defences and almost a mile of open ground lay between them and those they had abandoned.

Odin, her long night's watch complete, headed back to her old anchoring ground opposite Thyborøn.

*

The spell of mild weather ended at midday, wind building in the afternoon from the south-west, clouds piling, rain drifting in showers. One by one, the cooking-fires left smouldering in the abandoned redoubts, to give the impression of continuing occupancy, died in the drizzle. Yet even then, the enemy, intent on its own recovery from the misery of defeat, suspected nothing, made no move to investigate. It was only on the following morning that the first cautious Austrians were spotted on the ramparts of the abandoned centre redoubt. Prussians, and more Austrians, followed at the two others. Watching them by telescope from *Odin's* foretop, Dawlish could all but feel the disappointment of the Prussian officers who stood on the captured ramparts. Realisation was dawning that, without rear walls, construction of new gun-positions here would take weeks of work and, even then, long saps would be required if a new assault was to be launched across the intervening ground. The defence of the now-occupied redoubts had bled the Prussian and Austrian forces white, had devoured their stocks of powder, shell and shot. The Danes now lay in a stronger position than before, and continued supply from the lands north of the Limfjord could ensue that they could yet hold out for weeks or months to come.

The *Hulde* paddle steamer arrived that day from Aalborg – horsemen had been sent there along the norther shore after the failed assaults to ask for her return. She carried despatches, including one delivered to Lorance which he took directly to his cabin. She also brought medical personnel from Aalborg's hospital and canvas awnings had been rigged over her open decks for extra accommodation of wounded and sick. This time typhus victims were being evacuated too. Loading continued through the day, made miserable by persistent rain, and by evening the steamer had left again. None of the Croix Rouge personnel went with her.

Whoever remained at Thyborøn now would stay to the end, whatever that might be.

Except *Odin* and her crew.

Chapter 29

Dawlish would remember the first days of May as being suffused with satisfaction – even joy – that the ordeal had been survived with honour. It seemed too a time of hope, not just for him but for all Thyborøn's defenders. Neither Prussians nor Austrians had started any significant reconstruction of the captured redoubts and their guns were silent. Only a trickle of reinforcements moved up the isthmuses daily to join them. A possibility could be glimpsed that there might be no further assault before this war somehow ended, and even if one came it would be hurled against stronger defences than before. It was welcome that the loathed Radetzky had not been heard for days.

Spring had come at last. Bright warm days, long evenings, swallows darting northwards across the Limfjord – there was foliage on trees there now – and snatches of birdsong even in the camp itself. Danish troops, a company at a time, were rowed across to the northern shore to spend two days at farms there, a chance to sleep in dry barns, to launder clothing, damp and unchanged for months, to wash and shave and mend. They came back like new men, uniforms patched and ragged but clean, and another company crossed for its begrimed men too to be refreshed. Horses, all but walking skeletons, were brought across to graze. More timber was ferried south for construction of new shelters. And, best of all, the typhus itself was dying in the camp.

It was evening, Wednesday May 4th, sun sinking red, no ripple on the gently ebbing tide, *Odin*, anchored, steady as a rock. Dawlish was at the forecastle with Albemarle and Welborne, all off-watch and smoking cigars, a sense of shared achievement unstated, but comfortable and strong.

"Has Lorance still not let anything drop?" Dawlish was easy enough now with Welborne to be direct.

"You think I'd tell you if he had?"

"It was worth a try." Dawlish turned to Albemarle. "Has your father let anything slip?"

"The guv'nor? He's tight as an oyster when it suits him."

For Dawlish was now consumed with curiosity about where he would be in a week. Whitby and FitzBaldwin had been clear about the terms, but not the location, when he had committed himself. Discharge at a European port, a gratuity paid in gold sovereigns, travel expenses back to Britain. And an unwritten promise of favour.

"They know it by now, Lorance and the captain, both of 'em," Welborne said. "They'd be mad to say anything. Those last despatches they received, they didn't ask you to decipher anything, did they Nick?"

"No. I imagine Lorance and Mr. Bulloch have their own code."

"You're looking forward to your cruise, Welborne?" Albemarle said. "Warm seas and distant climes, rich prizes and dusky maidens under tropic skies?"

"Don't jest."

A pause, realisation of a boundary crossed.

"It's for our liberty," Welborne's voice cold. "The same war as on the Yazoo and the Mississippi and on the battlefields of Tennessee and Virginia. The *Alabama's* war too. For our homes and our honour and our womenfolk."

Albemarle was about to speak – some weak apologetic assurance, no doubt – but Dawlish laid his hand on his wrist to restrain him.

"Those fellows look cheerful." He pointed to a boatload of Danish soldiers stroking north towards rest and brief recuperation.

"The farmers'll be locking up their daughters." Albemarle took the hint and forced jocularity into his tone.

It fell flat. They smoked on in silence.

Welborne had grown more serious by the day. The possibility must be weighing on him, no less than on Lorance, that sufficient Confederate officers, or mercenaries like van der Horst, or more foreign seamen ready to sign on for a cruise of unknown duration, might not reach the unknown meeting point. Union pressure on neutral European nations must already be intense, perhaps irresistible.

But that would no longer be his own business, Dawlish thought. He had honoured his undertaking, had helped secure Thyborøn. Once back in Britain, promotion to sub-lieutenant would be but a formality – the favour of that illustrious personage whom even Whitby was careful of mentioning by name would see to that. There would be time, he hoped, before his next assignment. It would be a good one, he was confident, perhaps even to the Royal Yacht itself, an envied appointment such as marked so many well-patronised careers. And he would have money too, more than in his life, enough to take him in comfort to Pau, to honour Madame Sapin's grave and investigate what had become of Clothilde. He had time now to worry about her, as he would have worried about his own sister. He had promised his uncle to care for them always and –

A bugle call, staccato notes, repeated, another sounding from shore, unmistakable as alarms.

"There!"

Welborne was pointing towards the Danish defences. From here on *Odin* the rear of the ramparts could be seen obliquely. Figures were rushing up on to the fire-steps to join the picquets already there.

"Look!"

From the wrecked redoubt that was now part of the Prussian frontline, a team of horses was streaking north, across the bare sand of the new no-man's land, a rider on the right of each pair of the six, men clustered on the limber and gun bouncing in their wake. A horseman was galloping ahead, and now, from the captured redoubt, another team raced out, headed to the left of the other and strained to draw level.

Albemarle scrambled up the shrouds towards the foretop. Dawlish and Welborne followed.

"It's madness," Albemarle shouted as he thrust one of the telescopes stored there to Dawlish. "Look!"

For there was no cover, nothing to shield the Prussians from the Danish artillery pieces now being pushed out into their embrasures. The lone horseman had reined in, was gesturing to the teams. The first was slewing over, skidding wheels throwing up sand, the horses dragged to a halt and faced back as they had come. The gunners leapt from both gun and limber, uncoupling the weapon – the stubby barrel identified as a howitzer – and laying it towards Thyborøn. It was a drill that must have been practiced a hundred times at least, as perfectly performed as any ballet, and for all the haste there was no confusion. The teams remained harnessed to the limber but its doors were open, the charges and shells extracted, rammer standing ready to drive them down the bore. The second team had already swung to a halt and two more teams were drumming from the redoubt and deploying yet further to the left. The single mounted officer was ordering them to halt in line – some thirty yards separated each weapon from its fellow. It was a display that could have been the high point of a military review.

Satisfied, the officer wheeled his mount around and raised his cap towards the Danish lines. Even as he did, the first of his howitzers barked, the elevation high, enough to hurl its shell far beyond the defences to plunge down into the camp and village there. The gunners were firing blind, had no ability to know the point of fall but that was unimportant for this was a gesture of defiance, of honour, of arrogant and suicidal bravado.

Now the first Danish fire, a field gun in an embrasure leaping back in its recoil, trajectory low, the ball – a solid shot – ploughing a racing furrow that shaved close past the first Prussian weapon and showered its team with sand. They were pushing on the wheel-spokes to aim it north again, were then reloading, the drill as fast and faultless as before. The second Prussian howitzer blasted, leaped back. The horse teams stamped, shuffled, pulled against the men who struggled to hold them still. The Danes were returning fire, inaccurate in their first responses but with every advantage on their side. From the south came sounds of cheering – Prussian troops had rushed up on to what remained of the walls of the redoubt there and were urging on the insane heroism of the gunners. The third and fourth howitzers were uncoupled by now and they threw their own first shells. Puny they might be – Dawlish remembered how little more they had achieve than disturb sleep when he had served in a redoubt himself – but they were dropping at random among the unprotected tents and shelters of the Thyborøn camp and carrying terror with them.

A Danish weapon had switched to bursting shell and sent two rounds in fast succession to explode close to the second howitzer. One of the gunners there was down – a fragment must have caught him – and two comrades were carrying him back to the limber. It was not enough to break the rhythm of fire, not for this weapon, not for the others, for the Danish answer was ignored, indeed scorned.

"They're damn-well magnificent!" Admiration in Welborne's voice.

Dawlish felt it too, wished that, enemy or not, these men and horses might escape unscathed. For it was indeed magnificent, splendid for cool proud bravery, for defiance of shot and shell and destiny itself, for courage worthy of the Light Brigade at Balaclava. It could not last, and it was folly, not war, but while it lasted – less than five minutes – it was glorious, a half-dozen rounds hurled from each weapon.

The lone horseman rose up with his beast into a pesade, saluted the Danes again as its forehooves touched the ground, then pirouetted about and waved to his howitzers to withdraw. They were all but lost now behind a curtain of flashes and upthrown sand. Horses were plunging within the teams, some screaming in terror, and more gunners were running to help those holding them. The others were raising the howitzer trails, dragging them back to couple them to the limbers, then scrambling on board to crouch between the wounded already piled there.

The first team had drawn away, riders on the horses whipping hard, racing back towards the Prussian lines, cheers from there urging their headlong flight. The second team was lurching into motion as disaster struck it, a lucky Danish shell that crashed into the limber, its detonation shattering it, throwing out bodies and wheels and wooden fragments in the instant before its stored powder charges ignited also. The horse team raced on, dragging the remnants of the limber with them, leaving behind the howitzer and a half-dozen bodies strewn over a scorched circle, and stunned and injured men staggering away in agony.

Ruin enveloped the third team also, for the Danish gunners had mastered their ranges by now. It was yet to draw away – the howitzer was still uncoupled – when a shell fell among the horses, blowing half the team into bloody fragments, cutting down the others to struggle and scream in maimed anguish. Through the hail of falling sand another round – solid ball – smashed into the howitzer itself, tearing away one wheel, throwing down the barrel and scything through the gunners about it. The mounted officer spurred towards it. He must know in this instant that he had miscalculated, that he had allowed at least one salvo too many on the assumption that the Danes might not respond quickly enough, that his bravado was ending in tragedy. Then suddenly he too was gone, ripped from his saddle by a flying shard, and his panicked blood-sprayed mount bolted to follow the last team, the fourth, as it hurtled back towards the Prussian lines.

The guns fell silent.

"Poor devils," Albemarle said.

Dawlish too felt the pity of it. The wild dash and the lighting bombardment had been something no seasoned commander would ever approve – it was already easy to imagine Blackwood's contemptuous dismissal of it. Some ambitious young Prussian battery commander, desperate to draw attention to his courage, confident that success would disarm all criticism of disobedience, earn patronage perhaps, must have planned and done this on his own initiative. One brief moment of glory had ended with butchered horses, with burned and blinded men, with corpses – each somebody's rearing, pride and joy – slumped in bizarre postures on the sand.

Even the Danes must have felt something of that pity too, for there was a long pause before they began to cheer. None came from the Prussians, small groups of whom had run out to bring in the frantic horses. Long minutes passed before a single Prussian emerged from the redoubt, white flag raised. Dawlish focussed has glass and in his disc of vision saw a young officer, tunic open, chest bare beneath, his shirt tied by its sleeves to the lance that he was waving slowly. He waited, walked forward, waited again. He turned, beckoned to others to follow from the earthwork. Without hindrance from the Danes they ran towards the carnage, some with stretchers to collect the wounded and one, revolver in hand, to move from horse to wounded horse and shoot them.

The last survivors were carried back. Only still bodies remained. A wagon emerged from the redoubt, it too with a white flag, and advanced. It had gone fifty yards when a single Danish gun sent a ball to throw up a plume of and bounce away well clear of the corpses.

The wagon turned back. Notice had been served. Compassion went only so far.

If the Prussians wanted to recover their dead, they must swallow their pride and request a formal truce.

Night fell. That recovery must wait until the morrow.

*

Krag came across in the morning to agree arrangements for provisioning for *Odin*. She would sail with stocks of bacon, butter and flour, all drawn from the farms on Saabye's estates. It was according to the agreement for services rendered, but it must be bitter to comply with nonetheless. With spring just started, barns and stores were all but empty and Thyborøn's garrison needed every mouthful. That the ironclad would sail away, fully provisioned, two days hence must rankle. Dawlish sensed as much when he encountered the Danish lieutenant coming from FitzBaldwin's cabin. He looked flushed, even angry. The meeting might well have been a stormy one – apart even from the difference in rank, the captain was not a man to argue with.

"Was there much damage?" Dawlish asked. Fires had burned in the camp and village for much of the night.

"It might have been much worse," Krag said. "Half them fell on open ground. But eleven dead, more wounded, horses too, poor beasts and –" He seemed reluctant to go on. "You know the Croix Rouge people, don't you? The hospital was hit, some of them also. One shell, but it was enough –"

"Who?" Dawlish felt sick.

"Two of the nurses. I don't know the names. I haven't been there. An orderly too, and some poor fellow in bed, and Surgeon-Major Hartling was badly hurt."

FitzBaldwin gave Dawlish permission to go across when he asked.

"A bad business, Dawlish," he said. "The fellow should have been shot if he'd survived it, bloody fool. Sheer spite, nothing to be gained from it but to make the Danes dig their heels in all the more."

Seen from the boat, on the way across, the church looked undamaged. It was only when Dawlish approached it on foot with Krag that he saw the jagged-edged hole punched on the roof. It looked too small for the damage wreaked within.

They found Doctor Venel sitting, slumped, head drooping on a bloody apron, on the steps to the door. A Danish orderly lay full-length by him. Both were fast asleep. Dawlish, eager to go on and yet fearing to, moved to pass by but Krag reached out and touched his elbow.

"It's better to talk to the doctor first."

They had difficulty in wakening him, and when he came to, blinking, bewildered, he recognised Krag.

"Did Friherre Saabye send you? About Hartling?" Venel sounded past exhaustion, past despair too. "Tell Saabye that I had to take his arm off. Tell that I had no option, there were others besides, I had to hurry and –" He began to weep. "I thought it was over, that there was an end to it. We all did, the ladies too and –"

"Which ladies? Swiss? Swedish?" Dawlish had caught him by the shoulder, was shouting. "Which ladies died?"

Venel recognised him now. "Mademoiselle Chaudet." He was weeping again. "I studied with her father in Geneva. I knew her from a baby. I don't know how to tell him, or her mother either. And Mademoiselle Blomqvist too."

Anger, sorrow, pity. Dawlish's spirit screamed within him.

"Where is she?"

Venel gestured towards the shed where Killigrew's body had lain also. The question had been superfluous.

"Don't go there," Venel said.

"Listen to him." Krag held Dawlish's sleeve. His face told what he had guessed. "It'll do no good."

He pulled away, went anyway.

The women's bodies were distinguishable by the smallness of the bare feet protruding from beneath the blankets. His knees were weak, his hands trembling, but he forced himself to lift the first to see the face. It was serene, unmarked – she might have been sleeping – but it was not that of Eleonora Blomqvist.

He steeled himself to lift the second blanket, saw what Venel had tried to spare him. Half the head had been torn away. The other half was intact, still suffused by the great port-wine stain.

And beautiful.

Pity killed his anger. He looked down on the face for another minute before covering it again. It was no longer Eleonora Blomqvist.

Only the reminder of a noble life.

*

He spoke to nobody of it when he returned to *Odin* and was glad that he had the afternoon watch. The transfer and stowage of provisions demanded enough attention to keep depression from mastering him. Looking shorewards, into the no-man's land, he could see the Prussian wagons that were recovering the dead there under a flag of formal truce. The evening before he had been admiring and all but cheering on the daring of that young Prussian battery commander. Now he felt a savage joy that he was dead.

"Deck there!" The lookout calling down.

A vessel, still distant, moving southwards along the coast.

"A warship?" Dawlish shouted up.

One thought was in his mind now, must be in FitzBaldwin's and Lorance's also, he knew. The American, the *Conewago,* hoping to block exit under the Confederate ensign.

He went aloft, took the lookout's glass and focussed. Three masts, sails furled, smoke spilling from the funnel, a broad white stripe running along her fore-shortened flank. The *Conewago's* hull was solid black but the newcomer had the look of the *Niels Juel,* the large Danish frigate encountered earlier. And another Danish frigate, held up by engine-trouble, had been due to join the Elbe blockade. This could be her, but…

Better to take no chances. He hurried down and went himself to FitzBaldwin. Full manning followed, even though only one boiler was being kept at harbour pressure.

Hove-to a mile off the Limfjord mouth, the fork-tailed ensign identified the newcomer as Danish. She dropped a cutter. Three formally-uniformed officers could be seen in the sternsheets as it stroked closer. FitzBaldwin met them with as much ceremony as *Odin's* rag-tag crew could furnish and they went below with him. Shouted exchanges with the midshipman commanding the cutter confirmed the frigate to be the *Jylland,* all but a sister of the *Niels Juel.* She had joined the blockade off the Jade and Elbe only briefly. It had been abandoned yesterday, the midshipman said, and now the Danish ships that had maintained it were moving north. And no, he knew nothing else. His seniors must know, not him.

Those seniors remained on *Odin* only a half-hour They had no sooner dropped back into their cutter to head back than FitzBaldwin summoned his officers to his cabin.

"News," he said. "There may be an armistice soon, maybe in days. The government has seen the sense of it. It knows the situation's hopeless. The loss of Dybbøl settled it. They've opened negotiations."

FitzBaldwin should be smiling, Dawlish thought, but he was not. He hesitated, as if searching for words, before he spoke again.

"There's more. The Austrians. They've arrived, two frigates, bloody powerful ones, as expected. They've reached Cuxhaven, they're coaling there, making repairs, taking on supplies."

"What the hell has that to do with us?" Lorance spoke with anger. He must not have been included in the conference with the Danes. Even with others – subordinates – present, he seemed unable or unwilling to disguise his anger.

"We hold Danish commissions, Lorance" FitzBaldwin forced calm into his voice. "You, me, everybody here. And *Odin's* flying the Danish ensign."

"*Odin* be damned! She's *Galveston* in four days' time!"

"*Galveston* or not, we're joining the Danish squadron."

"The squadron that let those Austrians lift the blockade just like that? That let them sail unmolested into Cuxhaven? Even without this *Jylland,* the Danes had two damn powerful vessels to oppose them!"

"It's not that straightforward and –"

"The Danes let 'em slip through, or they backed down, it makes no odds. The Austrians' engines are damn-well weary, I'll warrant, and their bunkers all but empty from the haul from the Mediterranean! But the Royal Danish Navy will only face them if we're with them, is that it?"

"Watch your tongue, Lorance!" FitzBaldwin's temper was rising. "You hold the King of Denmark's commission, sir, you owe –"

"Nothing! I swore no oath, nobody here did! But we risked this vessel nonetheless, our lives too, time and again to the letter of the agreement, and we damn-well nearly emptied the magazines to smash the Prussians' attack last week."

Dawlish looked away, others too, embarrassed to see the confrontation. Only Welborne was nodding support for every word from Lorance. And yet there was logic in the American's reluctance.

"In four days, I'll listen to you, sir!" FitzBaldwin's face was flushed. "But until then I'm captain and – Dawlish! Find out what that fellow wants!"

A seaman had knocked on the door, had cracked it open, was standing there in trepidation. Dawlish went out.

"What is it?"

A report from the foretop. The lookout thought it important that the captain should know it without delay.

Another frigate, approaching from the west.

With no white stripe on her black hull.

Chapter 30

Noon, Friday May 6th, sun shining, a light breeze only, and *Odin* was moving northwards at quarter-revolutions towards the Limfjord mouth. She was leaving for the last time and there had been no ceremony, no parades, not even a celebratory meal, on board or ashore, to mark the end of her service here. The previous eighteen hours had passed in a hurricane of preparation – stoked furnaces, raised pressure, greased bearings, loaded guns, rotated turret, dropped bulwarks, fire-hoses laid, boats filled with water. *Odin* had been cleared for action and might have it within the hour.

For the USS *Conewago* was four miles outside the fjord's entrance, in meticulous observance of Denmark's territorial limits, and her captain's intentions were unknown. Her lights had shown her cruising slowly back and forth through the night but dawn had found her hove to – and waiting. Union agents must have learned long before now of the terms of the *Galveston's* temporary assignment to Danish service and of the date of its ending.

Dawlish was on his seat above the manned Armstrongs. Welborne, beside him, was hoping for battle – he had said so several times, relished the idea – but he might be the only man on board who did. Lorance, on the bridge with FitzBaldwin, showed no such joy. The differences between them had been settled – the demands of honour and of expediency had coincided.

Thyborøn was slipping past now, a desolate square mile of sand, littered with weather-worn tents and makeshift shelters, the remnant of the village at its centre. In its squalor, it seemed an unlikely site for an epic, Dawlish thought, but that was what it had been, and still was. He could not see it without emotion. Saabye's dogged refusal to accept defeat, his iron resolution to draw enemy forces here from the more important battles in the south, the stolid endurance of privation, disease and battle by regulars and peasant conscripts alike, had never faltered. The rows of hummocks around the church confirmed dedication unto death.

And not just the Danes either but – Dawlish's mind recoiled from the word, but it had to be accepted – the mercenaries too. Killigrew, Evenden, Eltham and almost a dozen others, their names already forgotten, some brought here through loyalty to Blackwood, others driven here by poverty, all had fulfilled the bargain. The three women of the Croix Rouge were there too. They seemed the saddest of all, the unbending Madame Racine, the Swiss nurse Mademoiselle Chaudet and Eleonora Blomqvist, untrained, undaunted by her blemished face, none with a personal stake in the conflict played out here. All had believed that a wounded man was not an enemy and they had died for that belief.

At this moment, even when battle might be imminent against a foe with whom he had no quarrel, Dawlish was glad he had been here, had stood with a small people defiant in the face of crushing might. He looked back, could see the defences Blackwood had conceived – even from the rear they were impressive. The colonel was there still, and Granville and his people too, waiting with the Danes for another attack. It might not come. No Prussian forces released from the siege at Dybbøl had reached here yet. An armistice could mean that they never would.

Odin was passing through the fjord's narrow entrance – at half-revolutions now – and the wide expanse of open sea lay ahead. The *Conewago* had not shifted, lay beam on, bows towards the south, smoke drifting from her funnel, yards bare, gaps in her dark bulwarks showing that her two great pivot guns had been unmasked. Brief sunlight flashes from the bridge and tops confirmed that half a dozen telescopes were focussed on the advancing ironclad.

Full revolutions now. *Odin's* turret was still locked fore and aft, direct fire ahead impossible due to the forward superstructure. Dawlish awaited FitzBaldwin's command to slew it over on to either beam, but no such order came.

"The ram." Awe in Welborne's voice. "He's going to use the ram."

And so too the Union captain must fear, for froth churned at the frigate's stern and she got underway, gathering speed as she turned into a wide turn to starboard. She held the turn, all but twenty-four points, before pulling out to parallel the coast on a southerly course. FitzBaldwin held his too, still due westwards. *Odin* was well clear of the territorial boundary by now. The *Conewago* lay a mile off her starboard bow, still driving south at a range long enough to pass ahead in safety but close enough to open effective fire with her pivot weapons.

Dawlish glanced towards the bridge. Every second's delay lessened the possibility of rotating the turret to bear in time. FitzBaldwin and Lorance were at either side of the helmsman, eyes locked on the *Conewago*. And silent.

Two minutes more and close enough to discern the figures on the American's bridge. Her gunners must have *Odin* in their sights, be waiting for the word to fire.

Then *Odin's* helm was over and she was curving to the north. The fork-tailed Danish ensign streaming from her mainmast gaff must be clearly visible. It proclaimed that this was no *Galveston* challenging Union power but still a vessel of the Danish navy, with her own war to fight and neutral in the conflict raging across the Atlantic. The turret locked fore and aft showed no open gun-ports to the other ship and proclaimed that there was no intent to offer battle. Nor should there be. Victory over a single Union frigate, perhaps at the price of sustaining serious damage, was of less value to the Confederacy than an intact corsair.

No challenge, no response.

The *Conewago's* captain – Joel Cutler, Lorance's friend forever – had been ready for battle, should it have been offered, but he had accepted the ironclad as *Odin* still, not *Galveston*. But it was clear too that he would wait, that he would dog her for the next three days, never lose sight of her by night or day, in calm or storm. Once the fateful midnight of *Glaveston's* rebirth had been passed, he would not hesitate to expose his wooden flanks to the devastation of the Armstrongs. Even a single explosive Union shell buried in the ironclad's unprotected upper works could be enough to end the prospect of a second *Alabama*.

The ring of the bridge telegraph told that FitzBaldwin was calling for reduced revolutions. *Odin's* bunkers were almost full only because the last sacks stored on deck had been emptied into them before departure. Coal was precious and must be conserved for the moment when even the slightest margin of speed over the *Conewago* could ensure escape.

The Union vessel had turned again, did not slacken speed as she too forged north on parallel course. Soon she was drawing level to port, nudging closer until a cable's length, not more, lay between her and the *Odin*. Her guns were still manned and trained, promise of battle to come, and her captain stood in the bridge-wing as before, hand raised in a salute that was returned by FitzBaldwin and Lorance. In the disc of his own glass, Dawlish saw that captain's face – bearded, firm-jawed, crow's feet confirming years of facing into wind and rain, a look about it of honest resolution, the face of a man under whom one would not hesitate to serve. The other officers on the bridge had something of the same seasoned determination too, and it was in the gun-crews and in the seamen on deck and in the lookouts in the tops.

Dawlish passed the telescope to Welborne.

"They'll make a hard fight of it, if it comes to it," he said.

"They're clever." A hint of scorn in Welborne's voice. "Yankees always are, smart and acute and calculating. It isn't any chivalry – they don't know the word – and it isn't any respect for Danish colours that's holding 'em back."

"What then?"

"They're hoping for the Austrians to do their work for them before we run up the Stars and Bars."

It made sense. Honour, commitment to a contract, was carrying *Odin* north to join the Danish squadron. The *Niels Juel,* the *Jylland* and *Hejmdal* were cruising in the Skagerrak, the strait lying between Denmark and the southern tip of Norway. There they were barring the Austrian ships now at Cuxhaven from entrance to the Baltic. The identity of those two steam frigates was known, the *Schwarzenberg* and – name of ill omen – the *Radetzky*. The officers from the *Jylland* who had boarded *Odin* briefly off Thyborøn had brought that information, knew too that the Austrian commander, Commodore von Tegetthoff, flew his flag on the *Schwarzenberg*. Both Austrian steam frigates, wooden, broadside armed, were even matches for their Danish counterparts. The support of the corvette *Hejmdal*, might slightly tip the balance in favour of the Danes – but *Odin's* presence could be decisive. But only if the encounter came in the next two days. After that, *Conewago*, not the Austrians, would be the enemy.

A half-mile to port of *Odin,* the Union vessel reduced speed, fell back a little, then held position. And there she remained as afternoon faded into evening, and evening into night. The sky clouded and the wind strengthened from the south-west, raising white caps and carrying rain squalls with it. *Odin* remained ready for action but half the turret crew was released at a time, leaving one Armstrong manned, ready for immediate firing. Dawlish and Welborne took it in turns to remain in command, cold and wet on the seat above the guns, unable in these circumstances to rig the tarpaulin cover across the drum. When they went below it was first to the engine room to dry and warm, and only then seek food and hot coffee and brief comfortless rest.

The glows shimmering above their funnels in the darkness marked the locations of quarry and hunter alike. They ploughed on northwards until, in the early hours, *Odin's* bows swung to the north-east. *Conewago* followed suit and they drove together towards the dawn, linked as if by an invisible chain.

*

The sky had cleared in the night and the sun rose above a choppy sea to show the hilly profile of the Norwegian coast low on the northern horizon. The port of Kristiansand lay north-east and the Danish squadron must be somewhere to the east. With lookouts doubled, *Odin's* search commenced. Regardless of the war – a local one that inconvenienced none but the countries involved – neutral traffic in the Skagerrak was heavy, steam and sail alike carrying produce from half the world into the Baltic, Finnish timber and Russian grain out. Their slow and steady plods identified the merchantmen, their slim lines and high speed the passenger and mail packets. Through the forenoon *Odin* steered south-east, doubled back to the north-west, turned south-east again, seeking and not finding long black hulls bearing broad white stripes. And all the while, still cleared for action, the *Conewago* trailed her. With only thirty-six to go, her captain must be counting the hours.

*

They met the Danish squadron in early afternoon, steaming south-west in line abreast, *Jylland* and *Hejmdal* two miles to port and starboard of the flagship, *Niels Juel*. They manoeuvred into line ahead at the sight of the *Conewago* – by appearance she might well have been Austrian. The American, with a larger ensign than before now raised, stood away to the north. She signalled good faith as she did, and curved over to lie two miles astern of the Danish line. *Odin* was recognised for what she was – her profile was unique among them – and, as the *Niels Juel* hove to, she did also at a cable's distance. A boat was dropped and FitzBaldwin went across.

He was back ten minutes later. Dawlish and the other officers were summoned to meet him on the bridge.

"I've spoken to Commodore Suenson, gentlemen," he said. "He's taking his squadron south. He's seeking out the Austrians, not waiting here for them. And *Odin's* joining him."

Lorance took out his watch, looked at it.

"Thirty-two hours," he said. "*Galveston.*"

"Thirty-two hours in which the *Conewago* won't touch us," FitzBaldwin said "And your decision after that, Lorance."

"What if we meet the Austrians in that time?"

"We'll fight them."

Lorance looked towards Welborne, towards van der Horst. His men. He sought their gaze and held it, then turned back to FitzBaldwin.

"We'll fight them," he said. "But there'll be more to it. What afterwards? What if the *Conewago* takes us on? Where will you and your people stand?"

FitzBaldwin looked to Dawlish and Albemarle, saw their nods.

"The *Conewago*? We'll fight her," he said.

*

The squadron moved out of the Skagerrak and into the North Sea, manoeuvring again into line abreast, *Odin* now positioned between the *Niels Juel* and the *Hejmdal*. Spaced three miles one from another – clear for signalling in these conditions, but close enough to form into line with speed – the Danish force headed south on a nine-mile front, the range of her lookouts broadening it another six miles again. Dusk was three hours before midnight in this month but as it fell the ships drew closer, each with her unique set of lamps aloft to identify her and help keep station. Three miles astern another set of lights trailed doggedly, the *Conewago*, relentless in her pursuit.

The turret was unmanned for now, its whole crew granted uninterrupted rest through the darkness. Dawlish woke in the early hours and found it hard to sleep again. It was Sunday the eighth of May, the last day in Danish service. He felt no great concern for what might come with daylight. He realised that death in itself no longer terrified him, though the manner of it did, and wounds and maiming most of all. His greatest fear was of flinching at the point of crisis, of failing the men who trusted him and gave him loyalty. That was every officer's unspoken fear, he sensed, worse even than loss of years of life and happiness, and he knew it would never leave him until his own end came. He prayed, but only briefly, asked God for himself only what a man should ask for, courage and fortitude until death itself. Remembrance troubled him – Killigrew's long agony, the slaughter he himself had wreaked on that open ground with *Odin's* guns, the Prussian artillery officer's insane and futile act of insubordination that had cost Eleonora Blomqvist her life.

Finding no rest, he rose and went first to the poop to look astern. The *Conewago's* lights still hung like bright dots in the darkness there. The Danish ships still lay off the port and starboard beams – good station keeping. It was half-past four, another hour to full daylight. Albemarle was keeping the morning watch.

"We've passed south of Thyborøn now," he nodded to the east, the unseen coast fifteen miles distant.

"Anything sighted?"

"We frightened the wits out of a few fishing boats. That was all."

Albemarle's tone indicated that he did not want to talk more. He too must have hopes and fears he did not want to share.

Dawlish walked out to the bridge wing, stood there, huddled within his greatcoat, face cold against the wind. The slow and gentle pitch was somehow pleasant, so too the throb from the engines reaching the deck beneath him, and the wash of the water alongside and the vee of the bow wave reaching out like grey streaks to be lost in the half-darkness. He was conscious of the silent men on watch, at the helm, in the tops above, the crew in the engine room, the stokers and trimmers feeding the furnaces, the others now sleeping in their hammocks. The ship was a living thing and the knowledge that he was part of her was satisfying. Untroubled now, he went back to his cot and slept.

*

A change of course at daylight brought the squadron ten miles north-west of Heligoland by mid-morning. By remaining in this area, it was well placed to detect any movement by the Austrians either north along the Danish coast or north-westwards into open sea. Sight of a single vessel – a large one, under stream – emerging from behind the high profile of the island brought a signal from the *Niels Juel* to maintain station but to ready for action. Dawlish's two great charges were already loaded and he was seated above them with Welborne

"Deck there!" *Odin's* foretop calling. "White ensign!"

The vessel came on steadily, then turned to pass across the Danish path – the Royal Navy's guardship, the steam frigate HMS *Aurora*, marking the tiny British possession's territorial waters' boundary. The message was clear – this far and no further. She doubled back, then hove to ahead of the *Niels Juel*.

Signals now from the Danish flagship to her two consorts, and to *Odin* also – Stand Off. She advanced slowly until less than a mile separated her from the British frigate, then hove to herself. *Aurora* dropped a boat and it stroked towards the *Niels Juel* over what was now a calm sea.

Long minutes passed. The *Conewago* too was standing off, never further from the *Odin* than three miles. Then the British boat headed back towards the *Aurora*. As it was hoisted, *Niels Juel* signalled again. The squadron would cruise north of the island, well clear of British waters

The *Conewago* followed.

An hour later a cutter, under sail, sent from the Danish flagship, drew alongside *Odin*. The officer who came aboard was grey-haired, bearded. Commodore Suenson's flag captain, Dawlish guessed. He went below with FitzBaldwin and Lorance, was closeted with them for an hour, left again with handshakes.

And *Odin's* last hours of Danish service ticked away as the *Conewago* watched.

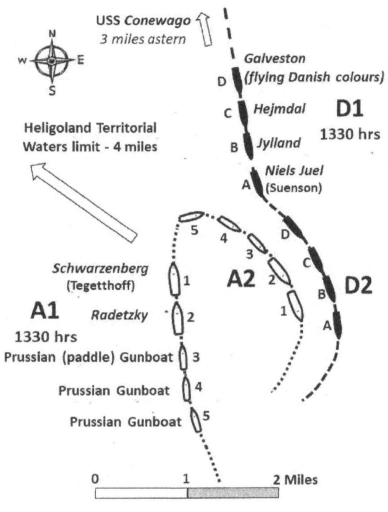

Battle of Heligoland

May 9th 1864

Opening Manoeuvres

Ships shown out of scale for clarity

D1, A1 etc : Show simultaneous
Danish and Austrian positions

Chapter 31

Just before midnight, a seaman brought Dawlish the captain's compliments and a request to join him on the bridge. Albemarle, Welborne, van der Horst and Nolan had received a similar summons. FitzBaldwin and Lorance were in quiet conversation in the wing, looking aft towards the lights of the *Conewago* and consulting their watches. Bright dots identified the lanterns of the Danish ships off either beam – *Odin* was still in line-ahead with them.

"Twelve o'clock, gentlemen!" FitzBaldwin snapped his watch closed.

There was no ceremony about the ending of the contract and the transfer of responsibility, but the moment was all the more solemn for that. FitzBaldwin reached for Lorance's hand and shook it, then the others' in turn.

"Damn-well done," he said, "damn-well done." He turned to Lorance. "An honour to serve with you, sir. She's yours now."

"Mr. Welborne!" Lorance said. "I believe you've brought something precious."

It was a thick rectangle of folded cloth.

Dawlish had not seen a Confederate flag before. Only when the Danish ensign had been run down – and folded and held by a seaman – did he glimpse the new ensign's cross and stars as it rose up to be lost in the darkness above. He saw tears in Welborne's eyes, something harder, prouder, in Lorance's as they, and the others, came to attention and raised hands in salute.

Now the telegraph relayed Lorance's first command as captain of the reborn CSS *Galveston* – reduction of revolutions. To either side, the lights of the Danish squadron began to draw ahead. Astern, those of the *Conewago* drew closer.

The small group remained in silence, and undismissed, on the bridge. The ironclad was still the ship she had been before, the crew unchanged – the great majority had committed themselves already to Confederate service. But for the officers this moment was different, Dawlish realised, for himself, for Albemarle, for FitzBaldwin most of all. Service, under aliases, to an established European monarchy, was different to service, however temporary, to a rebel state, unrecognised by any power. This was no unarmed blockade-running, as so many Royal Navy half-pay officers were engaged in, and to which the Admiralty and government alike turned a blind eye. Today could bring a battle. Honour, and regard for Lorance, would make it impossible to stand idly by, but Union diplomats would demand retribution for it, and Britain could not but give it. Careers would end, the possibility of prison loomed. FitzBaldwin and Whitby and the august personage who had financed the venture had not foreseen this situation.

Galveston had now dropped a mile astern of the Danish ships. Lorance rang for increased revolutions to maintain that separation. Astern, the *Conewago* had also fallen back, but was still pursuing. The Confederate ensign could not be seen in the darkness and the Union captain was avoiding a possible clash with what might still be a Danish warship.

"It's been thirty minutes. Long enough for the formality." Lorance nodded towards Welborne. "Haul it down and raise the other."

The Confederate ensign dropped and the Danish colours rose again to where daylight would find them.

FitzBaldwin – role now reversed with Lorance – must have seen the surprise on Dawlish's face.

"A legitimate *ruse de guerre*," he said. "Honourable until there's need to open fire."

"Let's damn-well hope there won't be," Lorance said. "Now, gentlemen – watch-keeping as before."

Van der Horst would stand the middle watch. Dawlish retreated to his cot. When, after daybreak, the order came for the turret to be manned, he yielded his previous position on the seat above the Armstrongs to Welborne and sat instead what used to be his place.

No longer my guns.

*

The sun rose, sky clear, a steady breeze from the south-east. The three Danish vessels had drawn in to close the gap left by the *Galveston* and she was trailing the *Niels Juel* in the centre of their line-abreast. Denmark's fork-tailed ensign still streamed above the ironclad. To the *Conewago's* captain, *Galveston's* station must look like part of some ingenious Danish cruising formation. The Union ship still followed, but drew no closer, even when the Danish vessels, and *Galveston* with them, cruised east-west-east back and forth north of Heligoland as they had the day before.

"You think Captain Lorance'll break free and make a run for it?" Dawlish said.

"Not when it's this clear." Welborne pointed towards the *Conewago*. "He knows that she's as fast as we are. We wouldn't lose her. He won't risk running and he won't risk fighting if he can avoid it, more's the pity."

"We can't shadow the Danes forever."

"Lorance won't need to. He's praying for wind and rain and high seas. We'll never shake her off otherwise."

The morning advanced. It was almost midday now.

"Deck there! *Niels Juel* signalling!" The foretop calling.

A string of flags was running up her halyard, and the *Jylland* and *Heimdal* were acknowledging.

"Smoke in the south-east!" Again the foretop.

It was a smudge, the smallest blemish on the blue horizon. It might be a merchant vessel straining towards the Elbe mouth, or a mail packet piling on coal to meet a fixed schedule, but almost directly beyond it lay Cuxhaven, where the Austrian frigates had been last reported. The Danes were well advised to view that smudge with caution.

Lorance sent Albemarle aloft to join the lookout. He studied the distant stain for a full three minutes before shouting down.

"There's more than one. Three or four. Maybe more."

The Danish ships were swinging off their eastward course to head just east of south. *Galveston* followed. Heligoland now lay off the starboard bow. HMS *Aurora*, unwearied guardian of its territorial waters, was loitering between the island and the approaching Danes.

More flags climbing on the *Niels Juel*. Then she was increasing speed, overhauling the *Jylland*, which lay on her port, then swinging in ahead of her. Then *Jylland* accelerated to follow in the flagship's wake and further to the west the *Hejmdal* too was arcing across.

"They're forming line of battle!" Awe in Dawlish's voice.

It was the manoeuvre that had dominated sea warfare for almost two centuries, the single line of ships advancing astern of a leader, seeking to lay their combined broadsides on any enemy to either flank. At Quiberon Bay, at The Saintes, at St. Vincent, it had carried the Royal Navy to victory, but at a pace vastly slower than the nine-knots at which the Danes were now ploughing towards the distant smoke. Even with the naked eye, individual black columns could be distinguished, two great thick ones in the van, then three slimmer identifying themselves beyond.

Dawlish's own glass was focussed on the ships approaching from the south – tall masts and bare yards, black hulls, white-striped, foreshortened beneath. Their ensigns were not yet visible but the resolution with which they were driving north left no doubt that they

300

were the Austrians. They also were settling into line ahead and the two leaders might have been sisters of the *Niels Juel* or *Jylland*, powerful steam frigates that carried their main armament broadside on a single deck. The black billows spilling from the funnels told of stokers shovelling like demons to feed the furnaces and build up speed yet further. With no less resolution than the Danish Commodore Suenson, the Austrian admiral – Dawlish recalled the name, von Tegetthoff – was welcoming engagement.

Three smaller vessels were following the heavy frigates and now their details too sharpened in Dawlish's disk of vision. Slighter, almost toy-like, he recognised them as Prussian gunboats, similar to those encountered in the Elbe estuary. Froth churning along the side of the foremost identified her as a paddle steamer, perhaps the very same that had courted death or glory in a vain attempt to save a consort.

The hindmost of the Danish ships, the corvette *Hejmdal*, now lay off *Galveston's* port bow and the separation was increasing. Dawlish looked back, could see the *Conewago* forging on astern, black smoke belching from her stack announcing that she too was building speed. He looked up – the Danish ensign still fluttered high above but the Union vessel had drawn near enough to bring her bow-chasers into range. Her captain's dilemma must be intolerable – the ship he dogged might be the Confederate *Galveston* under false colours, or she might still be *Odin* in Danish service, heading with full legitimacy towards battle with three sisters. Lorance's friend – and enemy – must be recalling shared days of service, peacetime decisions taken, innocuous choices made, and searching for some clue as to the course that the ironclad now might follow. Dawlish too was wondering as he glanced towards the bridge, saw Lorance and FitzBaldwin standing unflinching by the helmsman as they had during the Elbe battle. Their gazes were locked on the Danish line and not on the following Union frigate.

"Come about! For Christ's sake come about!" Welborne's muttering was just audible as he too was looking towards the Union hunter. He caught Dawlish's eye. "We can have the bitch! Lorance can double back, let her have both Armstrongs! We'll never have another chance like this!"

But for that, the turret must not be locked fore and aft, as it still was. It should be rotated to bear on the beam before *Galveston* would arc into a half-circle turn to risk the *Conewago's* broadside and flail her with the Armstrongs' full fury as they passed on opposite courses.

Now Lorance's decision.

The telegraph jingled on the bridge – he was signalling the engine room for maximum revolutions. Then the helm was over, *Galveston* swinging to port, gaining speed, racing on before lurching into a turn to starboard that carried her into the *Hjemdal's* wake. Still flying Danish colours, the *Galveston* had joined Suenson's line of battle and the two squadrons were closing at a combined speed of close to eighteen knots.

"This is Goddamn madness! This isn't our affair!" Welborne could not contain his anger.

"Keep your voice down!" Dawlish hissed. "You're under orders!"

He was no less surprised himself – was mystified indeed – for this was no longer a Danish vessel. But the idea of doubting a senior's judgement appalled him.

Welborne had no such scruples. He turned towards the bridge, his face flushed and angry. Even before he opened his mouth, Lorance caught his eye. His glance was adamant – no argument, follow orders to the letter. The turret would still stay locked fore and aft. *Galveston* was forging towards a battle with her main – and only – armament masked.

"Hopper! Stand by!" Welborne shouted the superfluous command down into the drum's interior. The gun-crews were at their stations, the Armstrongs loaded. They could do no more for now than stand and wait.

The *Conewago* had fallen back, lay off *Galveston's* port quarter now, far enough to distance her from the Danish line, a signal to the oncoming Austrians and Prussians that she wanted no part in the coming clash. But she still followed. And HMS *Aurora*, the other neutral, lay stationary some three miles off the starboard beam and Heligoland itself loomed behind her, another three beyond.

From far ahead Dawlish heard cheering, faint at first from the *Niels Juel*, stronger as the *Jylland's* crew added their voices, then the *Hjemdal's* men joining. For the first time in this war, whether by land or by sea, a Danish force was meeting its enemies on close to equal terms and welcoming battle. But on *Galveston* no voice was raised. Bewilderment, not elation, dominated.

The leading Austrian frigate – the *Schwartzenberg*, von Tegetthoff's flagship, Dawlish guessed – was swinging over, two points, no more. Then she was straightening on a course that must carry her west of the Danes on a track directly opposite but parallel. The lines would pass at a separation of about a mile, close enough for their broadsides to be murderously effective.

But that moment had not yet come and the *Schwartzenberg* was still two miles off *Niels Juel's* starboard bow. Then suddenly a flash ahead of the Austrian leader's foremast, a pivot weapon on the open forecastle opening fire, the deep rumble of the report following, and then a tall splash rising short of the Danish flagship. Now a ripple of flame ran down the Austrian's white stripe as her starboard battery came into action – too soon, for her broadside weapons could still not yet be brought to bear far enough ahead. Astern of her, the second frigate, the *Radetzky*, was also opening ineffective fire.

The range was closing fast, and then the *Niels Juel*, and shortly after her the *Jylland*, were firing also, their reports like rolling thunder. Shells from both lines threw up great curtains of spray and from the *Galveston*, far in the rear, it was impossible to gauge if hits were being scored. This was sea battle as Dawlish had always imagined it, lines hurling death at close range, and all the deadlier for the explosive shells and the heavier guns carried now than in the days of Nelson's glory. Ahead of *Galveston*, the *Hjemdal* was also joining in but, though Lorance was holding the ironclad steady in her wake, the turret was still locked.

A great flash close to the *Schwartzenberg's* bow, debris blasting outwards. A Danish shell had crashed through the white stripe's timbers, had found a gun's ready-use charges within and they had detonated. The smoke cleared to show a gaping hole – high enough above the waterline not to threaten stability but indicative of carnage on the gun-deck within.

"They're turning!" Dawlish yelled.

The *Schwartzenberg* was swinging over to starboard, still turning as the *Radetzky* followed, closing the range yet further, and holding the turn. The Prussian gunboats had fallen back, could not sustain the frigates' pace, but they were still following almost a mile astern. The Austrian line was running south-eastwards now, and the *Niels Juel* pulled closer to it to run parallel. The range had shrunk to two cables and the frigates on both sides were matched ship to ship, the Danish flagship exchanging broadsides with her Austrian counterpart and, astern of them, the *Jylland* and *Radetzky* running neck and neck, their fire continuous. Another shell had gouged into *Schwartzenberg* just ahead of her foremast. An internal fire had started there – flames, smoke, then clouds of steam as a hose was brought into action and the blaze died.

The Prussians were opening fire now also, their tiny contribution serving notice that their weakness would not deter them from the fight. Their shells were dropping well short of *Hjemdal* and *Galveston* but they were holding their place in line, baffled perhaps that the ironclad's turret had not swung over to bear on them.

Now a detonation on the *Jylland's* flank. Shattered timbers flew outwards, then smoke poured from a rent and her guns fell silent. She lurched to port, then pulled back into the *Niels Juel's* wake and a half minute later her battery was opening again, the *Radetzky* still her target.

Then the moment when the balance shifted.

A flash high on the *Schwartzenberg's* foremast marked a lucky Danish shell smashing above the foreyard. The smoke cleared but flames were licking from the topsail canvas furled along the yard above, then bursting into raging life. The blaze was running out to port and starboard, was reaching higher up the mast, was dropping burning fragments down on the foreyard and its own long bundle of furled sail. The ship's course was carrying her straight into the steady south-easterly breeze and fiery shreds of canvas were flying aft towards the mainmast and its yards.

(Reader: Please refer to the schematic at the end of this chapter).

There could be but one decision. The *Schwarzenberg* swung over to starboard, held the turn, only straightened from it as she headed north-west, directly toward Heligoland. Now the breeze was following her and blowing the burning debris forward on to the foredeck. A signal ran up the halyard from the bridge. In response, the *Radetzky* pulled out from the *Schwartzenberg's* wake and positioned herself off her port quarter to shield her from the Danish fire. The Prussian gunboats too had turned and were forming into line abreast to starboard of stricken flagship. The Danish line was following the turn and concentrating fire on the *Radetzky*.

"Welborne! Dawlish!" Lorance calling from the bridge. "Look up!"

And there the Danish ensign was dropping, the Confederate Stars and Bars rising, no doubt now of her neutrality in this battle. Then *Galveston's* helm was over and she was breaking from the Danish line, bows headed towards the gap between the *Schwartzenberg* and the nearest Prussian gunboat, the valiant paddle-steamer. Dawlish glanced astern – there, three miles distant, the *Conewago's* bows were swinging across also. The rebel ensign must have been spotted and, regardless of the Europeans' battle, the Union captain would not be deprived of his own.

The *Schwarzenberg's* plight was desperate now. High curtains of flame were roaring along the main and foresail yards and the mast above was itself alight. The foretopmast shrouds – tarred hemp – were ladders of fire. Undeterred by the sheets of burning canvas writhing down, a party on the foredeck had brought a hose into play on the glowing debris there.

304

Further aft, men, half-hidden by the funnel smoke, were scrambling up the shrouds to the main top. Several has already reached it and were dropping a line to the deck. It brought a hose-end with it when it was dragged back up and a half-minute later a weak jet of water sprayed forward towards the burning foremast which now looked close to collapse.

The *Radetzky's* fire had not slacked. Inaccurate it might be, like so much of the other gunfire fire on this day, but it was enough to deter the Danish ships from drawing close to batter the blazing *Schwarzenberg*. The ragged Austrian line abreast – the Prussian vessels were struggling to keep up – was maintaining course north-west. Two miles ahead another frigate lay in their path – HMS *Aurora*, hove to on the boundary of Heligoland's territorial waters. Von Tegettoff, the Austrian commander, had chosen the better part of valour. He had recognised not just defeat, but looming disaster, and he was heading into neutral waters where he could not be followed in anger.

But the Austrian resistance was not yet over. Even as the burning *Schwarzenberg* drove towards HMS *Aurora's* protection, the *Radetzky* still held the Danish van under fire. Her broadside battery could no longer bear and only a pivot-mounted weapon aft was still in action. *Jylland* had taken a hit at her stern and was struggling to maintain station.

And all this while, *Galveston* was far to starboard of the Danish line, her streaming Confederate ensign proclaiming that this was no fight of hers. Ahead of her a half-mile gap lay between the *Schwarzenberg* and the Prussian paddle-gunboat, the *Aurora* just beyond and drawing ever closer.

Then, without warning, A column of white water splashed high just off *Galveston's* starboard bow.

"*Conewago!*" Welborne yelled. "The bitch is still there!"

Dawlish glanced back. Half-hidden by the after superstructure, the Union frigate had closed the range and smoke was clearing from her forecastle. He raised his glass, saw the gun-crew clustered in frantic effort around a small bow-chaser, then stepping back. A stab of flame, wreathing smoke, and the knowledge that another shell was on its way. Armoured, *Galveston's* flanks might be, but her upperworks were as vulnerable as the Austrians' wooden walls.

Then the hit, the Union shell smashing into a water-filled whaler aft, blasting fire and liquid and wooden splinters across the deck, but sparing the hose-party crouched by the funnel. The *Conewago* had the range, could hit again, but Lorance was holding steady course regardless.

"Deck there!" Albemarle, from the foretop. "*Niels Juel's* turning!"

And so she was, swinging from her north-west course and into an eight-point turn that would carry her, and the *Jylland* and *Hjemdal* astern of her, towards the north-east, towards the Danish coast. Commodore Suenson, unwilling to follow the enemy into neutral waters, was breaking off the action.

The *Conewago* fired again, the shell dropping close off *Galveston's* starboard beam, and her course too, directly in the rebel ironclad's wake, had not deviated. The gunners at her bow were loading, ramming, pulling their weapon forward by her tackles and –

"She's turning away! The bitch is turning away!" Cheated of the battle he longed for, there was disappointment in Welborne's cry.

For the *Niels Juel*, now a scant two cables off *Galveston's* port quarter, was driving athwart the Union frigate's course. The *Jylland* and *Hjemdal* were following close, line-ahead still maintained. The *Conewago*, forced to avoid collision, was sheering away to starboard to parallel them. Her hope of crippling *Galveston* was ended.

HMS *Aurora* now lay but a mile ahead of *Galveston*. The ironclad had overtaken the extended Austrian and Prussian line and was pushing through. The Confederate colours had been recognised and no gun was brought to bear on her. She slipped past the still-burning *Schwatzenberg*, to port, and the Prussian paddle gunboat to starboard. Lorance and FitzBaldwin moved from one bridge-wing to the other, caps raised.

Dawlish swung his glass towards the Austrian's bridge and saw there a bearded officer, face blackened but indomitable, also with his cap uplifted. Then he gestured towards the burning foremast and shrugged with something like amused exasperation at the vagaries of chance. Von Tegetthoff had suffered a setback, not a defeat. Dawlish turned towards the closest Prussian gunboat and held her in his lens. He felt a surge of admiration, even affection. The captain of that paddler, little better than a Thames penny-steamer, had defied the ironclad's ram and Armstrongs before and had not hesitated to follow the Austrian line into close engagement with ships that could tear her apart in minutes. Were Prussia ever to build a proper navy, Dawlish thought, men like that could make it all but invincible.

The *Schwatzenberg* was slowing and creeping now over the invisible boundary as HMS *Aurora* advanced at a crawl to meet her. A string of flags at her main halyard signalled no hostile intent. The foremast was like a blazing fir tree, a cone of flame, the debris on the deck beneath still burning and billowing steam as hoses played on it. *Aurora* had dropped a boat and it was stroking across, most likely with an offer of aid. It had not reached the Austrian flagship before the last shrouds and stays burned through and her foremast crashed down in a shower of sparks. Debris piled on the forecastle and a tangle of yards, rigging and topmast toppled into the water to trail alongside.

But *Galveston* was still forging on at maximum revolutions, the reddish cliffs of Heligoland dead ahead. She too was crossing the unseen boundary, had hoisted no signal flags to request leave to pass, and yet there was no response from *Aurora*, as if her onset had not been observed. Her course would carry her astern of the British frigate at a cable's separation.

Dawlish glanced back towards the bridge, saw broad smiles on Lorance's and FitzBaldwin's faces, looks of triumph. Far off the starboard quarter he could see the receding Danes and, curving away from them the familiar profile of the *Conewago*, once more in pursuit, struggling to catch up her lost advantage.

Aurora's transom lay off the port beam – close enough to read her name – as *Galveston* passed. Though there were men on deck there was no hail, no acknowledgement, no attempt to deter *Galveston's* drive into British waters. The ironclad was on a heading that would carry her just south of the island.

And still no recognition of her presence – nothing but a single British officer in captain's uniform on the frigate's bridge-wing. Alone of all his crew he was turned towards *Galveston* and with slow deliberation raised a telescope to his eye, held it there for a long minute, then lowered it again and turned away.

"Frank McClintock, a capital fellow!" FitzBaldwin was all but shouting in delight at Lorance. "I told you! Midshipmen together! Blind in one eye when it suits him and damned if he'll give free passage to your Union friend!"

And Dawlish understood it now – a message passed from *Aurora* to *Niels Juel,* from *Niels Juel* to *Galveston*. The Danish officer who had so briefly come on board the day before had brought it. McClintock, *Aurora's* captain, national hero, Arctic explorer, was standing by his boyhood friend and would enforce neutrality to the letter for the pursuing Union ship.

Off *Galveston's* starboard quarter Dawlish could see the *Conewago*. She had completed a complete circle, was now bearing westwards, but her path would be blocked. McClintock would not allow her to pass across Heligoland's territorial waters, and she would have to curve around them to the south. *Galveston* had established a lead that would be hard, maybe impossible, to catch up.

Twenty minutes later, *Galveston* passed the southern tip of the tiny island at two cables separation. Dawlish could pick out the gun batteries that made it an all but impregnable British base. No challenge, no acknowledgement, and other blind eyes were turned to the Confederate ironclad now heading towards the broad waters of the North Sea. *Conewago,* forced to curve around south of the island, was lost to sight. *Galveston,* had established the lead she needed.

And, better still, the wind was veering, south-east to south, edging more slowly towards southwest and strengthening as it did. The sky was darkening there, grey clouds piling, squalls threatening.

Lorance's prayers for wind and rain and high seas were being answered.

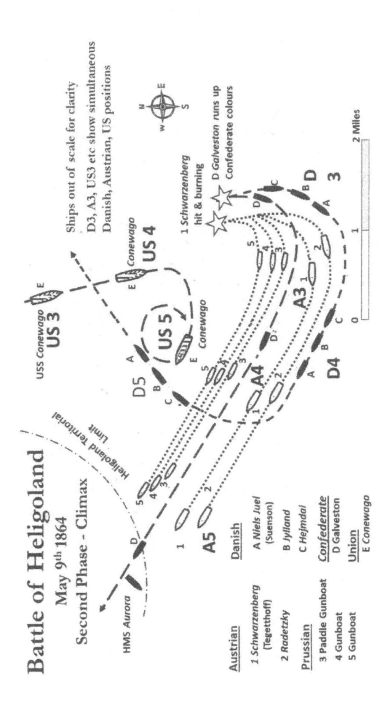

Battle of Heligoland
May 9th 1864
Second Phase - Climax

Ships out of scale for clarity
D3, A3, US3 etc show simultaneous
Danish, Austrian, US positions

HMS Aurora

Heligoland Territorial Limit

USS Conewago

US 3

US 4

US 5

Conewago

Conewago

1 Schwarzenberg hit & burning

D Galveston runs up Confederate colours

Austrian
1 Schwarzenberg
(Tegetthoff)
2 Radetzky

Prussian
3 Paddle Gunboat
4 Gunboat
5 Gunboat

Danish
A Niels Juel (Suenson)
B Jylland
C Hejmdal

Confederate
D Galveston

Union
E Conewago

0   1   2 Miles

N
W   E
S

309

Chapter 32

Dawlish had never seen a more desolate place, a vast body of open water, all but landlocked by low-lying windswept islands. Rain drifted across it beneath a blanket of grey cloud, and wind moaned in the rigging. Smoke drifted from a few miserable cottages close to the shores and a scattering of sheep dotted the bleak landscape. There was a small town to the north – Kirkwall, hidden by a low ridge. He had no desire to see it, or more of this anchorage, more extensive than the largest fleet might fill. One day at this Scapa Flow, amid the Orkney Islands, north of Scotland, was enough to do him for a lifetime. He wanted only to be gone.

Three vessels lay moored well inside the great natural harbour when *Galveston* had entered from the south at noon of May 12th. One was the familiar *Althea,* the second a collier, and the third – she lay two miles from the others – was a pristine steam yacht with clipper bows, a white hull and an ochre funnel.

The passage from Heligoland had deliberately not been direct – west at first, then north-east, north and finally north-west, shrouded in welcome mist and rain, whipped by strong south-westerlies that stripped foam from the wave crests. The *Conewago* had not been sighted – she might still be searching off the British, Dutch, Danish or Norwegian coasts. Once the replenished *Galveston* headed westwards from Scapa Flow into the broad Atlantic – as she would in one day more – the Union frigate's chances of finding her would be close to nothing. For now, only incurious crofters and shepherds could observe the ironclad. By the time word of her presence reached naval or coastguard authorities, she would be long gone.

Althea had brought men as well as food, munitions and other supplies. Five Confederate officers were among them – they had come out with blockade runners returning to Bermuda or Cuba. The two dozen seamen and engine room personnel with them were mixed, largely naval veterans from Britain, France and the Netherlands. Dawlish had no contact with any of them and did not wish it either. Bulloch had come with them, was busy with Lorance supervising transfer of stores, would return to Britain with the *Althea*. He saw Dawlish, clapped him on the back, thanked him, and got back to ticking items off a list.

Dawlish left the *Galveston* without ceremony. It was enough to shake hands with his gun-crews, with Hopper, with McRory and Crowther, with Welborne and with Nolan, wish them good fortune.

310

"Are you going to wish me luck, son?" Lorance said when Dawlish took his farewell of him. "I won't ask you. Slavery still bothers you, doesn't it?"

"Yes." No use denying it. "But I wish you well as a man, sir. As a fine officer and —"

Lorance cut him off. "Just let's say we hope to meet again. In better times." He extended his hand.

Dawlish turned to go but Lorance called him back.

"You've the makings of a damn fine officer yourself, Mr. Dawlish." Then he too turned away.

*

The yacht was called *Ariadne* and Dawlish never learned her ownership. Mr. Elmore Whitby had the use of her for now and he too was in a hurry to leave. FitzBaldwin, Albemarle and Dawlish were assigned cabins. They dined together that evening but neither Lorance nor Bulloch were invited, nor were they mentioned. The vessel's captain was also excluded. The meal, served by two white-jacketed stewards, was sumptuous — the vessel carried a French chef.

"It's all but over. The armistice should have gone into effect today," Whitby said. "For a month. Time enough to get the loose ends tied up, details agreed, a treaty drafted. A few signatures, and that'll be the end of the whole wretched business."

That was his only mention of the war. FitzBaldwin's references to recent actions did not lead to conversation and he soon gave up. Dawlish and Albemarle, as befitted age and status, sat as passive listeners while Whitby reminisced at length about meeting Giuseppe Garibaldi in London the previous month. The Italian patriot was the toast of society, its talk was of little else at present and hostesses vied to have him accept their invitations. FitzBaldwin was not interested — his silence was morose — and he just sat and drank. He seemed a lesser man than when Dawlish had seen him either in his own home or on *Odin's* bridge. A man who had received news of family bereavement might look like this.

Dawlish was glad that the evening ended early. His cabin was a single one — rosewood panelling, a writing desk inlaid with veneers, a washstand with a decorated porcelain bowl, an oil painting of highland cattle above the bed, crisp white sheets. Having it to himself brought a sense of finality, a full break with the last two months' experience. It seemed a dream already, felt as if it had been lived by a different person.

He was a Royal Navy midshipman again, hoping for quick news of promotion. He pulled from his valise the second volume of Gibbon that he had bought before leaving England. A century of imperial decline had passed since he had laid down the half-completed first volume in FitzBaldwin's library. It seemed almost as long since he had paid a half-crown in Taunton for the two orphan volumes. He fell asleep over Diocletian's division of the empire into east and west.

Galveston was all but blotted from view by a steady downpour when the *Ariadne* slipped out southwards the following morning. Whitby had been evasive at dinner when asked about her destination. "A Scottish port," was all he would say.

"Where are we headed, sir?" Dawlish asked it again over breakfast. He was alone with Whitby. FitzBaldwin's and Albemarle's heavy drinking through dinner must now be keeping them in bed.

"Wick. A most convenient place. There's a railway station there. Regular daily trains to the south."

It must be one of the most remote stations in Britain – Wick was a small fishing town on Scotland's north-east tip.

"The captain and his son will be disembarking there also," Whitby said. "You'll have good company on the journey home."

"You won't be joining us, sir?"

"No, Mr. Dawlish. I've a few more matters in hand." He paused. "By the way, you and I have some business to attend to before we part. After breakfast will do. No need to hurry."

Dawlish had known this moment would come, awaited it with both hope and trepidation.

My future.

They finished the meal in near silence, then went to Whitby's cabin – his saloon rather.

"Take a seat, Mr. Dawlish. A cigar? No? I agree, rather too early for it." Whitby opened a drawer in the desk, took out a small leather purse. "I thought that a cheque might be an inconvenience for you. Hard cash is likely to more welcome to a young man." He handed him the purse. "You'll find a hundred and fifty guineas there."

Half as much again as his six Shropshire farms had brought in last year. He had never seen more than five sovereigns all at once. But the sum surprised him.

"I understood that it would be just one hundred, sir."

"Just a small bonus, Mr. Dawlish. Some recognition for the inconvenience of an unforeseen formality. And no need for a receipt either. Not between gentlemen."

"A formality?"

"A very minor one." Whitby opened another drawer, took out a large envelope, opened it. Two sheets. He handed one across. "You might like to read it before you sign. And the copy also."

It was on thick paper, the script copperplate. No letterhead, no crest, just the single word 'Agreement'. Dawlish read it through. He had not expected anything like this. His word should have been enough. He looked up, saw Whitby looking at him and nodding.

"Read it again, Mr. Dawlish. So that there's no doubt."

An undertaking not in any time in the future to refer to actions or incidents in which he, Nicholas Ralph Dawlish, had been involved, or to undertakings or commitments he had made, formal or otherwise, under his own name or under an alias, in the period February 15th to May 15th 1864. To be signed on the basis of his honour as a gentleman. No mention of the word 'officer'.

"I'll countersign," Whitby said.

"What happens afterwards?"

"It'll remain in my records, nothing more. Just in case it's ever needed. Both copies."

"And if I won't sign, sir?" He felt insulted, humiliated, almost sick.

"That would not be wise."

"But Captain FitzBaldwin. And Colonel Blackwood and …"

"FitzBaldwin's signed already. He didn't like it either. But he did. So will Blackwood also, Granville too."

"Why?"

"Certain people don't want to be reminded, Dawlish. Not now, not in the future. They've been embarrassed. And they don't want it to go any further. They don't want to know your name, and if they do, they'll make themselves forget it. If it makes it any easier, it's not just your name. The others' also."

"So nothing ever happened, sir?"

"Nothing did that you had anything to do with." Whitby leaned forward. Something like a patient kindness in his tone now that had not been there before. "There's nothing dishonourable about signing. You're not being asked to lie. Only to keep silent."

"Does the Prince of…"

"Stop!" Whitby cut him off. "A certain gentleman has been precipitate, unwisely precipitate. His mother and his sister were not best pleased. He rather underestimated them, I fear. He has recognised now that he was made an error and he's been persuaded to comply with their wishes. He doesn't want to be reminded of it, not ever. You'd be well advised not to attempt it. It was an embarrassing matter and, as far as he's concerned, it never happened. That's the end of it."

Killigrew, Evenden, Eltham, the seamen who had smashed down from the foretop on to Odin's forecastle, others…

Whitby had sensed the depth of his distress. "I know the world, Dawlish, and you don't, not yet. There's no discredit in innocence. We were all like that once. It won't last. You'll learn all too soon." He reached a pen to him. "Here, sign. Get it over with."

Dawlish hesitated, but he signed. Twice.

"Will there be promotion?"

"Sub-Lieutenant. Already agreed. And a new assignment."

He realised already that it wouldn't be to the Royal Yacht. It never would be. Not now, not ever.

"What ship, sir?"

"HMS *Sprightly*." Whitby consulted a paper. "A gunvessel, I see here. She'll be heading for Esquimalt in ten days for duties on the Pacific Station."

Careers were not made there – that station was a backwater. And it was hard to be much further from Britain than Esquimalt, on Vancouver Island.

"And some advice, Dawlish. Worth remembering. Psalm 146, verse three."

He looked it up later.

Put not your trust in princes.

The End

A message from Antoine Vanner and a Historical Note

I'd be most grateful if you were to submit a brief review of this book to Amazon.com or Amazon.co.uk. If you're reading on Kindle you'll be asked after this to rate the book by clicking on up to five stars. Such feedback is of incalculable importance to independent authors and will encourage me to keep chronicling the lives of Nicholas and Florence Dawlish.

If you'd like to leave a review, whether reading in Hard Copy or Kindle, then please go to the *"Britannia's Innocent"* page on Amazon (Click on: amzn.to/33Le3OW). Scroll down from the top and under the heading of "Customer Reviews" you'll see a big button that says "Write a customer review" – click that and you're ready to get into action. A sentence or two is enough, essentially what you'd tell a friend or family member about the book, but you may of course want to write more (and I'd be happy if you did!).

You can learn more about Nicholas Dawlish and his world on my website dawlishchronicles.com and you may like to follow my weekly blog on dawlishchronicles.com/dawlish-blog in which articles appear that are based on my researches, but not used directly in my books. They range through the 1700 to 1930 period.

By subscribing to my mailing list you will receive updates on my continuing writing as well as occasional free short-stories about the life of Nicholas Dawlish. Click on: bit.ly/2iaLzL7

Historical Note

The armistice between Denmark, Prussia and Austria, signed on May 12th 1864, three days after the Battle of Heligoland, did not last. A conference of the major European powers, hosted in London by Britain, failed to broker a settlement acceptable to the belligerents. Fighting resumed two weeks later and continued, though at lower intensity than before, until July 1864. The war ended on August 1st, when King Christian IX of Denmark renounced all his rights in Schleswig and Holstein in favour of the rulers of Austria and Prussia. His agreement provided for Austria taking over administration of Holstein and for Prussia that of Schleswig. In 1920, in the aftermath of World War 1, in which Denmark had been neutral, plebiscites in these provinces resulted in North Schleswig choosing incorporation in Denmark again. South Schleswig and Holstein remain part of Germany today.

Denmark's army had performed heroically against overwhelming enemy might but the war of 1864 was in every sense a disaster – and one for which the country's politicians were responsible. It lost almost 3,000 dead and slightly more than that wounded – a heavy toll in a population that was reduced from 2.6 million to 1.6 million by cession of territory under the peace terms. The Council President – essentially Prime Minister – during the war, a bishop turned politician named Ditlev Gothard Monrad, was so unpopular that he left the country and settled briefly in New Zealand. He bought land, raised sheep and cattle, and hoped to attract Scandinavian emigrants. A dispute with the local Maori community ended this and brought him back to Denmark, where he again devoted himself to church and political affairs. King Christian IX, a largely passive player during the war, had more success as a father – his daughters included the wives of the future King of England and the future Czar of Russia while his sons ascended the thrones of Denmark and of Greece.

The Danish War was to be the first of three by which Prussia, driven by its "Iron Chancellor", Otto von Bismarck, united Germany, a collection of individual states up to that time. The Austrian Empire's alliance with Prussia in 1864 ended bitterly two years later in squabbles over responsibilities in Schleswig and Holstein. These provided Bismarck with an excuse for demonstrating Prussian dominance of Central Europe. Austria was quickly and comprehensively defeated in the "Seven Weeks War" of 1866. Prussia's mastery of logistics and railway management were as important as battlefield tactics in inflicting a crushing defeat – a hint of things to come. It would be France's turn for humiliation in 1870/71, leading to proclamation of King Wilhelm I of Prussia as the first German Emperor in the Hall of Mirrors in Louis XIV's palace at Versailles. Germany's own humiliation would come in that same hall in 1919 when it signed the treaty that recognised its defeat in World War 1 and, in the view of some, laid the foundations for a yet greater conflict twenty years later.

Small as the Danish War of 1864 was, by comparison with later conflicts, its tactical lessons were significant. Trenches and earthworks proved to be surprisingly resistant to artillery fire and allowed small numbers of rifle-armed troops to hold off much larger attacking forces. Massed assaults succeeded, if at all, only at the cost of high casualties. The same was found across the Atlantic when, that same year, Confederate forces entrenched at Petersburg, in Virginia, imposed a virtual stalemate, that lasted some ten months, on Union forces. Adoption of breech-loading rifles (which only the Prussians were using in 1864), and invention of machine guns, tipped the balance yet further in favour of defence over offence. The Turkish defence of Plevna in 1877 and actions in the Boer War of 1899/1902, and in the Russo-Japanese War of 1904/05, were further proof. Few of these hard lessons had however sunk in by 1914 and arrival of trench warfare on a massive scale came as an unwelcome and costly surprise to many military leaders.

The Battle of Heligoland was one of the last occasions when large wooden warships fought each other. Von Tegetthoff's defeat there was more than offset by his spectacular victory over the Italians at the Battle of Lissa two years later. Italy was an ally of Prussia in the Seven Weeks' War of 1866 and Lissa was the only Austrian success either by land or by sea. It had no impact on the war's outcome.

The CSS *Alabama's* raiding career, which had ranged over the Atlantic, Pacific and Indian Oceans, ended when she was run down and sunk by a Union sloop-of-war, USS *Kearsarge,* off Cherbourg, France, in June 1864. She had captured or burned 65 Union merchantmen, and had taken over 2000 prisoners, without causing a single loss of life. Her achievement inclined most navies to see commerce-raiding, or "cruiser warfare", as a promising strategy in future conflicts. The arrival of radio communications brought this largely to an end as regards surface raiders but the development of the submarine gave the strategy a new lease of life that has endured until today.

James Dunwoody Bulloch (1823 – 1901), the Southern Confederacy's agent in Europe, was responsible for organising blockade-running and for leasing or building, and for manning and supplying, commerce raiders. Of these, the CSS *Alabama* was the most successful. Classed by the Union State Department as "The most dangerous man in Europe", he was excluded from the general amnesty offered by the Union government at the end of the Civil War. He and his half-brother Irvine (who had served as an officer on the *Alabama*) remained in Britain thereafter, establishing a lucrative cotton importation and brokerage business in Liverpool. James Bulloch's half-sister Martha was the mother of the future President Theodore Roosevelt, who acknowledged with gratitude the advice he received from his uncle about handling ships under sail when writing his own history of the Naval War of 1812.

Denmark's only ironclad, the *Rolf Krake*, proved a priceless asset in its operations against Prussian land forces. She represented the future of naval warfare, by contrast with the wooden broadside-frigates that fought each other at Heligoland. The only surviving warship of the conflict is the Danish *Jylland*, which is on display, beautifully restored, in a drydock at Ebeltoft.

The saddest reminder of the war of 1864 is however to be found around Dybbøl, where the outlines of the main redoubts can still be seen. An examination of Google Earth's imagery of the area shows where thousands of brave men on both sides were sacrificed in a stupid, futile and unnecessary conflict. They deserved better of the politicians who plunged them into it.

Humanity does not learn easily.

Old Salt Press is an independent press catering to those who love books about ships and the sea. We are an association of writers working together to produce the very best of nautical and maritime fiction and non-fiction. We invite you to join us as we go down to the sea in books.

Our writers are Rick Spillman, Joan Druett, Linda Collison, V. E. Ulett, Alaric Bond, Chris Durbin, Seymour Hamilton and Antoine Vanner, all of whom write fiction. Joan Druett, in addition to her novels, also writes meticulously researched maritime history.

Visit: oldsaltpress.com/about-old-salt-press